Author of Green Mountain Boys, Daniel P. Thompson

The Doomed Chief

Two hundred years ago

Author of Green Mountain Boys, Daniel P. Thompson

The Doomed Chief
Two hundred years ago

ISBN/EAN: 9783337387631

Printed in Europe, USA, Canada, Australia, Japan

Cover: Foto ©Andreas Hilbeck / pixelio.de

More available books at **www.hansebooks.com**

THE

DOOMED CHIEF;

OR,

TWO HUNDRED YEARS AGO.

BY THE AUTHOR OF "THE GREEN MOUNTAIN BOYS," "GAUT
GURLEY; OR, THE TRAPPERS OF UMBAGOG,"
ETC., ETC.

PHILADELPHIA:
J. W. BRADLEY, No. 48 N. FOURTH ST.
1860.

CONTENTS.

CHAPTER I.

PAGE

Opening scene at Plymouth on the Meeting House Green, where a crowd were assembled in anticipation of the trial of three Indians for murder—A match of skill at target shooting between Vane Willis, a bold young fellow from the country, and Sniffkin, a young court lackey—Sparring and discussion between them, relative to policy of the Court of Plymouth toward the Indians, in which Dick Swain, the tool of the latter, takes a part—The coming of the Court announced by the ringing of the bell, and beating of drums at Head quarters—Sketch of the Indian tribes, and their position towards the colonists 9

CHAPTER II.

The Shadow, a church zealot, arrives with a secret message from Deacon Mudgridge, the chief instigator and manager of the prosecution against the Indians—The arrival of the procession—The introduction of Roger Williams for the defence of the prisoners—The trial and sentence of death 25

CHAPTER III.

The execution of the Indian prisoners in the jail yard—The appearance of Metacom, or King Philip, and Queen Wetamoo, on a roof overlooking the crowd in the jail-yard—their prophetic denunciations of the deed, and their virtual declaration of war in consequence 52

CHAPTER IV.

Moonlight scene in the street after the execution—The excitement and alarm of the people at the signs and omens seen in the heavens—Altercation among Sniffkin, the Shadow, Dick Swain, and Vane Willis—The ruse of the latter, to get rid of Dick, who was ordered to play the spy on his movements—Scene at Deacon Mudgridge's house—Confidential dialogue between him and the Shadow 72

5

CHAPTER V.

The scene at the house of Madian Southworth—The love passage between her and Vane Willis, which closes by his announcing his re-
olution of raising a company of his woodsmen comrades to defend the
settlement against the Indians, in the coming war—She gives him
her father's sword and bids him God speed—History of the family
of Colonel Southworth, who was the leader of Cromwell's noted regiment, and subsequently outlawed, self-banished, and lost in the
forests 88

CHAPTER VI.

The Deacon's plot to get Madian into the church—His persecuting
attempts, with the aid of the Shadow, to force her to marry Sniffkin
—Her sudden and mysterious disapearance, no one knew how, or
whither.. 105

CHAPTER VII.

Scene at the Pines on Charles river—The meeting of Captain Mosely
and Willis—The arrival of the Praying Indians driven by Captain
Prentiss and his troop from Natic to be taken in boats to Deer Island
—Their sad interview with their pastor, the apostle Elliot—The parting—and Elliot is left alone, sorrowing in the grove................... 125

CHAPTER VIII.

Metacom suddenly appears—His interview with Elliot and a Massachusetts commisioner, who also arrives—A war council, in a neighboring forest, and the forming of Metacom's first alliance with the
Nipmucks—His day vision on the top of Wachusett mountain and
the subsequent war dance.. 140

CHAPTER IX.

Willis distracted at the flight of Madian, raises his company, for the
double purpose of fighting the Indians, and recovering her whom he
supposes to have been taken by them.. 164

CHAPTER X

The breaking out of the war at Swanzey—The rallying of military forces,
and their march—Captain Willis detained and sought to be arrested
at Plymouth, for a heretic, by Deacon Mudgridge.,........ 176

CHAPTER XI.

PAGE

The first skirmish between Metacom's warriors and Captains Mosely and Willis' volunteer companies.. 192

CHAPTER XII.

The bold expedition of Captain Willis against the Pocasset Indians—Ventures in disguise into Metacom's camp, and witnesses his meeting with the Pocassets, led into his camp by their queen, Wetamoo—Willis detected, pursued, and with his company retreats to find a defensible position on the shore of the bay.. 212

CHAPTER XIII.

The arrival of the company at the shore—The furious assault of the savages, and the long and remarkable fight that ensued, with the escape of the company on board a ship providentially arriving......... 246

CHAPTER XIV.

Night, and terrific thunder storm on the bay—A dismasted vessel on which a female form is seen in a flash of lightning, crosses their path—a fruitless attempt to reach her as she is thrown on the rocky shore.;.. 256

CHAPTER XV.

A mysterious stranger partly in Indian garb makes his appearance at the old "Forge" of James Leonard, in Taunton, and holds a private conference with the latter, recounting his escape from shipwreck—Metacom enters in disguise—The stranger and Metacom waylaid by a band of kidnappers, but escape into the woods............................ 275

CHAPTER XVI.

Singular scene at a deserted house, a mile or two from Leonard's, between Deacon Mudgridge and the Shadow, while anxiously awaiting their party—The party at length arrive with alarming reports of a contest with evil spirits and Indians, and all flee for Plymouth....... 296

CHAPTER XVII.

Metacom's visit with the stranger to the secret cave of the Panisees or Powahs to learn the fortunes of the war—The mysterious ceremonies—The prophetic vision of Passaconaway, the aged seer, showing the destiny of the red men, and then that of their white conquerers to come.. 324

CHAPTER XVIII.

PAGE

A rapid sketch of the fall campaign, followed by a description of the Great Swamp fight at the strong hold of the Narragansets—The conflagration, massacre, and disastrous retreat—Captain Willis wounded, and carried off into the woods by the mysterious stranger, who suddenly appears at the close of the battle....................................... 342

CHAPTER XIX.

The sickness of Willis in the wintry forest—Bold counsels of Nanuntenoo—He is elected chief of the Narragansets—Willis removed to the island of Aquidneck by the stranger....................................... 373

CHAPTER XX.

Willis's long insensible condition at the house of a Quakeress—Her sad story—Willis's recovery—Visit of Captain Mosely—Gloomy news.... 391

CHAPTER XXI.

Scene at a house in Providence, of which the mysterious stranger and the lost Madian appear to be the occupants—Willis, Captain Mosely and Roger Williams arrive, and joyous developments transpire......... 412

CHAPTER XXII.

A scene at the Southworth Mansion—The fears and bodings of Deacon Mudgridge—The startling developments before the Court of Plymouth—And the awful fate of Deacon Mudgridge..................... 436

THE CONCLUSION.

Brief sketch of the melancholy situation of the doomed red men—Their last stand over the graves of their fathers at Mount Hope—the closing scenes of the deaths of Metacom and Wetamoo......... 460

THE DOOMED CHIEF.

CHAPTER I.

"New England, then, for many years
Had had both rest and peace;
But now the case was otherwise—
Her troubles did increase."
PETER FALGER, *the Pilgrim poet.*

IT was an anxious, as well as a stirring day with the colonists at New Plymouth. The public mind, for the last few months, had been laboring under a very unusual, and a constantly increasing excitement. Among all classes of men there evidently existed a deep, though unacknowledged consciousness, that the calculations of selfishness, craft, and fraud, instead of obedience to the simple dictates of justice and honesty, had latterly characterized their intercourse with the Indians. This, as in most other cases of conscious wrong doing, had made them, especially the leading men of the colony, peculiarly sensitive respecting the relations in which they stood with the red men, filling them with jealousies, suspicions, and apprehensions, lest the latter, impressed doubtless with the same or livelier convictions of their wrongs, should be secretly nourishing thoughts and schemes of redress and retribution. The colonists were also fully conscious that the injured race were now no longer the comparatively harmless and contemptible foes they were in times past, when bows and arrows and war-clubs were their most formidable weapons, whole scores of which were scarcely good against a single musket in battle; but that they had, at this period, almost universally supplied themselves with fire arms, in the fatal use of which, when occasion required, they had no superiors, even among the most expert sharp-shooters of the old world. And especially and painfully conscious were likewise the leading colonists, that in addition to the advantages thus possessed by their apprehended foes, there had now sprung up among them a Master Spirit who was believed to be fully capable of combining, and giving direction to all the various elements of their disaffection with fearful effect. That Master Spirit was Metacom, the King Philip of subsequent historic renown. And it was not without reason they feared that he, insulted, fined, and dragooned as he had been into hollow treaties of peace, would not long remain inactive or forego—unless prompt and decided measures were taken to prevent the execution of what was believed to be his bold and settled design—a war of extermination against the colonists of New England.

Something therefore it was felt should immediately be done. And something *was* done. But, as too often happens among people laboring under a high degree of excitement and apprehension, the colonists seemed madly intent on rushing into measures which hastened on the very event they were so anxious to avoid. And the consequence was that they soon plunged their hapless colony into those fearful scenes of blood and woe, which characterized the year that followed the opening act of the story on which we are about to enter.

It was a calm and sunny morning in the fore part of the leafy month of June, 1675. A crowd of loiterers, evidently awaiting some expected event, were scattered over the smooth and ample grass plat surrounding the Meeting House of the first planted village of New England, the noted Plymouth of

Pilgrim memories. Among the mingled and diversified company present on the occasion, consisting of villagers, and those who had come in from the neighboring towns to witness the public proceedings of the day, were a small party of young men who, to while away the time of their waiting, had entered into a contest of marksmanship, which being almost the only kind of amusement countenanced among the young men, by the over scrupulous elders, was generally engaged in with great zest, serving the young as a sort of standing exhibition, in all public gatherings, save those of a religious character. The contesting party in the present instance, were a half dozen youngerly men, of ages varying from twenty to thirty, all supplied with fowling pieces, or hunting guns, of the best construction for the use of the bullet. Deeming themselves among the best marksmen of the colony, they had agreed upon a target, and a distance, which should fully test their pretensions to nice shooting, the mark being a black ring, four inches in diameter, with two less visible inner concentric circles, and a black spot of the size of a half crown in the middle, all painted on a white board, and placed at the distance of one hundred yards from the shooting stand. Having all fired once round, it was seen that four of the contestants, though all making close shots, had failed to plant their bullets within the black ring. These having now, by their rules, no hope of bearing off the palm, voluntarily retired from the contest, which was thus left to be decided by the remaining two, who had both sent their balls within the ring, both bullets nearly alike grazing the next inner circle, and falling consequently about equi-distant from the centre. The attention of the crowd, who, by this time, had all gathered round the spot, was now especially directed to the two remaining candidates for the palm of victory. In personal appearance, these two rival marksmen were alike in nothing, save in the evidence of their similar ages, which were probably twenty-four or twenty-five

years. One was, for the times, richly and fashionably dressed.
And this circumstance, together with the contemptuous,
sneering expression that rested on his small, unattractive features, denoted that he was connected with some family of
wealth, and of real, or assumed consequence in the colony,
that he was disposed to plume himself on what he considered
his elevated position in society, and consequently to look upon
the common sort of men, as all well enough in their places,
to be sure, but not exactly fit to be counted among his associates. The other was a plainly dressed, but noble looking
young man, of a shapely, compact form, and of unusually
handsome features, enlivened with one of those clear, frank,
and firm countenances, which betoken intelligence, good motives, and cool courage.

"Dick Swain," said a bystander, beckoning to his side a
short, bustling, restless fellow, with a hooked nose, and a sort
of shiny, unsteady countenance, and at the same time pointing to the plainly dressed marksman just described, " Dick,
who is that fellow who is so confidently preparing to contest
the palm with Mr. Sniffkin, the English trained marksman ?"

" That fellow," replied the person thus appealed to, coming
up, and speaking in that low, confidential way, common with
men of secretiveness—" his name is Vane Willis, from one
of the neighboring towns,—a bold hunter, and a sure marksman, they say, he having practiced a good deal with the Indians, and proved himself a match for the best of them. I
know Mr. Sniffkin is well trained in shooting, and has the
most costly and high finished piece in the colony; but I am
really afraid this Willis, with his heavy, thick barreled gun,
will beat him."

" Afraid ! why afraid ?" asked the former. " Every man
has an equal right to the palm, if he can get it, hasn't he ?"

" Yes, yes; but then Mr. Sniffkin you know, is the ne-

phew of Deacon Mudgridge, and so connected with the Governor, who was related to the Deacon's wife before she died.
Besides that, Mr. Sniffkin is a member of the church, and that
fellow ain't. And then Mr. Sniffkin prides himself so much
on his skill in shooting. And then again, I suspect, there is
another reason why he wants to beat the fellow—to humble
him—something about a certain girl in this town—you understand, hey? But stay; they are about to fire!"

Sniffkin was evidently desirous that his rustic rival should
be the first to fire, and, in a tone sounding very much like a
command, requested him to proceed. But the other, with a
slight curl of the lip, and a little sprinkling of irony in his
manner, peremptorily declined that honor; when the privileged gentleman advanced to the stand, and, after having at
length found a place to rest his piece which satisfied him, he
took a long, careful aim, and fired.

Dick Swain, and four or five others of Sniffkin's obsequious
friends, sprang forward to the target, and soon announced
that the bullet had bored it within half an inch of the small
black spot in the centre.

"Yes, Vane Willis is as good as beat," cried the exulting
inspectors, as they came swaggering along back to the stand.
"He can never equal that shot."

"Don't boast quite so soon. We can tell better after Vane has
fired," retorted the friends of Willis, who were evidently a majority of the marksmen present, and who now gathered round
their tacitly acknowledged leader, with looks plainly betokening their confidence of his triumph.

Without pretending to notice the self-satisfied and super-
cilious airs of his rival, or the remarks of either party, Vane
quietly advanced to the stand, and, waving off those who were
preparing a place for him to rest his piece, like the one his
competitor had used, raised his gun at arm's length, and almost instantly fired. So quick and sudden, indeed, did the

report follow the upward movement of the barrel, that most of the company supposed that the gun had gone off by accident, and before it could have been brought to bear on the object of aim.   But on being told by the unruffled young marksman that he had obtained all the aim he wanted, his friends now, in their turn, bounded forward for the target.   There was a momentary silence among them at first; and then rose their exulting shout of victory.   The bullet had pierced the very middle of the black centre mark; and the triumph was complete.

"An arm's length shot against one with a rest, and a clean victory at that!" cried one of the exulting party.

"It is nothing more than I expected," added another. "The fact is, Vane Willis is the best shot in the whole colony."

"I dispute that," said Sniffkin, stung by the applause that had greeted his opponent, whom, in his ill-concealed spite and vexation, he was eager to disparage—"I dispute it. This was doubtless but a mere chance shot."

"Perhaps it was; but I am quite willing to try it over again with you," coolly remarked Vane.   "What say you, sir, shall we thus put the question to the test?"

"No," replied the other disdainfully; "I may prefer to choose my own company, when I engage in another contest. Nathless I dispute the assertion that you are the best shot in the country."

"So do I," rejoined the former; "there *is one* in the country whom I know to be my full equal, but his name is not Timothy Sniffkin."

"Who is it then, Vane?" asked the one who had made the disputed assertion.

"It is Metacom."

"King Philip?"

"Yes, King Philip, of Mount Hope. I have had repeated

trials with him both in the chase and at a mark. Neither could claim any advantage over the other from the quality of his gun ; for our guns, which were brought over by two German sportsmen, some years ago, and sold when they returned, are precisely alike, being the only ones of the same make in the colony, probably. They were made expressly for the bullet, which, by means of a curious winding groove inside the barrel, as you can see by mine here, is made to whirl as it goes through the air.* I was lucky enough to secure one ; and Metacom, who has a keen eye for such matters, somehow soon got hold of the other. And he has since practiced with such effect, that he has no superior, and probably not a single equal in quick and accurate shooting, this side of the great water.

"You seem to have been quite intimate with that vile, treacherous savage," maliciously remarked Sniffkin, winking significantly to his backers.

"Vile and treacherous!" repeated Vane, as with flashing eye, he advanced and boldly confronted his sneering opponent. "Would to heaven, that, for the peace and safety of our endangered colony,·the vileness and treachery were all on one side! But what meant you, sir, by that insinuating remark?"

"Oh, nothing in particular!" replied the former, evidently surprised, and at first, disconcerted at the fearless confronting

---

* The history of no invention is more obscure than that of the rifle. But it is evident that the invention is of German origin, and dates back nearly 500 years since; as early as 1381, we find it stated that a city in Franconia furnished thirty rifles, or guns with grooved barrels, in a war with the nobility. It is also stated that in 1498, guns with rifled barrels were in use at shooting matches at Leipsic. Their use, however, was very rare till long after the settlement of the American colonies. The Indians seem to have understood the principle, as shown by feathering their arrows, so as to give them a spiral motion; hence their eagerness to adopt the weapon as soon as they could obtain it.

of the other. "Nothing, in particular; but it may be well enough," he added, rallying a little, "to have it known, at this critical juncture, who those *are*, that have been consorting with, and still seem disposed to defend one, who, with his devilish heathen crew, may soon be arrayed against us in arms."

"Yes, sir, and if that time does come," retorted Willis, "and this piece, in *my* hands, with *my* knowledge of the enemy, does not as good service on our side, as *your* piece, in *your* hands, then I will agree to bear your taunts in silence. And I now challenge you, sir, in anticipation of such a time, to enter with me, on that condition, into the actual contest— a contest which will better show who is truly the man, and the marksman, than this by-play of shooting at a mark, where there are no dangers to be encountered. Yes, sir, I repeat the challenge; and I have a few friends here, I think," he added looking around on the little band of his hardy comrades, who, as the altercation progressed, drew closer and closer to his side, with increasing manifestations of their sympathy—" a few friends, perhaps, who are willing to vouch for me that I shall not be the first one to back out. Will you go my vouchers for that, boys?"

A hearty shout of affirmation was the prompt response to the appeal, which was thus made and answered with the more emphasis, doubtless, because they all wished to show the haughty court-minion that one of their number was not to be put down by sneers, or disparaged by groundless insinuations.

"There! Now you will please remember all this, sir," resumed the speaker, pointing to the visibly perplexed and disconcerted Sniffkin. "And you too, my friends, remember to hold me to my pledge, for making good my own offer in this behalf."

"O, yes," responded one of those last addressed. "Yes,

if times should really come, when there is any occasion for
making good such an offer; and it should then be necessary,
which it won't be, to jog your memory, we will do it. But
do you seriously suppose we are likely to see those times,
Willis ? Do you think there is actually any danger of our
being involved in an Indian war ?"

" Aye, I *do* think there is *much* danger of such an event,"
replied the other. " And if our people—especially our rulers—
persist in the course they now seem so intent on taking towards the already greatly irritated red men, I feel a bloody war
is inevitable."

" Take notice of that, good people of Plymouth !" eagerly
exclaimed the court lackey, looking round on the crowd with
an air of malicious triumph. " He has shown himself a seeker
of occasions to disparage our rulers and take the part of the
heathen salvages against them. Take notice of it, ye all,
good people, will you ?"

" Yes, take notice of it, all who wish," promptly responded
the other, with increasing earnestness ; " and take notice also
of the prediction I now, and here boldly venture to make,
that if these Indian prisoners, whom we are waiting to see
tried here to-day, for the alleged offence of taking the life
of one of their own tribe, who, by their laws, had become a
traitor and an outlaw,—if these prisoners, known to be the
leading men of the tribe, and the councillors of King Philip,
are condemned and executed, there will, before the month's
end, burst upon us a war which may not cease till the very
existence of these colonies is put in jeopardy !"

The startling import of this prediction, together with the
serious and decided manner in which it was uttered, fell with
chilling effect upon the whole company, producing a very
visible sensation, both among those who coincided with the
speaker, in regard to the mistaken .policy of their rulers in
their strangely mingled church and state government, and.

2

among those also who looked upon those rulers as all but infallible in wisdom and discretion; for it was but giving voice
to an apprehension by which they were *all* secretly impressed,
however they might differ about the best means of averting
the impending danger. Even the arrogant and self-sufficient
Sniffkin, who had found matter of accusation in the far less
pointed and objectionable remarks previously made by his
hated rival, was now too deeply impressed, or too much astonished by his bold words and fearless demeanor, to attempt to
gainsay them or renew his ill-natured and ungentlemanly
assault.

The silence that followed the dialogue thus impressively
brought to a close by the out-spoken young marksman, was,
however, soon broken by the startling peals of the church-
bell in the belfry, almost above their heads, which all understood to betoken the arrival of the hour of the expected trial,
that was to be held in the Meeting House, around which they
were assembled, and soon the roll of a drum at the head-quarters of the Governor, his assistants, and the church dignitaries,
of whom the court was to be composed, announced that the
military guards were then mustering, preparatory to bringing
out the prisoners and forming a procession for the place of
trial. All eyes were therefore expectantly turned in that direction. But the eager spectators were not to be very immediately gratified by the appearance of any coming procession.
The bell-man, in obedience to some signal made from the
Governor's house, soon ceased to ring the bell. The drum
ceased beating, and every thing indicated that there was to be
a temporary delay of proceedings at head-quarters. And instead of the expected retinue, a solitary man made his appearance, coming from that direction. His hurried motions, as
indicated, in the distance, by the rapid bobbing up and
down of his tall, steeple-shaped hat, and the quick, regular
outward flaunting of the skirts of his long, tunic-like coat, all

moving in correspondence with his steps as he advanced, seemed to show that he was bound on some mission requiring special despatch; and his appearance under the circumstances, consequently, very naturally soon attracted the attention of the expected company.

"Who is that tall man coming this way so hurriedly, Dick?" asked Sniffkin, beckoning the other aside.

"Why it looks like Deacon Mudgridge's Shadow," replied Dick carelessly.

"Deacon Mudgridge's Shadow! who do you mean by that, sir?"

"Crave your pardon, Mr. Sniffkin, meant no offence; but some call him so?"

"Call who so?"

"Why, Mr. Dummer, to be sure—Deacon Dummer, perhaps I should say, as I have heard that he had been advanced in the church—elected assistant, or supernumerary deacon, or something of the sort, may be."

"O, ho—yes; well I at first didn't know but you meant my uncle, Deacon Mudgridge himself, the strongest pillar of Church and State in the whole colony, and therefore a man not to be spoken lightly of by any. But you should be careful about picking up the nicknames, and cant phrases of vulgar schismatics and scoffers, even against Dummer, who is a very zealous and useful man, and is indeed talked of as a fourth deacon. And I think he will get the place, too, if he does as well in other things as he has in aiding Deacon Mudgridge to go through with this important measure on hand to strike a damper on that audacious King Philip."

"Glad to hear that of Dummer; for I am with the court party in this measure, you know, Mr. Sniffkin. And though I never mean to boast much; yet I think I may say, I have already done considerable myself towards helping it forward."

"Aye, you have done very well Dick, and won the praise of Deacon Mudgridge, who says you are a fellow of bright natural parts. But you may have a chance to do much more, to-day; for this matter must and will be carried through, notwithstanding all that has been said by that low caitiff, Vane Willis, whose treasonable words just now I hope you will remember and report to our rulers, whom he has so shamefully reviled. But here comes Dummer, and with some word or message from head quarters, I fancy."

The subject of this last remark, a lank, long, sanctimonious looking man, whom, as Dick Swain had inadvertently remarked, the people, or rather the more independent and outspoken part of them at least, had playfully dubbed Deacon Mudgridge's Shadow, on account of his well known subserviency to that important personage, whom he copied and followed almost as faithfully as the shadow its substance—now came striding forward with a countenance working with solemn anxiety.

"What is the news from head quarters, Dummer?" asked Sniffkin, as he and Dick advanced to meet the former far enough to be out of earshot of all others—"What is the news now? Have they got the jury together and everything rightly fixed there?"

"Mostly," replied Dummer, "mostly fixed, Mr. Sniffkin; and they supposed they had quite, and were on the point of starting for the Meeting House, but"—

"But what? Tell us at once, Dummer."

"Well, they have concluded to delay a brief time, on account of some untoward appearances."

"What appearances? What new thing has turned up now?"

"Nothing very certain, peradventure; but Roger Williams, that noted old schismatic, who is so prone to side with the powers of darkness now peculiarly manifest in the doings of the salvages, those children of Sathana, has arrived this morning from Providence, to see that the Indians have fair dealing in the coming trial, he says."

" That means, I suppose, that, instigated and hired by that damned sachem Philip, he has come on to defend and get them clear."

" Yea, truly ; and it is greatly feared that he has somehow got speech with some of the five Indians, who, to save all remarks of the ill-disposed against our fairness, and forever shut the mouths of the salvages in the same behalf, were, as yourself doth know, put on the jury with our twelve white jurors. For, although these five red men were selected with proper care, and have ever since been kept under righteous influences till this morning, yet some think they now see in them tokens of weakness and wavering. Moreover, the Indian witness, whose report and confessions so providentially led to the arrest of the murderers of our Christian friend, Sassamon, and who was ready to swear he saw the murder committed, and that he could identify the murderers, now seems strangely sullen and perverse."

" These things must be seen to immediately ; but what does Deacon Mudgridge think had better be done ?"

" Well, he thinks," replied the other, lowering his voice to a confidential tone,—" he thinks,—and that was what I came to see about,—he, I say, thinks that our friend, Dick Swain, here, might be the right person to see and manage these weak and doubting Indian jurors, who have been thus induced to come forward to help the Lord's side. He thinks also, that, peradventure, they might like their witness fees before hand, the amount whereof need not be stinted to any exact legal usage. And yet, furthermore, he thinks they may need strengthening in bodily firmness. And he has, therefore sent, by me, these instruments, whereby good may be wrought out," added the speaker, drawing out a handful of silver coin with

one hand, and a bottle of rum with the other, and covertly
passing them to Dick.

And the unscrupulous Dick as covertly took possession of
the proffered articles, and with an affirming nod to the Shadow,
and a knowing wink to Sniffkin, silently passed them under
his coat; when the three moved off, with an assumed air of
leisurely indifference, towards the Governor's quarters.

Before introducing the remarkable trial, to which we alluded as about to take place,—a trial which was destined, as
the fearless and sagacious young marksman we have introduced,
had hypothetically predicted, to be the precursor of the darkest day ever witnessed by the infant colonies of New England—
before introducing this eventful trial, we should, perhaps,
for the more ready appreciation by the reader of the scenes
next to follow, take a cursory glance at the character and conditions of the different tribes of New England Indians, together with the principal historical events, which grew out of
their relations with the whites, and which seem to have been
more immediately connected with the particular crisis we have
undertaken to delineate.

When the Puritan colonists had established themselves
in their different locations in New England, and began to enquire into the situation, numbers, and distinctive characters, of
the unknown wild people, by whom they were surrounded,
they found within what they esteemed their chartered limits,
three great, distinct, independent tribes, whose numbers and
power seemed to give them a controlling influence in the
country, and to command a sort of tacit submission from all
the various smaller tribes, and fragments of tribes, surviving
the great pestilence, which had evidently, a short period before the advent of the whites, swept untold thousands of them
into their forest graves.   These three tribes were the Pequods,
occupying the valley of Connecticut river, the Narragansetts,
occupying the western part of Rhode Island, and the Wam-

panoogs, or Wampanoags, occupying the eastern part of Rhode Island, and the southern part of Massachusetts, but exercising a nominal sway over all the other tribes within the territorial limits of the Plymouth and Massachusetts colonies. Of these, the Pequods, a fierce and sanguinary race of warriors, had, by the rare good fortune of a successful surprise been broken up, and almost utterly destroyed by the whites, nearly forty years previous to the time we have chosen for the opening of our story. This left but two of the only tribes much to be feared,—the Narragansetts, a numerous but not remarkably warlike tribe, perhaps, and the Wampanoogs, the most warlike and proudly independent of them all, to take their stand against the whites, in case the time should arrive, when the aggressions of the latter should awaken the jealousies and hostilities of the former, and induce them to combine and make a common cause in defence of their rights. And that time, in spite of all the efforts of the colonial diplomatists of that day, to dupe and over-awe the Wampanoogs, and keep them from an alliance with the Narragansetts, had now been for several years, gradually drawing near. For the first forty years after the arrival of the Pilgrims in the country, and while they were weak and consciously in the power of the natives, they earnestly courted the friendship of the stronger tribes, especially that of the influential Wampanoogs, and carefully abstained from all acts of injustice and causes of offence. And their first treaty with the sincere and noble-hearted Massasoit, king of that tribe, having been made with earnest and honorable intent, and carried out in good faith, was preserved uninfringed during his whole life, constituting a continually brightening chain of friendship between the contracting parties, and beautifully exemplifying the important truth subsequently confirmed and demonstrated by the pure and wise William Penn, that when the whites act sincerely and in no way become the aggressors, there is no difficulty in living in peace

and amity with the Indians.   But, at length, the good old
Massasoit passed away, leaving the succession to his two sons
Wamsutta and Metacom, both young men alike, ennobled by
birth and elevation of character, and well-fitted to sustain the
dignity of their father's throne.   These young men, during
the halcyon period of faith, honesty, and peace, that preceded
the death of Massasoit, had mingled freely with the colonists,
visited the court of Plymouth, received from the Governor the
complimentary names of Alexander and Philip,—were courted
on account of their high position, respected for their manly
deportment and unusual personal endowments, and afforded
facilities for information, which were rare with the natives,
and which, when improved as they had improved them, at
length made these princely brothers, doubtless the two most
intelligent, as well as naturally talented young red men then
to be found on the American continent.   And there is no reason to believe that, had they and their people continued to
experience the same respect and good treatment they had all
received during the life time of Massasoit, the chain of their
mutual friendship would never have been made dim by hostile
blood.   But a change had been gradually coming over the
colonists.   They had become comparatively strong and powerful, and with the increase of their strength and power, their
deference to the red men and disposition to treat them as
equals, either in trade or treaty, seemed strangely to undergo
a proportionate decrease.   All this Alexander and Philip were
not slow to perceive, and it soon so far operated on them as to
keep them aloof from the court of Plymouth.   And it was the
insulting and arbitrary attempt to compel their attendance and
required subserviency, which so mysteriously resulted in the
untimely death of Alexander, who, being the eldest, had succeeded to the throne, and preluded that series of wrongs and indignities on his successor, Philip, that finally led to the bloody
drama which is the ground-work of our eventful story.

CHAPTER II.

" The mind of the bigot is like the pupil of the eye, the more you pour light upon it, the more it contracts."—DR. HOLMES.

AFTER a long and anxious suspense, the company around the Meeting-House were again aroused by the renewed ringing of the bell and the beating of the distant drum, this time pealing out and rattling so loud and intermittingly, that all felt there was now little danger of another disappointment. And in a few minutes, as they had anticipated, the head of the procession consisting of the embodiment of Church and State, with their proposed Indian victims, jurors, witnesses, and others, hove in sight. Preceded by the Sheriff on a black horse, and a drummer and fife, came the Governor and his Secretary, walking side by side, next his assistants, who were to act as civil magistrates, and then the minister and elder of the Church, who were to make up the Ecclesiastic part of the court, formed after the fashion of the times for the trial of all important cases. And next to these came the jurors and witnesses headed by a constable, and then the three Indian prisoners, in their scanty native garbs, dejectedly, but firmly walking in Indian file, and enclosed before, behind, and on each side, in the hollow square of their well armed military guard. Immediately after these last, came waddling along, with an air of mingled meekness and wisdom, the thick-set, mealy, rough-visaged, and pig-eyed Deacon Mudgridge, the important personage, who has already been once or twice alluded to, and who was the volunteer manager of the forth-coming trial, on the part of the prosecution. By his side strode the long, never failing Shadow, who, as the

minister was to sit on the trial, had been, on account of his gifts
for prayer and impromptu, selected as a sort of Chaplain on
the occasion.   And last of all, followed a long line of citizens,
summoned into the ranks, to swell the retinue and give it the
most imposing effect.

This was a political or state trial, or at least made such by
its assumed connection with the public question, by which
the community, as before stated, were, at this time, peculiarly
agitated, and it was expected by all, therefore, that it would
be conducted with considerable ceremony.   But the authorities, not content with the usual ceremonies of such occasions,
had been at very *extraordinary* pains to have all the proceedings of this trial marked throughout with unusual parade and
great show of stern solemnity; for one of the principal objects
they had in view, in instituting the measure, was to strike a
dread upon the natives, and overawe their proud chief, the
feared and hated Metacom of Montaup.*   The whole affair
therefore, from the first—the marching of the procession,
the entrance into the Meeting House, the place appointed
for the trial, as the one most likely to be attended by Indian
spectators, and the seating of the authorities, with all others,
had been conducted with all possible pomp, and was thus
made to resemble, in appearance, some military trial and
execution, rather than the quiet proceedings of a court of
justice, exercising only the functions of civil authority.   And
thus nearly an hour was spent in the march of an hundred
rods, and in arranging matters for the opening of the court.
At length, however, all this had been accomplished, to the
apparent satisfaction of those in control, every thing had become settled down into quiet in the Meeting House, and the
anxious audience sat with keenly expectant looks, awaiting
the commencement of the important business of the day.

* The original Indian name, soon corrupted by the whites to Mount
Hope.

At this juncture, the attention of the audience was attracted by the quiet entrance.of an elderly gentleman, whose unobtrusive, yet firm and free deportment, intelligent look, and native dignity of manner, seemed at once to impress all classes of the mingled assemblage, as their enquiring gaze was turned towards him, with the involuntary feeling that they were favored with the presence of more than an ordinary man. Notwithstanding the snows of the seventy winters that had thickly powdered his high and noble head, and converted his once raven locks into the silver wreath that now entwined itself around his thin, rectilinear features and strikingly intellectual countenance, his step was firm and elastic; and little or nothing could be detected in his general appearance indicating any abatement of physical vigor. With a composed, self-possessed air, and an occasional quick, sharp glance around him, he advanced directly towards the platform on which the civil and church dignitaries had become seated, with the jury, prisoners, guards, and officers arranged below and along in front of them. Though evidently a stranger to most of the audience, he yet seemed soon to be recognized, and that, too, with manifestations of displeasure, by several of the older part of the assembly; and quickly the name and epithets, *Old Roger Williams!* *Williams, the banished heretic!* and *the half Quaker, half infidel Roger Williams!* was audibly whispered and buzzed from mouth to mouth, among the now continuing crowd. But without appearing to hear or notice these irreverent and unfriendly demonstrations, he proceeded deliberately along the aisle, until he reached the further end of the bench on which the Indian prisoners were seated, where he paused, and made some slight motion to attract their attention. They looked up, and while the twinkle of a smile lighted up, for the instant, their gloomy, saturnine visages, they simultaneously uttered a low, guttural exclamation of gratified feeling.

Williams, for the stranger was indeed no other than the persecuted and banished man, who was thereafter to become known as the first great champion of religious liberty in America, and who had now volunteered to come from his new home and freshly planted colony at Providence, to defend those from whose hospitable tribe he had once received protection and friendship. Williams then turned, firmly confronted the court, and stood silent, as if waiting to hear what they might have to say at his appearance before them.

"What may be your desire, sir?" at length, coldly asked the stern and severe looking Governor Winslow, affecting to have forgotten the other, or being unwilling to speak his name.. "Have you some favor to crave at the hands of the court?"

"Nay, your Excellency," replied Williams, in a deep, firm, and musical voice. "Nay, not a favor; yet I deemed it but proper, with a fitting opportunity of speech, to apprise the court that I appear here before them as the friend and counsel of these prisoners; not to defeat the ends of justice, but only to guard against its perversion to the detriment of *their* rights, as well as of the safety and good name of *your colony.*"

A frown was seen instantly to gather on the warty visage of Deacon Mudgridge, at the remarks, and a fidgety movement seemed to agitate the whole of his fat, dumpy person, as, alternately glancing at the speaker and the court, he did his best to look his aversion to the man, and his objections to the part he had proposed to act in the trial.

"Do you wish," resumed the governor, after a hesitating pause, "do you wish me, sir, to put it to vote with the court, whether you shall be admitted as counsel of the prisoners?"

"Nay; again I have to say, nay, your Excellency," calmly responded the other. "The constitution and laws of

England, and of this colony, of course, have always guaranteed, even to the worst of criminals, the right of being heard
by counsel, and I will not so far question the intelligence and
impartiality of this court, as to intimate any *necessity* of
asking such a thing of them. I only wait for the trial to proceed."

After a short, whispered consultation among the grave
personages of the court, which seemed to result in some perplexity and difference of opinion, respecting the admission of
Williams to act in the capacity claimed by him, the governor,
as the presiding judge, with much the air of one who finds
himself compelled to tolerate some nuisance which he lacks
the power to abate, at last turned to Deacon Mudgridge, and
suggested that, on the whole, it were better perhaps to let the
matter pass as it was, and proceed with the trial.

The Shadow, or Dummer, the deacon candidate, being then
called on for the purpose, made a long, loud and zealous
prayer, beginning with the fall of Adam, following the history
of the Church to the time when God's chosen Israel, in the
persons of the Plymouth colonists, began to antagonize with
the accursed Canaanites of the American forests, and ending
with praying every heathen savage out of the land, and King
Philip to an especial perdition.   •

When this introductory performance was at length brought
to a close, and the audience became composed, Deacon Mudgridge slowly rose from the conspicuous seat he had taken on
the right, but a little in front of the court, and, with an air
of exceeding solemnity, and a countenance big with the conscious importance of the trust devolving on him in the double
capacity of chosen captain of the church militant of the
colony, and the champion of its civil authority, began, by way
of a preliminary speech for suitably impressing the court, jury,
and all others with the right frame of mind before entering
on their duties, to dilate on the very great importance of the

case which had now come up for the solemn and prayerful
consideration of the court and jury. This trial would involve,
he believed, a most momentous crisis to God's favored people,
whom he had planted with his own right hand in this wilderness country, wherein to erect his tabernacles, convert or
drive out the idolatrous heathen, and make it a vineyard for
his elected heritage. And he could not forbear, he said, to
warn the court and jury, in advance, against the great danger
of falling into the fatal error of Saul, and also that of Achan,
the weak follower of Joshua, who brought sore judgments on
Israel by sparing some of the enemy, and being seduced by
the love of spoils, (to which our desire to gain the traffic of
the Indians might be likened,) and so fear to take decided
steps against the heathen prisoners; when the righteous
example of Samuel, who hewed the wicked Agag to pieces,
and moreover that of Joshua, who ordered the stoning to
death of the disobedient Achan—when these wholesome examples were still standing as beacon lights, whereby to avoid
incurring the guilt of any like offénces.

He then read the indictment, setting forth, in substance,
that the prisoners, one Tobias, a leading man of the Wampanoogs, and called by them Poggapanosso, one Wampaquan,
son of said Tobias, and one other Indian, instigated by the
devil and King Philip, did, on a certain day of March preceding, waylay, murder, and conceal in a hole cut through the
ice on the great pond bordering said King Philip's territory,
one John Sassamon, a praying Indian, with malice prepense,
and to the great displeasure of Heaven.

The deacon next read over his list of witnesses, whom he
divided into two classes: one to show what he termed the
necessary circumstantial matters bearing on the case, and the
other to give direct evidence of the murder. The first class
consisted of the more intimate white acquaintances of Sassamon, and the last of two Indians, Dick Swain, and the zealot,

Dummer. The witnesses embraced in the first division being then brought on to the stand and sworn, proceeded to give in their testimony, the aggregate amount of which was that the deceased Sassamon, formerly a Wampanoog, had been reclaimed, in the first place, from the devilish influences of his idolatrous tribe, became a praying Indian, and afterwards showed himself so apt at learning as soon to be able to read and write quite readily. But, after living several years with the whites, and receiving many favors from them, he suddenly disappeared, and was next heard of among his tribe, by whom he was again taken into full fellowship, and among whom he turned his knowledge and cunning to so good an account, that he soon was promoted to the post of confidential secretary to King Philip. This place he held many years, and until he appeared to have completely gained the confidence of Philip and his councillors; when, having committed some crime which by their laws was punishable with death, he fled for his life, and came back once more among his old white Christian brethren, who, moved by his loud lamentations for his late apostasy, and his earnest professions of renewed religious experiences, again received him into favor, and sent him to teach and preach among the praying Indians of Middleboro'. But, not content here with the exercise of his new calling, nor with the peaceable occupation of the land and house which his white friends had purchased for him, he at once began to play the spy on the movements of his old master, King Philip, when he soon appeared to become so burdened with the discoveries he pretended to have made of that chief's secret designs against the colonists, that he could rest no longer. He therefore repaired to Plymouth, sought a private interview with the governor, and, under the injunction of the strictest secrecy, made the startling disclosure that King Philip was actively preparing for a war of extermination against the colony—a fact which he pretended to have at first learned when he was the chief's secretary, and which was fully confirmed by his recent discoveries. Having made these revelations, he again earnestly besought the governor not to let his secret go beyond himself and council; for should a knowledge of the disclosure reach the ears of Metacom, his life would be sure to pay the forfeit. But it was not to be supposed that so alarming a secret could long be confined to the court. It soon passed from the governor and his consulting friends, and spread, with the rapidity of the wind, over the whole colony, and in a few weeks the luckless Sassamon was suddenly missing.

This part of the testimony having been at length brought to a close, the other class of witnesses, relied on for the direct testimony, were then called on to the stand. And the Indian who went by the name of David, among the whites, and who was announced by Deacon Mudgridge, as " the faithful Christian friend of the late lamented Sassamon, and the first discoverer of this hell-invented murder," was now directed to stand forward and relate the particulars of what was understood to be his story about the affair. Accordingly David, a small, demure, peaceful looking Indian, then moved himself along a little, and quietly proceeded :

" Find Sassamon gone, one day, and no come back. Much 'fraid him must be killed ; so go look all round in the woods; but no find him nowhere. Then go on Assawompset, big pond. Little way, see hat on the ice. Go there, find him Sassamon hat. See hole in the ice, get pole, feel him soon, and bring him up, pull him out, find where club strike him head Then go fetch white men, tell 'em Sassamon killed. They no believe, say him drown himself, and carry him off and bury him. Then me go and tell governor Sassamon killed, sartin. Governor look like believe some, order Sassamon dig up. Me there, show them, more time again, where club strike Sassamon head They believe this time, think

Indian tell right, and say Philip men did it, sartin, 'cause Sassamon break Indian law. Me know Sassamon 'fraid him be killed, long time. But me no tell, me no know who did it, 'cause me no see it. Can't tell lie—that make him bad Indian. Good book say God roast um liars."

All present being convinced that David had testified honestly, no questions were asked him on either side; and Patuckson, the other Indian witness, who was the only person pretending to have seen the deed committed, was then called on to testify. He was evidently an Indian of a very different character from that of David, being bolder, more forward, and exhibiting, both in countenance and manner, many indications of cunning and calculation. He commenced like one ready for his part, and glibly went on—

" Hoh ! me know all about Tobias and this two tother Indian kill Sassamon. Me go among Indians self, and find out. Metacom come home from long journey, hear how Sassamon been spying round there, and then hear how he tell governor bad story. He no like it, and tell him warrior Sassamon traitor, dog-spy; come round there to carry lie to white men. Metacom much mad, say him sorry Sassamon not killed for that tother thing, 'fore him run away; and so he call meeting of old men, at Montaup. Meeting all say Sassamon die this time; catch him, kill him. Tobias there, talk loud, say all good Indian watch him, kill him always. Me go off, watch too, for see what done. So, one day on hill near big pond, see Sassamon go across ice, and three Indians coming. Hide and soon see Tobias and this two tother Indian run fast, catch Sassamon, strike club hard, kill him; then cut hole in ice, put him in, then run away quick. Me no tell then; but when white men dig up Sassamon me tell all; show 'em where Tobias and this two tother Indian had camp, catch fish on tother end great pond; so they go, catch 'em all."

Deacon Mudgridge then, with the view of placing the tes-

3   •

timony of the witness in the strongest light possible, asked
sundry leading questions, which were so worded as to elicit
positive assertions of what were before left as matters of inference, and which were answered as he had anticipated and
wished; the court taking no notice of this violation of the
rules of conducting an examination, and no objection to the
course being interposed by Williams, who, from some policy
of his own, kept silence. The latter, however, evidently distrusted the truth and honesty of the witness, and resolved on
subjecting him to a close cross-examination. And in this he
was soon to be materially aided from an unexpected quarter.
Vane Willis, who knew something of the witness, and was
perfectly familiar with the localities of the murder, now
worked himself along through the crowd, took a seat directly
behind Williams, and whispered to him a few suggestions, of
which he might take advantage.

"You say, sir," carelessly commenced Williams, addressing the witness, of whom, he told the court, he would ask a
few questions by way of his privileged cross-examination—
"You say you saw Tobias coming over the ice, and I suppose
Tobias saw you, at the same time, didn't he?"

"Can't no tell," replied the witness, looking inquiringly to
Deacon Mudgridge, who, suspecting the question was put to
bring out an affirmative answer, which was to be used as some
trap, soon succeeded by his looks and motions in making the
former understand that he must answer in the negative.

"Can't you tell? don't you *know* he saw you?" again
asked Williams rather sternly.

"No; me don't know that—me think he no see me—me
know he no see me at all," answered the witness, fast growing
confident.

"How," persisted the former—"*how* do you know but
what Tobias saw you?"

"Know Tobias no see me," now positively affirmed the latter, impatiently; "me know him couldn't, 'cause me hid a great way off on the hill."

"Oh, not a great way I suspect," returned Williams. "But really, how far was it?"

"Can't tell," replied the witness; "but great way—as far as here to where governor house be."

"That, to be sure, is over a quarter of a mile," said the questioner. "But then Tobias and the others when you saw them were sometimes close to the shore, were they not?"

"No!" exclaimed the witness, "him great way out on the pond—more further from the shore than me back on the hill."

"That," now remarked Williams, glancing at the court, "would make the distance from the witness to the nearest point at which he swears he saw the prisoner under examination, over half a mile, and, as he says Sassamon ran some distance before he was overtaken, the distance to the spot where the deed was alleged to have been done, could not have been less than three quarters of a mile. And yet he positively swears not only to the commission of the murder but to the identity of the perpetrator! Enough of such a witness as that! I have done with him."

For the first time, both the witness and the prompting Deacon now saw the object of Williams' well managed man-euver to draw from the former the admission of the truth that he was at too great a distance from the scene to be able to swear safely to any thing. And the Deacon, seeing at once that it would not do to leave the testimony in this shape, leaped up and vehemently protested against the use of the cunning arts and devices of the godless lawyers of the secular and unsanctified courts, which his opponent had probably learned in the old world, where he learned his other heresies, and which he had now brought here, and put in practice to confuse and lead astray a simple minded native, and a truthful,

honest witness as there was in the world.   And then turning
to the witness, he sternly demanded of him, if he did not mean
to swear *positively* that he *clearly saw* the murder committed,
and that he *knew* it was Tobias, and the other prisoners, who
did it.'

" Ya-ya-yas—me know—me swear," responded the witness,
at first hesitating, but soon evidently becoming alarmed for his
own personal interests from what he read in the looks of the
Deacon—"yas, me swear—me swear hard—me swear two
times, again !   There ! guess me get pay now, sartin."

" Pay ?" exclaimed Williams significantly.   " Then he was
to be paid for swearing in a particular manner, and to have
no pay without so doing, was he ?   The court and jury will
please remember this."

" *Wo unto him that perverteth testimony !*" cried the visibly
disturbed Deacon in what he intended should pass for a 'scriptural denunciation of his opponent.   " But, peradventure, it is
no wonder that one who deserted the true church for damnable
heresies should resort to such means to shield the heathen,
with whom he has so long consorted.   No doubt he hopes to
make out the identity of the prisoners to be a doubtful matter.   But he will not prevail.   *The expectation of the wicked
shall perish.*   I will now introduce evidence, which, coming,
as I may say it does, directly from the ordering of Providence
for the detection of the guilty, he will hardly dare to impeach.
Brother Dummer, will you step forward and state what you
saw, with your own eyes, at the time Sassamon's body was
exhumed for examination, and the prisoner, Tobias, was
brought in to undergo the test then and there prescribed for
him ?"

" I did verily," said the Shadow, throwing his eyes around
and upward with an air of peculiar reverence and solemnity—
" I did verily witness, on that solemn occasion, a very great
marvel, touching the matter whereof I am now called to testify.

And I do affirm and say, that, when this child of Sathan, the prisoner Tobias here, was brought in where the dead body lay, to undergo the ordeal of confronting and touching it with his bare hand, he was forthwith smitten with the fear and trembling of conscious guilt, and could hardly be got near the body, much less be persuaded to touch any part of it.   Whereupon, the young man, Richard Swain, then and there also present, being moved thereto with the rest of us, but more prompt unto the duty of seeing the ordeal perfected, speedily seized the forefinger of the prisoner, and thrust it on to the naked body ; when, lo ! the mysterious and God-ordered result ! Fresh blood, which had started out at the touch of the guilty member, was plainly seen standing on the place of contact !"*

The now exulting Deacon next called Dick Swain, but, at the same time, remarked that he wished merely to ask him whether he agreed with the last witness and could confirm his statement.

" O, yes, be sure ; I saw the same blood he did," somewhat hurriedly responded Dick, rising, but manifesting no inclination to go into particulars.

" Very well, that is all," said the Deacon motioning the other back to his seat.

" Not quite all," interposed Williams, again acting on the whispered suggestions of the shrewd prompter behind him. " Were you sent by any one to be present at the examination in question ?"

" Sent ?—no, not in particular, as I know of," answered Dick, glancing around doubtfully.

" Well, sir, did you not go wholly for the purpose of witnessing the examination ?"

" I may say not—that is, not wholly so ; but hearing about it, and feeling some curiosity about the matter, I thought I

* See Cotton Mather and other early historians for the fact here testified to.

would skirt the woods along in that direction, with my gun, on the look-out for game, and stop there to see what was going on."

" Did you kill anything ?"

" No, nothing of any account; merely one gray squirrel."

" Did you kill the squirrel with shot, or with a bullet ?"

" With a bullet. I generally go into the woods with my gun loaded with a bullet, these days, as there are murderous Indians about."

" Yes, but what part of the squirrel did the bullet strike ?"

" Well, it went right through his throat, seeing you are so particular to know."

" It was a long time, wasn't it, after you shot the animal before you reached the place where they were examining the body ?"

" No it wasn't any such thing, sir," replied Dick, with an air that seemed to say, ' *you can't catch me in it that way.*' " It wasn't twenty minutes."

" Oh, well, but you had the squirrel in your hand when you took hold of the prisoner's finger and thrust it upon the dead body ?"

" No, sir, I did not; I *know* I did not, for I had just hurled the animal into the corner of the room where I had set up my gun."

" Well, you said you saw the blood on the spot which was touched by the prisoner's finger ?"

" Yes, I did, and will still swear to it. I saw it as soon as his hand was taken away, same as all the rest did. I *know* there was blood there."

" I don't dispute at all, that a bloody mark then became visible there; but," continued the speaker, suddenly turning a stern gaze upon the face of the quailing witness, while he raised his voice to a pitch of startling loudness, " but, Richard Swain, tell me, before God, who put that blood there ? Who,

sir, while his right hand was bearing the reluctant finger of
the prisoner to the dead body ?   Who drew the fingers of his
left hand, first purposely made bloody in the fresh wound of
his game, slyly over the spot of the coming contact ? Ay, sir,
who put that blood there with the sole object of making
evidence against this poor Indian prisoner ?"

"Blasphemy ! rank blasphemy !" cried the enraged
Deacon.   "He is trying to turn the miraculous intervention
of God for the detecting of an awful crime into mockery !
Are the sanctified Elders of the Church of Christ, who have
vowed to guard his authority against reproach, and our civil
rulers *who bear not the sword in vain*, to sit here and listen
to all this ?   For one, I do protest against such doings.   The
witness swore *distinctly* to the seeing the blood follow in consequence of the touch.   So did brother Dummer, whose word
none can question.   This is enough ; and I do most earnestly
object to this, or any other witness answering such entangling,
hell-devised questions, put to defeat the ends of heaven's own
justice.   Yea, as I said, the evidence is abundantly enough
to ensure a conviction ; but lest my opponent should claim
anything savoring doubt, or the weakening of the testimony
of the last witness by means of his ungodly arts, I will call
others who were present on that remarkable occasion of the
visible doings of Providence, and see what they will say."

So saying, the Deacon, to prevent Williams from pressing
his last questions further on the discomfited Dick, hurriedly
called on two more witnesses of the Dummer stamp, who, as
might be expected, unhesitatingly swore to the same thing ;
when, with an air of defiant exultation, he announced to the
court that he was through with the testimony, and that the
case was ready for argument.

There was now by common, tacit consent, a short pause in
the proceedings, which was made use of by the assembly, as
usual among congregated bodies after a tedious sitting, in

shifting positions, rising and moving from one place to another, or passing in and out the house. This naturally produced sufficient bustle and confusion to afford the active friends of the prosecution an opportunity for wire-pulling, which they were not slow to improve. The Deacon was seen conversing earnestly with the different members of the court, whom he successively beckoned aside for the purpose. The Shadow evidently had considerable business along the seats occupied by the white jurymen; while Dick Swain, on pretense of hunting for some lost article, might have been seen hustling about among the Indian jurors, and slyly passing something much resembling small bottles under their blankets. The audience however soon settled down into their former quietness and listening attitudes; when the Governor intimated to the Deacon, that he was now expected to commence the opening argument.

" Man is weak, and full of short-comings. Strength and wisdom are of the Lord. Let us invoke the Divine blessing," said the Deacon, suddenly throwing up his hands, and entering, with peculiar unction, upon a prayer especially devised for the occasion. After concluding his prayer, or rather his set of instructions to the Almighty how to influence the mind of the court and jury, and how to order the result of their deliberations, all disguised in the form of prayer, he cleared his throat anew, and commenced his great and long studied effort. But having already given several specimens of his mode of treating the case in hand, on religious grounds—a mode which appears to have been fully sanctioned in the colonial courts of the day, we will not follow him through his long, tedious, Scriptural argument, but only take notice of his speech, when he got round, as he at length did, to the alleged origin of the difficulties between the Indians and the favored people, who had been sent to this land, as he affirmed, to possess and improve it as their Heaven-bestowed heritage.

"These heathen salvages," he then went on to say, "after their lives had been mercifully spared—against the will of Heaven, I greatly fear—at length became perverse and stubborn, utterly refusing to hearken to the Gospel truths and beginning to harbor evil designs against our chosen people. This evil-minded, and rebellious spirit was first especially made manifest in that untoward Sachem, called Alexander, who, as his excellency here, then an actor in the affair, can bear witness, was signally chastised, and in a manner unmistakably showing the displeasure of Heaven at his perverse and wicked conduct. But Philip, the subtle and treacherous Sachem who succeeded him, instead of being warned by the rebuke he might have read in the fate of his brother, soon became guilty of still more untoward and heinous conduct. Encouraged in his audacious courses by our mistaken forbearance, doubtless, he hath gone on from year to year, in open violation of his solemn treaties, multiplying his offenses, by stirring up his tribe of Sathanic malignants to hostility against us, plotting with other tribes to join him, in his deeply meditated onslaught on the colony, and lastly by instigating the foul murder, now under investigation. And thus hath he careered it in his wickedness, until he hath at length reached that pitch of devilish doing and intent, wherein all have been brought to see that the public peace and safety loudly demand that he should receive a chastisement at our hands, which shall at once put a stop to his wicked and dangerous career, and serve as a lesson to all his heathen followers. Hence the present prosecution, and hence, also, the imperious necessity of a result, whereby such check and such lesson may be publicly given. And such result, since the guilt of prisoners stands clearly proved and established by the most indubitable testimony, in spite of all attempted perversions thereof by heretical sympathizers—such result, I say, I now, in the performance of my God-bounden duty, confidently urge and demand at the hands of this court and jury."

Having thus delivered himself, the heated Deacon dropped puffing and panting into his seat; when Williams, heeding neither the sneering whispers of the crowd, nor the cold and frowning looks of the court, calmly rose and entered on his speech for the defense.

" I do not deem it either meet or necessary," he said, " for me to follow the opposing speaker through that part of his discourse pertaining to the duties and mission of the church, which, he says, God has planted here to become his special heritage, and to act as his commissioned instruments in driving out the unbelieving heathen, or reduce them to obedience and belief in its behests and doctrines. I devoutly hope the church here *is* of God's planting, and that its waterings may be such as not only to bring it increase, but give it the light and grace to permit all, whether white or red, to believe and worship in accordance with the dictates of conscience, and not make the exercise of their rightful soul-liberty, a matter of accusation against them. But with all this I have nothing to do, and shall only begin on that part of his argument grounded on the alleged offenses of the red men, which first manifested themselves, he asserts, in the conduct of that hapless young chief, Alexander, (about whose fate it would have been better wisdom to have said nothing,) and to have been continually kept up by his successor, Philip, to the present time, in all sorts of misdemeanors and crimes, the last of which was the instigation of the alleged murder now under consideration. The existence of continued dissensions between the red men and the colonists, I fully admit; but as fully deny that the causes assigned for these dissensions are the true ones, or that they have any special bearing on this case. Of the origin and continuance of our difficulties with the Indians, my opponent has drawn one picture in colors wrought up from rumor, suspicion, and prejudice. I will draw another by the lights of certain knowledge, and in the spirit of even handed justice.

"Nearly forty years ago, a youngerly man, banished from his home in the neighboring colony for his advocacy of religious liberty, and becoming thereby a houseless, hunted outcast, who had not where to lay his head, nor wherewith to sustain life, at length found his only refuge among the children of the forest, and was especially taken in hand by the very tribe of whom we have just heard such sweeping denunciations. Here, finding a home and a welcome, the more cordially proffered for the very reasons which made him an exile, he studied the ways and characters of the red men, noted their virtues, and learned to make allowance for their errors. Being then in the family of the peaceful and honest old Massasoit, he could not but regard with interest the heirs apparent to this powerful Sachemdom, the old chief's two sons, Alexander and Philip, who have been branded in this presence as the great instigators of all the offenses of that branded tribe. They were then in the flower of their young manhood, and the exile thought them, as he looked upon their goodly persons, and noted their manly conduct and surprising intelligence, two young men of whom any monarch might well be proud, as successors to his throne.

"After a while, the exile made himself a new home, but maintained his relations and intercourse with these young chiefs, and was cognizant of all the events subsequently happening to each—of their movements and motives—of the accession of Alexander to the throne, and of his prompt repairing, with his brother Philip, to the court of Plymouth to declare their wish and intention to maintain inviolate the treaty of their father with the whites—of his then resting in entire confidence of their faith and fair dealing—of his deep surprise in being summoned to Plymouth to answer charges of meditating a violation of the treaty, confessedly founded on mere rumor, and of his still greater surprise at being soon after seized in his peaceful employments by a band of armed white men, and marched off a prisoner for trial, like some felon subject, instead of the independent sovereign their own treaty had acknowledged him. The exile also speedily became apprised of the young chief's strangely befalling sickness, while under arrest, and of his delivery to his friends on pledge for his return, if he recovered, that his degradation might be completed.

"Yes, the exile learned this, and with lively concern was hastening to the scene to avert the anticipated consequences of the outrage, when he met the weeping train, just landing from the river with their sick and dying chief. Here he stood by with deeply moved feelings, and silently witnessed the mournful scene. From minute to minute he noted the slower and slower heaving bosom, and the feebler and feebler groans of the departing sufferer, that rose low murmuring on the hushed wilderness, till his unstained spirit escaped to a land where persecution ceases, and love and forgiveness, with conscious rectitude of purpose, makes heaven for the red man as well as the white. The exile noted all this, and then the brief, awful silence that followed, the wild frenzied wail of anguish that the next moment burst from the convulsed lips of the bereaved young queen, the dark, but comely Wetamoo, then the low, ominous muttering of the old men, as they thought of the authors of this, their great sorrow and calamity, and then the fierce outcries of the up-leaping young warriors demanding to be led on to avenge the death of their idolized chieftain.

" And why were they not led on to execute their fearful purpose? They had good cause of war, and, as they believed, of a war of bloody, terrible retribution; for the Indians, who are the most unerring guessers of any class of people I have ever met with in the old world or new, then fully believed, and have ever since believed, that Alexander came to his death by the foul hand of the white poisoner!"

"Damnable falsehood! libel! treason! yea, rank treason!" shouted the here interrupting deacon, leaping to his feet, with a countenance blazing with holy wrath and indignation. "Was it not Major Josiah Winslow, who, in pursuance of bounden duty, bravely captured and brought home that vile Sachem, Alexander? And was it not at his own house that the captured wretch was seized with the fever, brought on by his heathen ragings? And, moreover, was not that duty-doing Major Winslow the same person who is now here presiding as our honored governor?"

"The gentleman forgets that I, myself, made no accusation against any body," resumed Williams, taking advantage of the first pause in the deacon's furious outburst. "I was merely naming the belief of the Indians respecting the cause of their chief's singular death. They did so believe, and repeated their conviction, in despite the rebuking words of the exile, who told them, as has just been intimated, that he must have died of the fever of passion, or grief and chagrin, though his suggestions met no other response than fiercely shaking heads, and the impatient question, '*Did ever Indian catch fever and die of that complaint before?*'

"But I willingly pass over that page of our history, which I only wish we had never been compelled to place there; for I gladly, Oh! gladly,

'Would tear that leaf—would blot it with a tear.'

I will pass over that sad page, and return to the only opinion I could be taken as giving, that the unwarranted transaction gave the tribe good cause of war. This I boldly repeat; for what nation is there on earth, heathen or civilized, who, if their sovereign were seized and carried off by another nation

with whom they were in treaty, would not instantly pronounce
it a war-warranting outrage? Not one. Yes, there *was* cause
of war; and, as I before asked, why did not war follow? I
will now tell you why. The exile—yea, the despised exile
and outcast—earnestly interceded for his old white persecutors;
and Philip, the still more despised and hated Philip, then becoming king, soon joined him in appeasing the wrath of the
red men. Such, at that dangerous crisis, was the course taken
by the forbearing Metacom, who then, as afterwards, honestly
tried to avoid war, the consequences of which, to both sides,
his far-reaching sagacity has ever fully appreciated. And he
not only quelled the hostile feelings of his followers, but soon
personally notified the court of Plymouth of the wish, on his
part, of still maintaining the treaty of his father, and of his
brother, notwithstanding his own deep sense of injury at what
had transpired.

"After this notification, Philip supposed, as his luckless brother had done, that this was sufficient, without paying attendance, like a vassal, at the court of Plymouth. But, like his
brother, he was mistaken about the double requirement of
that court, that would have him an independent sovereign
long enough to bind himself in treaty, and all the rest of the
time become the frequent homage-paying courtier, so that he
could be kept in subjection. Though not at first understanding this, yet he was soon made to know it. In a short time,
he, too, was summoned to Plymouth on charges founded on
suspicion, or the false representations of the runagate Indians
whom they had tempted by rewards for such communications.
He concluded, however, to heed the arrogant summons, for by
this time he had many just complaints of his own to make
known against the whites, for their inroads on his lands, and
for defrauding his people. But, warned by the fate of his
brother, he went with an armed escort, and held parley with
the court in the open air, but was, notwithstanding, entrapped

into the signing of a new treaty, which entirely passed over
his own grievances, they being no part of the object of the
astute framers, and by which he was unwittingly made to
acknowledge offenses never committed, and, as a punishment
therefor, to promise to deliver up the arms of his tribe to the
court. Nor was this all. At the very hour when he was
being detained by this one-sided and fraudulent negotiation,
the men of Plymouth were secretly mustering an armed force
to overpower his attendants, and seize him as a prisoner; and
they were only prevented from the execution of their design
by the remonstrances of the more conscientious pacificators,
then present from the sister colony. And this was but the
beginning of the indignities he was doomed to suffer. Within
a short period, he was again summoned to appear before the
court of Plymouth, under threat of war, for the violation of
the last so-claimed treaty, that he had not been permitted but
partially to understand, the charge this time being that he had
not delivered up the guns of his people, which they depended
on for their daily subsistence, and which he had no power to
compel them to surrender; and being still anxious to avoid
war, he consented to another conference, and met the court
again, but with a force of warriors sufficient for his personal
protection, well understanding the disgraceful plan which had
been started for capturing him at the previous meeting. But
the presence of warriors is but a poor shield against the
over-reaching of designing treaty-makers; and this time, another of those extraordinary documents was drawn up for the
occasion, by which Philip was made not only to consent to be
heavily fined for his alleged disobedience, but relinquish his
sovereignty, and submit himself and his people to the government of the colony! And the whole gist of all the complaints
since made against him, have been, not that he has committed
any acts of hostility, but that he has been *suspected* of meditating them, and of making preparations for defending himself

and people, in disregard of those one-sided, fraudulent, and
therefore void compacts, which, as if in insulting mockery,
are now claimed as solemn and mutually ratified treaties!

"Such is that other picture, which I proposed to draw, to
contrast with the one drawn by my opponent, and the exile I
have named as furnishing the materials is here, in the person
of him now speaking, to vouch for its truth and accuracy.

"Now, admitting that Philip, in view of the wrongs and indignities that have been heaped upon him and his hapless
predecessor, together with the well-warranted belief that they
were but the first steps of a policy to be pursued till he and
his nation should be entirely subjugated; admitting he has
been making military preparations, and courting alliances with
other tribes, for maintaining his sovereignty and defending
his people, does that very natural precaution place him in the
wrong?   Had he not a perfect right to do all this?   Would
not *you*, if a colony of strangers, with habits and notions repugnant to your own, should plant themselves near you, begin
to aggress on your rights, and manifest a disposition to reduce
you to subjection—would not *you* do it *yourselves?*   You
know you would.   Then ponder it, ye rulers of Plymouth, who
profess to be governed by the golden rule of doing as you
would be done by, ponder it well before you further denounce
Metacom of Mortaup for what he may have done, or rather
what he has been suspected of doing, and pause before you have
taken another step in your mistaken and indefensible policy
which shall make his cup of bitterness to overflow, and plunge
these colonies into the horrors of a savage warfare.

"Having thus disposed of the question of the true origin of
these difficulties with Philip and his people, and shown on
which side impartial justice would impute the greater blame
I now come to the present case which so manifestly grew out
of them, and which could not for a moment be of doubtful
issue but for the blinding mists of prejudice, and that most

reprehensible policy of retaliating anticipated wrongs in order to prevent their occurrence.

" The case is a plain and simple one, requiring but two points in the defense, either of which should be sufficient to secure the acquittal of the prisoners.

" FIRST, in that, I wholly deny the jurisdiction and right of this court to seize and try these prisoners, for the crime alleged against them. Sassamon, by his own confession, was a spy and a traitor. And it also appears he had previously committed some capital offence. And for these double crimes he was probably tried by Philip's Council, and voted an outlaw, whom it was the patriotic duty of every man of the tribe to try to seize and destroy. And that he was so seized and destroyed, may be equally probable. But the destroyers were only commissioned executioners of the law of an independent sovereignty, not murderers. And you have no right by the law of nations, or by treaty, to interfere with the execution; and especially so, as the deed was committed within the unceded jurisdiction of their government.

" SECOND, Provided that you had the right and jurisdiction you claim, and that Sassamon was slain by some of Philip's tribe, you cannot convict these prisoners without clearly identifying them as the perpetrators of the deed. Have you done so? Do you honestly believe, that your only professed witness of the act could identify them when standing more than a half mile distant from the scene? Would you hang a white man on such an identification? Let the consciences of the jurors answer, and direct them accordingly in the making up of their verdict. And what of the only other part of the evidence relied on—the so called ordeal of touching the corpse, and the claimed interposition of Heaven, in causing blood to issue from the already putrid body? Will you look to the agency of Heaven for the appearance of that blood, after noting the admissions and suspicious manner of that juggling

4

witness, Dick Swain; or will you believe it came there through an altogether different agency? Again let the consciences of the tryers answer. This ends the case. I have done, and will only add, let the jury beware how they render a verdict which will this day be recorded in the books of Heaven, to be forever open to the sleepless eyes of avenging justice, as well as among the records of earth, too often the habitation of blind prejudice and wilful error."

Great was the displeasure of the court functionaries and their supporters, at Williams' triumphant vindication of King Philip, the great Diabolus of their prejudice, fear, and hatred; at his fearless unmasking of their disguised policy for the subjugation of the Indians, and especially at his ungracious exposure of the weakness of their testimony against the already death-doomed prisoners. All this was abundantly manifested in the shocked and excited looks of the audience, and the vexed and angry appearance of the court, as all eyes were turned expectantly to Deacon Mudgridge, as the almost Heaven-commissioned champion who would now rush to the rescue of their endangered case. Nor were they disappointed. The Deacon with a countenance ominous of the total annihilation of his opponent, was instantly on his feet, hotly pouring forth a flood of denials, criminations, and anathemas, alternately on the head of " *the heretical Sathan-siding Williams,*" and on that of " *the wicked and God-accursed Sachem Philip, and his guilty instruments, the prisoners at the bar.*" But having pretty much exhausted his fund of these peculiar resources, in his opening speeches, he accomplished little more than travel again over his old ground; which he did with entire persistency and keeping to the end, and concluded with once more vehemently demanding the conviction of the prisoners. And the sympathizing and ready court, in a short charge much in the spirit of the Deacon's argument, submitted the case to the jury, who, in their turn, after a brief consultation among the white portion of them, and a hurried question or two to the maudlin and stupefied Indians of the panel, voted a verdict of guilty on the spot; when the court promptly pronounced the sentence, and, as if fearful their victims might escape by the usual delay, ordered that the prisoners all be *immediately* taken hence to the place of execution, and hanged, till *dead, dead !*

CHAPTER III.

Blood follows blood, and through their mortal span,
In bloodier acts conclude those who with blood began.

CHILDE HAROLD.

THE instant the death-doom of the poor, fated prisoners was
pronounced, the meeting-house began to vomit forth its crowds
of now freshly excited occupants. The court and jury had
evidently the popular tide in their favor, and accordingly,
their decision, however strangely they might have arrived at
it, was applauded by the majority of the assembled crowd,
with a unanimity and emphasis that effectually overpowered
the feeble murmurs of the less bigoted few, who were disposed to doubt the justice and wisdom of the measure. And
as the procession was being re-formed and put in motion, the
grim smile of satisfaction and inward triumph was everywhere
observable on the grave and well trained countenances of the men,
as they nodded knowingly to each other, and with quickened motions bustled to their places in the ranks; while the same exultant emotions found a livelier expression in the out-bursting
shouts of the boys, who, now as ever, the first to give voice to
any suppressed public feeling, ran trooping along in advance
towards the understood place of execution, the strongly enclosed yard of the public prison. Everything, indeed, seemed
to wear the air of rejoicing. The shrill fifes struck up their
merriest tune, and the unmuffled drums fiercely rolled their
jubilant clamors upon the air; and the procession swept on
like a triumphal march, graced with the trophies of war, to
the celebration of a victory. As the head of the column

neared the prison yard, a wide gate was thrown open, and the living mass, both those in formal array and the flanking crowd of eager spectators, together poured into the spacious enclosure ; when the first object that greeted their eyes was a new gallows, from which the workmen with their hastily snatched tools, were seen precipitately retreating, to make room for the in-rushing torrent. So well had the authorities anticipated the result of the trial, and the consequent need of such a structure to carry out the programme of the day. As this, and all similar arrangements, embracing both ropes and rough coffins, had been thus providently effected in advance, there was no need of any delay in proceeding at once to the eagerly sought consummation, and accordingly, therefore, the procession, after marching round the jail house, situated near the high fence on one side of the spacious arena, and then doubling in a smaller circle round the gallows, came to a halt, so as to bring the prisoners and their guard to the foot of the ladder leading up to the platform, which was made of rough, new planks, sufficiently extended to admit a dozen persons, and elevated about ten feet from the ground. The Indian prisoners were then at once pushed forward by the guard with the muzzles of their loaded and cocked muskets, and driven up the ladder to the platform, to which the sheriff, his few armed assistants, and the ever ready Dummer, again selected to make the customary prayer on the occasion, had all first ascended to take the victims in charge as they severally reached the top of the ladder. The prisoners were then placed in a row,,and made to stand so as to face the greater proportion of the thickly packed crowd of spectators below, when they were allowed a momentary respite, professedly to permit them to reflect on the awful fate so closely awaiting them ; but in reality, more probably, to make them an exclusive spectacle for a few moments, when nothing else was occurring to divert the attention of the spectators.

It was a strange, sad scene. First, and the most conspicuous of the motly group now occupying the scaffold, stood the
brawny savage captain and councillor of Metacom, Tobias,
glancing with proud defiance at his executioners, and now
frowning contemptuously down upon the gazing crowd below.
Next stood the son of this unflinching prisoner, a lad of perhaps eighteen, with a bosom visibly heaving with agitation,
but frequently glancing up to the dauntless countenance of
his father, as if to gain from his intrepid bearing the courage
that would enable him to die like a man and a warrior; and
last of the three doomed red men, stood a tall, straight, middle-aged Indian, with head erect, and a look of boast and
scorn, which seemed to challenge the gazers to detect in him
the least sign of fear or relenting. Next, and partly enclosing the prisoners, were arranged the sheriff's assistants,
with pistols in hand, keenly watching the former, but occasionally glancing, as if for expected orders, to their superior,
the sheriff, a severe, matter-of-fact looking man, with that
prompt, unquestioning cast of countenance which betokened
his equal readiness to make a prayer, or hang an Indian, as
the authorities might be pleased to direct. The latter important personage had taken his stand with a drawn sword in
his hand, a little in the rear of his line of assistants, and was
keeping his eye on Deacon Mudgridge, at the foot of the
ladder below, as if waiting for a signal to proceed; and last
among this contrasted group, apart from all, stood the pious
Shadow Dummer, with his folded hands raised to his chin,
his head meekly canted on one side, his eyes partly shut, and
his face devoutly turned heavenward.

Such was the contrasted picture presented in the important
few, who were now the focus of all eyes, either as executioners or sufferers, that were to furnish the materials of the great
exhibition of the day, as they stood there on the platform
above, in bold relief against the sky. Below the whole broad

acre, constituting the part of the enclosure more especially
devoted to the purposes of the occasion, was blackened all
over by the multitude of men, boys, and the spiritless, half-
civilized red men of the vicinity, going under the name of
praying Indians, with here and there a more erect, unerring
specimen of the same race, from the forests, who had neither pretension nor desire to claim any such distinction—all
here congregated to witness this widely bruited trial, and almost
as widely promised execution.   But they presented no such
appearance as that of a modern promiscuous assemblage, diversified by variety of habiliments, difference of deportment, and
faces of every expression, from sad and grave, to lively and
jocose.   For as they stood here in their broad-brimmed, sugar-
loaf hats, dark, long, and wide flapped round-abouts, trouser or
petticoat breeches, awkwardly furbelowed, or doubled over at the
knee, long, gartered hose, and buckled shoes, all of uniform cut
and color in the still unaltered fashion of the Puritan costume
of James the First—as thus garbed, they stood here, with their
stiff and measured motions, subdued demeanors, and countenances trained to the solemn, unvarying gravity which they
supposed could alone comport with the character of a Christian people, they seemed as much alike as a herd of animals
of the same species, with one general outward appearance, one
general expression of countenance, and one deportment among
old and young ; for even the boys seemed like men of a lesser
growth.   And there was no perceptible variation in the appearance of the whole vast crowd, except what might have
been occasioned by the bareheaded, blanketed Indians with
whom it was sprinkled.

But there was now a commotion among the expectant
throng.   Deacon Mudgridge, still the acting director of the
ceremonies, was seen making a signal to the sheriff, who, in
turn, was seen beckoning to some one else, standing near him.
And presently the Shadow was seen slowly advancing to the

front of the platform, when, after a solemn pause, he gradually upturned his cadaverous face, spread abroad his long,
bony arms, and raised his loud, heaven-aspiring voice in
thanksgiving and prayer. He thanked God for the special
care he had taken of his rock-founded church, and chosen
people in America—for the triumphs he had, from time to
time, vouchsafed them over the powers of darkness, as latterly
manifested in the raging of the heathen in the wilderness, and
especially he thanked him for the signal manner in which he
had made justice to triumph in their behalf, this day, through
the instrumentalities of wise and godly rulers and judges, and
the strong pillars of his church-household. And he prayed
that the auspicious result might be made to work a lasting
rebuke on the heathen malignants, now plotting the overthrow
of God's church and people, and teach their accursed sachem
a lesson which should strike terror into his black and guilty
heart, and make him to see that the Lord reigneth, and will
consume all those who may attempt to conspire against his
elect, like stubble in the fire, yea, like chaff in the fiery furnace.

All this, with great unction, he thanked God for, and all
this with equal unction and added fervor he prayed for, forgetting to offer one single word in petition for mercy for the
souls of the poor red men about to be launched into eternity.
And he, doubtless, really believed, that his effort would be as
acceptable to a just and merciful heaven, as he knew it would
be to his bigot-blind hearers on earth.

Scarcely had the loud, long-drawn voice of Dummer ceased
in the suddenly modulated double *amen*, before that of Deacon
Mudgridge, now mounted on a block about half-way between
the segregated group of court officials and the ladder, was
heard sternly muttering.

"Proceed! the prisoners have been allowed time for that
reflection, and repentance for their awful crime, which, if

rightly bestowed and truly felt, will serve, it may be, to soften their torments in the dreadful place to which they are about to go,—they have had ample time for this,—it is almost sunset,—time presses,—proceed at once with the execution."

"Proceed there!" echoed the sheriff, waving his sword to his assistants; "lead the oldest prisoner to his drop,—the furtherest there on the right,—adjust the noose round his neck, and let one of you stand ready with his hatchet to cut the cord holding up the drop, when the word is given."

The preparations had evidently all been elaborately made. Three separate drops, one for each prisoner, and all jutting out nearly a yard beyond the outer edge of the platform, had been constructed, fitted in, and made secure on a level, by a strong cord fastened to the front part, and running up to a round, elevated beam fixed up on the other side of the scaffolding for the purpose. Over these drops, dangling from the long arm of the gallows-tree, hung the fatal nooses, ready for the necks of the prisoners.

With eager alacrity, the obsequious assistants sprang to the execution of these designated preliminaries, and within two minutes, the still undaunted old warrior stood out alone on the drop, throwing his last look of contempt more defiantly than ever around him. An attempt was then made to draw a cap over his face, but by a sudden motion of his head, he brought it to his feet, and kicked it scornfully down upon the hooting crowd below.

"Strike the cord then!" shouted the sheriff.

It was done. The drop fell; and the old captain and councillor of King Philip was a contorted corpse.

The tall prisoner was next placed upon his drop and made ready for his fate, in the same way, and with the same hurried manner, as if the executioners were laboring under secret misgivings about the part they were performing, and were anxious to have the job over. His face wore a less stoical and a more excited expression than the one just gone before him. But he bore up bravely, proudly, and was turned off in the midst of his own death-chant, which he went down singing in full strain, till the jerk of the rope suddenly cut short his song and his life together.

The ready executioners then immediately laid hold of the last, whom we have named as the youthful prisoner. He was now more agitated than ever, started wildly, as the first hand was laid upon him, and hung back shuddering, and shrinking from the fatal drop before him. But finding this of no avail, he ceased his struggles, and, casting an agonized look up into the faces of his executioners, he broke out into the few English words of which he was master, and piteously begged for his life. He might as well, however, have appealed to the gallows itself; and the only response which his petitions received, was the quick lasso-like throw, and the tightening of the rope round his neck, and the violent push that sent him staggering forward on to the drop. And before he had time to recover his balance, came the sharp order of the impatient sheriff to the man standing with uplifted hatchet over the cord sustaining the drop.

"Strike !"

The rasping sound of the blow of the severing instrument instantly followed, and the drop and the prisoner went down together. But the next moment the crowd below was seen suddenly to heave like a billow, and a quick half-smothered cry of surprise and horror burst from a thousand voices. The rope had broken; and the paralyzed, but still life-whole victim had been landed, doubled and distorted, on the ground at the very feet of the shrinking throng. Two soldiers of the guard that had taken post near by, now quickly threw down their guns, sprang forward and seized the prisoner, just as he had succeeded, after several convulsive and ineffectual efforts, in gaining his feet; while another, with leveled and cocked musket, came up behind him. A glance at the ladder and the horrid implements, to which he was being forced along to undergo a second ordeal, now seemed to recall the poor fellow to his full consciousness; and he again broke out into wild lamentations and petitions for mercy.

"Stay a little," said the here interposing Deacon, to whom a new thought seemed suddenly to have occurred,—"keep your hold, but let him stand a moment. Wretch!" he continued, and turning sternly to the frantic and struggling victim,—"guilty wretch, after this foretaste of what so certainly awaits you, won't you now confess your crimes?"

The prisoner suddenly paused, and, in the first impulse of the moment, threw a look of scorn upon the other, in return for what was evidently deemed an insulting proposition, but he remained silent.

"Poor heathen," resumed the Deacon in softened tones, instead of giving, as all seemed to expect, a fierce order for the instant renewal of the murderous ordeal on the exhibition of such contumacy,—"poor benighted heathen, now if you will only say you were there and saw your father, Tobias, and that other Indian kill Sassamon, I will give you my promise that we won't hang you."

The poor, tried, and tempted sufferer again paused and seemed to be passing through a severe inward struggle between pride,—perhaps principle, and the love of life. The latter, however, as he glanced up to the dead bodies of his kindred, and the gallows, with the already substituted new rope awaiting his neck, at length appeared to prevail, and he repeated over in the affirmative the words which the other had shaped for him.

"Then you say, and truly confess, that you *did see* Tobias and the other Indian kill Sassamon, and put him through the ice?"

"Y-a-s,—said so."

"And you stood by yourself, saw the deed done, and did nothing to prevent it?"

"Y-a-s, but no help do it,—no touch him, one time, at all."

"There!" exclaimed the Deacon, triumphantly, mounting a block, and waving his hand to attract the attention of the whole assemblage, as well as that of all the court authorities,— "there! what will the blaspheming doubters say, now? He has confessed,—one of the very murderers themselves has fully confessed the foul deed! The verdict, sentence, and execution of the two dead, hell-deserving murderers, all now stand completely vindicated. It was but Heaven's justice upon them. They were both rightfully executed. And this poor wretch, also, who has just owned himself an accomplice in the deed,—what can he now say against his well-merited doom? 'Out of his own mouth will I condemn him saith my God." How shall we, then, dare incur His displeasure, by suffering the wretch to escape the death which the sentence this day so justly pronounced against him, and, which is now required at our hands? I confess," he added, looking round to those who had acted as the magistrates at the trial,—"I freely confess I do not see how we can avoid such a God-bounden duty."

"No, truly, brother Mudgridge," mildly responded one of the magistrates; "but you gave him your promise that he should not be hanged, if he confessed, as he did; and it were to be wished, in ordinary cases—not that I would contend that a promise to a heretic heathen, and made to bring about, as we are commanded, the ends of justice, should be deemed a conscience-binding matter—still, as I was about to say, it were rather, perhaps, to be wished that there was no necessity of contravening the literal words of the promise."

"I concur with the brother who has just spoken," said another of the court, a little more firmly; "but as the promise was made, I should prefer not to have it broken, at least, not in direct terms. If the governor, who withdrew just before the prisoners were swung off, was here, perhaps he would—"

"The promise need not be broken—I said he should not be hung, and he shan't," interposed the Deacon, lowering his voice, and looking knowingly to the magistrates—" leave that to me."

So saying, he turned round to the soldier standing with leveled gun, a few yards behind the prisoner, and hurriedly gave him some signal. The deafening report of a musket the next instant burst from the spot. And as the smoke rose, the hapless young Indian was seen prostrate and writhing in dying agony on the ground.

Thus was consummated a measure so unwisely begun, so questionably conducted, and so horribly concluded. As a matter of policy only, it was, under the circumstances, a measure of madness from its inception ; it was persisted in and carried on in violation of many of the most established principles of law and justice, and brought to close in a manner, about which, even some of the bigoted actors themselves, were evidently not without their misgivings. Especially was this betrayed in the case of Deacon Mudgridge, who, as soon as the last act was over, seemed impatient to have the crowd depart, lest, probably, his opponent in the trial, Williams, or others like him, who were perhaps present, should make a speech questioning some of the proceedings ; and, after fidgeting awhile at the delay of the spectators, who seemed in no haste to move, he sought the never failing Dummer, and suggested that perhaps a few words had better be said, as a sort of announcement that the proceedings were over, or as a dismissal of the assembly ; whereupon the ever ready Shadow, in a strange mingling of the announcement of a crier, with the benediction of a minister, jumbled together in accordance with the wording of the hint just received, mounted a bench and loudly exclaimed—

"The Lord reigneth, let the people rejoice ! The spectacles of the day are over. The assembly is dismissed, and will now retire to their homes; and may the Lord add his blessing, and suitably impress them all by the solemn scenes they have this day witnessed. Amen."

But contrary to the announcement of the Shadow, and no less to the wishes of the Deacon, the proceedings of the day were not to close without an additional scene, and one, too, which was as unwelcome to many as it was unexpected to all. As the crowd were beginning to get in motion, preparatory to taking their departure, individuals in different parts of the swaying throng were seen suddenly stopping short, and pointing excitingly up over the top of the tall fence on the western side of the enclosure. One after another rapidly caught the significant gestures; and soon the whole assembly were brought to a stand, and their eyes turned in the direction of the indicated spot.

There, in the last flickering gleams of the setting sun, planted on the flat roof of an old deserted building, a little removed from the other side of the fence, but so far overtopping it as to bring it within view of all, conspicuously stood, side by side, two persons of the different sexes, both garbed in dress and insignia which sufficiently betokened at once their race and individual distinction. The man, who was tall, strongly built, but in exquisite proportions, with a towering Grecian head, and features of corresponding shapeliness, wore on his head a snugly setting coroniform cap, composed of an encircling belt of bright wampun, and surmounted by a single tastily enwreathed plume of red feathers—on his feet and legs, gaily beaded, yellow gaiters; and on his body a blue broad-cloth frock, made whole like a hunting shirt, terminating in a red fringe at the knees, and confined round the waist by a broad wampun girdle. These, with the bright-bladed tomahawk, that gleamed from his girdle, and the long gun that stood resting in the hollow of his arm at his side, completed his dress, and all his visible equipment. The woman, once the belle and beauty of the forest, and still of a model figure, and finely cut features, was similarly accoutred, except in the lengthened skirt and high bosom by which the Indian female costume is mainly distinguished.

"It is King Philip !"—"Aye, King Philip and Queen Weetamo !" were soon heard buzzing through the surprised and agitated throng of gazers below. For a moment after he was discovered, the chief object of their riveted attention remained motionless, silent, and thoughtful. But now he advanced a step, his lips opened, and his voice, rising like the first low notes of a trumpet, rang out clear and distinct upon the air :—

"Listen ! listen, pale faces of Plymouth ! listen to the last words which Metacom has desire ever to say to you. The men that my father could have brushed into the sea with his hand, but instead gave them all the lands they wanted, protected them in their feebleness, and all his life stood between them and the hostile tribes who would have destroyed them—these men have grown *too strong* to remember his kindness in their treatment to his son. True, they have talked peace, but done the works of war, Metacom has talked peace and showed his good faith by doing the works of peace. They have made treaties with him as a king, and used him as a subject bound to obey them, and bear all they put upon him, without word or question. They have seized on his lands and hunting grounds, on claim of deeds from traitor Indians, that they knew had no right to sell them. They have got his people drunk and cheated them out of their furs and wampun. They have forced him to give up the hunting guns by which his people got their living. They have put heavy fines upon him. They have taken his bad Indians by the hand, and rewarded them for lying about him. They have thought to make him a slave, and once planned to seize him as a prisoner, and serve

him, may be, as they did his brother. All these things they
have done; and so broken their treaty, as many times as the
snows have come and gone, since he took the place of his father. But still Metacom wanted peace. He would not
listen to the words of war from his tribe, who knew there was
good cause of war; for he yet hoped that the pale faces would
soon show some of the repentance and good doing they so
much preach to the Indians. And he stood between them
and his angry warriors. Yet he found none of the good
doing, but much of the worse. He soon found them threatening war against him, unless he came to Plymouth to humble
and put himself in subjection. And because he did not come
they sent a paid spy among his tribe—one who was before a
traitor, and a criminal, but spared death in great mercy, and
who now died for his double crime. They then, guided by
other traitors, came within his treaty limits, seized the best
men of his tribe as murderers, who were no murderers. As
murderers they tried and sentenced them, instead of giving
them up to be tried by their own people as you were bound by
your treaty to do. And now you have dared to choke them
to death with ropes, after your own fashion, like dogs, or your
Quakers and witches. And there they hang, to tell the red
man the story of the way in which you would have peace and
friendship with his people. Metacom has been here to see
with his own eyes how you have made this black finish to
your high heaped insults and outrages. And he has now
opened his mouth to tell you he will hold back the hatchets
of his warriors no longer. And if they now be made red—
if your houses burn, and your people die—on your own con-
triving heads rest the blood of your slain men—on your own
affrighted eyes flash the light of your burning buildings, and
on your own guilty ears ring the cries of your perishing
women and children."

During the first part of this cutting and most unwelcome

expose, the red man's wrongs and their forbearing chief's grievances coming as if in confirmation of the uneasy Deacon's apprehensions, though from a far different source, that important
personage made no active demonstrations, and only stood
wincing, and frowning his pious indignation. But as the
bold speaker was drawing to the close, which involved a
virtual declaration of war, the pent wrath of the former began
to show itself in action. He started, looked fiercely around,
and then hastened in among the group of the amazed, but
more quiet officials, held a low, hurried consultation with
them, and then ran back, and made some communication to
the guard, the nature of which the next moment became apparent. A strong detachment of the guard was seen rushing
towards the entrance of the enclosure, and the rest, on a
fresher instigation, hastily cocking and raising their muskets.
But all in vain. The quick eye of the wary chief had detected,
and rightly divined the whole movement. And before the
sound of his last terrible words had died on the ears of his
dismayed and trembling listeners, he had disappeared, and was
lost, alike as a target for those preparing to fire on him from
within, and as a prisoner-prize for those sent round to seize
him from without. He had somehow strangely slipped away
and was nowhere to be found.

But though Philip, who had caused so much annoyance to
the court leaders, as well as the deep sensation everywhere
apparent among the general mass of the assemblage, had now
disappeared, and all seemed to breathe easier, like men suddenly relieved from the presence of some fearful apparition—
though Philip, the chief cause of the commotion, had disappeared ; yet neither the one class nor the other of the disturbed throng were to be let off without a finale of the strange
scene, calculated to sink deeper in minds imbued with superstition than anything in the one they had just witnessed.
Philip had indeed taken his final departure, but his companion

5

remained unmoved and motionless, standing up in the gray twilight like some antique bronze statue, frowning down upon *all*, but with looks particularly bent on the soldiers who had just been baulked of their noble game, and who still stood with their guns partly raised in the direction, and seemingly hesitating, in their evident surprise that she had not taken fright and fled also, whether she was to be made a substitute target for their bullets. In a moment she defiantly took a step in advance, and with wild gestures, and in shrill and frantic tones, exclaimed,—

" Let the pale faces fire, if they like. It would be a brave thing to kill a squaw, and a fitting close of their bloody days' doings! Aye, let them fire, if they will, and finish an old work on the queen-wife of the murdered Alexander! What! cowards, are you afraid of a woman? Then hear the curse and prophecy of the bruised and broken-hearted Weta-moo, who has been made strong enough to live only by the hope of seeing the hour when her terrible wrongs should be avenged! Base poisoners of my noble husband, that sweet hour is at hand. The day of the red man's reckoning has come. The bitter curse, which, in all her dreams, and in all her day doings, has for years been burning in the torn bosom of Wetamoo, is at last about to light upon your heads. You have at last aroused the old lion of his long angry tribe, and you will soon see the difference between Philip in the war-path, and Philip meekly asking peace in your council lodge. He will soon see for every drop of the blood of his people you have this day shed, a whole river flowing from your own. And the glad eyes of Wetamoo will soon see, too, for every hair of her murdered husband's head, a bloody scalp torn from the heads of the pale faces, swinging in the lodges of the red men. You made Wetamoo a widow, and you have made two other widows to-day, but for every widow you have made among the red men, you shall see a thousand wailing widows

among yourselves. Your houses and hearthstones shall all be
made red with blood, and your whole land heavy with tears.
This is the curse and prophecy of Wetamoo, and by her God,
and by your God, she swears that the one shall follow you till
every word and jot of the other be fulfilled."

She ceased. As she had been permitted, notwithstanding
the boldness of her denunciations, and the fearful import of
her prophetic maledictions, to proceed unmolested, so unmolested she was allowed to retire from her stand, and go where
she chose. And so ended the day, made memorable in Puritan history, as the precursor of the desolating and terrible
Indian war that so closely followed. Yes, the day, with all
its exciting scenes, had at length ended; but it had ended in
a manner which was as little anticipated by the movers of its
principal proceedings as it was relished by them. Their object in the arrest, trial, and summary execution of the poor vic-
timized red men, was far less to further the ends of justice,
than to overawe Philip and his tribe, and all other tribes
with whom he might otherwise ally himself for hostile purposes; and at the same time gratify the bitter prejudices of
their whole people, and impress them with the desired ideas
of their own inflexible justice, and fearlessness in executing
it. It was with the originators, therefore, what they doubtless deemed a very sagacious political measure, especially devised to intimidate the apprehended foe, and thus, to use a
modern phrase, to conquer a peace with the dreaded Philip
and his stubborn tribe, which they were conscious could, with
their own deliberately aggressive policy, be in no other manner obtained. And these astute managers evidently had, to
the end of the trial, even in despite the untoward appearance
and effort of Roger Williams, fully succeeded in keeping the
popular current, as before intimated, running strongly on
their side, as manifested in the fierce exultation of the whites,
and the trembling awe of the praying and other Indians in

attendance, at the result of the promptly conducted prosecution.   But the execution, especially the last act of the revolting scene, had obviously been an overdose even for Bigotry
herself.   A reaction of feeling was beginning to take effect;
and doubt and apprehension on the white, and kindling
resentment on the Indian spectators, were usurping the place
of the defiant exultations and over-weening confidence of the
one, and the abject fears of the other, that but a few hours
before were on all sides so palpably displayed.

It was of this altered state of feeling in the mingled crowd,
that the sagacious Philip, who had been an unseen spectator
of the whole scene, and whose discriminating eye had detected
the change of the moral current, had suddenly resolved to
take the advantage by boldly showing himself, and make a
speech intended no less for effect on his own recreant subjects
present, than on the superstitious and bigot-blind followers of
the court of Plymouth.   And he had counted not in vain.
His bold and skillful effort, falling, as it did, on the doubtful
and fluctuating feelings of the crowd, had brought the gathering tide against him at least to an ebb.   And the work which
he had so successfully begun seemed to receive a finishing
blow in the fiery and fearful words of the wrongs-treasuring
Wetamoo, whose weirdlike foretokenings of blood and desolation fell on ears and hearts too deeply impressed with the wild
superstitions of the times to resist the spell of fear and fore-
boding, which those words were so well calculated to throw
over them.

Thus did the outgeneraling chief turn the arms of the
court of Plymouth against themselves, in all that related to
the effect counted on from their measure, as was abundantly
shown, not only by the silent, thoughtful, and strangely altered
manner in which the mingled assemblage dispersed that night,
but by the general panic that immediately followed among the
whites, and the disappearance of large numbers of recreant or

praying Indians, who were found flocking to the standard of their old master, now, for the first time, thrown defiantly on the breeze.

"But, can this"—here, perhaps, asks the surprised and doubting reader, whose ears, from his youth upwards, have been continually regaled with the unqualified, stereotyped laudations of the intelligence and exalted virtues of the Pilgrim Fathers, which, almost from time immemorial, have been one of the accepted droppings of the pulpit, and one of the staple themes of Fourth of July and Pilgrim-day rostrums— "can this be a truthful picture of the treatment and policy of the colonists towards the Indians, or those of them, at least, who declined to part with their tribal independence? Can it be any thing like a fair representation of the proceedings of one of the courts of justice of that day? And, finally, can it place in a true light the hitherto unquestioned religious character of the rulers and chief actors in the public affairs of that peculiar era?"

We hope not, doubting reader; for the credit of our forefathers, we really hope it is an exaggerated picture, or at least one of a very limited application. But till you shall have traveled back with us, and, unbiased by all pre-conceived opinions, have carefully examined the records of those times, taken all the facts and circumstances stated and admitted by cotemporary writers, and, rejecting all modern eulogistic or palliating commentaries, have drawn for yourself all the fairly deducible inferences—till you have done this, and convinced us and yourself, by that only safe process of arriving at the truth, that our picture is an unwarranted and improbable one, we must let it stand, and bear the responsibility of its general truthfulness.

The great mistake of the pilgrim fathers consisted in making the civil rule subservient to the ecclesiastical. This, from the very nature of the case, ever *has* led, and ever *must*

lead, to grave errors in the administration of justice, and fatal
mis-steps in governmental policy; for the leaders of the
church less often attain their positions of influence by the
capacities which would qualify them to become advisers and
dictators in civil proceedings, than by the mere fervor of
their religious enthusiasm; and their counsels, consequently,
must ever be unsafe, and, however honestly intended, not
unfrequently lead to measures productive of public mischief
or individual wrong. This placing of the civil power under
church control would have been less dangerous, doubtless, if
the church had been built up on the best principles for in-
suring its purity. But this could not have been so here; for
here, again, the pilgrim fathers fell into another error, which
must often have been as injurious to the interests of true
religion, as it was unsafe in the administration of civil authority. They had established the rule, that no man should hold
any office unless he was a member of the church. If human
nature was the same then as now, this was virtually offering a
reward for hypocrisy, under which all the most cunning, calculating, and ambitious, without any reference to their secret
feelings or belief, would go through the forms of a profession,
and rush into the church. And the same unscrupulous ambition and lack of principle that had induced them to seek
admission into the sacred fold, would, when they got there,
induce them to strive for posts of influence, where they could
control the sincere and undiscerning, and, through the power
thus obtained, subserve their own wicked or selfish purposes
at the expense of private right and public welfare.

Under all these circumstances, therefore, why should it be
thought strange or improbable to find in control, at times, that
class of men of whom we have made Deacon Mudgridge the
representative, or that the latter should find ready instruments
in another and entirely honest class, represented by the sincere
but zeal-blinded Dummer, and still more ready tools in yet

another, and the most despicable class of all, represented by the pliant and unscrupulous Dick Swain?

The pilgrims closely resembled the Jews, whom they avowedly copied. But it should be said of both, that, with all their faults, the severe physical training they imposed upon themselves, and the high moral energies they cultivated, were admirably calculated to make nurseries of men destined to found great and powerful nations. The training of Moses made the soldiers of Joshua and David, whose achievements resulted in the establishment of the splendid empire of Solomon; and the training of the pilgrims made the soldiers of our revolution, and their achievements have also resulted, under a more diffused intelligence, and modified and more correct views of the offices and requirements of religion, in the still more splendid and beneficent fabric of our present American liberty.

With these remarks, intended to meet the scruples of the doubters at the threshold, and apprise all that we do not intend to follow the beaten track any farther than we think it leads to truth and justice, we will return to the thread of our narrative.

CHAPTER IV.

"His virtues being overdone, his face
    Too grave, his prayers too long, his charities
    Too pompously attended, and his speech
    Larded too frequently, and out òf time,
    With serious phraseology,—were rents
    That in his garments opened in spite of him,
    Through which the well accustomed eye could see
    The rottenness of his heart."

                          POLLOCK'S HYPOCRITE.

NIGHT had now cast its sable mantle over the earth, and the tumults of the day and the strong passions of human throngs had subsided in the darkness. But soon the great, round moon came rolling up from behind the seemingly long, watery mound that bounded the sea-ward limits of the scene ; and anon the whole extended view of land and waters, first gradually disclosed in the clustering pencils of her mellow beams, shooting athwart the broad expanse of the sleeping bay, and then tipping with silvered fringes the varied objects of the surrounding shore, stood revealed in all the solemn splendors of a moon-lit land-scape.

Perhaps there is no scene or situation that so much disarms us of the promptings of selfish or evil inclinations, and disposes up to pensive contemplation, as that in which we find ourselves, when looking abroad in a bright moonlight night. We feel that it is neither night nor day, and while we are tempted to forego the mental quiescence of the one, we are restrained from pondering the agitating schemes of the other, partly, it may be, from the conscious uselessness of then nerving ourselves for any action, but more, we believe, from the mysteriously softening and benign influences of the hour And that gravely humorous bard, who penned the couplet:—

—"then rose full soon
That patroness of rogues the moon,"

fouly libeled the character of the amiable queen of night. *Her* patronage is not sought by the prowling felon and evil doer, who love darkness, but by the lover and sentimentalist, who delight to appropriate her propitious influences. Job speaks of the sweet influences of the pleiades, but if any of the heavenly bodies possess and exert any such properties on the human family, the moon, we think, is clearly entitled to the pre-eminence. And if, under her sober and quiet dispensation, the thoughts of the imaginative and superstitious sometimes take flights not warranted by reason, or shape themselves into distempered fancies, it would hardly be fair to hold her chargeable for their vagaries.

The same bright luminary, which had thus brought into beautified prospect the varied features of the landscape, also brought into view scores of the good people of Plymouth, who, tempted by the beauty of the evening, and moved with an uneasiness and concern that led them to seek companionship for an interchange of opinions, had left their houses and gone into the streets. And here they were seen standing in scattered groups around the open doors, in the yards, or in the road-ways, discussing, with subdued demeanors, and low, suppressed tones, the incidents of the day, and the consequences which might flow from them. From the anxious and disturbed manner and tones every where observable among both speakers and listeners, the fact became obvious that a general feeling of doubt and perplexity had fallen on the people ; and that the boasted measure of their rulers, which had that day been consummated, and from which so much had been promised and predicted, towards intimidating King

Philip and his tribe, was not only felt to have proved a failure, but that what had been done would be likely to hasten on the menaced evil. Mingling with the rest of one of the principal groups thus assembled in the streets, were again found most of the personages who were introduced in the opening scene of the day; and among them stood the gab-gifted Shadow, holding forth in his usual strain, but with words particularly intended for those who had been timidly giving open expression to the general feeling of doubt and apprehension, now become too irrepressible to be longer concealed.

"It is," said he,—"it is from the sins of the people, and our lack of duty-doing courage to wash our hands of them, by fitting and acceptable acts of expiation, that we have only to fear. Every day I behold doings that will make us to stink in the nostrils of heaven. Every day mine eyes are pained with sights among old and young, that proclaim us in a loud voice—yea, in the voice of many thunders, to be a perverse and sinful generation. Our women are seen decked with vain ornaments. Our young men and maidens are seen familiarly walking together in the streets in open day, or riding, side by side, into the country for vain recreations, after the manner of the carnal minded and uncircumcised. The holy Sabbath is desecrated in our midst by cooking victuals, and secular conversation on that sacred day. The land has become full of heresies and abominable doctrines. And even we of the household of faith, I greatly fear me, have erred and done foolishly in that we have not frowned upon, and put a stop to these loose doings of the people; and especially in that we have not put down with the arm of the law, sanctified and made strong by the orderings of the Church, the damnable heresies of the Quakers, and other schismatics, as we formerly did, and as the law even now commands us to do. Yea, I greatly fear we have erred and gone astray by our want of faithfulness and mistaken omissions of duty, to wipe away the reproach brought upon us by these abominations. But there is now great reason to hope that our skirts will soon become cleared of the sin of our remissness. We have this day made manifest our determination to avoid and avert from our guilty land the curse that fell on Saul for sparing the heathen, Amalekitish Agag, whom God had ordered his people to destroy. We have this day executed vengeance on three worse heathen than the idolatrous followers of Agag, wherein our modern Agag of the wilderness will be made to fear and tremble."

" He did not appear to fear and tremble much to-day, methought, when he appeared before the whole court and people, at the close of the execution, and so boldly told them what they might expect from what they had done," carelessly remarked Vane Willis, the successful young marksman, before introduced, who seemed to have been listening rather impatiently to the Shadow's notions of duty and way of carrying them out.

" The young man mistakes the manifestations," rejoined Dummer. " The scourging of Sathana will make him to rave and howl, and the more he raves and howls, the stronger the token that he hath been hit and balked in his devilish designs. Now, *I* look upon the chafings and raging of that audacious Sachem, and that she-devil and heathen sorceress he brought with him, to alarm us with false prophecy, as a sure sign that our wise and fearless rulers have done that which has struck him in a vital part. It is a good omen, brethren. This chafing child of Sathana, as he clearly is, may rage awhile, but he will soon slink back to his place; and we shall hear no more of him, or his rebellions. And this I know, is Deacon Mudgridge's opinion."

So saying, the self-satisfied zealot turned and walked off to the residence of his oracle, the important personage whose opinion he had just quoted as something too infallible ever to

be gainsayed or questioned, leaving the rest of the company
to resume their discussion.

"Dummer is a man of great faith," observed one of the
more thinking and discreet of the group, after the subject of
his remark had got out of hearing; "and I hope his predictions about the effect and consequence of this day's work will
prove true ones. But—"

"But what?" interposed Sniffkin, the aristocratic young
court lackey of the opening scene of the story—"but what,
sir? Mr. Dummer is undoubtedly right. The court acted
wisely, and knew what they were about when they started this
measure. It was a grand stroke of policy; and what is better, they have carried it to the end in a manner well calculated to ensure the object. And the effect on the damned
Sachem will be just what Dummer predicts. I am confident
of it."

"If you knew better what stuff Metacom was made of, you
might be a trifle less confident, perhaps," responded Willis,
quietly.

"It is quite consistent," retorted Sniffkin, contemptuously,
without turning to the speaker—"consistent, and to be expected, that a fellow who showed so much sympathy for the
guilty heathen before their trial, and then at the trial assisted
a noted heretic to thwart justice and get them clear, should
now try to destroy the effect of the wholesome example of a
result he wished to prevent. If Mr. Dummer, whose face is
set like a flint against scoffers, and all those who consort with
heathens and heretics, had known the fellow he spoke to, his
just rebuke would not have been quite so mild a one, I fancy.
I think some folks had better look out, lest they soon find
their feet on slippery places."

"I think so, too," chimed in Dick Swain, still smarting
under the remembrance of the hazardous dilemma in which he
believed Willis had assisted Williams to place him at the

trial. "I think just so myself; for now the guilty heathen dogs are disposed of, the Quakers and heretics, I understand, are to have their turn next."

"And hypocrites, knaves, and fools are then to have their own way without let or hindrance, I suppose," rejoined the marksman, with an air of undisguised disdain, as he whirled on his heel, and left the group, on his way up the street.

"Dog him, Dick," whispered Sniffkin, into the ear of the other, pointing after his retiring rival; "dog him; see where he goes. And as matters now appear to be in a good shape to leave, I will go home."

The two last named persons then departed on their different destinations, leaving the rest of the company to continue the discussion unbiased by the words or presence of either of the contending parties, to whom they had been listening.

"I am afraid," at length remarked the man who had ventured to intimate some doubts respecting Dummer's confident assurances. "I am afraid that young man, though rather rough and irreverent, perhaps, towards Mr. Sniffkin and Dick Swain, is right in what he evidently believes will be the consequence of hanging these Indians. I am afraid our rulers have been a little too fast."

"And so am I," responded another, who had also been smothering his convictions. "I didn't think so much of it till I heard King Philip, standing up there so calm and dignified like, tell over how he had intended to keep peace, and then come out so bold and square for war at last, on account of what he had seen there to-day. I couldn't help thinking that there was something kinder reasonable in what he said; and then to hear the Indian woman, who is, like enough, a witch, as Mr. Dummer says, and can foretell things, to hear her curse and prophesy! Why, it enymost made my hair stand up on my head!"

Others, now all restraints on giving free utterance to their

feelings were removed, were beginning, all at once, to give expression to the boding fears with which *their* minds were also
laboring; when they were cut short by the sudden appearance
of a man running towards them from another group that had
been standing at some distance, and in a more open part of the
street.

" Have you seen the great mystery?" he almost breathlessly
exclaimed ; " have you here noticed the strange appearance of
the moon to-night?"

" No, what is it? what is it?" eagerly demanded a dozen
excited voices.

" Here, come to this open place, you can see it between the
houses—there," continued the herald of the strange tidings, as
the others all now rushed to the spot, " there, only look there,
a blood-stained human scalp, right in the middle of the
moon !"

All eyes followed the eagerly pointed finger, till they rested
on the innocent face of the luminary that had so suddenly become an object of suspicious interest ; when, surely enough,
a scalp seemed, to their startled and distorted visions, to have
grown out of that scraggy, opake spot in the moon which has
so often attracted the eyes of wondering childhood, at all
times, but which now, owing to the peculiar state of the atmosphere, was seen marked and defined with unusual distinct-
ness. First one, then another, and then all, assisted by
their excited imaginations, recognized the shape and appearance of that horrid token of savage ferocity, and unanimously
proclaimed it an omen of coming war, which could no longer
be mistaken. But they were not to be required to rely alone
on the evidence of this monstrous prefiguration for proof of the
near approach of such a calamitous event. In a few moments
the amazed and shuddering gazers were aroused by the sounds
of multitudinous footfalls ; and turning, they saw a dusty horseman, with a mingled crowd of excited men and boys hurrying

along, behind, and on each side of him, in full march towards them.

"News, news !" shouted a man, who now started forward in advance of the rest of the new comers by way of heralding their approach ; " great news from the other colony ! Here is a man straight from Boston. Form a ring, form a ring, and then we can all hear him relate the strange tidings he brings us."

A ring was accordingly formed, and the news-monger, still sitting on his horse, proceeded to relate to the gaping crowd, how, one or two days before, "in a clear, still, sunshiny morning, there were divers persons in Maldon, who heard in the air, on the south-east of them, a great gun go off, and presently thereupon, the report of small guns, like musket shot, very thick discharging, as if there had been a battle." In another town, the people had been astonished by " the flying of bullets, which came singing over their heads; after which the sound of drums, passing along west-ward was very audible." And in several other places, invisible troops of horses were heard riding to and fro, like squadrons charging in hostile conflict.*

Great was the fear and perplexity that fell on the minds of the crowd as they listened to the narration of these prodigies, which, with the one they themselves had just witnessed they all, with one accord, and without one thought of attempting to account for them on natural principles, set down as unmistakably portents of war. And thinking of their wives and children, in their agitation and dismay, they immediately broke up, and hurried to their homes, as if the dreadful tomahawk might be already busy there in the work of death.

But, while these things were thus agitating, with doubts and fears, the common people without, there was one within

* See Cotton Mather's Magnalia for the prodigies here related as the precursors of King Philip's war.

doors that evening, who, wrapt in his own self-sufficiency, was never more assured and exultant in his life; and that one was the chief mover, and the most active participator in the events of the past day—the untiring Deacon Mudgridge, to whose affectedly plain, but really very costly mansion, we will now take the reader.

The Deacon, having finished his supper, and visited his private cupboard for that little addition to creature comforts, which he occasionally took just "for stomach's sake," had repaired to his usual sitting room, where he was accustomed to receive the numerous calls of those daily coming to consult him on matters of church and state; for so important in the public mind had his opinions become, that few things of any moment, in either, were undertaken without his advice or concurrence. He was now slowly pacing his room and soliloquizing half aloud, in that kind of strange jumble of prayer and self-gratulation, to which the scathing genius of Burns subsequently gave form and habitation in "Holy Willie," and his prayer—

> "O Lord, I bless thy matchless might,
> When thousands thou hast left in night,
> That I am here before thy sight,
> 　　For gifts an' grace,
> A burnin' an' a shinin' light,
> 　　To a' the place."

"Ay, here, firm as a rock, while others faint, or would succumb to the powers of darkness. And then the great matter of this day—Lord, I bless thee for carrying me through it, and exalting my horn in that thou hast given me the triumph—(Well, I think they will see, now, that but for me, the heathen had never been thus signally chastised and discomfited, to the saving of the people and the glory of God. But that accursed schismatic Williams! verily, I did not know, one while, how the thing would befal.) Yet thou,

Lord, didst rebuke my want of faith by giving me the victory. Nevertheless, Lord, do not let that vile man come between me and thy helping hand again, lest, peradventure, the people in their weakness be led away by him. Lord, put thy hand upon him, and all thine enemies, and continue to build up thy servant, whom thou hast so much blest, and particularly aid and assist him by thine orderings, in that other matter which thou knowest he has in mind to see perfected, and—"

A gentle rap, rap, on the outside of the door opening from the street into the apartment, here interrupted the Deacon, and quickly assuming the meekly wise and sanctimonious air, which he usually wore in public, he responded—

" Peace be with you ! come in."

The door opened, and the Shadow meekly entered.

" Well pleased at thy coming, friend Dummer, inasmuch as it gives me opportunity to thank and congratulate thee on thy faithful and opportune public services, during the day just brought to such a triumphant close."

" I did not come expecting such praise, Deacon Mudgridge, and I greatly fear me, I do not deserve it. I feel myself but a poor weak vessel, Deacon Mudgridge."

" And therein consisteth your strength, because it maketh you to lean directly on the Lord, who turneth trusting weakness into a strength to the overcoming of the children of Belial. Your prayers, to-day, friend Dummer, were full of holy power, and had an extraordinary adaptedness."

" I will not try to disguise how much it pleaseth my heart to hear such words from one who hath it in his power to advance those who are found worthy, to posts of greater usefulness in the Lord's household ; and I have sometimes thought that if—"

" Ay—ay—I know, and it shall be brought about speedily,

6

friend Dummer. But how do men say *I* acquitted myself, to-
day, against the adverse powers brought against me ?"

" With admirable wisdom ; and it was of that I principally
came to congratulate thee ; and I think *we* of the household
of faith ought all to feel great and exceeding gratitude, that
we have such a buckler and shield to ward off the arrows of
Sathana, whose presence methought was never more visible
than to-day."

" Your last remark shows you to be a man of discernment,
friend Dummer. You are verily right about the devilish
manifestations of to-day, especially in the untoward coming,
and through all the subtle managings and arguings of that
man of sin, the schismatic and dangerous Williams."

" Yea, truly ; but then, with what astonishing quickness
and power you met his devices, and overwhelmed him at every
point, Deacon ?"

" Ay, you must bear in mind I am an old soldier in the
Church Militant, friend Dummer. I saw from the first moment of the trial, from tokens well known to me, that Sathan
had come up to defeat us, and was already busy with his invisible instigations, at the ear of Williams, as was another I
could name. But arming myself in the panoply of prayer and
divine promptings, I followed the old sarpent in all his doub-
lings and windings, and think, as you say, that I completely
circumvented him at every point, and carried the battle glo-
riously ; yea, even unto the righteous termination thereof. But
not mine the praise—not mine the glory, friend Dummer."

" Truly not, Deacon Mudgridge ; but then we cannot help
admiring the chosen and honored instrument of such achieved
glories, whereby both church and state were crowned, as to-day,
with righteous judgment unto the manifest averting of calamities."

" Thus much I don't know that I should try to prevent,
friend Dummer. But did you perceive anything in the goings

on at the execution, betoking to your mind the presence of Sathan there also ?"

" Verily I did think I perceived his promptings in the ra vings of the audacious Sachem, and moreover in the false prophecies and vile cursings of the red sorceress, as I think she must be, who was with him, at their mysterious coming. Yea, I did perceive tokens of his presence, and have already asserted it, in my laborings with the people, in the street, this very evening."

" You did right, both in the assertions, and in your labor- ings, which, as I suggested, when we left the scene, seemed to be required to calm, and put confidence into the minds of the people, who, through their weakness, were, I perceived, troubled with some misgivings. But you might have gone further and pointed out to them the marvel of the breaking of the rope, when the last of the damnable trio was swung off; for what but Sathan's own hand could have sundered that strong, new rope ? Nothing. It was scorched and made rotten by the hot grasp of his fiery fingers. But you saw that I did not allow his cunning device to serve him ; for the young imp, he had thought thus to save, as soon as we had got his confession, was sent to hellward almost as quick as his accursed companions. Yea, I saw all that clearly ; and when the impudent Sachem and his she confederate so strangely appeared up there, as if they had been transported to the spot through the air by the taking of one under each arm, methought I could distinctly see him standing bodily, in the shape of the great Apollyon himself, leaning over from behind them, and grinning and gibbering into their ears. It was then I gave the order to the soldiers to fire, and had they done so quick enough, the Sachem had died; since I had breathed a hasty blessing on the undis- charged bullets. And I an't so sure but the infernal prompter himself would have been grievously wounded."

" These things are truly marvelous, Deacon, and fill me

with amazement at your penetrating ability. But do you
think we have done all we must do, in the purging out of
diabolisms and heresies in the land, before the Lord will fully
accept us and make us to be wholly victorious over our
enemies?"

"No, of a verity we have not; and it rejoiceth me exceedingly to find one at least, who, like you, seems to have a just
and holy sense of what is required of the church and rulers
in these times of evil omen. We must first wrestle mightily
with God by prayer and fastings, and at the same time be
doing the works of faith by putting down, with a fearless
hand, all kinds of heresies and misdoings."

"It is a truth, Deacon Mudgridge—a sad truth, and one
that should shame us to be up and doing. We are over slack
and timid in our marked lines of duty, and I concur with your
opinions, even unto the full measure thereof. Something *must*
be done; but where do you think it were most expedient to
make the beginning of the needful and wholesome work of
sin-purging and acceptable expiation?"

"On just the like of that dangerous schismatic, (and a rank
heretic, also, I doubt me not,) who made us so much trouble
to-day, whom I think our rulers erred in admitting to speak,
and who, instead, ought to have been put under arrest for
meet punishment. But our governor, though ready to put
down the heathen savages with an iron hand, and with a will
and courage that knows no trembling nor hesitation, seems not
to understand the devices of Satan and the dangerous workings of heresies on a people, and so is timid and doubtful in
these matters."

"Then *you*, Deacon, must be the man to move in the
matter of these crying abominations."

"I suppose I must; for duty is duty, and seeing wherein it
ought to be done, I should not, it may be, shrink from the

doing thereof. And you, brother Dummer, must take hold with me."

"The Lord helping me, I will not be laggard; but whither more particularly pointeth the finger of duty among the multitude of offenses requiring the hand of correction?"

"I have already hinted what should be done with those steeped in damnable heresies, like the man Williams and his confederating disciples. There is another class that I consider even more dangerous—I mean that pestilent sect called Quakers. There is a law still in force requiring the branding of them—boring with hot irons their tongues, which had uttered false doctrines—whipping them from town to town on their way to banishment, and the inflicting of the just penalty of death if they returned. That wholesome law was once commendably executed, and the land was blessed accordingly. But now, in our guilty remissness, it has become but little better than a dead letter. Quakers, and even returned Quakers, I grieve to say, walk among us unmolested."

"Yea, Deacon, I greatly fear this thing is so."

"But what would you say of one who was both heretic and Quaker, or at least was deeply tainted with their abominable doctrines?"

"I should say of him, *anathema maranatha*, and count it a God-bounden duty to move against him."

"And yet, such an one, as I know, through the praiseworthy faithfulness of our trusty, albeit sometimes a little irregular brother, Dick Swain, appeared in the streets this very morning, and openly took sides with the heathen prisoners, and reviled our rulers. And then, to add to his contumacy and wicked intent, the fellow unblushingly went to the side of Williams, and prompted and aided him through the trial, in perverting the evidence unto the defeating of justice and judgment."

"Surely that were a grievous offence. But, who is he?"

" A youngerly, but very froward fellow, called Vane Willis, from some place out of town, though often here, it is thought, and I fear with no good design. In truth, I have the most painful surmises, that he is trying to tamper with some who have been especially placed under godly influences, and the protecting care of the Christian household. You well knew our worthy sister, in the Lord, the widow Southworth, who left us a few months ago ?"

" Surely, I did,—a godly woman, eschewing all false doctrines, and full of spiritual obedience."

" You knew, likewise," resumed the Deacon, drawing near the other, and speaking lower, " that this family, on the fleeing of her unfortunate husband, afterwards slain by salvages no doubt, was put under my sole charge and guardianship, which I discharged to the great satisfaction of our duty doing sister, who always depended on me for advice in all that related to the spiritual and temporal affairs of herself and her daughter, now left behind her. But that daughter is not like her mother in many things, being more inclined to doubts in some of the matters of sound doctrines, as I have thought I sometimes perceived, and less inclined to give ear to wholesome counsel. Now her mother and I both labored to get her into the fold of the church; but failing in that, we, at length, fully agreed on betrothing her to my nephew, Timothy Sniffkin, for her temporal advantage and spiritual safety, and then, when her mother was taken away, I invited her to take up her residence at my house, knowing that then she would not have there any proper protectors; but she seemed strangely perverse in all these matters. Now I greatly fear that this pestilent fellow that I spoke of, with whom she confesses to some acquaintance, has had some hand in her perverseness."

" Heinous! how heinous, if so!" said the shocked Dummer,— "I see,—I see the thoughtless and straying lamb of our flock is to be saved from the devouring wolf. But, the means,—the means, Deacon ?"

" In my holy anxieties, I have pondered the thing diligently, and have hit upon a course. As a first step, I would have you to-morrow go and labor with her, with counsel and prayer, to induce her to come into the sacred fold. Peradventure, with my backing, she will listen; and the path will then be opened to almost certain success. Meanwhile, we must narrowly watch the base beguiler. If he is a Quaker, as Dick thinks it is clearly certain he is, then——"

Sharp outcries, and the sounds of hurrying footsteps in the street, here cut short the conference of these worthies, who, running to the window, soon gathered from the hurrying passers, that a man, supposed to be Dick Swain, had been seized by some of King Philip's crew, just outside the town, and carried off; when the Deacon and his Shadow snatched up their hats and joined the throng rushing on to the rescue.

CHAPTER V.

"O luve will venture in whaur it daur na weel be seen."

THE alarm mentioned at the close of the last chapter, had
proceeded from the loud cry of "*Help! help! Indians! Indians!*" heard rising from some point in the bushy pine plain
swelling up from the rear of the village. On almost any
previous evening, no general alarm probably would have been
thus created; for the person or persons hearing the outcry,
would have fearlessly gone alone to the spot indicated by the
noise, to see what was wanted. But on this evening, so
deeply excited and apprehensive had all classes become, from
witnessing the spectacles of the day, and hearing of the attendant omens, that those whose ears the cry had reached, instead
of proceeding to the place, had turned and ran the other way
into the village, spreading the alarm through the streets, and
then facing round to lead those whom they had thus rallied
out, to the locality of the supposed trouble. And on rushed
the confused throng,—the Deacon, the Shadow, and all, each
armed with a musket, old sword, pitchfork, hoe, cudgel, or
such other defensive implement as most readily came to
hand.

"There! it was somewhere about here that I was passing
when I heard the outcry, and the sound came out from those
low scattering pines," exclaimed the man that had led the
way, stopping in an open field a little beyond the last house
on that border of the village, and pointing to a line of scattering bushes about forty rods ahead.

"Let us form a line and advance then," cried one of the more resolute of the company.

"Wouldn't it be meet on this alarming occasion first to have a prayer?" asked the Shadow, in a quavering voice, beginning to raise his shaking hands to suit the action to the word.

"Stay a little, brother Dummer," interposed Deacon Mudgridge; "let us first collect our minds and reason together on the matter. And firstly, is there any certainty as to the man thus boldly snatched from our midst by the audacious salvages?"

"Why, I thought to be sure, that the voice sounded greatly like unto the voice of Dick Swain," responded the man who had first spoken.

"He is right," sung out Sniffkin, who had prudently stopped some half dozen rods in the background, but was now venturing considerably nearer. "He is undoubtedly in the right about it, for I have reason to know myself, that Dick Swain is the man. But it will be of no avail to go into the woods after him. There is, likely enough, at this very moment, a whole line of hostile Indians lying in ambush in yonder pines to cover the retreat of the miscreant abductors, who, no doubt, are now far on the way to King Philip's camp, and I pretty well know who is at the head of them."

"Things being so," after a long pause, began the Deacon, who seemed to comprehend the allusions of Sniffkin, and who had been casting about for a decent excuse for backing out himself—"things being so, and it sometimes being but a wrongful tempting of Providence to rush into the dangers where our righteous indignation would carry us, I would rather counsel, lest we act without due consideration, that we all now return to the meeting-house yard, for a more fitting consultation, wherein the conclusion, peradventure, may be arrived at to recommend the calling out of our brisk company of armed troopers."

This motion being eagerly seconded by the Shadow and Sniffkin, was soon unanimously carried, when the crowd, now promptly led forward by the last named brave personage, all took their way to the meeting-house, many of them evidently breathing much easier than when on their outward march towards the suspicious thickets where the luckless Dick had so strangely disappeared.

But leaving this excited assemblage to their discussions respecting the fate of Dick Swain, and the most advisable steps to be taken for his rescue, we will now take the reader to a scene enacting in another part of the village, which will, perhaps, sufficiently elucidate the pretty little fright of the Puritan populace which we have been describing, and, at the same time, develope another step in the progress of our eventful story.

In a somewhat secluded location, on a different border of the town, stood, at this period, a substantial dwelling-house, so constructed as very happily to combine, in the general appearance, the architectural characteristics of the best class of English cottages with those of the American farm house. Although not a very ancient building, it was yet old enough to have allowed time, since its construction, for the full growth of the well arranged shrubbery that embowered it. Standing back some distance from the road, it was enclosed by the long, shaded yard in front, a garden on one side, a fruit orchard on the other ; and extensive cultivated fields extending all along the rear. Along the front of the house ran a wide verandah, which was enveloped in a cloud of clustering vines in full foliage, through which, at the particular hour we have chosen for the introduction of the reader to the scene at hand, a small light, from one of the front rooms, was fitfully gleaming. In that room, and by that light, placed on a small table standing near

an open window, sat the now sole mistress of the establishment, a dark-eyed girl of about twenty. She was attired in
the habiliments usually worn by the wealthier of her sex, but
which, on her finely turned figure, were made to appear, as dress
ever will on some persons, to unusual advantage. She held in
her hand a richly bound old volume, from which she occasionally raised her eyes and turned her head to listen—sometimes,
it was evident from the wondering and puzzled. expression
that for the moment rested on her beauteous features,
to the distant noises of the tumult in the streets, and
sometimes, it was equally evident from very different expressions of countenance, for the nearer sounds of the footsteps of
some expected visitor. Presently those sounds appeared to
strike upon her quickened senses. She started, and while
her whole heart seemed jumping into her kindling cheeks,
rose, advanced a step towards the door, and stood expectant.
The next moment, the young marksman who had left the
crowd in the street so abruptly, an hour or two before, stood
in the entrance, with looks that spoke a gratification which
his tongue would have in vain tried to utter.

" The brightest of good evenings to you, Madian," he said,
respectfully extending his hand.

" And as pleasant an one to you, Sir Vane, if I am to let
you off without a scolding for calling on a lady at nearly ten
o'clock in the evening," she replied, accepting the proffered
hand with a sort of half bantering, half serious air. " But
now you are here, you may be seated and tarry long enough to
answer me a question or two. Our serving-man, Taffy, has
been out to witness the public proceedings, and has informed
me what occurred during the *day.* But I would inquire
what has happened this *evening*, to cause so much commotion
in the streets ?"

" Oh, nothing, or nothing very alarming, I think, Madian."

"Nothing! Then they made much *ado* about nothing, it appears to me."

"They did—much more than I expected."

"Expected! Why, was it about something of your own moving that you could go into a calculation of its effects on the populace?"

"How sharp you are upon me to-night, Madian!"

"Ah! you look roguish, sir—you stand suspected—yes, convicted, nearly, of something, I know not what—now confess, sir, that your punishment may be the lighter."

"Well, Madian, as you certainly should have some excuse from me for delaying to this unseasonable hour the call that Taffy doubtless told you I proposed to make this evening, I may as well give you the true one, and especially so as it may concern you to know it."

"Proceed; prithee, proceed, sir."

"Taffy perhaps told you of my bout with Sniffkin this morning, at target shooting, and afterwards at word shooting?"

"He did; and I could not but fear that you gave him as much advantage over *you* in the latter, as you gained over *him* in the former, for I think he will be likely to try to turn your bold language to your detriment."

"Be it so, then; for it is not in me, Madian, to hold my peace under false accusations, much less if they come in the shape of insulting insinuations. Nor will any fear of the Plymouth regency deter me from expressing my disapprobation of a course of policy which I feel to be so certainly hazardous to the peace and safety of this colony. But that is not what I was about to tell you. Soon after this bloody day's work was over, I started out to come here, when I fell in with a crowd in the street discussing the matter of the execution, which, now it is over, seems to have filled the fickle people, who were at first so urgent in getting up this mad proceeding, with great

fears for the consequence. Here also I found Sniffkin and
his tools, who all assailed me again. I was, however, determined I would, this time, have no altercation with them, and
so walked off and was proceeding on my way, when I soon
found myself dogged by Dick Swain; and having, as I glanced
back on my retreat from the crowd, detected Sniffkin whispering some directions to Dick, I readily comprehended the
object, and so contrived up a little scheme to defeat it."

" Yes, but what was the object of dogging you?"

" To see whether I came here, Madian," replied the young
man, bending an earnest, significant look upon the other.

" So that is the way," responded the spirited girl, with her
thin nostrils distending, and her black eyes flashing with suppressed indignation—" so that is the way, then, they would
treat the guests I choose to admit here! Well, perhaps I have
no right at all in the house my father left me! But go on
with your account of this nice affair."

" Yes. Well, I then altered my course, proceeded to the
border of the pine barrens, where two of my red friends who
had come on with me to the trial were encamped, pointed out
to them the dogging tool still lurking in the distance, and
directed them, when I should have decoyed him along against
them, to rush out, gently take him in tow, lead him a mile
into the woods, detain him an hour or two, and let him go.
Standing in a neighboring copse, all this I saw done—heard
his uproarious outcry of ' Murder! Indians!' &c., as they
drew him into the bushes; then, soon after, to my surprise
and vexation, I perceived half the town rushing in wild alarm
to the spot, when, after listening from my covert to the consultation of the valorous pursuers of the supposed abducting
Indians, as they drew up in a line at a safe distance from the
wood, and hearing them, at the suggestion of Sniffkin and
Deacon Mudgridge, decide to return to the meeting-house to
hold a council of war, I took my way by a round-about path

very quietly hitherward, to fulfil an appointment, if not too late, which it would have grieved me much to have been choused out of, but even more to have kept it in a way that would have added to the embarrassments of my fair enter-tainer."

A low, silvery peal of merry laughter burst from the lips of Madian, as the narrator closed his account of the night alarm, which had so awakened her curiosity; but she made no other comment than by asking,

" But will not this Dick Swain suspect who was the insti-gator of his odd abduction ?

"No, I think not. It was so managed that he could see no signs of any communications between me and the In-dians, who were made to go round in the bushes so as to appear to rush upon him from a different direction from the line he and I were taking."

" What then will the affair end in ?"

" Smoke. They have contrived to let him escape, by this time, and probably he is now back to the meeting-house, an-nouncing to the crazy crowd his marvelous escape, which he will doubtless swear he effected by disabling a good half-dozen of Philip's warriors. And to-morrow you will hear his exploits, I presume, bruited from mouth to mouth through the town."

" I hope, *all* the events of this day will result in no worse consequences."

"I *hope* it, certainly, but hope against conviction. For I feel that the fatal die has this day been cast."

" Then you count on the approach of troubles for us all ?"

" I do, Madian, I am deeply impressed with the apprehen-sion, that times are at hand such as the people of this colony have never seen. Indeed, I feel so certain of it, that I am about to enter on immediate preparations, so that when the

storm of war shall burst, as it doubtless will soon, and suddenly, it shall not find *all* unprepared and helpless."

" Surely, Mr. Willis, you cannot be anxious to plunge, un-
called by the rulers, into the perils of a savage warfare ?"

" If such as I am do not come forward, to stand between
the helpless of our unguarded homes and the exasperated savages, who will be likely to do so, or do it in a manner which
can only be effectual ? The court of Plymouth, and those
they will be likely to appoint to lead their troops to battle, know little or nothing of the modes of Indian warfare,
and before they will have learned by experience, hundreds of
families may perish. I shall ask no appointment of them,
while they remain under their present influences; but, Madian, I must go."

" What, alone, and single handed ?"

" No—in anticipation of this crisis, I have already talked
over the matter with a few of the young men, who entertain
my views, and who would not hesitate, they say, to follow
where I would lead. And I am thinking, therefore, to organ-
ize a select band of volunteers to be ready for the emergency.
But if I do this at all, I should do so immediately; for as I
look upon affairs, every moment's delay may be fraught with
peril. And within this very hour, therefore, I shall be on my
way to Boston, to enlist from that colony some I know there,
whom I would like to have with me, in the proposed service."

" To-night? O Vane Willis, Vane Willis, how your words
pain me !"

" It must be so, Madian. It is a patriotic duty. You are
the daughter of one who was reputed a brave soldier, and
can better appreciate than many others, perhaps my feelings
and motives. Yes, dear Madian, I must go; but before I
leave you, to see you I know not when again, I would carry
with me some comforting pledge that you——"

" Why, you know already, Vane—how can you but know,

on whom my choice will fall, if I can be left free to make it ?
You are agoing to fight battles abroad, *I* remain to fight battles
at home. If we both come out conquerors, and ever live to
behold the light of peace again————"

" Then I have your promise ?"

" I know not what I *ought* to say, Vane, and yet I know
not what to say, but yes."

" It is settled and sealed then. But, Madian, cannot you
give me some token of this our plighted faith, to look upon
when alone in the wilderness, to give me strength and hope in
the hour of battle ?"

Madian dropped her head a moment in thought, when
starting up with an animated look, she begged to be excused
for a brief absence, and hastily left the room. In another
minute she appeared, bearing in her hand a richly mounted
rapier, whose blue bright Damascus blade gleamed in the light
like a polished diamond.

" Here," said she, pausing before her wondering lover,—
" here is the trusty blade that was worn on many a hard fought
field by Col. Richard Southworth, in the voluntary service of
his idolized master, the lion-hearted Oliver Cromwell of England. On whom can his daughter more fittingly bestow it,
than on one who also voluntarily proposes to encounter no
less perils for the public safety ? Vane Willis," she added,
holding up the blade with both hands, and imprinting an
ardent kiss on its burnished side, " Vane Willis, this is yours ;
and I pass it to your hands, consecrated by the love of the
giver. Keep it, and with her ever-attending prayers, and in
her name, as the last representative of a brave warrior, and in
the name of that true man, Sir Henry Vane, whose name you
in part bear, use it worthily. And may heaven bless and
watch over you. But now go—in mercy, go ; I can bear this
no longer. Adieu, adieu !"

And the proud, but deeply moved maiden hurried him to

the door, and scarcely waiting to receive his parting words, turned to hide her gushing tears, and fled to her chamber.

It is now time that we should pause in the action of the story to give the reader a more particular account of the family last introduced, than he or she can have learned from what has been said of them in the preceding pages.

Col. Richard Southworth, a man of wealth and family, was at the opening of the revolution, which resulted in the overthrow of the British monarchy, in 1642, a resident of the banks of the Severn, in the west of England. In religion a puritan, and in politics a follower of the noble Hampden, or something still more republican, he was among the first to take arms against the infatuated Charles and his corrupt advisers, in their reckless attempt to subvert the constitutional liberties of the people. And having entered Cromwell's noted regiment as a captain, he displayed so much devotion to the cause, and such gallantry in deeds enacted under the searching eye of his daring leader, that he was soon promoted to the next succeeding military grades. And, when that great leader, through the force of his overtowering genius and energy, rose to the post of commander-in-chief of the Parliamentary army, the well-tried Southworth was placed at the head of his regiment—a regiment which had already laid the foundation of its old master's fortunes, and which, for high discipline and unwavering courage, has rarely been equalled by any other body of troops in the world.

In the great struggle that now ensued, Richard Southworth, with his invincible regiment, became the scourge and terror of the quailing monarchists, by the irresistible fury of his charges in battle, and in the untiring perseverance of his efforts everywhere to crush and destroy them. But no sooner had he seen his revered leader and pattern firmly seated in authority, with the prostrate royalists at his feet, than he sought, and at length obtained the reluctantly granted per-

7

mission to retire from the army, to the enjoyments of private
life on his estate, only replying to the earnest solicitations of
Cromwell to take posts of honor and profit under his government, by saying that he had seen all the desires of his heart
satisfied in the downfall of the hated Stuarts, and in the elevation of a God-appointed ruler, who could be safely trusted
with the rights of the people.

With the exception of an occasional visit to the court of
Cromwell, the colonel, having married and settled down on
his estate, now maintained a life of seclusion during the whole
rule of his beloved sovereign, evidently contented with his
quiet pursuits, and well satisfied with the situation of public
affairs.   But on the death of Cromwell, he immediately became distrustful and uneasy, for he had the sagacity to perceive that with the departure of the controlling spirit of its
great champion, the life and soul of the anti-monarchical party
in England had gone also, and that in the amiable and yielding Richard, now succeeding to his father's authority, the
ever secretly plotting, and now hopeful royalists would find
an unconscious instrument to help them again into power.
The advent of the latter contingency would, with his settled
convictions and unbending disposition, render his further residence in England insupportable, and probably be as dangerous
to him personally as it would be repugnant to his feelings.
Having taken this view of the subject, he soon formed a new
plan for his future ; and with his accustomed promptitude,
proceeded immediately to execute it.

In pursuance of his scheme, he lost no time in converting
his whole property into available funds, and preparing to leave
the country.   And with so much energy did he prosecute the
object in view, that within three months he had made everything ready for the departure of himself and family.   When
taking his wife and only child, the spirited little Madian, together with a trusty Welch couple, who, man and wife, with-

out children, had lived some years with the family in the capacity of servants, and were still willing to follow its fortunes, he proceeded in a private manner to the coast, and took passage to Holland. And within another month, having safely deposited the larger part of his funds in the bank at Amsterdam, and everything else there favoring his projects, he and his family were on their way to America.

Having arrived in Boston, and tarried a few days with a relation of Mrs. Southworth, they proceeded to Plymouth, to which the Puritans in Holland had very naturally, from their greater knowledge of the colony settled there, directed the attention of the colonel as the most desirable for a permanent settlement. Here, when it became known that he was a Puritan and a man of means, he was kindly received, and assisted in the purchase of the best tract of land to be had adjoining the village. Of this, the independent new emigrant took immediate possession, put the land under a thorough system of cultivation, and at once commenced building the dwelling-house which we have described, and in which, so rapidly was the work prosecuted, he had the pleasure of seeing himself and family, in a few months more, quietly ensconced, and settled down, as he supposed, for a peaceful and unmolested future; for having seen in the old world enough of bloody strife and political bitterness and wrangling, in the former of which he had only engaged from a stern sense of duty, while in the latter he never would take part, he now had no favors to ask of the public, except to be left to his own private pursuits, and the free enjoyment of his own opinions. But before he had been many months in the country, he discovered entirely contrary to what he expected to find here, that, in the matter of religious doctrines, at least, he could not speak and act as he pleased, without being taken to task by the straight going churchmen, who here had control, and who required that the opinions of all others should be squared by their own.   He had himself often risked his life in battle, in a good part to secure the immunities of religious freedom ; he knew that his old sovereign, Oliver Cromwell, had ever tol- erated a diversity of religious belief.   And for a while, he could not conceive how men, who had suffered so much from persecution themselves, and periled so much for the right to worship in their own way, could ever become the persecu- tors of others for claiming the same privilege.   But at length he found too much reason to believe that.

> " In the school of oppression, though woefully taught,
> 'Twas only to be the oppressors they sought ;
> All,—all but themselves were be-devil'd and blind,
> And their narrow-souled creed was to serve all mankind."

Colonel Southworth had, while in England, several times listened to the burning eloquence of the celebrated George Fox, the founder of Quakerism, and had become deeply impressed with the truth and moral beauty of many parts of his creed, and finding, on his arrival in this country, that the Quakers here were undergoing the most bitter persecutions for no other crime than their belief, he hesitated not openly to con- demn the course of the colony towards them.   This soon brought upon him the denunciations of the church, which, in- stead of awing him into silence, only made him the more bold and determined in the defence of the persecuted.   And still persisting in his course, he, in a short time, was accounted a Quaker himself, prescribed and put upon the list of those against whom a decree of banishment had been procured. And the decree would have doubtless been immediately en- forced upon him with the same promptitude, with which it was upon others, but for the intercession of a few friends, or those who had chosen to call themselves such, among the church of Plymouth, who gained for him a short respite. The chief of these intercessors was Mudgridge, who, from the first, had taken great pains to ingratiate himself into the

Colonel's favor, and who now, by this act of seeming friendship, and by pretending to sympathize with him, instead of
trying to reform him, as he had promised the church, succeeded in completely gaining his confidence. Mudgridge
then, though then youngerly and comparatively poor, was yet
a very active and ambitious member of the church; and he
had the address by frequently making encouraging reports of
his progress in rescuing the Colonel from his heresies, to keep
him along on sufferance nearly a year, and until an event occurred which made all efforts of that kind unnecessary.

The restoration of the Stuarts in the person of the despicable
Charles II. had now nearly two years been effected in England. Those who had had anything to do with the trial and
execution of Charles I. had been summarily condemned to
death, and all executed, except the three so-called regicides,
who escaped to America—Goff, Whaley, and Dixon. But
with the death of this class of men, the royal vengeance was
not satisfied. Others, like Hugh Peters and Sir Henry Vane,
who were accounted influential promoters of the revolution,
were, from time to time, added to the list of the doomed, till
the early career of Colonel Southworth was in some way called
to mind, when he, too, was condemned to death, his abode
ferreted out, and a warrant, with a large reward for his apprehension, was, as before in the case of the three regicides, for-
warded to Boston. Luckily, however, a friend in that city
got an intimation of the arrival of the warrant before it reached
the hands of the officers, and despatched a messenger to the
prescribed Colonel, who, on receiving the timely warning, instantly commenced preparations for immediate flight. But
with whom should he entrust the charge of property and family ? Between himself and his wife, a cold, incapable, rigid
religionist, there had long been but few intermingling sympathies, and in business affairs, no community of knowledge.
As he grew more liberal, she grew more bigoted ; and since

he had fallen under the displeasure of the church, whose
opinions with her were both law and gospel, she had actually
sided with them against him. She knew little of the situation and extent of his property, except that he owned his present
establishment, and had sufficient money in the house to last
the family, with the profits of the farm, several years to come.
For these reasons combined, he resolved to place the charge
of his whole affairs in the hands of another. And the person
selected for this purpose, was, as might be expected, his confidential friend, Mudgridge, who was immediately summoned ;
when the two spent most of the night closeted together in consultation, the result of which was that all the colonel's property
here, and paper evidences of funded property abroad, with
authority to draw the latter as needed, was placed in the
hands of Mudgridge, in trust for the sole use and benefit of
his family, over whom he was also to have the oversight and
virtual guardianship, unrestrained, as it very naturally happened, in the hurry and anxieties of the moment, by either
witnesses or written guaranties for the faithful discharge of the
important trust.

As soon as these hasty arrangements were made, the pro-
scribed patriot filled a pack with clothing, took a good supply
of coin, bid his family a hurried farewell, and under cover of
the night departed for some undecided destination to the
westward. The next day the officers of justice made their
appearance, and scoured the country, far and wide, in pursuit
of the fugitive ; but wholly in vain. For several months,
nothing was heard of him by any one. But at length Mudgridge received a letter from him, brought by an uncommu-
nicative Indian, from some unrevealed locality, and saying that,
" resting, as he now was, under a double ban, for the rightful assertion of his principles in England, and the honest
expression of his religious views here in the colonies, he had
become thoroughly disgusted with the conduct of his race,

and it would be very doubtful whether he should ever again make his appearance in any so called civilized community ;" and that " he neither cared for, nor wanted any more property than he had with him. Let all that go to his family, who need take no further thought of him." In this way matters rested some time longer; when some hunters, who had come across the wilderness from Connecticut river brought word that they had learned on their way, from the Indians, that the white man who had run away from Plymouth, the year before, and who, from the description given of him, could be no other than Colonel Southworth, had died of sickness, a few weeks before, and had been buried by the Indian family with whom he had been living.

From this time, Mudgridge became the sole supervisor and undisputed director of all the affairs of the Southworth family. And from this time, also his own circumstances in life commenced a great and rapid amendment. House after house, for renting, to say nothing of his own costly mansion, were, during the next ten years, seen going up under his directions; and farm after farm were added to his fast spreading domains, till he was accounted by all, the richest man in the place. All this was attributed to his commendable business sagacity, and the blessings that followed his Christian virtues, the last of which had long since made him a Deacon in the church, and now one of the most influential men in the colony.

And in this manner, affairs continued to go on till the death of Mrs. Southworth, which occurred the winter before the time we have chosen for the opening of our story. The Deacon had succeeded to his entire satisfaction in getting along with the widow. But the daughter, who was now grown to womanhood, he had long since perceived, was altogether a different person, both in intellect and disposition; and with him it appeared to become a great object that she should have the right kind of husband. His nephew, Timothy Sniffkin, had therefore been imported the year before, from the neighboring colony, but with what success will better be shown in the progress of the tale.

Having thus in a digression, far more extended than we at first proposed to ourself, given a history of the remarkable fortunes of the family we had introduced, we will now resume the thread of our narrative.

CHAPTER VI.

" Was this religion pure and undefiled ?
Was this religion for a little child ?
Can tender, trembling spirits thus be driven,
By whips of living scorpions into heaven ?"

THE next morning, as Madian Southworth sat at her window
pensively revolving in mind the tender passages that had occurred between her and her gallant lover, at their last night's
interview, the whole of which now seemed to her so sweet, so
entrancing, and so transient, that it appeared more like the
bright and fleeting representations of a dreaming fancy than
a tangible reality, her eye caught a glimpse, through the clustering shrubbery, of the tall, stooping figure of the Shadow entering the front gate, and approaching the house. She slightly
started, and a sort of recoiling shudder seemed to pass over
her ; for, as the grating sounds of his slow, solemn tread upon
the graveled pathway fell upon her ear, she instinctively felt
that his early visit had something to do with the subject of her
thoughts, and the new born, and, as yet, almost ethereal ties,
which her heart rose up jealously to guard against the rude
touch of all others, whether the opposing or the careless.
Soon schooling herself into composure however, she respectfully saluted Dummer as he entered, and invited him to a
seat, in which, after sundry awkward flourishes and sprawling
movements of his long, ungainly limbs, he at length became
pretty fairly settled. The native dignity of Madian, now
made the more imposing, by the cool reserve with which her
demeanor had become involuntary invested, very evidently

discomposed the intruding zealot, and it was some moments before he could get his thoughts sufficiently in working order to open upon the matter of his mission.

"I came," he at last rather falteringly began—"I came—the best friends of the family thereunto consenting and advising—to hold friendly communion and kindly counsel with the daughter of our late well-beloved sister Southworth, in matters pertaining to her spiritual welfare."

"Indeed, sir," responded Madian, in a sort of non-committal, enquiring tone.

"Yea, young woman; for, in our holy anxieties for the spiritual safety of one, who is now left without any proper Christian guide in the family, and therefore continually liable to be deceived and led astray by the Evil one, who watcheth by day and by night to seduce the young and unwary by his manifold devices, we of the household of faith are filled with a very great desire—yea, with inexpressible yearnings, to see you come into the sacred fold."

"Perhaps I should be thankful, sir, for so much attention to my condition, if it be attended with the perils you intimate. But let me ask if the fold you speak of is the same as the one in which, as I have been told, was once originated a decree for banishing my father from his home and family, only for disapproving of the persecutions of the harmless Quakers?"

"You are in grievous error, young woman. The Quakers are *not* a harmless sect, but schismatic and pestilent, the spreaders of false doctrines and dangerous heresies. And your father, if not one of them, did commit a heinous offence in upholding them, as he himself did admit and confess, as I was told by Deacon Mudgridge. And hence, on account of his repentance, he was graciously spared the banishment you mentioned."

"I have never before heard of any such repentance on *his* part. And as he was not driven from his home, as it had been intended, I had supposed that the repentance must have been on the part of the movers of that Christian measure."

"The movers repent! the church guilty of repentance, young woman! verily thou talkest like one of the unregenerate whereas thou art reputed to have been piously inclined, disagreeing with us only in the matters of sound doctrines. But this questioning of the doings of the elect betokeneth, I greatly fear me, that there is still a chain of hell about thy neck, drawing thee away unto all sorts of Sadducisms and heresies. And I feel it my God-bounden duty to warn thee of thy situation. By the terrors of the law, persuade we men unto repentance. Wherefore I speak unto thee as one in the gall of bitterness and the bonds of iniquity—as one in danger of being given over to the buffeting of Sathan, and at once snatched away to that awful hell of everlasting burnings where the worm dieth not and the fire is not quenched. O repent ye, repent, and straightway come out from among the workers of iniquity, lest the terrible Avenger of sin come like a thief in the night speedily upon thee for thy awful contumacy, and the righteous wrath of an offended Heaven fall quickly on thy guilty head, and utterly consume thee, like stubble in the fiery furnace, which may God in his mercy avert.—Let us pray."

Before the astonished maiden had time to utter, had she felt disposed to do so, one word in self-defence, or in deprecation of this storm of crimination and warning, which she had so inadvertently brought down upon her own head, the excited zealot had thrown himself upon his knees, and began to pour forth the loud, wordy torrent of one of his most heated invocations. And now feeling relieved from the disquieting effects of the calm, searching looks he had been compelled to encounter, and taking advantage of the privilege usually accorded to this exercise—that of being permitted to utter, unquestioned, whatever may best subserve the purposes of the speaker, he redoubled his efforts to frighten and overawe the fair object of his holy onset. By a long and terrible tirade on the enormity of her sins of commission and omission, he prayed her to the depths of hell, and then, by a pretended wrestling and wrangling with the Almighty, to snatch from him the victim as a reward for his assumed faith, he prayed her out again; and finally he prayed her into the church, where, in a sort of prophetic rhapsody he claimed he now clearly beheld her; and thereupon fell into shouts of thanksgiving to God that she was at last safely placed beyond the reach of the snares and devices of the devil in hell, and all his schismatic, Quaker, heretic, and false-doctrine spreading emissaries on earth.

Having thus brought to a close his desperate effort for driving Madian into the church, in part performance of the plan which he and the Deacon had the evening before concocted, the Shadow now rose with a self-satisfied air ; when, without adding a word by way of retiring civility, lest it might weaken the effect of a performance, which, if left to work its full power on her mind, could not fail, he thought, soon to result in the desired consummation, he demurely took his hat and departed to report progress to his great exemplar.

Madian scarcely knew what to make of this strange visit of one with whom she had not the honor of hardly a passing acquaintance, and still less of the stranger manner in which he had conducted it. She had early been deeply impressed with all the generally received tenets of the Christian faith, and sincerely loved and admired the pure and simple teachings of the Evangelists, and those of St. John more than the rest, because they breathed more particularly through the whole of them, that trustful and childlike love to her God and Savior, which was so much in unison with the feelings of her own heart, and which, she felt, was all the religion she possessed. At that period, she might have sought admission to the church, had she deemed herself worthy. But viewing that establishment through the bigoted eyes of her mother, she esteemed it too pure, exalted, and infallible to make it proper to receive into fellowship one so unworthy as herself. But as she became older, and began to see with her own eyes, and reflect for herself, she witnessed such a want of what she thought to be the requirement of Christian charity in the church, as then conducted ; so much intolerance, as exhibited particularly in the case of her father, which she had begun to call to mind and investigate, and so much wrangling and disputation about the niceties of doctrines—all which she felt to be distracting her mind and dampening her heart's devotion, that she at length lost all desire to become one of them; fearing, indeed, if she did so, that not only whatever of the Christian spirit she possessed would be smothered in the profitless polemics then in vogue among all church members, but that on account of their intolerant notions, she should find herself among those who would not be likely long to extend her their fellowship, and to whom she certainly could not extend full fellowship herself.

These views she had not latterly hesitated to express openly, and for this reason, the visit of Dummer, coming with the avowed object of urging her to join the church, had taken her by surprise. She could not understand, and the more she reflected, the more was she at a loss to comprehend, why the church or any of its members should *desire* her to take a step which, according to her views, should be entirely voluntary, and which, if not so, would be little less than a sacrilege. Yes, why should such a measure be urged upon her, especially just now, unless there was ulterior and unworthy motives somewhere at the bottom of the movement? What that motive was, and by whom, and with what object entertained, she believed she knew ; but what she had as yet witnessed was not sufficient to reduce her conjecture to a certainty. She theor-

fore resolved to keep her own counsel, act with prudence, and wait for further developments.

And for such developments, she was not kept long in waiting.

The next day, a good and pious matron of the village paid her a formal visit, during which the lady urgently advised Madian, not only for her own good, but as the means of more extended usefulness, to make a public profession of religion. And this was followed up on the day succeeding that, by another female church member, who urged, as an additional reason for the step recommended, that it would be a safeguard against the scandals which otherwise would be likely to get into circulation against a lone and unprotected young lady. On the next day to that, she had to entertain yet another visitor on the same errand; and on yet the next, two, both evidently freighted with similar loving duties, to be discharged towards the persecuted Madian. And so it continued through the week; when Deacon Mudgridge himself, by way of bringing up the rear, was seen, towards night, leisurely approaching the house.

To all these besiegers, Madian had thus far given very civil though rather evasive answers. But having, while so treating the subject with them, succeeded in fishing out from one and another of them enough to satisfy herself who was either directly or indirectly the moving spirit of their conjoint labors of love and duty, she resolved, that she would now, if the Deacon gave her an opportunity, bring the matter to an eclaircissement; for she began to tire under an appliance which she felt to be as insulting to her, as she was determined to make it useless to all others.

The persistent Deacon, consequently, found her, evidently much to his surprise and vexation after what had been done, a very intractable subject. And when, after he had paddled round to the point, and repeated the proposition which his

emissaries had made before him, and which he now put in the
form of a request, savoring much of the air of a command; when
she told him respectfully, but decidedly, that she must be her
own judge in the matter, and decide for herself when, and
whether ever, she should seek admission into *his* church or
any other, he seemed greatly disturbed, shook his head
gravely, and solemnly throwing his white pig eyes upward, in
seeming ejaculation, muttered something about "a lost sheep
of Israel."

For some time he appeared quite determined not to give up
beat in this important preliminary to success in his main object, after taking so much pains to pave the way for its accomplishment; and he returned again and again to the charge.
But finding himself completely foiled in every new attempt,
he at length appeared to be convinced of the uselessness of
further effort in that direction, and soon evidently made up
his mind that he might as well now as ever, hazard the
chances of the main assault.

"The Scripture," he said, after some boggling in fixing on
the manner of introducing his subject—"the Scripture moveth
us in sundry passages thereof unto the searching out our duty
pertaining to our relations as man and woman.   It is not good
for man to be alone—much less helpless woman, as we are
everywhere in the *Word* led to infer; hence we find Bethuel
and Laban giving their daughters to wife, when they arrived
to woman's estate.   And I, standing in place of father in this
family, am minded, in sense of duty, to speak to you in the
matter of changing your condition to one more fitting, and
less encompassed with the snares that beset the young and
unwary, than the unprotected one you are now standing in."

"But *I* am not at all troubled about that matter, Deacon
Mudgridge, and have no thought of changing my condition at
present," promptly responded Madian, though not without a
slight tremor in her voice.

"The feeling that prompteth to that is peradventure but maiden reserve, which is not unbecoming a young woman, albeit soon overcome, as I trust it will be in the present case, for you are now arrived to woman's estate, and it is meet you should have a suitable protector. In view of these things, I confess I have for some time been exercised with many anxieties in this behalf. Wherefore, it has given me great pleasure to hear that my nephew, Mr. Timothy Sniffkin, has made honorable proposal to raise you to the marriage estate."

"I am glad, sir, the proposal gave pleasure to *any* one. I am sure it did not to me."

"Now, verily, young woman, you cannot have been so hasty and inconsiderate as to have answered Mr. Sniffkin in a manner savoring forwardness and opposition to his advantageous proposal ?"

"As Mr. Sniffkin has seen fit to disclose part of what occurred, I choose that you should look to him for the rest."

A visible frown passed over the hard, warty visage of the Deacon, at the equivocal remark of the other, but without deigning any direct reply to it, he proceeded:

"As the law of God and the regulating of men made in conformity therewith, as abundantly established by the various precedents of infallible Scripture, fully empowereth the father to bestow the daughter on whom it may seem to him meet and proper ; and as those properly authorized to represent the father in the matter thereto pertaining, and moreover, as Mr. Sniffkin did not move in this thing without my knowledge, and without my consent and approbation first fully obtained, it remaineth only for me to say, that I expect thy acquiescence in the measure, young woman."

"Then, Deacon, it only remains for *me* to say, that you must be sorely disappointed."

"Nay, I am *not* to be disappointed in this. It is not a new thing, the fitness whereof is now to be discussed, but one that has been advisedly agreed on, yea, and definitely settled, months ago."

"Settled, sir! How can a case, in which you make me one of the parties, have been either settled or agreed on and I know nothing about it?"

"Natheless, it *has* been settled."

"Settled, I again ask? Settled how, and by whom?"

"Your mother and myself, perverse young woman, and that many weeks before her lamented departure. Yea, she and I, by fair and understanding agreement then and thereinto entering, did betroth you to Mr. Timothy Sniffkin."

"My mother!" almost shrieked the astonished girl. "My mother! Impossible! I will not believe she acted such a part, without one hint, one word of consultation with me on the subject. No, I will never believe it, sir, till she come up from the dead to confirm the slanderous story."

"Woman is a weak vessel," at length responded the relentless Deacon, in a moderated and commiserating tone, rallying from the surprise and momentary abashment into which the bold reply and the bolder intimations of the aroused maiden had thrown him—"yea, woman is verily a weak vessel, else the word of a high and never-before-doubted officer in the Church of God had never thus been so irreverently gainsayed. But I am not here to bandy vain words with the perverse and petulant on the question of my own truthfulness, or the fitness and wisdom of your godly mother's doings, for it is not needful that I should do either. I am here myself, and, in her absence in another and better world, stand clothed with full authority to act in the premises, and carry out her wishes unto the working out of your temporal welfare."

"You, sir? What right have you, sir, to dispose of me in marriage without my consent? Please show me your authority for such a strange proceeding."

"Peradventure you will not find me wholly unprepared for

8

to meet the demand, and I will forthwith do so, albeit thy
arrogancy and forwardness little deserveth my condescending
thereto," replied the deacon, with an air of cool triumph, as
he drew out a paper, and, passing it to the other, directed her
attention to the last clause of the instrument.

The whole of it was in the hand-writing of Deacon Mudgridge, but signed "Richard Southworth," and in the bold,
well-known characters of the colonel's chirography; and the
clause referred to ran thus:—

"*And in addition to the aforesaid appointing of the said
John Mudgridge to be sole agent and manager of my property,
I hereby appoint him also the guardian of my daughter
Madian, to be operative in case her mother should die before
she arrives at the lawful age of twenty-one, and then to hold
during her said minority.*"

With paling cheeks and growing dismay, the trembling girl
slowly read the fatal paper to the end; when, spurning it from
her, she rose and stood a moment confronting her persecutor,
with a look that made him, with all his self-assurance, quail
and shrink, as some foul spirit may be supposed to do from
the rebuking gaze of an angel of light. She then turned
away with chilling dignity, and, without uttering one word of
comment or courtesy, immediately swept out of the apartment.

The disconcerted Deacon sat waiting some time, often uneasily glancing towards the door through which Madian had
so unceremoniously departed for her expected reappearance.
But he waited in vain, and finally rose, took up his hat and
church-going cane, proceeded with a noisy tread to the front
door, and there also stood lingering a while longer, purposely
hitting his cane against the casing, and rattling the latch to
apprise her, if within hearing, that he was on the point of
going. At length finding, however, that none of these arti-
fices was likely to induce her to return, he reluctantly made

his way homeward, increasing his speed, under the goadings
of his gathering vexation, every step of his progress and
fiercely muttering to himself as he went :—

"Now, who would have thought it, that she would have
broke away in such a huff? But mayhap it is better as it is,
than if I had charged her obstinate standing-out against my
plan, to her secret leanings to that pestilent Willis, as I intended, if she had not run away, and as I still more than ever
opine to be the true reason of her contumacy. Yea, I think
it better left as now; for the prospect looks dubious enough
at that. Well, well, matters are safe enough I think, even if
this plan should miscarry. She, nor any one else now alive,
can know much about the amount of that property at the beginning, except the farm and things visible here, which, of
course, she can have when she becomes of age. But then,
again, how much better it would be to have one of my family
and under my control placed at the head of the whole matter,
in case of doubts and contingencies sometimes strangely arising! Then the farm itself, with the rest of the property here
—why, is not that worth bringing into my family, and keeping within the line of the church, unto the strengthening of
God's heritage? Of a verity it is. And why can't it be secured yet? Am I thus to be foiled and thwarted in this vile
manner, by a silly forward girl? Am I in such power in
church and state for nothing, that I must submit to such a
vexatious rebuffing at such feeble hands? And is it not all
the work of Sathan and that accursed Vane Willis? And
haven't I enough shrewdness to meet and whip both of them
on their own ground? Is it John Mudgridge that can't do
this? We'll just see— ay, by the Lord of Sabaoth, and it
shall go hard, if I don't yet see my plan, even to the last jot
and tittle, all carried out and accomplished."

When Madian ascertained that the Deacon had fairly
made good his exit from her premises, she repaired, it

being by that time in the dusk of the evening, to the room where usually were found sitting, after the labors of the day, her two faithful domestics, Taffy and Maggy; who, though now on the downhill of life, were both vigorous and active, and still found competent to conduct all the out-door and in-door labors and duties of the establishment, which now, since the death of Mrs. Southworth, more fully than ever devolved upon them. She had often taken a seat with them when she had no company of her own to entertain, to while away the evenings and enjoy their society; for though their manners and dialect still betrayed their purely Celtic origin, they were quite shrewd and intelligent. But this evening she had a particular motive for holding communion with them; and, in pursuance of her object, she, after a few commonplace remarks had been exchanged, turned to the man and said hesitatingly—

"Taffy."

"What's your wull, my young leddy?" responded the little, brisk old Welchman, respectfully.

"Nothing of much consequence perhaps; but I thought I would ask you, Taffy, who do you consider to be in control here—in other words, who do you consider mistress or master of this establishment?"

"Who mistress of this dwalling-stead and land gear?" asked the honest Celt, throwing a look of surprise on his idolized young mistress,—"Why, who should it be, but my young leddy?"

"I had rather supposed so, myself, Taffy. But Deacon Mudgridge, I find, claims to be my guardian, as well as manager of all the property."

"Aweel, he's frequent speeched that to me, whan he's come speering about the wark an' things,—an' I list to what he said respectful-like, to plase your mother, whan live, though the wark an' all's jist as gude done without him. But you!—

gardian you, is it he wud? Why, what is the long-faced carl minting at, Madian?"

"I've kenned what he's minting at, this long while," here interposed Maggy, glancing knowingly from her husband to Madian. "He wants a good maik for one of his kin,—the short-faced carl, that he got on here a-purpose. But he's ganging for more than he'll ever get, I hope.",

"I hope so, too, Maggy," said Madian,—"And I hope you and Taffy will stand by me, in case of need; for I fear he intends to make me trouble about the affair. He has got a paper, which appears to have been signed by my father, and which he pretends gives him authority to dispose of me as he pleases."

"Then he's got a paper the kurnel wud never hev writ his name to, an' he had thocht twud force his dochter to wed agin her free wull. That wud not be kurnel Southworth, God bless the noble man! But he were so hastened and fashed up, in getting away that night he so handsome chated the gallows, the cuss't tyrants over the water thocht they had got sure made for him, that he might not hev seen the effect of what was fixed up for him to sign by that cunning church carl, that has so much preach about *the dervices of Sathan*. It might be that same, or it might be some tother way the thing got fixed so; the whilk I wud rather not explicit."

"Then, Taffy, your thoughts are running in about the same direction as mine; but let us all keep our own counsel."

"That I wull do; but if he comes speering and ordering great deal mucher about the wark and bizness things, with the leave of my young leddy, I'll not budge a fot for him."

"Nor need you; for if you are content to go on, and be as trusty and capable, in the labors and management of the place, as you and Maggy have always shown yourselves, I shall be happy to be the mistress here, without much help, either from Deacon Mudgridge or his hopeful nephew."

"Ah, now! that is the old kurnel hisself, speeching through his own, whole-blud dochter!" exclaimed Taffy, who had long secretly disliked and distrusted Deacon Mudgridge, and was consequently highly gratified with this discovery of his young mistress's views and feelings. "Maggy! my dule and doubt are over! It is all right with her, she shall be top of the hape, in spite of long-faces or short-faces, deil or dummy. Yes, my braw young leddy, you shall be *whole* mistress here till you tak one of your own chusing to hold the reins with you."

"And whan she do chuse," added Maggy, with a roguish glance to Madian, "I hope he will be a nary worse one than the goodly young man that helped her and her mother through the snow-storm, on their visit to Boston two year agone."

"Tush! tush! Maggy," said Taffy, jocosely, "you mak my young leddy look rud in the cheek. But she needn't shame about it; for Vane Willis is a young man the kurnel hisself wud be proud of."

"I thank you both," said the blushing, but gratified girl. "And now, as I think we all understand each other, I will bid you good night, and retire. But one word more," added she, lingering and hesitating in the door-way,—"I have some reason to suspect that there is a plot afoot to work mischief for Mr. Willis,—by whom, you can guess, perhaps. Now if you go out into the street to-night, Taffy, you might gather something about it, perhaps. You remember the attempt they once made to banish my father on charge of Quakerism?"

"Certes, I do; but they daur not come to drive him away; an they had, I wud hav gin my old flint-lock a warming with gunpowder. An they wull as little daur touch Mr. Willis, I opine. But we'll find out what they're at," he added, taking his hat, and on the hint thus received, immediately leaving the house on his way to the village.

"Let others do the talking, and you the listening, Taffy, if

you wud succeed in speiring out anything," said the shrewd
Maggy, calling after him.

Having thus seen love's garrison at the Southworth dom-
icil put in as good a state of defence as the circumstances
would permit, we will now follow Taffy in his news-gathering
rounds through the village, to see, with him, what might there
be going forward.

Sauntering along the street, with an air of indifference, but
with all his senses intent on whatever came within their
reach, the cautious Welchman at length reached the central
square, where the street scene described in the opening of
the last chapter occurred, and where a crowd was again assembled, discussing the events of the preceding evenings, and
recounting the omens and prodigies which had then come to
light, together with others that had been since heard of as
constantly occurring in almost every part of the country.

When Taffy joined the group, Dick Swain was proceeding
in full blast with a description of his adventure with a prowling band of King Philip's Indians, and his marvelous escape,
which he attributed solely, as Willis had predicted he would,
to his own prowess.

" But the instigator of that foul deed, which came so near
costing me my life," he added, in conclusion,—" the instigator is well known ; and he is a marked man, too, as you might
judge for yourselves, maybe, if you could see all the papers
now in the constable's pocket."

Others then held forth on the alarming portents of the
times—of the sights seen in the heavens, and

> "Sounds that had come on midnight blast
> Of charging steeds careering fast,
> Along the mountain's shingly side
> Where mortal horseman ne'er might ride."

But as many and alarming as had been these prodigies, the

list was not yet completed. While the excited crowd were
still engaged in discussing those that had occurred, their attention was arrested by a solitary voice, which was heard rising
from some elevated point in the distance.   All wildly started,
and then fixed themselves in an attitude of intense listening.
For a moment all was silent; then the voice came swelling on
the gentle night breeze louder than before.

Who, or what could it be?   It could not be a man, they
thought, for it seemed to come from some point far above the
level of the earth ; and besides that, there was a strange and
awful solemnity in the tones, that recalled the conceptions
they had formed of the voice of a warning angel. But
" Hark ! hark !" they cried, in eager, half-whispered exclamations.   " How clear and distinctly it comes now !   It utters
words ! there ! listen ! listen !"

" Woe to this wicked land ! woe ! woe to the inhabitants
thereof !   They have polluted the altars of the Lord, and made
many to stumble at his law by their works of injustice and
oppression.   Woe ! woe to them all, for fiery judgments are
at hand, and they shall be humbled, for that they have gone
astray and done wickedly—for that they have— !"

Here the words became too inaudible in the dying of the
breeze that had wafted the sounds to the ears of the dismayed
listeners, to enable them to make out any connected sentence.
But the voice for some time continued to reach their ears, and
enough was distinguished to tell them that the burden of the
strange message was one of solemn warning, and predicted
woe.

It were, perhaps, a hopeless task to undertake to make
readers, in this present age of almost entire disbelief in aught
not explainable on natural principles, realize how great was
the effect produced on the public mind at that time, by incidents of the character we have introduced here and in some
of the preceding pages.   But it must be recollected that it

was then on the eve of the great moral epidemic which, a few years later, seized on the public mind, and became fully developed in that strange and fearful delusion now familiarly known under the appellation of the Salem Witchcraft, and that all the elements that produced it were already generated, and would have now, probably, burst into action, but for the powerful diversion of the current in which the thoughts of men were running, caused by the terrible realities of the desolating war that intervened. The class of theologians—*demon*-ologians they might more properly be called—who then controlled public opinion, becoming bewildered in the fogs of mystic philosophy, and launching out on its sea of uncertainties till they were hopelessly beyond the moorings of reason, had been, for many years previous, palming on the too willing ear of the multitude, their distempered imaginings, for the doctrines of truth and revelation; and the crop that ere long sprang up was but the natural result of broad-cast dissemination. The public mind became—only more intensely like that which had formed it—dark, mysticised, bewildered. Men saw and heard strange and ominous sights and sounds in all the heavens above, and on the earth beneath. To their distorted conceptions, all space had become peopled with dark, indefinite, mysterious, and questionable incorporeal agencies. Spirits, sprites, goblins, gnomes, demons, and devils, of every class, size, shape, and degree, were all around, above, below, upon, and within them; and the consequence was, that a whole people came near perishing—not from the lack, but the repletion of vision.

But to return to the incident above narrated. Not one in ten of those whose senses had thus attested it, probably, had the least doubt that the voice and words that had so mysteriously fallen on their ears had proceeded from other than the human organs of speech. This conviction alone was enough to fill them with fear and perplexity, while the words, so sig-

nificant of coming evil, completed their amazement and alarm.
The affair, therefore, as well might be expected, spread like
wild fire through the town and surrounding country, and
became almost the sole topic of conversation, both in private
circles and public gatherings, through the next day. There
were a few, it was true, who ventured to suggest that there
might be some misapprehension or mistake about the alleged
fact that a voice, uttering intelligible words, had been heard.
But the doubts of this class were all silenced when the now
almost dreaded darkness had again shrouded the earth; for
then the same clear, trumpet-like voice was again heard rising
on the night air, and pouring forth, in solemn and pitying
accents, its burden of prophetic woe. And on the next, and
on many of the succeeding nights, the same awe-inspiring
mystery was repeated; and then it was heard no more. But
it had been heard enough to complete the work of agitation
and alarm among all classes, which the preceding prodigies
and other ill-omened incidents had put in such rapid progress.
The court of Plymouth were called together, to take the
alarming aspect of public affairs under consideration. The
leaders of the church also held a special conclave, in which,
although Deacon Mudgridge expressed the opinion that the
voice, which had been the greatest cause of the general alarm,
"was only that of the *Man of Sin*, or *Great Deceiver*, come
to distract the people and frighten them from their duty," it
was yet at length decided to appoint a day of public *fasting
and prayer*. And the Deacon and his Shadow thereupon
immediately set to work in drawing up an enumeration of
subjects to be made the special themes of humiliation and
prayerful confession to the offended Heaven; among the
principal of which was "the wicked laxity latterly shown by
the church and state in not bringing, as formerly, all Quakers
and heretics to the condign punishment they deserved, and

thereby incurring that displeasure of Heaven which was now threatening to visit the land in judgment."

As soon as this was arranged by the church leaders, they joined the civil functionaries; and their united deliberations soon resulted in the determination, not only to appoint a public fast, and carry out the suggestions of Mudgridge in regard to Quakers and other heretical persons, but to raise a company of soldiers, and also to despatch at once fast-riding couriers to the sister colony of Massachusetts, to invite their co-operation and assistance, by sending on one or more armed companies, to aid in the war which had now been shown to be inevitable and imminent.

But as deeply and exclusively as the subject of the impending calamities of war were occupying the minds of all others, there was one man with whom these matters appeared to be a secondary interest. During all the commotion, the untiring Deacon Mudgridge had never, for one hour, lost sight of his determinate project of uniting his nephew and Madian Southworth in marriage. And instead of being willing to await the softening influences which time and gentle means might work on her feelings, he seemed strangely intent on pressing the matter to an immediate issue. After brooding a day or two over his chafed and chagrined feeling, occasioned by the resolute resistance with which the spirited girl had met his infamous requirements at the interview we have described, he at length worked himself up to the determination of staking all on a bold and desperate measure to forestall her opposition, believing the strength of his position and his influence to be sufficient to enable him to carry it out with safety and success. This new and bold plan was, without consulting or apprising Madian, or apprising her or any one else of his intention, to cause the bans of the projected match to be proclaimed in church the next Sunday. And it was done—to the utter astonishment and blank dismay of the unapprised maiden, it was shamelessly done in her own presence in church, at the close of the services, while the people were already in motion to depart. Under the first impulse, she tried to speak out to forbid the bans. But so great was the tumult of her feelings that her tongue utterly refused to do its office. And deeply muffling her face in her veil to hide her emotions, she hurried home with a heart bursting with indignation and outraged pride and delicacy.

But we do not propose to follow the doughty Deacon through all the measures he now actively put in motion, under the supposed advantage of his last resort for sacrificing the girl to subserve his own selfish purposes. Suffice to say, that although, through his various emissaries and tools, he worked untiringly and desperately for the speedy accomplishment of his base purpose—although, through the mistaken construction of the obstinate silence, into which the menaces of himself and the persecuting importunities of his minions had at length driven the poor girl, he had taken so much courage as to fix on the day for the wedding, and supposed the victory was now as good as won—he was yet destined to disappointment. He was doomed to undergo the mortification of witnessing the failure of his plans in a manner he had little anticipated, and to guard which he had made no calculations. One morning Madian Southworth was unaccountably missing from her home; and no one could tell where she had gone, or what fate had befallen her, even Taffy and Maggy professing to be as ignorant and anxious on the subject as the rest. And notwithstanding all the efforts of the enraged Deacon and his active satellites, not the least trace of her could be discovered, nor any satisfactory explanation found for her mysterious disappearance.

CHAPTER VII.

" Give me the man of upright heart
Who dares the truth to utter,
And act the noble, manly part
Though enemies may mutter !"

THE next successive step in the progress of our eventful
story, will take us to the quiet banks of that beautiful but
singularly sinuous river of eastern Massachusetts, which, after
meandering its way full one hundred miles to gain one fourth
of that number in direct distance, and thereby embracing
within its doubling folds more than twenty of the best and
most populous towns in the state, comes gently urging its
tranquil waters to its briny estuary, where now lie, in the
parent city and its clustering appendants, those thronged
marts of trade and wealth, going to make up the proud em-
porium of New England.

In an extensive grove of scattered pines, on the banks of
the stream just described, near the point where the brackish
and turbulent waters of the estuary subside into those of the
pure and gentle river, might have been seen, on a pleasant
evening, a few days subsequent to the events narrated in the
last chapter, a mingled multitude of men and boys from the
neighboring city, occasionally interspersed by a few shy, ab
ject looking natives of the forest—some listlessly sauntering
along the banks of the stream upward, some gathered round
a number of light shallops and skiffs moored to the shore at
the lower part of the grove, and others standing in scattered
groups further in shore, and, while engaged in conversation,

frequently turning an eye or ear towards the southwest, as if awaiting the sight or sound of something expected to approach along the road from that direction. In one of these groups stood our young hero, Vane Willis, who, it will be recollected, had avowed his purpose of coming to this quarter to enlist some chosen friends to stand ready to engage with him in repelling the first onset in the war he so confidently anticipated. He was conversing with a stoutly built, middle-aged man, with a bronzed, weather-beaten visage, and a frank, resolute countenance. Although the two had met for the first time but an hour before, yet they had heard of each other, and were now conversing with a freedom and confidence, which a mutual appreciation of character will often at once beget between the greatest of strangers.

"I have now," said Willis, at the point of the conversation which it concerns us to report—"I have now privately enrolled in your colony, Captain Mosely, a dozen choice fellows that I have been with enough in forest hardships and dangers, to know the mettle they are made of; and, within another week, I will have twice that number in my own colony, equally well fitted for the service. And having appointed a midway rendezvous, we will all be ready to take the field, or the forest, as the case may require, within twenty-four hours after the first act of hostility shall have occurred."

"The first act of hostility!" exclaimed the other, repeating the words in surprise—"Why, that has already occurred."

"When and where do you make that out?" asked the former.

"Last week, in Plymouth, as I supposed you knew," replied Mosely. "The cussed hell-hounds, they say, came boldly into that town and carried off one of the citizens; and though he escaped with his life, I believe, he found the woods full of the red devils preparing to fall on the settlements. It was that news which the messengers brought, with what was known before, that led our court to authorize me to raise the company of volunteers I have been telling you about."

"That! Oh, that was no very serious matter, I fancy," said Willis, smiling. "But after all, it is well, perhaps, that it happened; for it may arouse the Plymouth leaders to a sense of the dangers they have incurred by their own short-sighted policy, and teach them the necessity of preparing for a blow which is now sure to fall upon us soon; and if it is delayed, it will only be to make the stroke more certain and heavy."

"Well, people are so excited and crazy these days that one scarce knows what to believe. I didn't think it a very likely story, myself: nor have I believed any thing in their cussed mummery about the signs and omens. But I fully agree with you, that your stupid Plymouth managers have brought trouble on us all. And it will probably be found that you and I have moved none too early in the business. You and your company of woodsmen, I plainly perceive, will be just the fellows to cope with this kind of foe, in all the bush-fighting, at least. You have a commission, I suppose?

"No; I and my boys are agoing to fight on our own hook. I have not asked for a commission, and having openly condemned the course of the Plymouth Court, I should not get one if I had."

"I shouldn't think you need have much trouble about that, my young friend; you belong to the church, of course?"

"No, captain, I have not that honor."

"Oh, that's it,—I see now,—there's the secret of your difficulty, Willis. I could not have got up a single peg in this colony, an' I had not thrown my anchor on a church bottom."

• "You a church member?—You who was brought up a swearing soldier in the English army that took Jamaica from the Spanish; and then, if they didn't belie you, Captain, sailed some time with the West India buccaneers, and always was in the habit of cursing and swearing enough to throw old Shimei himself into the shade.—You in the church?"

"You talk rather plainly about past matters, it strikes me, young man. And if you was one of your mealy-mouthed hypocrites, you and I would see who was the best man. But as you are one of the sincere, out-spoken sort of fellows I like, I wlll take no offense and answer your question. I *am* a member, and, for anything I know, in regular standing in the church."

"But how could you get in, Captain?"

"I will tell you, as it may be some use to you, hereafter, perhaps, though the less you mouth it the better. Well, when I gave up roving, about ten years ago, and settled down here to be something, I soon saw I should be little better than nobody at all, unless I got into the church; and so I offered myself. But, for some time, owing, I was told, to that cuss'd habit of swearing you speak of, I found the gate shut against me. Well, as I did not like to give in beat, and as I could not break up the habit, I cast round for some safe outlet for it, which I at length found. For having noticed that these particular church gentry had a sort of orthodox fashion of swearing themselves, about the men and things they hated, I improved on the hint thus obtained, and at once turned all my heaviest batteries upon the Quakers and heretics, whom I then fell to cussing and damning like the house a-fire. And the result of it all was, that I soon sailed into the church-harbor with flying colors."

"I can't say, Captain," remarked Willis, good-humoredly shaking his head,—"that I quite approve the principle you apear to have acted on in the matter."

"Nor I," bluntly responded Mosely,—"I know well enough that it was a cussed mean principle; but it was as good an one as the strait-laced times would admit. If it was a wrong one, the responsibility, I hold, should be on those, who, by making church-membership the only stepping-stone to office, tempted me to resort to it. They could not expect a fellow of any gumption was a-going to sit down contented to remain at the bottom of the heap forever."

" But you must surely feel a reverence for religion ?"

" Religion ? To be sure I do. It is my best private comforter. But what has that to do with the church? I hold religion to be quite too good a thing to be mixed up with church matters; and they shall never have mine, I swear to them, to use for that purpose."

" Some such notions, I confess, have often been forced on *my* mind ; for, as deeply as I love and reverence the gospel of our Saviour, I cannot agree with the practical construction so often put upon it by our church and state rulers, in their persecutions of dissenting sects, and in their violation of the rights of the Indians, even where the poor, trusting creatures have become their own converts, as in the cruel and unnecessary measure which we are now waiting to see executed, and which will probably make scores of them enemies, who, if let alone, might be made useful friends in the approaching war."

" Yes, a cussed foolish buzziness, as I have told them," responded the blunt captain. " But, hark ! was not that the blast of a trumpet ? Ay, ay, there they come ! Captain Prentiss and his red brood just heaving in sight, yonder," added the speaker, pointing up the road, round a distant curve of which a well mounted military officer, with a trumpeter at his side, followed by a strong company of cavalry, enclosing a motley body of two or three hundred Indians of all ages and sexes, hurrying along on foot, came sweeping into view.

The occasion of this unwonted spectacle, as may have been already partly inferred from the closing words of the foregoing dialogue, as well as of the assembling of those here present, to witness it, was the removal, under an order of the Gen-

9

eral Court, of the large body of christianized Indians who had
long since been peaceably located at Natic, and who were now
being conducted by a military force to this place for embarkation, in boats, for their destination on Deer Island, lying
outside of Boston harbor, at too great a distance from the
main land, it was supposed, to permit of their escape.

Nearly a quarter of a century before the period of which we
are writing, the self-sacrificing John Eliot, the St. John of
the new world, who, instead of aspiring to the positions of
honor and influence among his own people, to which his acknowledged talents and learning would have doubtless elevated
him, devoted all the energies of his life to the work of christianizing the natives of the forest, had seen the great wish of
his heart realized in the permanent settlement of a large body
of his red disciples at Natic.*

After the most unwearied efforts, he had succeeded in obtaining the cession of the five or six thousand acres of land,
which was to constitute this Indian town, from the inhabitants
of Dedham, who appear to have claimed the tract as part of
their own territory.   Next, he procured a quit claim convey-
ance of the tract, from one Speene and his associates, who, on
their part, claimed the original right of soil; and, finally, to
make the grant doubly secure against future contesting claim-
ants, he had obtained for it the formal confirmation of the
General Court of the Colony.

Here the indefatigable apostle to the wild children of the
forest, as he has been so justly called, had gathered in his
disciples from all quarters, joined them, with the labors of his
own hands, in building a bridge across Charles river, which
ran through the town; in erecting a spacious meeting-house as
the general centre of their Christian worship; and lastly, in

---

* So named by the Indians at the time of its occupancy. The word *Natic*, in their own language, signifying *a place of hills*. See Spark's life of
Eliot.

building permanent dwelling-houses for a village, and for an agricultural independent community, which no earthly powers had the right to molest, so long as engaged in the peaceful pursuit of their avocations.

Here the gratified leader had spent months and months, through a period of more than twenty years, in privately instructing his trusting and devoted followers in the arts of civilized life, in civil polity for the government of their community, and especially, in the simple but sublime truths of Christian revelation. Here, he statedly preached to them in the loved tabernacle which he had helped them to build and consecrate, and to which, on each hallowed Sabbath morning, they came flocking at the beat of a drum, like loving doves to their windows. In short, he had labored and lived to see his hopeful flock here permanently settled—gaining year by year in temporal thrift and moral elevation, and in making such a progress in Christian knowledge and virtue, as to have gained for them as a church, the full acknowledgment and fellowship of all the white Christian churches in the colony. And he had not only beheld, as he did with unspeakable satisfaction, the practicability of his great experiment for christianizing the red men, thus measurably demonstrated to the doubting world, and his labors of love crowned year after year with a more and more perfect success; but he had lived to enjoy the additional gratification of beholding the natural antipathies of the people at large against the objects of his affectionate solicitude, to all appearance, nearly overcome, or so far, at least, that they began to be looked upon as fellow-men, and entitled to the ordinary privileges of humanity.

But latterly, a change had come over the spirit of the people. The jealousy and hatred which had been long springing up between the colony at Plymouth, and King Philip and his subjects, and which had now come to a crisis, had, within the last year or two been rapidly spreading among the colonists of Massachusetts, who hitherto had treated the natives with much more fairness than had been shown them by the people of Plymouth, and had so little sympathized in the fears and suspicions of the latter as to have often interposed to rebuke and quiet their growing disaffection.

At the present juncture, however, the old antipathies of the Bay colonists seemed not only to have been fully revived, but now to have been fanned to a flame by the startling news from Plymouth. They everywhere began to look upon the natives with distrust, and whatever their tribal relations, or whatever their character for friendliness or Christian conduct, to place them all in one and the same category—that of the natural enemies of the white men. And the General Court, sharing in the prevalent excitement and alarm, had not only taken steps to raise military forces, but passed a decree for the forcible removal, or rather virtual imprisonment of the praying Indians. Accordingly, the thorough going Captain Prentiss had been promptly dispatched with his company of cavalry to their principal establishment at Natic, to drive them from their doubly guaranteed homes and possessions, and conduct them off, like a gang of slaves, to a barren island which could afford them at best, but a pitiable subsistence.

In a short time the showy and domineering cavalcade with their long line of sorrowing victims, came pouring along against the landing, where the boats were in waiting to receive them; when the sharp, stern voice of Captain Prentiss was heard commanding a halt, and issuing his orders for an immediate embarkation.

At this moment a plainly dressed man of a clerical air, and a meek, pleading countenance, was seen hastening, with the quick, tremulous steps of age, from a neighboring coppice, and eagerly making his way through the crowd towards the spot where the officer just named sat on his horse, giving directions to his subordinates respecting the business on hand.

It was the good Eliot, the Indian Apostle, whose body, worn
and exhausted in the willing service of benefiting the red man,
was now tottering on the brink of the grave, but whose soul
was still glowing with the intensity of his love and yearning
solicitude for the únfortunate race, for whose eternal welfare
he had spent, without hope of any earthly reward, all the best
part of his laborious life. He had heard of the project of
their cruel and unwarranted banishment with deep surprise,
and with feelings of unspeakable anguish. He had remonstrated with the leading men of the court, and persevered in
his intercessions until he had brought upon himself the contumely of both the rulers and the people, who had now become
so crazed with fear and excitement, as not only to look upon
all the praying Indians as secret plotters in aid of the impending war, but to regard, with dislike and suspicion, every
white man who ventured to speak a word in their defence.
But he might as well have remonstrated with the angry billows of the ocean for dashing over their usual limits when
lashed into blind fury by the power of the natural tempest.
And having found all his remonstrances and intercessions
wholly ineffectual, and having that morning seen, with an
aching heart, the troops depart to carry the despotic order
into execution, he had come here to take a sad farewell of his
beloved flock, minister to them the consolations of the gospel,
and offer up for their future welfare and safety his prayers
and intercessions to Him, with whom, he felt he might plead
unrebuked for that answer of peace which he had failed to
receive from men who professed to worship the same God
with himself, and who, at that very hour, perhaps were thank-
ing him for the success of their unholy doings in the present
outrage.

As the venerable man passed along through the yielding
throng, who seemed to shrink from his presence as from the
contact of a leper, many a spiteful hiss reached his ears, and

many a pointed finger of scorn greeted his eyes; but, heeding none of them, he pressed on to the side of the stern commander and meekly asked his attention in listening to "a respectful request for a small favor, the granting of which would be received with much gratitude."

"Favor! what favor, old man?" gruffly responded the officer, looking down with an air of mingled impatience and disdain upon the meek suppliant.

"These once wild but now well meaning people, Captain Prentiss," respectfully but earnestly urged the aged intercessor, "have for more than a score of my weary years, been the especial subjects of my ministerial labors. I love them as children; and they have come to look on me as their father and friend; and the favor I have to ask, is to be permitted, for one short hour, to hold a little meeting with them, in some secluded corner of this shady grove, where unmolested, I may commune with them, pray with them, and give them my parting counsels. I cannot think the General Court would refuse."

"Yes, yes, I hear you, sir," impatiently interrupted the other. "But instead of receiving such an undeserved permission, to enable you, for ought I know, to preach to them a little more of the sedition you are suspected of by some, shouldn't you be well satisfied with the favor the Court has already mercifully vouchsafed you, in that you are not driven off with them?"

Repeated bursts of laughter ran through the crowd, in savage approval of the words of the last speaker, who, after glancing around with a gratified air a moment, was about to resume; when Captain Mosely, who had stood by witnessing what took place, promptly stepped forward, and in his abrupt, bold manner, exclaimed,

"Avast! there, Captain Prentiss. This, to be sure, is none of my commands, or my business—thank God for it!—and I

don't wish to interfere; but, natheless, I may suggest whether
we had better do any thing that will make the Indians themselves blush for us. We must recollect that these poor
creatures have not, as yet, done any thing blameworthy; and
as they are about to be shipped, both they and their preacher
very naturally want a little talk and worship together, and I
move they have the permit. I will be answerable for all the
sedition Father Eliot will preach to them; for, to say nothing
about you, captain, I wish to God I was half as good a man
as I believe him to be."

A visible frown passed over the sternly grave countenance
of the military bigot who had been selected for the present
service, but he was evidently staggered by the plain remarks
of Mosely, who, whatever his faults, was a great favorite
among the common people, and who, as the former perceived
from sundry manifestations of applause with which his remarks
were also in turn received, was not without a strong party in
the crowd to sustain him; and the result was, that Captain
Prentiss, after a brief consultation with his lieutenant, commanded the attention of his company, and announced to them
that, "as Captain Mosely had agreed to become responsible
for the Indians in charge, while they and their minister should
hold a short prayer-meeting, the troop might now take a respite
of one half hour, at the end of which they must all be in
readiness—one half to take the horses round to Boston, and
the other half to go with him in the boats to take the suspected heathen crew to their destination."

"Captain Mosely," said Willis, who had retained his place
at the side of the other, and had been the most out-spoken of
all in approval of his course, "I shall always honor you for
your fearless and humane interposition. They not only meant
to insult Father Eliot, but deprive him of all chance to speak
to his flock. But here he comes to thank you himself, I
presume."

"It is truly so," said the good old man, feelingly, as he warmly grasped the rough palm of the captain, while a tear was starting to his eye, and his lips began to tremble with his grateful emotions. "Sir, I th—ank you,—thank you for this! May God bless you. Yea, and you, too, young man, for approving the kind act. You both shall have my prayers."

"Well, we need 'em bad enough—at least I do," responded Mosely; "but no thanks, Father Eliot; I don't deserve 'em, for I spoke out for myself, being riled all up to see them use you so, like cussed Arabs."

"Oh, don't curse them," said the other, "don't curse them. They knew not what they did. Let it all pass. But they have allowed me brief time—I must improve it," he added, turning away and hastening to a little elevation, where he could be seen and heard by all of his dusky flock.

"My children!" he then cried, in the most touching accents of affection, "we have found friends, and they have prevailed. We are to be indulged in a short meeting. So follow *me*, now—follow *me*, my children."

The gratified apostle then with hurrying steps led the way to a place in another part of the grove, which he seemed to have already selected for the purpose; while the agitated mass of his devoted followers, with eyes gleaming with joy and love, and with the confiding alacrity of a brood of chickens running at the call of the feathered parent, went streaming along after him. When he reached the allotted place, which was an open grassy plat, surrounded with low evergreens, he took his stand in the centre, and, with a countenance working with emotion, he motioned them to arrange themselves around him. He then commenced the loving ceremony of taking them, one after another, individually by the hand, exchanging with them, in broken utterance, the mutual salutations, and ministering to them all the words of faith and Christian consolation.

"Hard, hard, farder Eliot," said these sobbing children of

persecution, as they came up to grasp the proffered hand of their idolized pastor, and to water it with their tears—" hard go away so ! never, may be, come back again ! then no more Natic home, no more green fields, no more good houses, no more meeting house, no more pray there, no more preach, no more see good farder Eliot—Oh, hard, hard !"

" Yes, yes, my beloved children," would reply the weeping pastor, to remarks like these, " it is indeed a sore trial, and hard to be borne ; but we must all bow to the will of the Great and good One above, who has doubtless ordered it for wise purposes, and our own benefit. It has often been so with the followers of the Lamb, who has told us, that through much tribulation we must enter the kingdom of God."

At the conclusion of this touching scene, in which more than half the allotted time had been spent in thus commingling their sorrows and sympathies, he asked them all to kneel on the ground closely around him. Readily comprehending the object, they immediately gathered up, dropped upon their knees in thickly encircling lines, and reverently bowed their grief-bedewed faces to the earth ; when, with his thin, trembling hands widely spread over them, the silvery locks of his uncovered head, rising and falling in the fitful evening breeze, and the fast coming tears coursing down his furrowed cheeks, the good and guileless old man lifted up his broken voice and prayed—

" O thou good and merciful God, who hast proclaimed thyself the father of all, are not these poor, suffering, and sorrowing ones, all thy children ? Are they not as dear to thee, and as much entitled to thy kindly regard, as those, whom, in thy ever wise dispensations, thou hast permitted thus to afflict them ? We entreat thee, then, O heavenly Parent, as much of the red man as the white—our Father, and their Father—our God, and their God—we entreat thee, in the faith and love thou hast planted with thine own hand in the yearning bosom of thy unworthy servant—we earnestly entreat thee to take them under thy especial care and protection, doing unto them, and for them, according to their need and their weakness, to enable them to bear up under the heavy hand of the strong that has now been so grievously laid upon them. Give them of the fullness of thy grace and love. Make good unto them all the peace and satisfaction of which their misguided oppressors may now perchance be deprived, for their offences towards these little ones, of the same Christian family. Take them by thy fostering and fatherly hand, and lead them in pleasant places. Provide for all their temporal wants. Vouchsafe to them thy choicest blessings. Minister unto them, and comfort them in all their trials and afflictions. Guard them from all the forms of sin and temptation. Constantly reveal thyself to them in thine unerring Spirit, as a light to guide their feet in their strivings onward along their dim pathway, to a more perfect righteousness above. Guide them safely through this thorny vale of life; and finally, O merciful Redeemer, gather them all to the great fold of thy loved and accepted ones in heaven."

The last word of this impassioned appeal to heaven in behalf of this injured flock of converted and affiliated Indians, had scarcely died away among the whispering pines, before the stern, harsh voice of Captain Prentiss, now seen galloping, with fiercely waving sword, towards the spot, was heard authoritatively exclaiming—

"Turn out! turn out there! ye moping mischief brewers. Your time is up. Budge along here, then, to the boats; and step lively, every soul of ye, or I'll have a platoon of troopers at your heels!"

With the hurried, apprehensive motions of a gang of slaves, sharply threatened with the lash of the master, the Indians bade their now doubly dear, earthly shepherd a hasty farewell; for they saw he was too much overpowered by his emotions to follow them on their thronged way to the landing, where they had hoped he would repair to give them his final blessing. But though deprived of this satisfaction, they were not to be left without a compensating comfort. Through the openings of the swaying shubbery, they occasionally caught precious glimpses of his revered person, still standing on the consecrated spot, where solitary and silent, he was now affectionately stretching out his arms towards them, and now raising them aloft, as if to snatch from Heaven one more blessing on their departing heads.

If there is *any* form of worship among men acceptable in the sight of heaven, it must be the secretly offered incense of a trusting and devoted heart; when words and thoughts are breathed and shaped in the conscious absence of all human witnesses. If men ever pray worthily, and in the unalloyed sincerity of their hearts, it is then; for who shall say, how many detracting thoughts,—how many shades of unworthy feeling, or vanity, the lurking love of approbation, or the fear of giving offence, may throw over the petitions of men praying in public? Many a public prayer, we fear, has been framed less for the acceptance of Heaven, than the admiration of men.

After father Eliot had stood some time indulging in his grief, and in the outpourings of his heart in secret prayer, he turned, with heavy steps, to depart; when he, for the first time, became aware that the scene just described had not been without a concealed witness, whose searching scrutiny above that of all other men, he would, under the peculiar circumstance, have been the most anxious to avoid. But for a new scene, let us take a new chapter.

CHAPTER VIII.

"Kind nature's commoners, from her they drew
- Their needful wants, and learn'd not how to hoard;
  And him whom strength and wisdom crown'd they knew,
  But with no servile reverence, as their lord.
  And on their mountain summits they ador'd
  One great good Spirit, in his high abode.
  These simple truths went down from sire to son,
  To reverence age,—the sluggish hunter's shame,
  And craven warrior's infamy to shun,—
And still avenge each wrong to friend or kindred done."

EASTBURNE.

WHILE father Eliot, as mentioned at the close of the last chapter, was turning away from the place where he had been mournfully lingering, with thoughts still dwelling on the departed objects of his solicitude, his attention was suddenly arrested by the sound of a footfall behind him, and almost at the same instant, by a light tap on his shoulder. Wheeling quickly around, in the surprise, he found himself confronting a tall, commanding figure, garbed in an English dress throughout, and so little darker in complexion than many of the bronzed seamen every day to be encountered at the neighboring port, that he might well have been taken for one by those who had never before encountered him, and noted his peculiarly piercing, yet mild and pleasant countenance. But Eliot had done both ; and, after gazing a moment, doubtfully, upon the intruder, who had receded a step, and stood with folded arms, smilingly waiting to see if he could be recognized, the former said—

"King Philip! Is not this King Philip of Mount Hope?"

"Yes, Mr. Eliot."

"But, King Philip, what has brought you here so unexpectedly?"

"I came into this colony to see for myself what was doing here about things needful for me to know, Mr. Eliot. I came to this spot for the same purpose, it may be, as you did."

"And have you witnessed the little meeting I have just had with my Christian flock, at this place?"

"I have—I stood in the bush near by, saw all—heard all."

"I feared so—I am sorry, King Philip."

"Why should *Mr. Eliot* be sorry? *His* words were good —they were very kind to the red men."

"I am sorry, because I fear you will argue wrongfully about our religion, on account of the treatment you may have seen some Christian white men bestowing on the undeserving red men, to-day."

"Why argue wrong, if *I did* argue, as you may well say you fear I would? Your Bible say—you preach yourself—the tree is known by the fruit it grow. I told you, Mr. Eliot, when, many moons ago, you come to Montaup to see you could make me praying Indian. I told you then your religion not worth one of the buttons on your coat. I had often seen what it made white men in Plymouth. I now have seen what it make them here."

"Oh, you must not judge our religion by the mistaken conduct of its professors in some cases," responded the other, in evident distress, and in no small strait to know how to repel the inference, which his conscience told him the conduct of his people had given his shrewd opponent too much reason for drawing. "Professors often go astray, and do very wrong.

But if they are so prone to do wrong with religion, what might they not do without it ?"

" You may best answer that question yourself, Mr. Eliot; and I will put another to go along with it :—If Indians be such devils, hell-hounds, damned bad men, as you whites call them, *without* your religion, what would they be if they *had* it ?   No, no, Mr. Eliot, though *you* be a good man, I don't want your religion for my people—certain not while there are so many white Christians in the land to bring it into disgrace in the eyes of Indians.   If we red men, as in times long gone, were all the people this side of the great water, it might be different.   In such case, I sometime said, may be I would like to *try* it for my people."

"Oh ! the misconduct of professing Christians that are thus bringing our religion into reproach among those who would otherwise receive it !   King Philip, you judge erringly.   The treatment you may have received from a few has embittered you against all.   We have taken no part against you in your difficulties with the Plymouth people ; and yet, it is now said, you are about to wage a bloody war with us all.   The people of this colony are greatly alarmed ; and the court have ap-pointed a commissioner to set out immediately for Mount Hope, to see you, remonstrate, and treat with you.   That com-missioner applied to me, this very morning, to go with him ; and I was to give him my answer at this place, where I pre-sume he is still lingering about the landing to receive it. Shall I tell him you will be there to receive us ?"

" No; too late.   Your colony are doing things that make it not possible to treat with them.   Tell him no use to go. I shall not be at Montaup."

" Then why not hear him here ?"

" I said no use,—I say again.   But I would hear his talk if he came alone, or only with you, Mr. Eliot."

" Then I will straightway go and see if I can find him.

But see !" added the anxious intercessor, pointing to a well dressed man imperfectly seen through the shubbery making his way in that direction, and peering around him as if in search of some one,—"See there comes the very man,—in search of me probably. I will go forward and speak to him; when we will both immediately come here for the interview."

Eliot thereupon hurried away, met the commissioner in question, when, after apprising him of the circumstances just related, and holding a brief conversation, the two advanced to the spot where the proud chieftain stood waiting to afford the promised interview.

Eliot, in a kind and courtly manner, went through the ceremonies of the introduction; when Metacom, with the dignity and grace for which he was so remarkable on these occasions, advanced, shook hands with the commissioner, and then, receding a step, respectfully awaited the expected communication.

" King Philip," said the commissioner, after a long, hesitating pause, " news has reached us, that you are about to make war against the colonies. Our governor and council, who have appointed me to hold parley with you, cannot understand how you can have any cause of war against the colony of Massachusetts, who have always tried to stand peace-makers between you and the Plymouth colony. And they instruct me to ask you why you have thus declared war against us ?"

" I have not declared war against your colony," responded the chief, with cool dignity. " My war is with the court and people of Plymouth. But if the court of Massachusetts make movement looking to join the Plymouth men, then they make themselves all one of my enemies."

" But we have made no such movements," deprecatingly said the commissioner.

" May-be," replied Metacom with increasing coolness and an air of irony. " May-be the court have sent a commissioner to treat of peace without letting him know they are all the while preparing for war. If that be not so, what looks it to, the forcibly driving away the peaceable red men of Natic from the homes and lands they own as much as your rich men own their houses in Boston? And what looks it to, the raising of a war-armed company, under Captain Mosely, to march to help the Plymouth colony? The commissioner does not appear to be well instructed about what his colony is doing."

"You wrongly interpret these movements," replied the nonplussed commissioner, who, as was evidently the case with nearly all the public men of that period, had greatly under-rated the Indian character, and especially that of Philip, and therefore was not prepared to find such a knowledge of the secret movements of the court in his opponent—"You make too much out of them, and I hope you will still consent to treat for peace with our governor."

"Your governor?" haughtily responded the proud monarch of the Wampanoogs—"Your governor is a subject of King Charles of England. I shall not treat with a subject. I shall *now* only treat with the king, my brother. When he comes, I am ready."

This unexpected declaration of Metacom—who, believing he had now fully fathomed the secret designs of Massachusetts to take part with the colony of Plymouth in the war against him, felt consequently not a little indignant that the former, while privately instituting hostile movements, were hypocri-tically pretending, in public, to desire to treat with him for the continuance of a peace which he had never violated—this declaration, as he intended it should, brought to an abrupt termination the conference with the commissioner, who at-tempted no reply. Father Eliot, however, began earnestly to entreat Philip to pause before he should take any steps which should involve alike, perhaps, all the white men and the red men of New England, in a war of blood and desolation. But the immoveable chief interrupted by saying—

"No use—no use to talk, Mr. Eliot. Your people are not like you. You may speak for yourself, and I will tell you, that whatever come, you, family, property, will all be safe from the red men. But speak no more for *them*. *They* have told me in deeds, which always speak louder than words with the Indian, what they will do. It is not my fault. They will have it so. And as they have chosen their own path, let them walk in it."

With this, and a distant parting bow to the commissioner, and a kindly one to father Eliot, he turned away and disappeared in the nearest thicket, on his way to the then unbroken forests of central Massachusetts, whither, for awhile, at least we propose to accompany him.

The great leader of the Wampanoogs, whose warlike achievements, during the terrible year now close at hand, were destined to carry death and dismay into every white settlement in New England, was, at this period, in the very flower of his manhood, his age being not much, if any, above thirty. And in him might be seen the rare spectacle of a man uniting in himself the highest grade of intellect with the most perfect physical conformation of body, and the greatest degree of exterior grace and manly beauty. He was, indeed, in appearance, as in reality a king—every inch a king, having descended from a long line of royal ancestors, who, contrary to the precedents of most or all other tribes of North American Indians, had, at some distant point in the past, established, and had ever since successfully maintained an unbroken hereditary succession of the crown in their family. He was deeply sensible of the tremendous hazard he incurred for himself and people, by engaging in a general war with the white men. And he had accordingly watched, with a sovereign's solicitude, and with a sovereign's jealousy and alarm, the aggressive policy of the colonists, which he believed, was intended to be consummated in reducing him and his people to a state of the

most abject submission, if not unconditional slavery, or in
their entire extermination. For himself and his proud tribe,
they had already decided on the Roman alternative of death
before slavery. But were they to maintain the fight single-
handed and alone, without the aid of the other New England
tribes, who ought to see, he thought, the same fate in reserve
for themselves? And having spent the whole of the past
week in a laborious reconnoissance of the condition of both
the Plymouth and Massachusetts colonies, he was now about
to enter on the next step of his plan—that of obtaining, if
possible, the promise of a favorable answer to the above question.

As soon as the cautious chief, who, on leaving his company,
had steered in a direction nearly opposite from the one he
intended taking, found himself safely beyond the reach of
their senses, he struck off in a line parallel with the upward
banks of the Charles. Making his way with long, rapid steps
and amazing celerity, he pursued his undeviating course three
or four miles, and until he reached the point where the stream
comes down from a considerable sweep to the northward; when
he paused, and fixed his course through the woods across the
bend, so as to strike the river again where it touches, or
rather passes through, a cluster of lakelets, which it had
reached near its last great bend from the south to the east.
Another hour of his rapid walking brought him to the pine-
clad shore of the largest of these ponds; when he paused,
drew a small bone whistle from his pocket, and blew a low,
long, and peculiarly modulated blast, that thrilled far and wide
through the gloomy recesses of the silent forests around. In
a moment, the call was answered from a dense thicket bordering the western extremity of the pond, about a quarter of a
mile distant. Bending his steps towards the spot indicated by
the answering sound, and by the gleams of light which now
soon occasionally shot through the dense undergrowth from

the same direction, Metacom in a short time came upon a large camping bower, with a cheerful fire blazing on the ground before it. The next moment, ten well-armed, noble-looking Indian warriors emerged from the shantee, and falling into a dressed line before him, respectfully saluted him as their sovereign master. They were, with one exception, a band of his most trusty and sagacious Wampanoogs, come there, by his appointment, to hold with him a council, and receive from him such missions as could best be determined on after the completion of the reconnoissance in which he had been engaged. Having returned their salutations with graceful dignity, he followed them into the camp, when they all sat down to a plentiful repast, consisting of fresh fish and venison, which had that afternoon been taken from pond and surrounding forest by the devoted band, and prepared and kept in readiness, untasted, for the expected reception of their royal leader. With the usual taciturnity of their race, they dispatched their meal in almost unbroken silence. Then followed, with an almost equal absence of conversation, the customary filling, lighting, and smoking of the neatly carved stone tobacco pipes, with which they generally, as now, were found well provided. After this, Metacom rose and commenced the expected narration of the discoveries he had made among the Bay colonists, minutely describing every event and circumstance believed to have any bearing on the object of their common solicitude— the evident suspicion and alarm among the people, their growing bitterness towards the Indians, their secret preparations for aggressive warfare, and lastly, what he considered more significant than all, the outrageous policy they had so unexpectedly adopted towards the praying Indians.

Low exclamations of alternate surprise, indignation, hatred, and defiance, had burst from the lips of the swarthy warriors, during the speaker's recital of the different parts of his subject; and as he closed the last one, respecting the course taken towards the praying Indians, their eyes gleamed with savage delight, and their exclamations rose to a loud yell of exultation; for their sagacity at once told them, that the colonists in this short sighted measure, had given them an advantage in the game of war, which might easily be turned to good account.

"Good! my brothers understand," resumed the speaker, after a long, significant pause, in which he glanced approvingly round from one face to another among his keenly appreciating auditors, as they sat round the flickering fire with their burning eyes fixed intently upon him. "My brothers see it all now. My brothers see that the men of Massachusetts, in speaking smooth things, and the words of friendship to Metacom and his people, have been speaking with forked tongues. My brothers now see how these smooth-tongued pale faces can talk peace when they mean war. My brothers see how they must hate the red men—so much hate that they rob and seize for prisoners even those they have made praying Indians, taken by the hand, and called friends and brothers. My brothers here are convinced; for they see now what the white man's faith is when given to the Indian—the frost of a spring morning that turns to mist before the noonday can come to see it. But will these cheated, praying Indians see it with the same eyes? They *must* see it all now, and be ready to come back to the ways of their fathers. Metacom would then have some of his warriors go to them—go to-morrow to Squantum; take over canoes to them so that they can escape from the island before they are shipped off and sold as slaves. Tell them to come and join Metacom, and he will make them men and warriors. Let two of my brothers do this, and let two others go and tell the same story to all the praying Indians at Punkapog, Neponsit, and Nonantum.*

---

* Locations in Stoughton, Dorchester, and Newton, where small communities of praying Indians were also established.

"Metacom has now done, till some of his brothers have spoken. What news brings Annawan from Montaup? Annawan is my father's old friend, counselor, and war captain, and with an old warrior's eye has no doubt noted how the young warriors feel since Metacom left them, and what preparations they are making for war? Let him speak. The ears of Metacom are open."

On this, a warrior of sixty winters, but with a frame of iron, and an eye glowing with the fires of youth, slowly rose and said :

"The young warriors are ready. They are more than ready. They burn for battle and blood. When Metacom came home from Plymouth, and told them at the council and the war-dance how the court had choked their friends and brothers, they howled ! Metacom knows how loud they all howled for revenge. And when Metacom told them they should have it, and if they would wait till he had made the preparations, he himself would lead them to war, they rejoiced—every Wampanoog in the land rejoiced. They all fell to sharpening their knives and hatchets, making bullets, and getting their guns ready for the onset. They now only wait the signal from Metacom."

"It is well," resumed the former—"it is well to be ready. But the young warriors must not be so impatient as to hurry them on to deeds of war before the time. This is what I fear. Metacom thinks it is for Annawan to see to this; for he only may be able to restrain the fiery young braves.. Let him therefore, hasten back to-morrow, and tell them we are yet ready only for some *small* blow, that, if struck now, may prevent the *great* one we intend. Tell them we shall have now to meet the more powerful Bay colony as well as the weaker Plymouth, and therefore have a double preparation to make ; and tell them more, that Metacom is laboring for his life to make his side strong. He is now going to the chief village of the Nipmucks, at Wachusetts mountain, to hold a war council, before the Massachusetts commissioners, who are to start in three days, can get there to make a treaty of peace. He must then go to other tribes till he has visited every one from the great rivers of the east to the long river of the west,* to hold war talks with them, and make them take up the red hatchet he will lay at their feet.†

"But now," continued the speaker turning from the oldest to the youngest of the band. "Now Metacom would be pleased to hear Quinapin, whom he is glad to see here among his warriors. Quinapin is a sachem and friend to the Wampanoogs. Does he bring good news from his tribe? or will his tribe be better pleased to stand with folded arms in the coming war and see the Wampanoogs carry off all the glory?"

The Indian thus flatteringly and skillfully addressed, was a tall lusty, showy young Narraganset, who being but one of the smaller sachems of his tribe, was ambitious of preferment, and courting an alliance with the renowned king of the Wampanoogs, who, in the fiery but beautiful Wetamoo, had a queen sister who had driven off her last husband for his friendship to the whites, and whose hand, if it could be obtained, would ennoble the proudest warrior of the land. Metacom had known his desires without encouraging his hope; but he now evidently resolved to favor his suit as a means of bringing about the close alliance he was anxious to establish with the powerful tribe of the Narragansets, whose co-operation in the coming war was of the utmost importance.

"Quinapin believe the young warriors all right," replied the obviously flattered young sachem. "They all little love

* The Connecticut, the name being an Indian word signifying *Long River*.
—SCHOOLCRAFT.

† The mode of courting an alliance among Indians, is for the chief requesting it to approach the other party in council, and lay a hatchet painted red at their feet; when, if the hatchet is taken up by the latter, the alliance is regarded as fully consummated.—CARVER.

the pale faces, and would love the fight. But Ninigret, the chief Sagamore of the Narragansets, is very old,—his eyes are dim. He is like a little child, and does not like to hear about war. Young Nanuntenoo is the panther of the tribe, and will soon be the great chief. Metacom should see him."

"Metacom will see him and see the young warriors," responded the former, cordially. "Let Quinapin go home to-morrow, and tell his people what he has heard ; and tell them, also, Metacom will be there in four days with the pipe of peace for *them*, and the red hatchet for his enemies. Let Quinapin prepare for the council, and Metacom is his friend in all his wish."

This appeared to end the conference or council of the warriors, which, though but three of them had made any continuous remarks, had yet been so interlarded, at the various pauses of the speakers, by the significant monosyllabic expressions of the rest, as to make it evident, that the whole subject under consideration was too well understood and appreciated by all, to require any further discussion. All matters of public concern being now dropped by common consent, the band slightly replenished their fire, refilled their pipes, and commenced the dreamy regalement of their native weed, for the last time before betaking themselves to their nightly repose. When this once peculiarly aboriginal process of narcotic imbibition, which, strangely enough, is about the only habit we have ever borrowed from the Indians,—one vice to not one of their virtues,—when this process was completed, these stoic philosophers of the woods closely gathered their blankets around them, threw themselves down upon their primitive evergreen couches, and lulled by the drowsy monotony of the piping frogs along the shore, mingling with the Eolian music of the pines above their heads, were soon all locked in those sweet slumbers which are alike the boon of the savage and civilized wood-man.

The next morning the invigorated warriors sprang from

their sylvan couches with the first broad flush of the dawn, rekindled their fire, prepared their breakfast, speedily despatched it, and packed up for an immediate departure. Their leader then briefly repeated the instructions of the preceding evening, and sent six of their number away on their allotted missions; he next drew out from his well-filled wardrobe pack, which had been brought to this place by his orders, a light Indian traveling dress, and donned it in place of the English disguise-garments he had been wearing on his tour of observation among the whites. And thus equipped for the start, he led the way for his four remaining followers into the forest, and set his course for his destination beneath the lofty Wachusett, whose looming summit even there was seen peering up, for their land-mark, just over the long, blue, misty line of the western horizon.

Instead, however, of following them, as one after another, with ceaseless tread, they silently and swiftly threaded the continuous recesses of the diversified forest, during that long summer day, we will now change the scene to the mountain village of red men, which circumstances had made the object of their forced and weary march.

On a sunny plateau, at the foot of the majestic mountain we have named, where the uniting streams of crystal waters come dashing down from the precipitous heights above, to form the extreme sources of the romantic Nashua, stood the sixty or seventy wigwams which constituted, at the period of which we are writing, the favorite and most populous village of the numerous Nipmucks, whose whole territory embraced all, and more than all, the present great agricultural county of Worcester.

On the evening of the day in question, this village was swarming with an extra population of red men, who had gathered, and were still fast gathering in from other villages or scattered residences in the country round about, for the

purpose of being present, evidently on some unusual occasion.
On an open and well-smoothed piece of ground, near the centre of the village, a score of men were busily engaged in
erecting a capacious arbor-fashioned structure, nearly sixty
feet long, fifteen feet wide, and of a height corresponding to
the width, the frame work of which was formed by bending
very long, slender poles, and inserting the ends in the ground
at equi-distant spaces.   While such numbers were engaged on
the spot, an equal or greater number were employed in bringing from the surrounding forest, another and smaller set of
poles to weave in laterally for ribs to the structure, together
with large quantities of freshly pealed bark boards to serve
for its covering.   An air of anxious haste, so unusual with
the red men, was every where perceptible among the company
thus employed, who, up to this time, had been working with
the eager alacrity of a community of beavers, prompted evidently by their wish to get their fabric completed before dark,
to be in readiness for the reception of some great assemblage
then expected to occur.   But as the descending sun to which
for the last hour, they had thrown many an anxious glance
while plying their work, now sunk behind the mountain, and
the shades of evening began to gather over the long reach of
spreading forests lying beneath them on the east, they ap--
peared to see that the idea of accomplishing their task that
night was a hopeless one.   They gradually relaxed their
efforts, and at length wholly abandoned the work, and stood,
some looking with pride on the result of their labors, some
wandering listlessly around the grounds, and some engaged in
conversation about the arrival which, a messenger had the
evening previous apprised them, might about this hour be expected.

   At that juncture, a loud, shrill, long drawn sound rose
from the forest below, arousing every man, woman, and child of
the thronged village from their listlessness ; and they were all

now seen hurrying forward with excited looks to join the central gathering of the eager expectants.

"It is his whistle ! Metacom! the brave Metacom ! the Great Sagamore is coming !" at length passed rapidly from mouth to mouth; and the next moment the wild hurra of savage welcome burst from five hundred voices, ringing merrily along the steep sides of the overhanging mountain, and filling its hundred glades and glens with the multiplying echoes of the glad acclamation.

In a short time, the tall and noble figure of the Wampanoog chieftain, now garbed in his richest Indian dress, and his person decorated with his most imposing regalia, emerged into view, and followed by his four attendant warriors, slowly advanced within thirty yards of the long line of admiring people, who had been drawn up to receive him; when he was again greeted with another loud and prolonged shout by way of welcoming his arrival. With a low and graceful bow, he acknowledged the courtesy, and then put himself under the lead of the four Nipmuck sachems, who now advanced to conduct him to the lodge which had been appropriately fitted up for his reception.

The summer's sun had again culminated, and was again slowly sinking towards the western horizon. On the topmost cliff of the towering Wachusett, sat alone and in moody silence, the proud chief of the Wampanoogs. He had, after his arrival the preceding evening, partaken the bountiful repast brought for him and his warriors, smoked the pipe of peace with the sachems who had called at his lodge, enjoyed his night's repose, and again invigorated himself with a morning repast; but with a policy which probably many another public speaker has adopted, he declined mingling with the people, lest the effort he was intending to make before them in public, should be weakened by the familiarity. And as the new council lodge, which had, the day before, been begun in special honor of the occasion, could not be finished to the satisfaction of the builders much before night, he had given notice that he would defer his speech until evening; and he had then betaken himself alone to the woods, to pass the day in solitary reflection, or perhaps in nerving himself with the war-spirit, which it was his aim to infuse into the bosoms of the people he had come to address and enlist in his cause. But whither should his uncertain steps now be directed? According to a very natural superstition of the Indians, who, more than any people on earth, perhaps, are prone

" To look through nature up to nature's God,"

the mountain tops are peculiarly the dwellings of the spirits; there are the most auspicious places for gaining the ear of the great or ruling spirit of all; and, consequently, that whatever of high resolve may be made there, will, if not directly prompted by him, at least be more likely to receive his sanction and blessing. He had therefore climbed the highest peak of this bold and majestic mountain, and, hour after hour, had been sitting on the highest rock of its commanding summit, with his grieved spirit brooding over the wrongs of the past, and his teeming mind revolving the projects of the future.

But he now rose to his feet, and, with his rifle and tomahawk lying carelessly at his side, pensively ran his eye over the magnificent panorama which the place everywhere presented to his wandering vision—on the east, in the thousand woody hills, with sparkling lakelets interspersed, stretching away in lessening perspective, till they melted into the misty light of the distant ocean—on the south and west, in the dotted landscape of solitary hills and interwoven ridges of mountain elevations, more conspicuously represented in the gray, bald Mount Holyoke, and the more distant and lofty Saddle-back, with the bright Connecticut occasionally gleaming up through the mountain gorges between them, like a silver thread in a dark embroidery; and finally, on the north, in the nearer form of the bold Monadnock, standing like a solitary sentinel of an advanced guard, to guide the vision to the shining pinnacles of the far off White Mountains, lifting their majestic heads from the azure depths of the encircling horizon.

It was evidently, however, not on the magnificent scenery that his thoughts were now intent. His wandering eye, in sweeping the horizon, has lighted on the habitations of the white men. He everywhere catches glimpses of their solitary openings in the wilderness, marking the front lines of the encroaching army. In the rear of these, he notes their smiling villages, with their tall church-spires shooting upward, giving certain indication of the increasing thrift and growing numbers of the invaders thickly crowding on behind, to seize upon the domains of the retiring red men. He turns to the south, but only to be greeted by the same painfully significant indications; for relief, he turns to the west; but as his eye follows up the broad valley of the Connecticut, his vision is there also met with the no less saddening prefigurations of destiny, which he sees in the white settlements, fast spreading themselves along up the fertile banks of that favorite river of his red brethren in the west. He again turns back to the east, and once more mournfully traces round the encircling line of civilization, which now, to his alarmed imagination, begins to assume the form of a monster white serpent, enclosing the whole wilderness home of his people with its vast, terrible coil, and drawing its fast contracting folds closer and closer on the victims of the hideous embrace. He sudddenly pauses and recoils. His eye becomes troubled, and his cheek pales; for in these demonstrations of the steady march of the white man's thrift and power, he instinctively reads the doom of his own people. Mark the gathering conflict of his perturbed and wrestling spirit! His mind quickly turns back on the long line of the

countless generations of his ancestors, who have successively
lived and passed away, the undisputed tenants of all these
broad primeval forests.

"Are not," with gloomy pride he exclaims—"are not the
big trees standing on the graves of my fathers? Has not the
Great Spirit whitened these hills with a thousand returning
snows, to thicken the coat of the beaver to clothe, and bring
the moose to feed, my people? Who, then, are these coming
over the great waters to seize, with robber hands, our rightful
possessions, destroy our hunting grounds to make them fields
where, with scoff and jeer, they shall plough over the sacred
bones of our dead warriors, and finally to drive us, like timid
deer, beyond the mountains of the setting sun?

"Oh, Manitou!" he cries, in the anguish of his feelings,
and with arms thrown wildly above, as if for aid to shut out
the unwelcome picture of coming destiny which had thus
come, like a baleful shadow, over his maddened soul—"Oh,
Manitou! is this, indeed, thy decree? Is this thy love and
justice to the poor red man? I will not believe it! My eye
shall be shut against the fearful vision. My ear shall be
stopped against the lying voice. It was *not thou* who said it!
It was the *white* man's God that was mocking me. No! no!
good Manitou, it is *none* of *thy* work. *Thou* art the great
friend and *protector* of the red man! I was wrong to doubt
thee. I see it now," he continues, as his faith begins to shape
itself to the current of his wishes, and he feels that kindling
glow in his bosom which the Indian ever interprets as the
promptings of a propitious spirit, and to which his fancy now
gave voice in the visible omens of nature—"I see it now in
this small bush, which thy wind has just bent forward towards
my hand, that I might thus wrench it up from the earth
before it grew strong in the ground and its branches spread
to cover the whole land. I hear it in the roar of the mountain waters, that comes in anger on my ear because the war-

riors are not ready for the fight. I hear it in the sharp screech
of yon soaring eagle, the totem bird of my tribe, whose cry
sounds vengeance to the white enemy. I hear it in the winds,
that murmur their rebuke for our coldness and loitering in
the war-path. I see it in the sun, that looks down with a sad
and bitter smile upon the red men every where lying idle in
the wigwam, when dangerous animals are gathering around to
destroy them. I hear it, I see it, in every thing—all speaking
thy voice, and showing thy will, that we make war on the pale-
faced aggressors till the last one is driven into the sea, and
the red men again become the lords of the country." He
ceases, but his quivering muscles and flashing eye speak the
determined purpose of his heart; and grasping his rifle and
tomahawk, he rapidly makes his way down the mountain, now
fully nerved to act his part in the gathered council of warriors
awaiting his presence below.

The shades of evening were once more fast gathering over
this mountain home of the red men, and the bright stars were
beginning to twinkle down through the branchy tree-tops of
the deeply foliaged forest. The new and unusually capacious
council lodge—now finished and appropriately ornamented
with all the emblematic devices of savage ingenuity, among
which the stuffed eagle, the totem badge of the Wampanoogs,
was, in compliment to that tribe, conspicuously suspended from
the ceiling—the new lodge was filled with the flower of the
Nipmuck warriors, awaiting in silence the promised appearance
of their illustrious visitor. At length, a commotion outside
the thronged building betokened his approach; and the warriors quickly arranged themselves on either side of the long
room, leaving a clear avenue through the centre to a sort of
block-work platform, raised at the further end for a stand for
the orator of the evening. Presently the distinguished guest,
now splendidly attired for the occasion, made his appearance
at the entrance, and, under the guidance of the oldest sachem

of the place, marched proudly up the well-smoothed avenue,
and lightly mounted the platform. For a full minute he sur-
veyed the hushed and expectant assemblage in silence. He
then, in low but clear and musical accents, entered on the history of the white settlements, since the first feeble and suppliant bands made their appearance and humbly craved of the
red possessors a small lodgment on these shores. He skillfully
demonstrated that every village, hamlet, or dwelling they had
erected, and every acre of land they had cleared, had been at
the expense of the best interests of the red men. He showed
that just in proportion to their growth, in every step of their
progress, from their little beginning up to their present greatness, their arrogance had increased; and that their settled,
though at first carefully concealed, intention to dispossess and
drive off all the original owners of the land, had every where
been betrayed in deeds which stamped their fair professions as
things of cunning and falsehood. With these facts staring
them in the face, then, he asked who could be so blind as not
to see that the artful aggressors were only waiting for a little
more increase of their number and power, to drive back every
tribe of the east from their time-honored homes and the sacred
graves of their fathers, to lands already occupied by other
tribes, where they could find no permanent homes, and, if
they were received at all, it would only be to starve and die
for want of game to support the doubled population? He then
drew a vivid picture of the insults and injuries which, from
time to time, had been heaped upon himself and his tribe by
the Plymouth colony, up to their last great outrage, so unblushingly exhibited, in seizing and hanging up with ropes,
as they would so many of their thieving dogs, the best of
those who bore the proud name of Wampanoog.

From the sad story of his own wrongs he passed to those
of the long suffering tribe he was addressing. He reminded
them in moving terms how often and shamefully they had

been cheated and overreached in trade; how, under one pretence or another, they had been crowded from their best lands, and driven back to the mountains; how large numbers of their tribe had been inveigled, under promise of protection and friendship, to settle near the whites, and become converts to their religion; and he then related his late discoveries of the treachery of the Massachusetts colonists; what he had seen of their preparations for war; how, in proof of the fact, he had seen them, as the first step in carrying out their hostile intentions, seizing upon and making prisoners of these very praying Indians, and he concluded this part of his subject by asking his auditors if these praying Indians, for whom so much friendship had been professed, were thus treated, what they supposed was in store for the rest of them?"

The universal burst of indignant denunciation which from all parts of the swarthy assemblage, followed this *ad hominem* question, told the gratified speaker how well his remarks had counted; and after the commotion had subsided, he proceeded next to relate to the excited throng his day-dream on the mountain, which his glowing eloquence, building on the ground-work of their peculiar superstitions, readily impressed on their willing minds as an undoubted revelation of the Great Spirit to his red children, in this their hour of danger. He pictured to them in vivid colors, his vision of a huge white serpent coming up from the sea, and gathering with its mighty coil, stretched all round from the north to the west, the devoted red men within its fatal grasp—then his agonized cry to the Great Spirit for assistance to escape from the threatened doom, and finally, the responsive command that came to him in the winds, that moaned reproachfully over the mountain—in the frowning sky—in the angry sound of the distant water falls, and in the fierce scream of the war eagle above his head, all bidding him arouse from his fatal lethargy, and go forth with his warriors to destroy or drive the monster from the land before it should be forever too late.

"It was the command of the red man's God," he added, in tones that swelled up like the ringing notes of the bugle, sounding the charge to battle. "Metacom bowed in submission to the high behest. His vow went up to the Great Manitou to execute the bidden vengeance on the mustering foes of his red children. Metacom's heart is now strong. His arm is nerved for the great struggle. He will soon go forth on the war-path with his brave Wampanoogs. But shall he go alone? Will the other tribes stand idly by, and with folded hands look coldly on to see him fight their battles and his own, and lift not a hatchet in the common cause?—see him struggle, and fight, and die for their rights, and they themselves shy away like a flock of frightened squaws from the conflict? What say the brave Nipmuck warriors to a charge like this? Will *they*, too, be found loth and laggard when the great day of vengeance arrives? Will *they*, too, turn themselves into weak, trembling women, and hold their hands to their ears when the war cry of their red brothers is ringing around their green hills, and calling them to the rescue?"

"No! no! no!" rose in one wild, universal shout of reprobation of the degrading thought from every young warrior of the agitated throng, which, by this time, was swaying and surging under the power of these maddening appeals, like the storm-lashed billows of the ocean. "No, no; the Nipmuck warriors shall be found neither coward nor laggard on that great day, but stand by the side of the Wampanoog brave, and keep pace with him in the race of the battle."

The chief looked around on the workings of the tempest he had raised with a grim smile of satisfaction. He saw that the auspicious moment to avail himself of the fruits of his effort had arrived, and that from words, it was time to proceed to

11

that binding, emblematic action from which no true Indian ever thinks of receding.

He therefore descended from his stand, and slowly marching down the open space to the spot where the four sachems of the tribe were seated, paused a moment before them with reverent air; and then drawing his painted blood-red hatchet from his belt, cast it down at their feet; when receding a step, he stood calmly, but with a look of proud confidence, awaiting in silence the result.

But these elderly personages, less carried away by the fiery eloquence of the speaker than the younger portion of their tribe, and deeply sensible of the responsibility they should incur by the action to which they had thus been challenged, for the first few moments sat mute and motionless, demurely looking down on the ground beneath their feet.

A murmur of displeasure ran through the crowd at this unexpected manifestation of doubting or indifference; and the sachems, evidently disturbed by the expression, began to glance uneasily around them. But still they moved not from their seats; and for another full minute sat doubtful and hesitating, when another and far more significant burst of displeasure rose from every part of the room, and brought them to their feet.

With a quick glance over the crowd, which seemed to say, we take this as a vote of instruction, but on you be the responsibility, they together leaped forward, grasped the red emblem of war and alliance; and each with a hand on a part of it, held it up to the crowd, who now sent up a shout in confirmation of the act, that shook the startled wilderness for miles around them.

" A war dance ! a war dance !" shouted the exulting chieftain, himself leading off with fiercely chanted war song, while the customary chorus rose wild and loud from every mouth of that dark assemblage.

After Metacom had danced awhile alone, first one, then

another, and then yet others fell into the area kept open for the performance, till the whole mass, with their flourished knives, tomahawks, and war clubs, and with yells and war-whoops intermingled in the chorus, were involved in the frightful mazes of that ominous exhibition of the wilds, which has so long been known as the certain precursor of blood and desolation to the hearths and homes of the white men.

Thus had the great chief triumphed—thus succeeded in making this numerous tribe so firmly and immovably his allies in the coming war, that when, a short time after, the Massachusetts commissioners came to enlist them against the Wampanoogs, or at least to secure their neutrality, these over-confident messengers of peace were met with surly silence, and, on a subsequent misjudged attempt, with a shower of bullets that laid eight of their escort dead on the earth.

But this was but a specimen triumph of this sagacious and powerful chieftain,—the first in the series of moral victories, which, while passing from tribe to tribe, with a celerity and boldness never before witnessed, he achieved over the minds of a divided and hitherto often mutually hostile race, in bringing them into league with himself to be ready to meet the anticipated crisis. And there can be but little doubt, that, had he been allowed six months longer to consummate his plans, as he had intended and hoped, he would have had the pleasure of beholding nearly every tribe, from the Atlantic to the great lakes, united in one great and irresistible confederacy, as the fruit of his gigantic plans and untiring exertions in maturing them. But, to his unspeakable grief and disappointment, he was suddenly cut short in the full tide of his successful career in this important part of his great scheme, by the unexpected outbreak of hostilities between the whites and his impatient Wampanoogs on the immediate borders of his own domain, which called him at once to the scene of action, and which, also, now calls us there to note the events which belong to another part of our story.

CHAPTER IX.

"Ah! who could deem that foot of Indian crew
Was near?—yet there, with lust of murderous deeds,
Gleam'd like a basilisk, from woods in view,
The ambush'd foeman's eye,—his volley speeds."
CAMPBELL'S GERTRUDE OF WYOMING.

"O MADIAN! Madian!—What dark fate has befallen my loved and beautiful Madian?"

It was the voice of the half distracted Vane Willis, as he turned in despair from his fruitless search to discover the retreat, or fate of the persecuted maiden, whose mysterious disappearance was mentioned at the close of a former chapter.

We parted with Willis, it will be recollected, in conversation with the rough-and-ready Captain Mosely, on the banks of Charles' river, in the vicinity of Boston, where they both appeared to be present to witness the embarkation of the praying Indians. As he was retiring from that scene, he was, for the first time, apprised by a friend, who had come from Plymouth, of the disappearance, or rather reported elopement of Miss Southworth. As might be expected, he was surprised, but in no way alarmed at the unexpected news. For, though he but imperfectly knew the circumstances by which she was surrounded, he yet was well aware that Deacon Mudgridge and his hopeful nephew were using their united exertions to force or inveigle her into a matrimonial alliance with the latter. And he thought it quite probable that to avoid their persecuting importunities, she had privately left her home for a short residence in the family of her relative in Boston, where, he secretly congratulated himself, he should now have the pleasure of seeing her, before his return to the other colony, for which he was then already on the point of starting. Getting clear of his bantering friend, therefore, as soon as he could decently do so, he hurried into the city, and after a little excusable attention to his toilet, at once repaired to the residence of Madian's kinsfolk, where he confidently expected he should find, and, he hoped, agreeably surprise her.

But when he had arrived there, and questioned the family, he found, to his great disappointment, that she was not there,— had not been there, and that nothing had been heard from her, nor of her, for several months, by any of the family. He felt deeply perplexed at the strange circumstance. He could not comprehend nor account for it. And the more he reflected, the more did his doubts and perplexities become mingled with apprehensions, that something very unusual, to say the least, must have befallen her. He prudently, however, kept his uneasiness and misgivings to himself, and contenting himself with the mere expressions of regret and surprise at not finding Miss Southworth here with her relatives, he soon withdrew from the house and hurried back to his lodgings; when, making the few preparations which were only necessary, he announced his departure, mounted his horse, and within one hour, though it was then bed time, was far on his nightly journey to Plymouth.

Arriving the next morning at the house of an intimate friend, of the name of Noel, who was a member of his prospective company, and who resided in the town next northwardly of the one to which he was destined, he there stopped to refresh and rest himself and his over-ridden horse, till evening; when he rode into Plymouth, and repaired at once to the Southworth mansion, where, he felt confident, he should be kindly received by the old domestics, and where he believed he could not fail to learn something which would enable him at least to form some probable conjecture on the subject which was so deeply engrossing his solicitude. And so far as regarded his reception there, he had reckoned rightly. Taffy and his wife were overjoyed to see him; for, from the want of any better solution of the mystery, having fallen in with the prevalent opinion that their young mistress had privately left, after they had retired at night, and gone off with Willis, whom they believed to be her accepted lover, they were look-ing to *him* for the very information he was hoping to obtain from *them*, respecting her otherwise wholly unaccountable absence. And when he informed them that he had neither seen her, nor heard from her, since he parted with her at that house, nearly a fortnight before, they heard him at first with incredulity, and, at last, with astonishment and dismay; becoming in their turn, also, deeply concerned for her safety. But they could tell him nothing satisfactory in regard to her unexpected flight, except to express their decided opinion, that it was caused by the despicable course which Deacon Mudgridge had pursued to force her into an abhorred union; and which they then proceeded to relate to the excited and indignant lover, in all its disgusting and contemptible parti-culars, including his last high handed act of causing a legal notice of her marriage with the thrice rejected lover, to be proclaimed in the church, the appointing of a time for the ceremony, and lastly their plot to dispose of the accepted lover by banishing him for a Quaker, the first time he should make his appearance.

The last intimation concerning the designs of the conspira-tors on himself, Willis treated with open derision and defi-ance; but on all the rest, he felt too deeply exasperated and alarmed to make it prudent for him to attempt to give any expression to the emotions of his laboring bosom. And hav-ing gained all the information he could expect from the warmly sympathizing Taffy and his wife, he cautioned them against disclosing to any one the fact of his visit here, and assured them that he would know no rest until he had found their mistress, or ascertained her fate, he took his leave of the anxious old couple, and, mounting his horse, rode slowly and thoughtfully back to the residence of his friend, which he now concluded to make his headquarters for the further investigation, which he was now sternly determined to pursue.

After anxiously pondering the whole subject, and carefully weighing all the circumstances which he thought could have any connection with Madian's disappearance, he at length reached the conclusion, that one of three things only, could have befallen her :—Either Deacon Mudgridge or some of his minions had abducted her, and conveyed her to some place where they could control her, or she, driven to desperation by her persecutions, had committed suicide ; or finally, that, in attempting to make her way to the house of some friend out of town, she had been seized by the Indians and carried away to some of their distant villages to be kept for ransom, or an hostage, in anticipation of approaching hostilities.

From what Willis already knew of the despicable schemings of Deacon Mudgridge, he felt strongly inclined to look upon the first of these suppositions as the true one ; and he resolved to contrive some means for forming a definite opinion on this part of the subject. But he readily saw, that he, himself, under the circumstances, would not be the right man to succeed in drawing anything reliable from the Deacon, or any of his servile clique, and he therefore determined to depute another to perform this service. Accordingly, the next morning, he laid the whole case before his friend Noel, who was a shrewd, trusty man, and who, deeply sympathizing in his anxieties, readily undertook the task, and went off immediately to Plymouth with that object, leaving Willis to take a tour of inspection round all the ponds in that town or vicinity which would be likely to be resorted to for the purpose of suicide by drowning.

At night they both returned, and sat down to make their mutual reports, and compare notes made in the different fields of observation.

"Well, Noel," said the impatient Willis, as soon as they were alone, "my day's work has resulted in no discoveries; must your report be as empty?"

"Not quite. Though I have discovered no clue to the girl's whereabouts, I have yet been able to satisfy myself, at least, on the point you wished me to investigate."

"What—in relation to the agency of the Mudgridge combination in her disappearance?"

"Yes—any immediate agency; for I am fully satisfied that none of them know any more what has become of her than yourself."

'How have you ascertained this, Noel?"

"In a dozen ways. Not from the saintly Deacon himself, it is true—for he keeps himself pretty close these days, they say—but from his understrappers, and the news-mongers of the town, with some of whom I was well acquainted, and with all of whom I contrived, on one pretence or another, to have during the day a conversation on the matter in question."

"And the result of all was—?"

"The result of all was, that the Deacon and his nephew, and all they can influence, are death on you, Vane Willis; and you had better look out, for you are a marked man there."

"A marked man! For what reason?"

"For snatching the game from their hands; for there is no kind of doubt but they really believe you have eloped with her and gone to parts unknown."

"Ah! that is my crime, then? I had suspected as much.

And if the Deacon *really* believes this, as you say, I suppose he lays the defeat of his darling scheme much to heart."

" He lays something to heart, evidently. They tell strange stories about the Deacon, Willis."

" Indeed ! Why, what are they ? "

" Nothing very definite, to be sure, but something, after all, which affords room for speculation. They *all* seem to understand that something unusual has come over the man ; and among some, there are mysterious whispers afloat, to the effect that he has recently been haunted by a ghost or an evil spirit, and that he keeps the Shadow to watch and pray with him every night."

" That, friend Noel, if true, is a strange story—strange, at all events—perhaps a significant one."

" I thought so, Willis ; and, coupling the affair with some things you told me last night, I studied upon it all the way home, but came to no conclusion. What inference do you draw from the circumstance ? "

" I don't know," responded the other, thoughtfully; " I am not prepared to say much on that point at present. But, taking all your accounts together, they have removed the most maddening, though not the most melancholy, of my apprehensions—that was, that the Deacon and Sniffkin had somehow spirited Miss Southworth away to some place where they supposed they could control and eventually subdue her to their purposes. And yet it will throw me on to another conclusion, which any but a lover would probably pronounce more alarming."

" What is that—the supposition of her suicide ? "

" No, I was not thinking of that. My researches have to-day been conducted with particular reference to that question. I have skirted every body of water within five miles of Plymouth, and all other places where such a deed would be likely to be consummated. But I have made no discoveries ;

and besides, on recalling the firmness, resolution, and other noble traits of Madian's character, I cannot really bring my mind to the revolting conclusion that she could be driven to that desperate alternative. I am therefore forced to adopt the only other conclusion that I have been able to form respecting this mystery of mysteries."

"And that is what I should think the scarcely more probable one of her abduction by the Indians—is it not?"

"Yes, Philip's tribe, since the mad and unwarranted execution of their brethren at Plymouth, probably consider themselves in a state of war with the colonists. And this act may have been purposely intended to provoke the whites, as I suspect is their plan, to take the first step in open hostilities."

"It may have been so, possibly. But where could they have taken her? Not from her own house, certainly?"

"No! She must have thought to have gone to the house of some friend, several miles off, perhaps—and on foot, so that she could not be traced."

"But is it likely she would have gone on foot? She could have ordered her man to attend her on horseback, and have trusted him with her secret, could she not?"

"Why, yes, I should suppose so; and I am free to admit that this, my last conclusion, is not without its improbabilities; but I can reach no other."

"How do you know but what she *did* reach some friend's house, and is still privately remaining there?"

"Because, by this time, she would have found means to communicate with me, or her trusty domestics at home; though at first, till the Deacon and his emissaries had given over the search, she might think it best to leave them in ignorance, so that neither their words nor manner, when questioned, could betray any knowledge on the subject. She was acquainted with but three or four families out of town—all living within a circuit of ten miles ; and Taffy has already been to every one of them."

" Well, Willis, though I still cannot help doubting whether you have even now hit upon the true version of the affair, yet, as I can't at present offer any better one, I will say no more, except to ask what movement you next propose to make by way of following up the investigation ?"

" It is this—to repair to-morrow morning to Indian Pond, where there are still encamped the small band of friendly Saconets, whom, as I before told you, I design to attach to my proposed company, to be employed as runners and scouts, in case we are called into service. These I will put in pairs or singly, including myself in the arrangement, on all the roads and by-paths running out of Plymouth, to search every piece of woods by the way-side, several miles in each direction outward, for trails or other indications, where ever an Indian would think of making a capture, or leading a victim out into the forest; when, if any such capture has been made, we can hardly fail, I think, to discover the trail of the captors."

" And supposing you *do* discover what you judge to be such a trail, Willis, what will you do then ?"

" Make instant preparations to follow it up. And follow it I will too, Noel, to the furthest depths of the wilderness, before I stop short of the rescue."

To those who can appreciate the intense anxieties which a gallant and resolute young lover would naturally feel under the circumstances, it will not be necessary to tell how faithfully and untiringly Willis, with the efficient aid of his keenly observing red associates, carried out the next day, the plan of operations which he had so sanguinely marked out for himself. But it was all in vain. A little before sunset, having himself made no discoveries, he reluctantly relinquished the search, which, on his part, had been wholly fruitless, and repaired to the place he had appointed to meet his Indian scouts at sunset, and hear the reports of the observations which they severally might have made through the day. The spot thus designated was the summit of a high hill, situated two or three miles westerly of Plymouth, and so elevated as to command an extensive view of the surrounding country, including that village and all the roads running into and out of it, especially the great throughfare from the southwest which ran but a short distance from the southern base of the elevation.

Punctual to their appointment, the Indian scouts, from some of whom, at least, Willis still hoped to hear favorable tidings, all arrived at their elevated rendezvous before sunset; when one after another they related to their anxious employer their doings, minutely describing the routes they had taken, and the manner and amount of their observations made on each through the day.

By way of enhancing the value of their services, some of them, indeed, asserted that they had discovered trails in certain localities, such as might have been made by Indians carrying off a captive. But all their representations of this character, when sifted by cross examinations, turned out to be merely some very inconclusive circumstances, amounting in fact, to little or nothing towards indicating an abduction of the missing maiden or affording any clue to her fate.

Disappointed, sad, and now this last hope of being put on the track of Madian having thus vanished, more than ever perplexed to account for her disappearance, Willis turned away from the spot, despondingly murmuring the words with which the present chapter was commenced—O, Madian, Madian, Madian ! What dark fate has befallen my loved and beautiful Madian ?" And he began slowly and musingly to descend the hill on his way back to the place from which he had so hopefully started out that morning.

Before he had proceeded many steps, however, his eye accidentally fell on the distant harbor and its indented shores, stretching far away on either side of the village ; and he soon paused and stood hesitating. A new thought had suddenly occurred to him. Madian, he now felt satisfied, could not have been taken away on the land side of the village ; but might she not have been seized on some part of her own lands, and taken to a boat concealed by her Indian captors for the purpose, in some of the coves along the shore, and rowed off by them, under cover of the darkness, to some point of land several miles to the south, from which she could be led across the country, then mostly a wilderness, to some of King Philip's villages ? Yes. Why not? It was in effect the same hypothesis for the solution of the mystery in question, which he had the night before settled down upon, as the only one then left having even the sanction of probability, varied only by the manner in which the abduction had been effected. It must be so ; and the thought instantly revived the dying hopes of his bosom, and aroused his mind to its wonted activity.

Half-formed schemes for a rescue were in a moment float-ing over his busy brain ; and he was retracing his steps to consult his Indian friends on their willingness to join in an excursion into Philip's territory, when his eye caught sight of an object which instantly riveted attention. It was a long cloud of smoke or dust arising in the distance along the great road from the west. An exclamation of surprise at once brought the Indians to his side, when they all hastened to the western brow of the hill, and fell to scanning the unu-sual spectacle, which they soon ascertained to be a thick cloud of dust raised by horsemen making their way with all possi-ble speed along the road to Plymouth.

Instantly comprehending that the men must be the heralds of important tidings, which they appeared to be proclaiming at every house they passed, Willis, followed by his attendants, hurried down the hill towards the road to get near enough to hail them as they came by. This they had scarcely effected, before the heralds, covered with dust, and lashing their foaming horses swept along the road, loudly exclaiming:—

"To arms! to arms! The Indians have risen! Twenty men have been shot down in Swansey, and Rehoboth is in flames!"

The impending storm had indeed burst on the unprepared colony in all the peculiar horrors of savage warfare. That day had been the one on which the general fast, named in a former chapter, had been appointed at the village of Swansey, near the head of Narraganset bay.

As the people were coming out of the meeting house, they were met by a volley from concealed foes that brought many to the ground, while others scattered and ran to their homes only to share the same fate. And those who fled out of the place for safety were soon met by fugitives from other towns, which had also been doomed to the same terrible visitation. And the news, flying like the wind, had, almost with the hour, thrown all the southern part of the colony into a state of the wildest commotion and alarm. Runners were instantly dispatched in every direction to spread the note of warning and alarm, and the fleetest horses put in requisition to speed to the court of Plymouth for military assistance.

"It has come then at last," said Willis, after standing a moment mute and half paralized, under the first effect of the startling announcement which had just been made—" sooner indeed than I *really* expected, but not sooner than I feared; and the blow as I predicted, has fallen suddenly and without warning. Heaven only knows what tidings will next reach us from the scenes of these horrors. Well, every man, who *is* a man, will have but one path to pursue in a crisis like this. We shall soon see who will take it. For myself I shall quickly be ready to do my part towards breasting the storm. And love as well as duty shall now be my incentive to action."

So saying, he turned to his Indian followers, who had, as readily as himself, comprehended all that had occurred, and in a brief and pointed address told them all his arrangements for forming a company of rangers for the war; and then he made known his wish to enlist them all, and as many more as were inclined to join him, to serve for scouts, runners, or fighting men, as circumstances might require, and to be rewarded according to their faithfulness and the value of their services. As he expected, they all promptly responded to his appeal, and declared themselves ready to enter upon any duty he might see fit to assign them. Taking them at their word he dispatched them immediately to all the different individuals, far and near, about the colony, who had given him encouragement of joining his company, to request them to meet him with the least possible delay, at Noel's farm house, which he had appointed as their rendezvous. And so little preparation did these simple and hardy men of the forest require, that within half an hour, every one of them had disappeared on their respective missions, leaving their new leader to make his rapid way back to his quarters, at the hospitable abode of his friend and coadjutor in the enterprise on hand.

CHAPTER X.

Men of the north ! look up !
  There's tumult in your sky,
A troubled glory surging out,
  Great shadows hurrying by.

Your strength—where is it now ?
  Your quivers—are they spent ?
Your arrows in the rust of death,
  Your fathers' bows unbent.

Men of the north, awake !
  Ye're call'd to from the deep ;
Trumpets in every breeze—
  Yet there ye lie asleep.

JOHN NEAL.

THE alarm of the sudden outbreak of the savage foe, described in the last chapter, had spread over the country with
such amazing rapidity, that within twelve hours from the
time the first hostile volley was poured upon the unsuspecting victims at Swansey, every family of the colonies, both of
Plymouth and Massachusetts, to the remotest log-house of
their frontiers, was in possession of the fearful tidings, with
the thousand exaggerations incident to such occasions. Although the most far seeing men of the country, and especially
those best acquainted with the Indian character, had repeat-
edly warned the public of what would be the inevitable consequence of the policy of government towards the natives,
particularly that of the court of Plymouth ; yet for all that,
the news, when it at last came, as predicted, fell like a thun-

der clap upon the people, filling them everywhere with the deepest consternation and dismay.

In this emergency, Massachusetts, notwithstanding she had severely censured the court of Plymouth for a policy towards the Indians, believed to be calculated to involve the country in an unnecessary war, and more than once interposed her peaceful offices, yet now, when war was come, acted with promptitude and despatch. The governor and council met in the night immediately after the news of the outbreak reached them; and after a short and exciting debate on the question, whether they should send their commissioner for a further attempt to pacify King Philip, or troops to fight him, at length concluded to do both, and send them all along together, to act as the circumstances might require. Accordingly, Captains Henchman, Mosely, and Prentiss, were sent for; when Henchman was ordered to rally out his company of regular infantry, and be ready to march early in the morning, Mosely to follow with his volunteers as soon as he could collect them, and Prentiss, with his cavalry, to start soon enough in the day to overtake the rest by the time they should halt for their first night's encampment. And with such promptness and energy were these orders executed, that before noon the next day, the last of the designated forces were on their march to the scene of action.

Equally expeditious and fortunate, in the meanwhile, had been our young hero, the determined Vane Willis, in collecting and organizing his promptly responding associates, preparatory to an immediate march for the defence of the imperiled inhabitants of the southern frontiers.

On the second morning after the alarm, there stood paraded in the green lane in front of the house of their rendezvous, thirty athletic, resolute, young woodsmen; while a little distance aloof, were seen lounging, in irregular groups, about twenty Indians, who had by this time also come in to attach
12

themselves to the company. Of this promising band, Willis had, the night before, as all both wished and expected, been unanimously chosen captain, and Noel, the second in command; while all the subordinate offices had been filled with almost equal unanimity. The usual drill and the few simple military evolutions through which the company had just been taken, had ceased; and their leader now stood proudly glancing along their ranks, with the gleaming talismanic blade, which Madian had bestowed, and which had now become invested with a double interest in his mind, for the first time openly displayed at his side.

"Captain Willis," said Noel, coming forward from the other end of the line, and taking his superior a little aside. "Captain Willis, do you still persist in your resolution of marching into Plymouth, this morning, instead of proceeding directly on towards the scene of action?"

"Yes,—though I neither expect, nor, indeed, at all covet a commission from the court, considering who rules the roast there, yet I think it but right and proper to report myself and company to the governor, that he may know what forces are in the field."

"Under ordinary circumstances I would certainly do so; but you know the combination they have there got up against you; and I really fear they will try to detain you on their absurd charges, or otherwise delay or embarrass you."

"Then there will be fighting much nearer than Swansey or Rehoboth; for I will neither be detained nor delayed a single hour. Yes, Noel, I shall go there."

"Very well; if you are determined on the experiment, you shall not want for one backer, at least; and I think every member of the company, indeed, may be counted on with equal certainty. But hark!"

The conversation was here interrupted by the distant roll of drums, whose "stormy music" came fitfully swelling on the morning breeze from some unseen point along the road coming in from the north. And presently a stout looking horseman made his appearance, leisurely approaching alone in the same direction.

"Can it be," said Willis, after listening a moment to this indication of the approach of some military array, and scanning with interest the advancing horseman—"Can it be, that the Bay colony have rallied, and pushed on their forces so expeditiously as this comes to? It looks like it; and if so, I will venture to say that we shall find Captain Mosely and his volunteers leading the way. Yes, yes, and yonder horseman, I suspect, though mounted for some temporary purpose, can be no other than the go-ahead captain, himself."

Willis was correct in his conjecture. In a few minutes the captain rode up, heartily greeted the other, and was introduced to Noel; when he warmly complimented them both, on the fine, and, as he termed it, business like appearance of their company.

"Is that the way you are going into the fight with the Indians, Captain Mosely?" said Willis jocosely, as he glanced at the rather sorry looking horse on which the other was mounted.

"Yes, if *every* day's march must make me as foot-sore as the tough one we had of it, last night."

"Why, did you march all night?"

"To be sure we did. We never left Boston till nearly noon; and being determined to overhaul Captain Henchman, who marched with his regulars in the morning, we pulled on through the night, and did not overtake them till day-break."

"Where *is* Henchman and his company, now?"

"Where they encamped, near one of that cluster of ponds in the hilly country, four or five miles astern."

"But we have just heard drums, not half that distance from us. Whose company did they belong to?"

"Mine—my company of spunky volunteers, who, by their famous fatigue march, are covering themselves with dust and glory."

"I don't understand it. If Henchman's force has had the rest and refreshment of a night's bivouac, and your company none, how came your company so much in advance?"

"Well, Willis, I am ashamed to tell you; and for the credit of the Bay troops, I hope you will not believe a word of the story."

"Ashamed, Captain Mosely? Why, what has happened?"

"What has happened? Why, there was an eclipse of the moon last night, or rather this morning."

"I understood there was to be one. But what had that to do with your story?"

"A good deal. That same moon, in her mumps this morning, came near playing the very mischief with Hichman's whole company. When I reached them, I found their camp in a complete panic, and seriously meditating a retreat homewards. The cussed fools, it seems, had been looking at the eclipse, and their frightened fancies had converted the odd appearance of the moon at the time into all sorts of bloody omens—some seeing in it nothing but scalps; some, Indian bows; some, clouds of smoke hanging over burning villages, and some—the devil knows what; and the result was, that the very men who would probably be brave enough in any *real* danger, were scared half to death by the bugbears of their own raising."

"But their captain—what was their captain about, in the meantime, to suffer such foolish fancies to possess them?"

"Why, he was as mum as a fish; and I'll be hanged, sir, if I did not think he looked almost as glummy and down in the mouth as the rest!"

"And what did *you* say to them, Captain Mosely?"

"Well, I scarcely know myself, for I never was so mad and

mortified with the conduct of any set of fellows in my life. Before I worked myself up to the swearing point, however, I tried to reason with them, telling them that such eclipses had happened a thousand times—that there was now nothing unusual nor unnatural in the appearance of the moon, for such an event. Then I laughed at them, and told them I thought they were slandering the poor, innocent moon in her troubles, for even if there were any omens in the case, she would not be such a partial, scurvy jade as to give out signs all on one side—that the Indians must take half of them to themselves, at all events, which would leave the matter no worse than before. Then I tried to shame them for being frightened by scare-crows, like a parcel of children before their clouts were off.´ And finally, proceeding next to serious talk with them, I waxed rather warm, probably, for a church member in regular standing, as I am; and if I swore outright, I don't believe Gabriel has put it down on the debtor side of my account, for I could not keep the old man down, and so at last cussed them up hill and down for a pack of ninnies and cowards."

"How did they bear all that?" asked the surprised and greatly amused young officers.

"Well, a good deal better than I expected. The fact was, they began by this time to see that the supposed sure omens were, after all, mere matters of guesswork; and the more that idea prevailed among them, the more they got ashamed of themselves. And so, the mischief-making eclipse going off, to help the matter, about the same time, they soon became more cheerly, and set about cooking their breakfast, which they invited us to partake; and by the time all was over, and my company prepared to move, I had the pleasure of seeing them in something like a soldier-like condition again, and packing up to follow us. They will now soon be on the march, I think, especially as they would wish to be off before Captain Prentiss, who stopped with his troop at a house but a few miles in the rear, should overtake them and learn the cause of their tardy movements."

"There, captain, your company are just heaving in sight," said Willis, pointing to the head of a column of men just emerging from a copsewood on the road about a mile distant. "And now Lieutenant Noel, we will, if you please, be putting *our* little band in motion."

"Stay a moment," said Mosely.—"Where is to be your next halting place ?"

"For our midday halting place, some part of Middleborough, probably ; but I have concluded to march first into Plymouth, to report my company to the governor."

"That will be a mile or two out of the way," observed Mosely.

"Yes, and that is not all," interposed Noel. "There are those about Plymouth court who are looking for a chance to pick a quarrel with Captain Willis ; and I have been advising him to steer clear of them."

"O, yes, I bethink me now," responded Mosely. "Willis told me something about it. But they wouldn't be so inveterate in their sectarian dislikes, as to rake them up against a man coming to help them,—especially in a crisis like this ? If *I* had any wish to go there, I would not be deterred by any fears of that kind."

"Nor will I, Captain Mosely," responded Willis, with a determined air. "I shall give them a call."

"For all that," rejoined Noel, "I am not without apprehensions of difficulty."

"Difficulty !" said Mosely, in surprise at the serious assertion of the other, "I should like to see them try to make it,— I will think of this matter."

And so the officers parted, Willis and Noel with their brave little band, which they now at once put in motion, to march to Plymouth, and Mosely to sit on his horse in waiting for his company to arrive.

It was about nine o'clock in the morning; and a group of the most active members and attaches of the court of Plymouth, consisting of the cold, stately and severe Governor Winslow himself, several of the magistrates, and all the several personages before introduced in that connection, were standing on the green lawn in front of the executive mansion, where they had assembled, as they had often done during the two past days of excitement and alarm, to hear the news and discuss the condition of public affairs. Deacon Mudgridge, who, as usual, had engrossed the attention of the governor, was remarking,—

" I think the people yesterday, albeit very natural on the receiving of such startling tidings, were overmuch alarmed. But now that our valiant Captain Cudworth and his trusty company are far on their way towards the kenneling holes of the hellish crew, their confidence will revive."

" Ay, that is a good company of the captain's, truly," responded the governor ; and I think we may count on them for good service, in chastising the audacious Philip and his murderous gang."

" Of a verity we may. They have gone forth to battle armed by the panoply of the prayers of the church. They are like the God-selected band of Gideon, for they have all lapped the water of righteousness, and will surely prevail. How brother Dummer did wrestle in that exceedingly able prayer he made on the eve of their marching, yester noon ! I felt in the fervor and faith of that wondrous outpouring, that the time had indeed at length come, when we were to be permitted to fulfill the command of Heaven, to drive out the heathen and possess the land that has so long been polluted by their abominations."

" I am glad, Deacon, to see you getting up to the point of

your old faith and cheerfulness, again. I have thought you appeared rather cast down of late."

"Peradventure your excellency may not be wholly in error in that regard. I confess, as you do know, governor, that my Christian patience has been sorely tried, lately, in the matter of the scandalous outrage enacted by that shameless heretic, called Vane Willis, in abducting or, by his devilish arts, enticing away from her home, and the lawful protection of her friends, that young lamb of our Christian flock, the daughter of our good and worthy sister Southworth."

"But I should think Mr. Sniffkin would have the greater reason to be sad and dejected, if I have rightly understood the matter."

"Mr. Sniffkin is justly and properly indignant, and has already arranged to bring the contumacious villain to punishment, for that, and his other public offenses, should he ever again make his appearance. Nathless it could hardly be expected he would feel so sensibly as I the deep disgrace thus brought on the good name of the deluded maiden's family, whereof I was responsible, and also on the church, under which through me, its first officer, she was in a sort of tutelage. I have lain awake nights, and grieved, and grieved, over this terrible reproach, governor, and earnestly prayed that the base author of it be made to meet the punishment he deserves."

"You lay all the blame of this untoward affair, I perceive, on the young man, who, as I have heard, is not without friends and influence in some parts of the colony. Why should not the girl be made, in some degree, at least, to share it with him? And there are some other things about this case, which I am not quite sure I fully understand, Deacon Mudgridge."

The Deacon cast an uneasy glance at the governor; and was about to reply; when he was interrupted by the inspiriting strains of martial music, indicating that some military .

array was approaching. And in a few minutes more, a small, but well armed, and fine looking company of foot soldiers, headen by a tall, handsome young officer, wheeled round a corner into full view, and advancing in dressed column, and steps all timed to the tune of piercing fife and rattling drum, came sweeping down the street in bold and gallant style towards the spot where the Governor and his attendants were hastily arranging themselves for a reception. Supposing the company to be Henchman's infantry, of whose march out of Boston, the morning before, they had been apprised, they all joined, on the first appearance of the column, in a welcoming hurra; and then stood, with gratified looks, silently awaiting their approach.

"A fine company!" exclaimed the governor, who was a man of military tastes. "A fine little company, that!" he repeated, with unwonted animation, as he glanced approvingly along the line. "What noble and hardy-looking fellows! Ah, there's service in that company! But," he added, with a puzzled expression, as they drew near—"but can that officer in command be Captain Henchman? I know Henchman; that is not him—that is a much younger man. Who is he, Deacon Mudgridge?"

But the Deacon was quite too much disturbed by his own feelings, by this time, to heed the question. He had that moment identified the young officer with the hated Vane Willis; and the expression of trained meekness which first sat upon his flat, meaty visage, and which was then banished by the surprise of the unexpected discovery, had now settled into a look of wolfish ferocity. For a moment he stood mute and hesitating, with his features fast contracting towards a focus, and working with suppressed passion. Soon rallying, however, he addressed a few low, earnest words to the governor, and then hastily went and whispered some order in the ear of Dick Swain, who, with a knowing, affirmative wink and nod, hurried away from the place. Captain Willis now came up, commanded a halt, and, uncovering his head, bowed respectfully to the governor, who seemed not a little confused and at a loss how to act in the unexpected emergency.

"I came," said Willis, in a clear, calm voice, after a pause sufficient to ensure attention—"I came here to report myself and company to your Excellency, as I deemed myself in duty bound."

"I—I have not, I believe, the honor of your acquaintance, sir," responded the governor, in evident embarrassment. "What company do you propose to report to our court, for inspection or otherwise?"

"A company of volunteers, your Excellency, who have seen fit to honor your humble servant, Vane Willis, by placing him at their head; and who propose immediately to march to the post of danger, hoping, by the blessing of God, to do some service in defence of the colony against the savage foe."

"We have already dispatched a sufficient force for the occasion, we trust; and they marched yesterday, under the command of that brave and skillful officer—Captain Cudworth— and with the most happy auspices," was the hesitating and equivocal response of the cold and haughty Winslow.

"We came," promptly replied the unflinching young officer, with a slight spice of ironical bitterness creeping into his tone—"we came but to report ourselves, that the court might be duly apprised what forces were in the field—ours among the number—voluntarily exposing their lives to save the helpless families of the frontier from the torch and the tomahawk of the merciless enemy ye have aroused, and," he added, glancing significantly at the Deacon, his Shadow, and Sniff-kin—"and to ensure safety to those who see fit to stay at home."

"Be mindful of the presence you are in, young man," said the governor, secretly stung at the rebuke to his friends, and perhaps himself, involved in the words and unsubmissive manner of the other.

"I am, your Excellency. But our business is completed, and I have nothing further to offer," responded the captain, now turning with a flashing eye to his company, and exclaiming, with that sudden and startling energy which suppressed excitement always imparts to the human voice, "Attention, fellow soldiers! Shoulder arms! To the right about face!"

"I can hold my peace no longer; no, not a minute —not a minute longer," here interposed Deacon Mudgridge, trembling all over with pious indignation, and advancing with hands rapidly sawing the air, towards the glum governor. "No, I can't; and I protest, if there was nothing else to be said and done — yea, I do earnestly and solemnly protest against our holy cause against the heathen being endangered by the least connection with the ungodly wretch. But there is something else to be said and done. I charge," he continued, with increasing vehemence, as his eye caught sight of his supple tool, Dick Swain, followed by the constable and his posse, hurrying towards the scene. "I charge this same Vane Willis with numerous high handed offenses, among which it is sufficient, for this time, to name the crime of his being a heretical and pestilent Quaker, (whereof, to avert the anger of an offended God, it has been decided to purge the land,) and the still more heinous and crying offence of abducting a worthy young maiden of this good town—for all which crimes and offenses the proper warrants are in the hands of our trusty officer, here just arriving, and I demand the criminal's immediate arrest."

"Does this look like being a Quaker?" demanded Willis, who, the moment a threat was made to arrest him, stopped short in his preparations to march, and boldly confronting his accuser, seemed resolved to face the charges on the spot. "Does it look like a peace-sworn Quaker, to be here in arms,

and voluntarily on my way to the war? Away with the absurd charge ! And as to the other specified offence—that of
abduction," he added, advancing a step towards the quailing
Deacon. "You, sir, may count yourself a lucky man, if you
can clear your *own* skirts, when the day of reckoning shall
arrive, of everything chargeable on you, connected with that
mistreated young lady's disappearance."

"I can testify," interposed Noel, stepping forward to the
side of his superior, and waving his hand to attract the attention
of the governor, who was evidently becoming ill at ease at the
aspect affairs were assuming. "I can safely testify to Captain Willis's innocence, and even entire ignorance of the manner of the disappearance of the person whose alleged abduction constitutes the last charge ; and but for myself, he would
have to this hour, believed that the abductor was no other
than the accuser himself."

"It is false !" exclaimed the Deacon, fuming like a tiger
about to be cheated out of his prey. "It is false ! It is a
combination to screen the contumacious villain, who is verily
guilty of both the charged offences. And they, moreover, are
but a part of his crimes. He has reviled and spoke evil of
our rulers, as I do know. He has committed treason against
the State, in that he took part with the enemy at the late
trial of the Indians. He is a scoffer of our holy church. He
is a heretic—yea, a rank heretic, as well as pestilent Quaker,
and I command you, constable, to do your duty !"

"Back, sir! lay no hand on me !" exclaimed Willis, in a
determined tone, as the officer and his attendants made a move
towards him. "Though I do not intend to run away, nor be
frightened away by your threats and demonstrations, yet I now
give you, one and all, to understand, that I will not submit to
an arrest on such false and foolish charges, nor will I be detained one moment longer than I choose."

"Do your duty ! Why don't you do your duty? Do your

duty, I say !" shouted the enraged Deacon, brandishing his clenched fist towards the officer.

" Advance at your peril, sir !" again cried the undaunted Willis, in a tone that brought the officer a second time to a pause.

" Soldiers," now vociferated Noel, in the sharp tones of military command, " Soldiers of the rear ranks ! advance, here on the right and left, for the protection of your captain !"

"I denounce !" rejoined the infuriated Deacon, as with astonishment he saw the two files of armed men resolutely arraying themselves on either side of their commander—" I denounce ! I anathematize ! I protest against this high handed resistance to authority ! And I appeal to the governor, who beareth not the sword in vain. I appeal to him to see the law executed."

" Hold !" sternly cried the governor, obviously anxious to avoid an open collision, which his conscience told him would redound little to the credit of the court and colony—" Hold ! I command the peace ! I command you all to desist from your demonstrations, till the matter can be duly considered !"

"But is the course of justice," said the Deacon, turning with ill-suppressed irritation to the other—" Is the course of justice, I should like to know, to be turned aside by threats and treasonable demonstrations ?"

"Certainly not, Deacon," responded the governor, deprecatingly, as he glanced uneasily from one party to the other like a man between two fires—" that is, it certainly ought not to be ; but it should be peaceful and deliberate ; and I was about to say, that the warrants having been duly placed in the hands of the officer, though the accused may be able to extenuate, and I hope purge himself of the charged offenses, yet now, as the matter is situated, I see no other way but he must submit to arrest."

"Well, *I* do,"—here promptly rose the loud, grum voice of a brawny looking man, who, before unnoticed, had been sitting on a horse, on the outside of the now accumulated crowd, an attentive witness of the altercation—"*I* do, *I* see another way to get along with the foolish flareup; and that is for the meddlesome movers to back out, and let Captain Willis and his company go about their business."

"Who is that who presumes to gainsay the order the governor has just so deliberately given?" demanded the unyielding Deacon, turning with a look of mingled surprise and anger, to this new and unexpected interposer.

"Don't fret," coolly returned the other—"don't fret, mister, all in good time; though you are not quite the one to deserve an answer to the unmannerly question. But hark'ee, governor, I am Captain Mosely, of the Massachusetts volunteers, now resting a bit on the plain up yonder, while I rode in here."

"Indeed!" responded the governor in surprise, while something like a blush passed over his austere visage, at the thought of what the other must have been witnessing—"very well, sir, I will hear what you may have to say."

"I intend you shall," bluntly rejoined the captain, whose brow gave unmistakeable tokens of a storm. "I intend you shall; for having been listening to this trumpery affair as long as my patience will hold out, I am ready to let off. And this is just what I have to say—no more, no less—that if such officers as Captain Willis, here, who, with his company, promise to be the most efficient little corps in the field—if such officers as he are to be harassed, snapped up, and detained by malicious prosecutions or charges, growing out of your miserable, strait-laced, sectarian mummeries, I swear by the God that made me, I will, within one hour, be on the march home again, to disband my company, and let the savage hell-hounds come on and work their will on ye. But, for the sake of the defenceless families of your frontier—not you—I'll be cussed if I'll allow you *even that* alternative. Captain Willis," he added, drawing out two pistols, and cocking them, as he threw a significant glance at the recoiling constable and his posse, "Captain Willis, put your company into motion, sir! I'll take the responsibility of covering your rear."

The last words had scarcely escaped the lips of the bold captain, before the sharp commands of Willis, "Prepare to march! March!" rung out upon the air, and the next moment his exulting band moved defiantly away from the disgraceful scene, leaving the governor biting his lips in chagrin, and the baffled Deacon fairly foaming in his speechless rage.

CHAPTER XI.

"Not ink, but blood and tears, now serve the turn,
To draw the figure of New England's urn,
New England's hour of passion is at hand;
No power, except divine, can it withstand."
                    BENJAMIN THOMPSON, poet of 1675.

AFTER the last described impotent and despicable attempt
to detain, and, at least, disgrace the patriotic young captain,
made by the malicious and bigoted schemers, who had, unfor-
tunately for the public interests at this time, obtained a controlling influence over the court of Plymouth, no further molestation was offered him, and he led his company triumphantly
out of town, followed by his intrepid friend, Captain Mosely,
who still claimed the honor of covering the rear till they
reached the spot where his own company had halted.

"Well, Captain Willis," said Mosely, now spurring his
old horse forward, with a look of grave humor, "for this important and dangerous service, in bringing you so handsomely
out of your battle with deacons and dunderpates, I shall
expect to be remembered by you, and your fine fellows here,
when you may see me and mine in close quarters with the red
devils of the woods."

"Ay, ay, Captain Mosely," responded the other in the
same spirit. "There shall be no backwardness on my part;
and if I rightly read the looks of our boys here, I can answer
for them also. What say you, my lads," he added, beginning
to twirl his cap as a signal, "have you a cheer for the gallant
captain and his company?"

The cheer was given and several times repeated in a queerly blended tone of fun and earnest, which more significantly told the state of feeling which the late scene, and its half ludicrous termination, had created among the men, than a whole page of description.

" Will you take the lead, Captain Mosely ?" asked Willis, observing his Indian scouts now coming forward from the bushes, and falling into his rear in readiness to march.

" No," replied Mosely, laughingly; " there's no knowing what will happen to you, till you get a little further out of the shadow of the august court of Plymouth. No, move ahead, and we will follow. But hold on a few minutes, till I have mustered my men. I'll be hanged if I won't tell them this cussed droll flareup we just had. There's nothing like a good laugh for a soldier before going to battle."

In spite of the remonstrances of Willis, Mosely rode off, arrayed his company, and was soon heard relating to them, with his own peculiar coloring, what had transpired to give rise to the demonstrations, of which, standing at too great a distance to understand the words exchanged on the occasion, they had been the wondering witnesses.

A loud laugh simultaneously burst from the lips of the rough captain's hundred congenial followers, as he concluded his humorous description ; and this, at his instance, was followed up by three lively cheers for Captain Willis and his company. And with this odd introduction to each other, the two forces were both immediately put in motion for their destination.

Much of the road now ran over dry pine barrens, making, with the sand yielding under their feet, and the clouds of suffocating dust continually rising to the heads of the soldiery, the most toilsome and disagreeable marching which an army can be called on to encounter. And yet so vigorously did these hardy men push forward through the day, that by sunset

13

they had reached the western point of that cluster of large ponds lying about half way between Plymouth and the northern heads of Narraganset bay, which had been appointed for their rendezvous. Here they encamped for the night. But the rising sun of the next morning looked down again upon a rapid march for the scene of action.

As they drew near the localities of the outbreak, on this day's march they began to see evidence going clearly to show, that the reports of the alleged outrages, which had been spread abroad, were not, as many had hoped and believed them to be, either false or exaggerated. The indications of the perilous situation of the inhabitants all along the southern borders of the colony, thickened with every mile of their progress. And soon spectacles were often encountered on the road, well calculated to bring these melancholy convictions home to the bosoms of the men, to arouse their spirit, and make them eager to press forward for retributive vengeance on the authors of the havoc and desolation, which had so evidently been spread, and which was still being spread, in almost every direction over the country. Now they were met by a fast speeding horseman riding to announce the massacre of a single family residing in some secluded location, and now by others bringing the tidings of the devastation of whole neighborhoods. Now they encountered on the road a bleeding fugitive, who perhaps the only survivor of his family was fleeing for safety, and now scattering companies of wailing women and children, recently escaped from scenes of slaughter, and hurrying towards the older settlements for places of refuge; while far and wide, over the low-lying country around were every hour seen shooting up at different points, slender columns of vapor, denoting the yet unannounced destruction of solitary dwellings, or broader clouds of smoke, showing the conflagration of freshly assaulted villages or hamlets. It seemed indeed as if every piece of forest concealed within its thickets an unseen band of the lurking foe, who were every day and hour somewhere bursting from their fastnesses upon the unsuspecting inhabitants, spreading death and destruction over one place, and then disappearing, as suddenly as they came, to repeat the same awful tragedy in another.

All discerning men could now see before them, the consequences of the blind policy which had been pursued by the court of Plymouth—a policy founded in self-exaltation over the despised Indian—in a misapprehension of his character and intellect—in a careless disregard of his rights, and in a but too illy disguised desire for his subjection. They could see that this policy, with the acts of injustice and oppression which it indirectly sanctioned, or at least very naturally led to, had driven the red men to take that final stand from which there would be no receding, till either they or their opponents should be swept from the land. They saw all this; but they saw at the same time, that the hour for regrets and criminations had now passed by, and that it was the duty of all to unite in the common defence of the imperiled colonies.

At a seasonable hour that evening, all the Massachusetts' forces together with the hardy little band of Captain Willis, reached the late scene of carnage at Swansey, and at once united themselves with the Plymouth troops at the garrison house near a bridge leading over a slender arm of the bay into King Philip's dominions. Here they were welcomed with great rejoicings by the alarmed garrison, who had already lost several sentinels by the fire of the Indians everywhere beleaguering them from coverts in the forests around, and with wild war whoops and other demonstrations of rage and defiance, threatening a general assault. Nothing, however, but a little ineffectual skirmishing, or rather alarms, on the part of the pickets, and the empty, though terrific demonstrations of the besieging hordes of the invisible foe, occurred to call the troops from their repose, at any time during the night. But early the next morning a large band of painted Wampanoogs, armed with musket, tomakawk, and scalping knife, boldly crossed the bridge in open view of the garrison, and with menacing gestures and loud yells of defiance, stood for some time, challenging the hesitating troops to come out and meet them in combat.

"I am not a-going to stand that, by a jug-full!" impatiently exclaimed Captain Mosely, who, with Cudworth, now promoted to the post of commander of the united forces, had been witnessing the impudent bravado of the Indians. "If but twenty men of my company, or those of any other, will join me for a sally, I swear, it shall be made before I am half an hour older."

"Why,—your life, and the lives of half your men, would pay the forfeit of your rashness, captain," responded the timid and overcautious general, with a look of blank surprise.

"Well, general, suppose it should be so, wouldn't an equal number of the enemy be likely to share the same fate? And even if they did not, do you think our lives, so sold, would go for nothing? I, who count myself considerably better than a green one in matters of war, have always noticed that ten lives lost in a bold dash will often, by intimidating the enemy, save a hundred in the general results of a campaign. It will probably be so here; and I think this is just the time to make a push on those red, vaunting devils, which will show them a specimen of the mettle we are made of."

"Yes, but for sc perilous a step as that, Captain Mosely,— really, sir, as the commander here, I hardly dare incur the responsibility of"—

"Never mind, general, don't fret your gizzard about that, in the least. When the court of Plymouth haul you for it, just say to them that the lawless old Captain Mosely insisted on shouldering the whole responsibility of the affair. I shall go,—good morning, sir. Ho! there, my merry volunteers!"

continued the captain, hastening towards his company, and shaking his fist significantly towards the enemy, do you hear and see that yelping litter of hell yonder, daring us to our teeth? Now, how many of you will follow me to give them a lesson which shall show them the difference between our cold lead and their empty bragging?"

"All! all! shouted fifty resolute fellows, seizing their guns and rushing forward.

"Just what I expected of you, my hearties!" exclaimed the gratified officer, with a proud glance at his followers. "Now all you that are in earnest about this business, take ten minutes to equip yourselves; and, at the end of that time appear here on the ground, with your guns all well primed and loaded, knives where you can lay your hands on them for instant use, and powder and ball enough for a day's battle. I never heard of a soldier who came off any the worse for being well provided."

"Aha! how is this, Captain Mosely?" cried Willis, who, having perceived what was going forward, from a little distance, now came hurrying to the spot,—"How is this, sir? are you a-going to be exclusive towards your friends, in this movement?"

"O no,—the more the merrier: but I did not know that you and your boys would crave the honor of facing the pokerish prospect."

"Well, we do, sir. We had just been hatching up something of the kind ourselves; and would all gladly participate."

"Really?"

"Yes, give us a chance, and ——"

"You shall have it, sir! Your very offer shows you deserve it. And it shows, also, I have not been at all mistaken in you, Vane Willis."

For the ardent young officer to fly to his own company,

notify them of the proposed sally upon the taunting foe,
obtain their eager response for a participation, see them set
about their preparations, and return to the side of his intrepid
friend, Mosely—occupied him but a few minutes. The two
congenial spirits then together went to a loop-hole which commanded the whole ground, and speedily arranged a plan of
attack, and the different parts which each of their companies
should take in carrying it into execution.

The new movement, by this time, had been noised through
the whole garrison; and all those who were not to be partici-
pants crowded to the loop-holes and every other spot which
might answer for a look-out, and with intense interest awaited
in silence the appearance of the expected sortie, the exact
plan of which yet remained a secret with the projectors.
Presently, Captain Mosely and his men, gliding noiselessly
into the yard in front, and with trailed arms, and in irregular,
broken, and seemingly confused lines, made their way rapidly
to a partially screening hedge about half way from the garrison house to the water, and within short musket shot of the
enemy. To the wonder of the spectators, Mosely's men were
suffered to gain the hedge, and throw themselves down beneath
it, without receiving a single shot from the enemy, whose attention seemed suddenly to have been drawn to the right and
the left. The secret, however, was the next moment disclosed.
Captain Willis, having divided his band and placed the two
divisions at the different ends of the enclosure, had sallied
out at the head of one of them, while Noel led the other, and
come into open view of the enemy before Mosely and his men
made their appearance. And these two flanking parties, who
had at first struck out laterally some distance in opposite directions, to divert the attention of the Indians from the force
advancing in front, were now seen bounding forward from
stump to stump in converging lines towards the bridge, occa-

sionally discharging their pieces, and receiving shots from the now aroused enemy in return.

At that juncture, a sudden movement was seen along the hedge, and the next moment the stentorian voice of Captain Mosely was heard—

" Front line prepare to fire !—rear line to charge by, with loaded pieces ! Fire ! Charge !—in the name of God, charge !"

The explosive crash of fifty blazing muskets instantly followed, and the next moment Captain Mosely, with his rear line, leaving the front one to re-load and come on, leaped the hedge, charged furiously forward, and disappeared in the smoke, which, rolling down the hill, completely screened them in their course from the aim of the astonished foe. Then rose, from under the drifting smoke cloud, the commingling shouts and yells of the combatants, and the reports of rapidly discharging musketry, showing the fury of the conflict that now ensued. But before the startled spectators at the garrison could realize the scene that had so suddenly burst upon their view, the brunt of the battle was over, and the fate of the field decided. With the lifting of the sulphurous veil that had shrouded the spot, the now uniting forces of Willis and Mosely were seen hotly pursuing the terror-stricken savages, who, like a herd of wild horses, were rushing pell mell over the bridge to gain the coverts of the bushy plain beyond.

Shout after shout of exultation now burst from the elated troops of the garrison, on beholding so complete a rout of an enemy from whom, ten minutes before, nothing but the destruction of half the numbers of their assailing friends was expected. And they suddenly grew valorous, formed in front of the garrison house, and began to move towards the bridge ; while a still more elated squad of fifteen or twenty troopers, formed from the cavalry of Captain Prentiss, mounted their horses, and, under the lead of a subaltern officer, dashed down the road and went thundering over the bridge to join in pursuit of the now despised enemy.

"Now, Captain Mosely," said Willis, coming up, after having halted his men at a point in the road where the woods were becoming thick enough to afford places of concealment for the Indians—"now, captain, I would not dictate, but would certainly advise you to adopt a different mode of pursuit. We have left a number of the foe on the field, but thus far, providentially, have not lost a man ourselves."

"No, thank God; and so have fully made good what I told that quivering old granny of a general, at the outset. But do you think the scared devils, that have made such good use of their legs to get out of our reach, will muster courage enough to make another stand?"

"Not on the road, openly, nor in a united band anywhere, probably."

"How then, or in what places? There is not now even a shadow of the whelps anywhere to be seen."

"And therein lies the greatest of our dangers. You see those scattered little thickets, with bushy hillocks, and an occasional old log, which begin to skirt the road on either side, two or three hundred yards ahead, don't you?"

"Yes, but the road is clear for four times that distance."

"That may be true, and yet behind every one of those dark objects may, and probably does, lie an Indian with cocked musket, waiting for us to approach near enough along the road, to enable him to make sure of the victim he shall single out for his murderous aim."

"Aha! That is their game, is it? Well, Vane, I have all along told you, I should have to knuckle to you in the mysteries of the bush fight. So, now for the plan you would propose, what is it?"

"Simply for every one now to become his own keeper, and

fight his own battles ; that is, for the men to scatter widely into the woods on both sides of the road, and advance, in something like a general line, perhaps, but rods apart; so that each, keeping a tree or some object between him and all suspicious looking coverts, can, while taking care of himself, be in the way of doing effectual service in killing or routing out the foe from his lurking places. It is *their* fashion of fighting, and the only one for *us* to adopt, if we would conquer, or even successfully resist them."

" What say you, boys ?" said Mosely, turning to his company. " Captain Willis, here, though young in years, is an old scholar in the matters of which he speaks, and probably knows better how to circumvent the red sarpents we have now to deal with, than any man in the army. Perhaps we had better follow his advice. So, break ranks, and be on the move."

" Let your men take the centre, then, Captain Mosely," rejoined Willis. " Noel and myself will again divide our command, and move a little ahead of you, on your flanks, leaving you to deal with such game as we may drive into your beat."

As the men of both companies were about to betake themselves separately to the woods in accordance with this politic arrangement, the squad of cavalry, whose new-born zeal had fired them to join in the pursuit, came furiously galloping along the road, and, in spite of the timely warnings of Captain Willis and others, dashed heedlessly onward to overtake the foe, who, as they still persisted in believing, must be, like other beaten enemies, flying in the open road, some distance ahead. And being confirmed in this impression by the fact, that nothing was to be seen in the way, as far as the first reach extended, they rode on in conscious security, and with increasing speed, till they arrived at a sudden turn in the road ; when pulling up to cast forward for new objects, they descried a little band of Indians, a few hundred yards in advance, looking wildly around them, in the greatest seeming agitation and terror, and ostensibly hurrying away to escape the threatened pursuit.

"Charge! charge upon the skulking rascals!" exclaimed the officer in command, drawing a pistol and fiercely waving his sword for the onset.

It was the last word he was destined ever to utter. At that instant, a scattering volley, streaming out from a dozen coverts in the forest around, was poured upon them by the invisible foe. The officer reeled in his seat, dropped the reins, and in the flouncing and turning of his unchecked horse, soon came to the ground, writhing in the agonies of death. Several of the men were also severely wounded, but being able to keep their saddles, all turned and fled in wild dismay from the fatal scene.

"Hold!" sharply exclaimed Captain Willis, who anticipating the result of this rash and heedless advance, and far outstripping his companions in the woods to keep as near the endangered party as possible, now burst suddenly into the road,—"hold! Would you leave your dying leader to be scalped and tomahawked in the road? Come back, if ye be men! Come back, some of you, and help me bring him away!"

But the panic-struck troopers paid no other heed to the humane appeal, than by spurring their horses to greater speed in escaping from the vicinity of danger. The heroic young captain, however, whom no sense of personal peril could deter from the performance of any duty which he believed humanity demanded at his hands, hesitated not a moment, but ran to the speechless and gasping sufferer, raised him from the ground, clasped him round the chest, and bore him, regardless of the fresh shower of hostile bullets which were directed towards the spot, resolutely back to a place of safety.

"That was a brave deed of yours, Captain Willis," said Mosely, now seen hastening to the spot, where the former had laid down his charge, and was searching for the fatal wound. "Yes," he continued looking down with an air of deep commiseration on the last struggles of the expiring victim,— "yes, a brave, but, as far as life is concerned, a useless effort. See! the poor fellow is gone!"

"I see he is. Shame on the cowards who deserted him, with a wound from which for aught they knew he might recover; but I am resolved to see, before I give over the chase, if his death cannot be revenged."

"You are right, my brave friend. It will never do to leave the murderous hounds with the idea that they have repulsed us. We will leave the body of this luckless man to be taken by his friends, who, as we pass on, will doubtless come to look for it. We will leave the dead in spirit, to bury their dead in the flesh, and fall into our places with our men, who are now getting abreast of us. This ambush and mishap, Vane, have made me a full convert to your notions of fighting Indians; and, as bad as I hate skulking, I shall hereafter unhesitatingly adopt them for my men."

"And yourself, too, captain,—much more strictly than I have perceived you to be doing, since we entered the bush. And particularly cautious must you, and *all* of us, now become, as the enemy are lying concealed, doubtless, at no great distance in front."

"Well, the nearer the better;—I am aching to get my eyes on the infernal scamps."

The two officers then hastened away to their respective lines of advance. Mosely repairing, with deliberate step, to take the lead, a little in front of the centre of his extended line, and Willis, swiftly threading the woods to the head of his slow and stealthily-moving flanking party on the right.

Leaving his men to move directly on without altering their pace or relaxing the caution, which he knew was now especially needed, Captain Willis took a wide, outward sweep, but with a speed sufficient still to keep him considerably in advance of the foremost of his men; and then tacking short to the left, soon gained a thickly covered elevation, which overlooked all the principal coverts that shielded the enemy in their fatal assault upon the discomfited troopers. Creeping cautiously along to the edge of the thicket on the brow of the elevation, he fell to inspecting, one after another, every dark spot and depression in the ground, within the reach of his vision, where any of the foe could possibly lie concealed. At first he ran his eye successively over all such objects and places, without discovering anything calculated to excite the least suspicion. No motion was anywhere perceptible, and no object anywhere in sight presented other than a perfectly natural appearance. Presently the sharp cracking of a dry limb under some heavy tread, away to the left, reached his ear, and almost at the same instant, a slight, quick movement of something somewhere within the area which had just undergone his fruitless inspection, flitted indistinctly across his half averted vision. He therefore again closely bent his gaze in the direction; but for some time with no better success than before. At length, however, he detected what appeared like two small humps or hummock, ranging in a line, one before the other, standing up just in sight out of a little hollow so thickly fringed, on the side next to Mosely's advancing line, with low, leafy shrubs, as to afford a perfect concealment of what might be lying in the hollow behind them. Feeling very confident that those hump-like appearances, though seemingly as immovable as the ground itself, were not there at his previous inspection, he taxed his vision to the uttermost to see if he could detect anything there which had effected the change, when he soon discerned something which

seemed like a straight rod, or stout staff, extending, as the
exactly corresponding sections, seen through the interstices
of the leaves, clearly indicated, from the forward hump,
through to the other side of the bushes. And the next moment the truth came like a flash to the mind of the startled
officer. The two humps were the upraised shoulders and
head of a crouching Indian, and the rod, his gun, leveled at
some one of the approaching line of white men, and its fire
but delayed for a fairer exposure of the marked victim, or the
lessening of the intervening distance, to make more certain
the result of the shot. As Willis cast his eye in the direction indicated by the suspicious tube, his heart leaped to his
mouth on descrying the stalwart Mosely advancing in the
same range, not more than thirty rods from the concealed foe,
using little or no precaution, and evidently unconscious of the
proximity of danger. Although his own stand was even
more distant from the savage, he hesitated not an instant to
bring his rifle to an aim, and lay, with his finger on the trig-
ger, awaiting the first movement of the foe, to breathe a
prayer for the success of his bullet, and send it on its destination. Not long had he to wait for the critical moment. The
hitherto motionless foremost hump now gradually rose into the
distinct proportions of a human head, and the next instant
the sharp report of the young officer's rifle rang through the
forest; while the brawny object of its deadly aim was seen
leaping high into the air, and then pitching heavily forward
to the earth. It was a shot which none but a marksman
could have made, and it not only destroyed a dangerous foeman, but was the means of deciding the fortunes of the day;
for, with the report of the rifle, and the death screech of its
victim, a dozen painted warriors, alarmed at this unexpected
attack on their flank, and its fatal result on one of their leading braves, leaped quickly from their seemingly impossible
concealments around, and in their surprise and dismay, stood

for a minute looking confusedly about them, and exposing themselves as fair marks for the fire of Mosely's line, who were now drawing near, and who, but for the timely shot of Willis, must have been, for all their supposed vigilance, very soon, and to a fearful extent, perhaps, fatally surprised. And the opportunity was not suffered to go unimproved. All of that line within sight poured in their volleys upon the bewildered savages; and the alarm being thus communicated to others, who were lurking further within the woods, and who were started out from their coverts in the same manner, the firing spread rapidly along the whole line of the assailants, and ended only with the last man of the other flanking party led on by the resolute Noel. The effect was instantaneous and decisive. The Indians, surprised at finding themselves thus assailed in front and flank, and what was equally unexpected, in their own fashion of fighting, fired a few shots in return, and fled into the remote recesses of the forest.

· Captains Mosely and Willis, now seeing the uselessness of further pursuit, called in their men; when finding none to be missing, and but two wounded, and those only very slightly, the two companies marched back to the garrison, with that keen sense of inward exultation which men usually feel, when they have done a proud deed without the aid, and against the warnings and discouragements, of those who claim to be their superiors.

The army at the garrison-house, who, from the alarming accounts brought in by the discomfited little band of troopers, had expected nothing less than that the two companies who had gone in pursuit of the Indians into the fastnesses of the woods, would be cut to pieces or destroyed, again became brave and jubilant, on beholding them all returned in safety, and especially so, when they learned that the enemy had been put to flight and driven entirely from the vicinity.

"I congratulate you, Captain Mosely," said the general,

coming forward, among the other officers, to compliment the victors, "I heartily congratulate you on your successes. Your escape from the enemy, with so little damage to yourself and men, seems little less than miraculous, and would appear like a direct answer to the earnest prayers we put up, after you went forth into the peril, for your safety and deliverance."

"Your prayers were all well enough, general, doubtless," bluntly replied Mosely. "But to my notion, they would have been quite as likely to be answered, if they had been made on the field of battle. St. James says, *faith without works is dead.* And I am free to say I am a good deal of his opinion."

"The captain speaks plainly, but not without force," interposed Parson Miles, a patriotic Baptist minister, who owned the garrison house, and who had shown great resolution in defending it on the late assault on the town. "I cannot but think that those who would look for blessings on their prayers, should not themselves shrink from actions corresponding to their petitions."

"Give us your hand, friend," warmly responded Mosely. "You are the parson for me. I hope for your better acquaintance, sir."

The general, not pretending to understand the rebuke which one of the last speakers had intentionally, and the other unwittingly, given him, made some general remark, and retired after notifying all the officers present, that a council of war would be holden that evening, to decide on a plan of operations for the next movement to be made against the enemy.

Both the officers and men of the little army having become assured, and confident of future triumphs, from the successes of the day, insignificant as the Indians themselves, who came there only for the purposes of espionage and intimidation, probably considered them; the council of war, who convened that evening, unanimously voted to make a bold push at once directly into the heart of King Philip's dominions.

Accordingly, the next morning, General Cudworth mustered the troops, and, with the exception of a small force left to man the garrison house, put them all immediately in motion for Pokanoket, as was then called the whole of that romantic little peninsula, which from time immemorial had been considered peculiarly the seat of empire, and the fatherland of the proud and powerful Wampanoogs. This sea-girt territory, which, though but little larger than an ordinary township, now embraces a numerous and thriving population, including its chief port, the beautiful village of Bristol, was then an unbroken wilderness, except the southern thousand acres which the successive chiefs of the Wampanoogs had mostly divested of forest, and converted into cornfields.

The army in the course of their difficult and toilsome march through the woods, encountered many a windfall of tangled trees lying upon the ground, and many a dark, jungly thicket, which were all their wily foe might have desired for surprises and ambuscades, and which the troops approached with no small fear and trepidation. But none of their apprehensions were realized. No signs of any ambuscades were discovered; nor did an enemy, through the whole of their forest march, anywhere make his appearance.

"The whole Indian army must be concentrated around Mount Hope, the home of their hell hound leader, the accursed author of all this mischief," remarked General Cudworth to Captain Prentiss and the other officers he had exclusively made his military counsellors, as the dignified bevy were riding along at a safe distance from the front of the advancing column. "We shall be sure to find them there, all prepared to meet us, and full of their heathenish confidence, no doubt, that they shall be able to defeat us."

"Nathless, they will soon be taught, I trust," responded Prentiss, "the difference between the power of our God, and their God, who, I make no doubt, is no other than Sathan himself."

"Truly, captain," rejoined the former, "and it is a most comforting reflection to feel and know that the Lord Omnipotent is on our side."

"Yea, even so, general," said the warmly consenting captain. "And we must not, for a moment, harbor a single doubt or misgiving, that our arms will signally triumph in this righteous war, which these red sons of Belial have stirred up against an innocent and God-chosen people. But see! we are coming out into the open country, and cannot now be but a mile or two from the stronghold of the enemy. I must ride to the head of my troop to be in readiness to take my place in the line of battle."

The officers now parted to repair to their respective posts; and the troops pushed forward with quickened steps and beating hearts, in full expectation of emerging from the woods but to see a long line of the savage foe drawn up to dispute their further passage to Mount Hope, at which their last desperate stand, it was thought probable, would be made round the home of their present great leader, and the honored graves of his royal predecessors.

To their agreeable disappointment, and the great relief of many a trembling neophyte of the bloody Mars, they beheld, on entering the opening, instead of the anticipated host of painted savages yelling out their rage and defiance, only broad fields of green corn waving in the breeze, and stretching away as far as the eye could reach in every direction, over the rolling country that intervened between them and the dreaded Mount Hope, now seen rising in the distance.

Here halting and forming in two columns, the troops continued their march through the corn fields, still expecting to

14

see drawn up behind every swell or knoll they passed over, a formidable array of their foes ready to greet their first appearance with a storm of fire and death. Swell after swell succeeded, however, as they went trampling over the growing maize, and yet no enemy was encountered. Presently the numerous wigwams of the royal village, spreading along the green slopes of Montaup, rose distinctly upon the view. Here, at least, the enemy must be found; and, though not a wigwam in sight exhibited any indications of the presence of either open or concealed foes, yet the army was again brought to a halt, and carefully formed into an extended line of battle by the astute commander. The line then slowly advanced till within two hundred yards of the village, when a general charge was ordered, and the troops, with leveled and cocked muskets, made a desperate rush upon the whole range of wigwams, which they reached only to find them every where silent and deserted! Nothing being found here, detachments of infantry and cavalry were then despatched to scour every nook and corner of the promontory, all round the borders of the water, from east to west, in search of concealed enemies. But they all in a short time returned with the same story, reporting that not an Indian—young or old, sick or well—was to be found, nor even the trace of one any where to be detected, in all that end of the peninsula. It seemed to have been a preconcerted national exodus, and not an implement of peace or war was left behind to indicate an intention of any future return. But the valorous general was not to be balked in this manner; and, for lack of living foes on which to expend his martial energies, he employed the troops for the remainder of the day in beating down and trampling into the earth the growing corn of King Philip's extensive plantation, the whole thousand acres of which, before sun-down, was utterly ruined or destroyed. The army was then recalled.

ordered to take possession of the deserted wigwams, and encamp for the night.

In the estimation of General Cudworth and most of his officers, the Indians, frightened by the military array brought into the vicinity, had scattered and fled into the distant wilderness, to return no more—in short, that the war was now over. Others, however, were of a different opinion; and, as a compromise between the two parties, it was decided, at a general consultation the next morning, that a small force should be left at Mount Hope to build a fort, and, for the present, hold the station, while the rest should return to Swansey. Among those who wholly dissented from the opinion of the general and others that the war was over, was Captain Willis, who believed that the war, instead of being over, was as yet but hardly begun, and that Philip, justly believing that Mount Hope would be untenable, had crossed over to the extensive forests on the east side of the bay, and was now there concealed with all his forces; and he petitioned the general for liberty to lead his own company— strengthened by the force proposed to be left at Mount Hope, who could be of no use there—round into that part of the country, to ferret out and engage with the enemy. The obstinate general, however, though at length he reluctantly gave Captain Willis permission to take his own company on a scouting expedition, would not allow any other force to accompany him. Thankful even for this permission, Willis at once decided to avail himself of it, and lost no time in making his preparation for starting on the hazardous enterprise, whither it will best suit the objects of our story to accompany him and the gallant little band of which he was the idolized leader.

CHAPTER XII.

"They saw their injured country's woe;
　　The ruined home, the wasted field ;
　They rushed to meet the insulting foe ;
　　They took the spear, but left the shield."

"Guards of a nation's destiny !—
　'Tis yours to shield the dearest ties
　　That bind to life the heart,
　That mingle with the earliest breath,
　　And with the last depart."

PERHAPS there is no prospect or spectacle on earth, that so pleasingly combines the finest elements of the grand and beautiful, as a view taken from one of the lofty mountains rising from our New England landscapes, which, lying spread out beneath and around the summit stand-point, extend, mellowing away in the dim distance, beyond the furthest limits of the wandering vision. This will be found generally to hold good, we believe, of nearly all our high mountains, even as now standing in their interior locations. But had some of their most lofty and commanding peaks been situated on the seaboard, the grandeur of the scene they might have afforded, must have been almost immeasurably enhanced; while there need have been, when taken as a whole, little or no diminution of the beautiful. Had Mount Washington, that out-towering giant among the cloud breaking elevations of the north, stood beetling over the sea, at Cape Elizabeth, what conception can compass the magnificence of the scene, which its tremendous summit would have presented to the entranced be-

holder, in its beautiful and boundless, variegated landscapes on the one side, and the smooth and tranquil, or
rough and tumbling waters of the illimitable ocean on the
other.

No high mountains, however, rise any where in the near
vicinity of our sea-board, to afford us views of such a supposa-
ble character. Only eminences of two, three, and, at the utmost, we believe, four hundred feet, can anywhere be found
from one end of our long line of coast to the other, situated so
near the broad ocean, or any of its extensive bays, as to give
us the opportunity to look down and abroad upon its liquid
plains, in any such sense, as we look down and abroad from
the mountain peak upon the subjacent plains of a country
landscape. And even these elevations are not only few and
widely scattered, but generally rise at too great a distance
from the outward line of coast, to give us anything like a clear
and uninterrupted view of the ocean. But among all those
eminences in our coast country, that *do* afford such views,
there are none, perhaps, more favorably located for embracing
those extensive land and water views, that combine the requi-
sites of a perfect landscape, than Pocasset Hill, which rises
abruptly from that low lying country around, to the height
of three hundred and twenty-three feet, and which, at the
same time, is situated within half a mile of the great eastern
arm of Narraganset Bay, in the northeastern corner of
the State of Rhode Island, and only about fifteen from a
long reach of Buzzards Bay on the east, and another of the
open ocean on the south. Here the eye of the spectator, as
he stands on the summit of this conspicuous eminence, wanders on the north and west, over the bright waters of the
broken and fantastically indented bay, and the thriving villages seen glimmering from various points along the serpentine
coasts, and stretching away to the distant capital of the state,
and even beyond to the far off highlands of Massachusetts and

Connecticut; and all around on the south and east, over extensive reaches of sombre forests and glittering lakelets, with the scores of villages and hamlets every where variegating the scene, till all the lessening objects of the vision become blended and lost in the long light line of the encircling ocean.

On the summit rock of that conspicuous eminence, on the second morning after the fruitless invasion of Mount Hope, described in the last chapter, sat two men intently engaged in scanning the various aspects of the forests, then stretching away from the hill on the east to the vicinity of the seaboard, without break or opening, except in the long bright chain of the Watuppa ponds, whose nearest points were but two or three miles distant. Both these men were here in the guise of Indian dresses and native accoutrements; and one of them, the most youthful and finely formed of the two, had so skillfully metamorphosed himself by these, and the application of some kind of coloring matter to all the visible parts of his skin, that it would have required far more than any ordinary closeness of observation to have discovered him to have been other than what his general appearance indicated.

"There, Noel, I think I have it at last!" exclaimed the last named person, after a long and close inspection of a particular locality in the forest before him, which he had selected as the most promising for the discoveries he was seeking— "I think I have hit upon the place at last."

"Whereaway, Captain Willis?" asked the other—"whereaway are you detecting any indications of their encampment? I have discovered nothing of the kind."

"I will direct your eye to the spot in question, Noel. You see that long swell of oak forest land, lying something like two miles off, perhaps, and running north and south about half way between this first little appendant sheet of water down here to the southeast, and the great South Watuppa pond—do you?"

" Yes,—I have now got my eye on to the spot you mean, I suppose."

" Well, by comparing the peculiar hue of the atmosphere along the line of the swell with that of all the surrounding localities, you can easily detect quite a difference in the appearance—do you distinguish it now ?"

" I think I can. Ay—now you have directed my attention to it, I do very plainly perceive the difference you name; but what is your version of the matter ?"

" My version is that the peculiar appearance of the air all along over that swell, is but a thin, filmy cloud of smoke, which has gradually risen up through the trees from small innumerable fires, such as would naturally be built at an Indian encampment in cooking their morning meals. And I will venture to express my unhesitating belief, that Metacom and his two thousand warriors are all encamped on that single swell of land."

" I think you may be right, captain—a single fire, kindled by a hunting or fishing party, would, if as large as usually made, rise up through the trees in a distinct column ; at all events, it would not be apt to diffuse itself over but a small space ; while the smoke from numerous small fires scattered over a space half a mile in extent and imperceptibly stealing up through the trees from a hundred different places, would, probably, gradually unite in the air above, so as to produce the blue, hazy appearance, which certainly *does* hang over that tract of the woods. And if our conjectures are correct about the cause of this appearance, the place is probably the camping ground of the Wampanoogs, who are doubtless concentrated somewhere in this vicinity."

" Yes, that is my conclusion ; for Queen Wetamoo's tribe would not be numerous enough to spread over so large a space as I judge this encampment to embrace ; besides, the principal seat of her tribe is still a considerable distance to the south of us."

"Ah ! does her territory extend as far north as that south-ernmost chain of ponds yonder ?"

"Just about, I suppose, but why do you ask ?"

"Because, when you called my attention in this direction, I was scrutinizing appearances in that quarter, and if I am not very much mistaken, I saw a large number of Indian ca-noes lying along shore at the extremity of that pond. Let us examine what I took to be canoes, a little more particu-larly."

They did so, and were soon rewarded with an additional discovery. They not only clearly made out the objects pointed out by Noel to be canoes, but soon saw a large body of In-dians coming down to the shore, a part of whom took the canoes and struck out over the pond to the north; while the main body, as became evident by occasional glimpses of them which were obtained as they passed through open spaces ad-joining the water, moved rapidly along the eastern shore in the same direction.

"I understand it all," said Willis, turning away with the air of one who deems the subject of inquiry fully settled. "I understand the whole arrangement as well as the red plotters themselves."

"Well, then, captain, on putting all these things together, what is the amount of your conclusions ?"

"It is this—that body of Indians we have just discovered passing on north, are Wetamoo's four hundred warriors, the queen herself and a small band for her guard, being those we saw putting off in the canoes. They are all on their way to King Philip's camp, to perfect an alliance, and concert mea-sures for the next series of outbreaks. Such, at least, is the indication of their intentions; but the exact character of the meeting, and the plans of Philip, cannot be ascertained except

by skillful espionage. All this is most important to be known,
but who will undertake to go into their camp unless I do it
myself?"

"Into the camp itself, Captain Willis—into the den—nay,
the very jaws of the lion ! Why, surely, you have not been
meditating anything so daring as this? A reconnoitering
close enough to obtain a pretty good idea of the character and
numbers of the enemy, if we discovered their locality, I was
prepared for, but not for this. Are you really serious about
making such a perilous attempt?"

"O yes. I thought when we left our camp, that circumstances might require more of me than an ordinary reconnoissance ; and that was the reason I was so careful to perfect my
disguise."

"But, why not send one or two of our Saconet scouts?"

"In the first place, they could not be induced to venture
directly into the Wampanoog camp; and if they could, they
would not be likely to obtain all the information which I
want, and which I have faith to believe I can obtain by the
proposed visit. I can both understand and speak their language. I can interpret their movements and general appearance, and draw my own inferences. And, as my disguise is
complete, I shall, while running little risk of detection, subserve a most important public object. At all events, Noel, I
have made up my mind to try the experiment."

"Then, friend Willis, we may as well call you a lost man.
Your courage, it seems to me, wholly outstrips the ordinary
bounds of prudence."

"You should have more reliance on an over-ruling Providence, Noel. The enterprise is sanctioned by its importance.
Who knows what bloodshed and suffering may be prevented—
what villages saved from destruction, and what countless
families snatched from an awful death—by the timely discovery of the designs of a foe, who ever come without warning,

and are sure to fall on those places where they are least expected? The motive which moves me to prevent, if possible, calamities like these, will surely command from heaven the protection of my life."

" Then, if you *will* go, it should be my duty to go with you—at least, into the near vicinity, to be at hand to aid you in case of detection and trouble."

" No—one will run less chances of detection than two, even though one of them keep at a distance behind."

" What would you have me do, then, Captain Willis ?"

" Go down to our company on the shore; and then, if you please, you may march them silently around—say, to a point about a quarter of a mile west of the south end of this little pond down here, where we just saw the Indians passing. You will there be sufficiently distant from the trail not to attract the attention of any stragglers following after the main body."

" It shall be promptly done, captain."

" Very well; I will then make to that point for joining you, after I get fairly clear of Metacom's camp. But let us agree on the exact location of your halt for the purpose. There! do you notice that green clump of pine trees, with a tall, dry one shooting up in the midst, all standing not far from the point I named ?"

" Yes, very distinctly."

" Well, whether I am pursued or not, I will make my way to that tree. Now, Noel, keep up faith and courage, and within two hours expect to see me at that spot. Good bye."

" Good bye, captain—good bye, my friend Willis. May God keep you."

A few words may here be necessary, perhaps, to fill the apparent break between the last and present chapters. After Captain Willis obtained permission to detach his little band from the main army, which was not to return until the next day, he immediately left Mount Hope, and made a forced

march back to Swansey that night, for the purpose of supply-
ing his company with the food and ammunition necessary for
the projected expedition into the great forest on the east side
of the Narraganset bay, in search of King Philip's forces,
whom he felt so confident he should discover to be there
concentrated. And having thus supplied themselves the next
morning, and made all other advisable preparations for the
enterprise on hand, the company struck across the then but
partially cleared country, to a point on Taunton river some
eight or ten miles from its outlet, passed over the broad stream
in boats procured for the purpose, and, turning short to the
right, proceeded slowly and cautiously down the thickly
wooded banks on the east side of that wide-spreading outlet,
towards Queen Wetamoo's dominions, lying nearly opposite to
those of King Philip on the opposite side of Mount Hope
Bay.

As the way was often extremely circuitous, the extensive
intervening swamps compelling them to make wide detours to
the east, it was nearly sunset before they reached the shore
of the bay, near the western base of the sightly eminence,
with a description of which was accompanied the opening
scene of the present eventful chapter. And no signs betokening the vicinage of the enemy having been discovered
anywhere above, Captain Willis soon determined to encamp
at this place for the night, and make it his head quarters for
the reconnoissance; he proposed to set on foot the next
morning, feeling very confident, from his knowledge of the
country, that Metacom and his collected warriors could not
now be far distant.

Accordingly, they cast about them for a place for encampment, which would afford them the best advantages for defence
in case of an attack by night, and soon were fortunate enough
to find one enclosed on three sides by the overhanging shelf
of an encircling ledge of rocks, and the water and an almost

impenetrable tangle of fallen trees on the other; and, for-bearing to kindle any tell-tale fires, they partook, each from his well stored pack, their evening meal, and lay down on their mossy carpet for their welcome repose, which, happily, was not disturbed till the bright morning sun, peering over the eastern hills, looked down into the fastness of their bivouac, and roused them from their slumbers to enter upon the untried scenes of the day before them.

Before deciding on any plan of action, however, Willis decided on taking his lieutenant with him and ascending to the top of the hill, believing they might there make disco-veries which might decide the plan of operations to be pur-sued; when, on the suggestion of the captain, they both ex-changed dresses with two of their Saconet scouts, with additional disguises on the part of the former, and set off for the summit, where we introduced them in the new characters they decided to assume to favor the important discoveries they were intent on making.

Leaving his anxious and apprehensive subaltern to return to his company, on the shore below, Captain Willis, after the parting we have described, immediately set forth to execute his daring purpose. He well knew his personal safety must necessarily be more or less involved in the undertaking. Yet the public interest, he believed, demanded the risk at his hands. And this, he persuaded himself, would have alone decided the question of the bold attempt, if he had no other object in view.

But he had another object in view, which he had not chosen to reveal, and which was more potent in inciting him to the undertaking, perhaps, than he would have been ready to ac-knowledge. He fully believed that his lost Madian was somewhere retained as a captive among the Indians, and he had resolved that he would, in some way or other, penetrate into every Indian village or encampment in the country, before he would relinquish his hope of her recovery. Armed, therefore, with this double motive, he pushed on to the execution of his purpose with a resolution which knew no turning, and which never for one moment wavered.

Setting his course, when he reached the termination of the eastern slope of the hill, so as to keep clear of the northern extremity of the small pond before mentioned, he proceeded, with light, rapid steps, through the thick and swampy forest for more than a mile ; when, finding himself on ascending ground, he paused to ascertain his position and bearings.

Soon perceiving, from certain landmarks he had noted before leaving his lookout on the hill, that he had reached the foot of the oak ridge, on the other slope of which was the supposed encampment, and believing it would be safest to approach it through the thickly leaved forest covering the whole length of the swell, he passed on a half a mile to the north, and then, turning short to the right, proceeded directly over the rise, and soon found himself in the leafy and thick undergrowth of the deciduous forest, through which no object was but a short distance discernible. Here he made a pause, and called into exercise all his senses to enable him to form some opinion of the distance he might now be from the location he had marked as the central point of the hostile camp. And very soon the low, confused sounds that reached his ears, and the fresh smell of smoke that pervaded the forest, told him that a large body of men were collected at no great distance to the south of him ; and that he had been very nearly correct in the calculations he had made respecting the location they occupied. Having made these observations, he cautiously made his way towards the place, stopping every few rods to listen and reconnoitre. After proceeding in this manner nearly a quarter of a mile, he began to obtain occasional glimpses of men in motion, only a few hundred yards in front of him ; when knowing that he was now in the immediate vicinity of the enemy, he took a long and careful survey of the woods on his right and left, to ascertain whether there were any outlying scouts, or Indians straggling without the limits of the encampment, in that direction. But perceiving none, he cast about him for some impervious thicket, or other screening object further ahead, which would enable him to look into the camp before he could be seen, that he might the better judge whether, or in what manner, it would be expedient to enter it. And he soon discovered the thick top of a tree, which had recently been blown by the wind across a knoll, about half way between him and the place where the movements had been perceived. To this leafy screen he now, while continually throwing keen, searching glances in every direction around him, silently and stealthily made his way; and having gained it, he crawled under the lowest branches, and then gradually rose to his feet; when finding himself effectually concealed, he edged himself along to a small opening in the branches, and applied his eye for the long sought observation. The first imperfect glance disclosed to him numbers of the enemy so unexpectedly near, as to cause him hastily to withdraw his gaze, lest some roving eye among them should chance to meet his, and thus detect his presence. The encampment lay directly, and in plain view before him, reaching, indeed, nearly up to the foot of the narrow knoll on which he was standing in his fortunately impervious concealment. A second, and now more cautiously made observation, revealed the whole scene, and fully confirmed all his previous conjectures respecting the numbers and character of the enemy. On an area of less than two acres of level ground, from which the undergrowth had been very recently cut down and cleared away, were assembled all the flower and strength of the proud and sternly independent tribe of the Wampanoogs, numbering not less than two thousand brave and able-bodied warriors, all armed with guns, and wholly unencumbered with women, children, or infirm old men, who, on their exodus from Mount Hope, a few days previous, had all been sent to the villages of the Narragansets on the western shore of the great bay which derives its name from that once powerful tribe.

Near the centre of the encampment, in front of a large temporary wigwam, stood the master spirit of them all, the princely Metacom, arrayed in his best costume and most showy royal insignia. He was conversing with a group of his confidential counselors and war captains, who stood around him reverentially listening to his remarks, and occasionally sending wistful glances towards the south, as if awaiting the approach of visitors from that direction ; while the main body of the warriors were scattered over the whole grounds, some smoking their pipes near the decaying fires of their respective messes, some leaning against trees, and some passing slowly . from one group to another, but all with their arms at hand, and maintaining the same expectant attitude as their great leader and his officers, to whom their eyes were frequently turned, and from whom they were all evidently looking for some public announcement. With the most intense interest, did our young hero scrutinize every part of the wild scene before him. Impelled by the first solicitude of his heart, he carefully inspected, one by one, the light, unsubstantial and open bough structures, which had been made to serve as sleeping tents for the assembled Indians, till he at length became fully satisfied that no one of them all could contain a female captive, and that, consequently, the object of his secret anxieties could not be in this encampment. But might she not be with the tribe of Queen Wetamoo, whose expected approach, he judged, from his discoveries on the hill, it must be, which was now engrossing the attention of the red multitude before him ? If so, would she not be likely to be brought along among the female personal attendants of that haughty queen, as a trophy

whom she would like to display? There was at least a probability in the supposition. And knowing there could be no
exigency more favorable for diverting all attention from himself, than the excitement and confusion which would naturally attend the ingress of Wetamoo and her numerous train
into camp, he resolved to seize on the occasion to put his daring project in execution. This point being settled, and the
manner of his consequent procedure being arranged in his
mind, he patiently awaited the advent of the approaching
company. His suspense, however, was of short duration. A
great shout rose from the woods, a short distance to the south,
modulated to that peculiar tone by which the Indians usually
announce their approach when drawing near their destination
on visits of peace and friendship. The shout of the advancing
warriors was instantly returned by a loud and hearty acclamation of welcome on the part of the gratified Metacom and
his warmly sympathizing Wampanoogs, who all immediately
hurried forward from all parts of the encampment to array
themselves in lines on each side of their great chieftain to
witness, or participate in the ceremonies of the reception. A
single glance at these movements, told the adventurous young
officer, that the critical movement for making his meditated
attempt to mingle unnoticed in the crowd, had arrived. Accordingly he noiselessly backed out from his tree top screen,
glided round it into open view, and with his rifle in hand,
and with an air of perfect unconcern about every thing, except
the objects which were causing the common rush, hastened
forward a little in the rear of the last of the incoming warriors,
and was soon jostling and jostled about in the thickest of the
changing volumes of the eager crowd, who had no eyes for
any thing but for the sight of their distinguished royal visi-
tant and her warrior train, then seen just emerging from the
thick forest below into the more open grounds of the encampment. First came the stately and beautiful Queen, magnifi-

cently attired, but in a manner which she evidently designed to be emblematical of the character she intended to sustain in the pending conflict,—that of the woman and the warrior united in her own person. Next, and immediately behind her, marched the small, grave-looking band of her chosen counselors, and then, in two separate columns, the far extending lines of her swarthy warriors.

After advancing within the limits of a dozen paces from the spot occupied by Metacom and his counselors, she paused, and, without uttering a word, turned to her followers, and first waved her hand to her counselors to take their places at her side, and then to her warriors to come forward and form themselves into lines on the right and left, corresponding with those of the opposite party. Having seen all her forces thus properly arranged, she turned round, advanced a step and confronting her royal host, stood silently awaiting the salutation which their etiquette required he should be the first to offer.

"Queen Wetamoo," at length rang out the trumpet voice of the chieftain host, breaking the profound silence which for the last full minute had pervaded the confronting ranks. "Queen Wetamoo, thou, whose woman form holds the soul of the great warrior, we kindly greet thee, and bid thee and all thy braves a warm welcome to our encampment."

"Noble Metacom !" responded the other, with queenly dignity, "thy words please us well. Thy greeting is warm, but only such as our friendship deserves at thy hands. We are glad to find it so ; for we come to offer thee the words of peace and good will ; and we hope the chain that shall unite our people will never grow dim by the moth of jealousy, or the rust of age. My noble brother's words are good—may the words of Wetamoo be as pleasing."

"But our queenly sister is wise," rejoined the chief, with a kind but searching look. "She knows there is a friendship

15

of words, and a friendship of deeds. The friendship of words is very pleasant, and, when there are no dark clouds in the sky, may answer a good purpose; but when the angry storm cloud hangs over us, we are not satisfied with smooth words; we want the friendship of deeds."

"Does Metacom suppose," replied the former, almost indignantly, "that Wetamoo would, at a time like this, offer any other than a friendship which is meant to show itself in deeds? Does he not know how the fawn was turned to the panther by that one terrible wrong of the pale faces, which took from him a noble brother—from her a loving husband? Can he remember his *own* wrongs, and believe she has forgotten hers? Can he have heard the cry of mortal anguish which then burst from her crushed heart, and believe that the never dying curse will not always ring out from the iron into which the foul deed, from that black day, turned it? Does Wetamoo ever lie down at night, or rise in the morning without thinking of this? Does she ever have a dream which does not shape itself into a bitter curse on the white man? Would she suffer herself to live a single day, but for the hope of seeing her wrongs avenged?"

"The heart of Metacom beats to the words of his wronged, but still strong hearted sister," replied the chief with an air of mingled sadness and indignation. "He remembers *all* her wrongs, and joins them with his own, as things laid up for the day of the terrible atonement. He enters into all her feelings. He knows her thoughts; and he well knows, also, how she, of herself, would gladly act at this great turning point of the red man's destiny. But he does not yet know what her counselors and warriors would do. They have suffered wrongs, but no such wrongs as Metacom and Wetamoo; and *they* may not see that the wasting thunders which the pale faces are everywhere preparing, are as much intended for them as the more hated Wampanoogs. They may not be tho first the whites have marked to die, or be driven from their hunting grounds and the graves of their fathers; but their day of trouble will come next, and their destruction be the more certain, because, having neglected the only opportunity they could ever have of joining their red brethren in rolling back the thunder on the heads of the destroyers themselves, till all perish, they will then have none to stand between them and the storm of death come to sweep them from the land. These are the words of truth, but they may not see it so."

"They do see it so, noble Metacom!" exclaimed the excited Wetamoo. "They know the words of Metacom to be the words of wisdom and truth. They, too, have their wrongs and insults to remember and avenge. They see what fate is intended for *all* the red men; and they *will not* refuse to help the Wampanoog roll back the thunder till the destroyers shall themselves find the fate they are intending for others. They know it all—they see it, they feel it with their queen. Then, try them, Metacom, and see if they make no sign of their will for the right action."

"It is the favoring moment! It shall be done," said Metacom in a tone so low that none but those immediately around him could hear the words, as he drew the blood red symbol hatchet from under his broad wampum belt, and advancing and waving it on high in sight of both armies, threw it down at the feet of Wetamoo.

The eyes of the warrior beauty sparkled with savage delight as she witnessed the significant deed, but without offering to touch the implement lying before her, or to give the least utterance to her laboring emotions, she turned to her counselors and bent on them an anxious and imploring look, more eloquent than words, of her wish for their approbation, before she took the responsibility of performing the solemn and binding act, to which she and her tribe had been thus officially challenged by the great warrior of the Wampanoogs. And her countenance soon broke into a grateful smile at the kindly looks and visible expressions of approval, with which these grave men met her enquiring glances. She then raising herself to her full height, spread out her suppliant hands to the whole mass of her assembled warriors, who fully comprehending the purport of the mute appeal, and being deeply stirred at what they had already heard and witnessed, instantly responded in an universal burst of all the varying tones and expressions of encouragement and applause. Scarcely waiting till this welcome demonstration had died on her ears, she turned, and, with trembling haste, seized on the typical hatchet, eagerly kissed the red blade, and then raising it on high, fiercely waved it over her head towards her admiring warriors, who sent up a hearty shout in ratification of the war-league involved in the symbolic, but, in their eyes, the no less sacredly binding performance. And the next moment the startled wilderness shook with the wildly responding acclamations of the delighted Wampanoogs.

"It is well!" exclaimed Metacom glancing along the serried lines of the now confederated warriors, with a look of intense gratification—"it is well! it is enough!"

"It is well; but it is *not* enough!" quickly responded the ardent Wetamoo, proudly advancing to the other with looks beaming with high resolve—"No, it is not enough, brave Metacom. *We* feel—all our united warriors feel, to-day, that none will turn back or grow faint while a pale face lives to wrong us. Let us swear that the feeling of to-day shall be the feeling of to-morrow, and forever. For ourselves and our tribes, in the presence of the avenging spirits hovering over us, let us swear it, Metacom, let us swear it!"

Metacom—even the lion-hearted Metacom—could not but hesitate at the thought of taking the unalterable oath of devoting himself, without reserve, to the desperate purpose he saw involved in the bold proposition of the relentless Wetamoo, which was no less than that of entering on a war of extermination with the united colonies of New England. Although, in brooding over his wrongs, he had often secretly made resolutions to the same effect, and always foreseen that the war, when once begun, would probably never cease short of the entire overthrow of either one or the other of the belligerent parties, yet he too well knew and appreciated the means and power of the colonists not to make him pause and tremble in view of the fearful issue, and consequently to hesitate to make the irrevocable declaration in presence of the assembled warriors, and under the sanction of the awful invocation which had been proposed.

But every doubt and shadow of hesitancy, which, for the moment, might have caused the far-seeing chieftain to pause before this Rubicon of his fate, was destined to be banished forever from his mind by the unexpected incident that now suddenly occurred to interrupt the proceedings. Two of the Wampanoog scouts, who had hovered along the skirts of the English forces invading Mount Hope, witnessed from their distant coverts all that had transpired there, and remained till they saw the main body of their troops far on their way back to Swansey, now rushed wildly into camp, and announced the devastation of all the beautiful corn fields of their chief by the white men, who had been there in great numbers with no other visible object. The news fell with terrible effect on the mind of Metacom, who at once saw in the destruction of his growing crops, on which he was depending for the winter supplies of his army, the extent of the calamity that had thus befel them. By the entire evacuation of his tribe of the peninsula of Montaup, he supposed he had removed all the object his foes could have in invading the place; and even if a few should come there, he never dreamed they would think of wreaking their vengeance in the wanton destruction of his growing crops. But the destruction of his property was not

all he beheld in the deed : he read in it the determination of
the whites to cease hostilities only with the extinction of his
people.   And the deed and the inference were abundantly
sufficient to bring him to an instant decision.

"Warriors!" exclaimed the exasperated chief, in a voice so
loud and determined that even his own followers were startled
at the sound, while he hastily motioned the ready Wetamoo to
his side—"Warriors, all!—not only the braves of our own
tribe, but those, too, who, with their warrior queen, have so
nobly joined us this day in the wampum league of war—open
wide your ears; listen to the words of Metacom and Wetamoo.
The mountain of injuries which the white robbers of our lands
have for years been heaping on our heads, you have heard of
before.   Yesterday you heard how many of our braves they
had killed at Swansey; to-day, you hear how they have tram-
pled down every acre of our beautiful corn fields at Montaup.
Now, listen, warriors! For every one of the braves they
have slain, a dozen white scalps shall be seen dangling in our
wigwams! For every acre of corn they have destroyed, a
dozen houses of the white men shall be seen blazing from the
torches of our braves! The words 'peace and friendship'
with the double-tongued destroyers of our rights and property,
are never, from this hour, to pass our own lips or be breathed
in our presence; but in havoc and blood we will pursue them
over the whole land, making their days busy in burying the
dead carcases we have left on our battle fields, and their nights
light from the fires of their burning towns and villages! By
the Great Manitou, we swear it! These are the words of
Metacom and Wetamoo. They are things that are not to be
changed or ever taken back. The Great Spirit has heard
them, and will guide his red children on the war path.
Have all our warriors also heard them, to approve and remember?"

The united war-cry which now wildly burst from the lips

of more than two thousand half-phrenzied warriors, mingled with the sounds of their fiercely clashing knives and tomahawks, was their terribly significant response to the dread appeal of their now oath-bound and desperate chieftain.

" It is well—it is good !" exclaimed the chief with an effort to appear calm under the fierce delight with which he had so evidently witnessed the welcome demonstration. " It is very well. The war whoop of the wronged red man is music to the red man's god. It is settled. The Great Spirit told me in a vision that if the red men willed it, the red men should conquer. The red men *have* now willed it, and the promise will not fail. I see it all now coming up in the future. The pale faces fade away. The red men remain to guard the bones of their fathers, and enjoy the land their fathers gave them. Warriors, I have done. Go now to kindle your fires and prepare the great war-feast, which deserves to crown the great doings of the day. With to-morrow's sun your dividing bands shall be put on their war-paths."

It would be difficult to analyze the mingling emotions of surprise, alarm, and horror, with which our disguised hero had witnessed from his place in the hostile but unobservant crowd, the scene we have just described. He had, it was true, made no discoveries leading to the remotest clue to the mystery which engrossed so many of his secret thoughts; but of the strength of the enemy, their desperate resolution, and the plans, resources, and sagacity of their great leader, he felt he had learned more in that one hour, than months of bitter experience might have taught him. So absorbed had he become, indeed, by the thoughts to which the unmistakable significance of much he saw and heard, gave rise, that he almost ceased to realize the perils which he knew attended his situation in the midst of an exasperated foe, and forgot his resolution to withdraw himself before the ceremonies should close, till recalled to it by the closing words of the chief, and the instant breaking away of the crowd that followed. Trusting, however, to his own fertility of expedients, in case he should have occasion to use them to ensure his escape, he borrowed no trouble, but hurried along, with his well assumed air of stoical indifference, with those moving in the same direction, till he had nearly gained the end of the encampment at which he had so unsuspectedly entered. Here he paused, and sent a quick, searching glance around him. Perceiving that all the Indians who took the same course with himself, on the scattering of the crowd, had all stopped or turned aside, and had begun to busy themselves in collecting fuel or building fires, he passed carelessly on, and cheered by the thought that one moment more would place him beyond the danger of detection, was on the point of entering the protecting coverts of the leafy undergrowth, when, to his no small disquietude, he encountered a Wampanoog warrior, who was returning from some near point in the woods, whither, it seemed, he had proceeded unnoticed before the assemblage had dispersed. The Indian, however, did not appear to act as if he supposed there was anything noteworthy in the encounter, and sheering a little, continued listlessly to advance. But his eye happening to fall on the muzzle of our hero's rifle as he was passing, he stopped short, and after pausing a moment, with a sort of puzzled, enquiring expression, looked up and said—

"That Metacom gun, sure. How you have him here?"

Willis instantly perceived both his error and his danger—his error in so thoughtlessly appearing here with a gun, the like of which, he knew, was nowhere to be found in the country, except in the possession of King Philip, and consequently his imminent danger of being thereby detected. His hand, which he had purposely kept thrust within his dress, was grasping the handle of the murderous knife that hung there concealed. But hoping to be spared the necessity of using it, since the worst suspicion of his unwelcome interrogator, as yet probably involved only the theft of the gun, and knowing that everything might depend on his reply and manner at this critical moment, he affected at first an air of slight surprise, and then bestowing a sort of boastful look on his gun, carelessly said—

"Then you no hear about it—gun mine—bought it of praying Indian come from Boston."

"Ugh!" exclaimed the doubtful Wampanoog, bending on the down cast and well schooled face of the other, a look of deep, though still not very well defined suspicion. "No believe—go see," he added, hesitating, but finally moving off towards the chief, to ascertain the truth of the doubted assertion.

Willis could almost feel the burning gaze, with which he knew the Indian was regarding him, but without venturing to return it, or make any reply, he faced about, and with an indifferent, swaggering manner, stood as if waiting to hear the result of the threatened inquiry. But not long was he content to remain in this attitude. Believing the Wampanoog, whose suspicions had been dangerously aroused, would return for a further scrutiny, which would probably result in the still more certainly fatal measure of being compelled to confront the eagle eyed chief himself, he instantly resolved to run the risk of a precipitate flight rather than remain to undergo such a hopeless ordeal.

Waiting no longer, therefore, than to see a few intervening trees placed between him and the receding Indian, he cautiously edged himself along into the bushes, glided rapidly round to the rear of the thick tree top, which had before so effectually screened him, and then bounded forward, in the same direction, thirty or forty rods into the forest without stopping to listen, or look behind him. Here throwing himself behind a large tree, standing on a small rise, he paused tu take breath, and listen for any sounds which might reach him from the scene he had just left; hardly expecting, however, that in the two or three minutes that only could have elapsed since he lost sight of the suspecting Wampanoog, that his story, whatever it might have been, could have possibly been communicated and understood, so that any alarm should as yet be thus created.

But he was not long in discovering his mistake, or in being convinced that his escape had not been one moment too soon effected. A confused murmur of excited voices, in the direction of the camp, quickly apprised him, that his foes were in commotion; and almost at the same instant, a low, sharp yell of exultation, evidently rising near the spot where he entered the thick woods, saluted his startled ears, plainly telling him that a band of pursuers had already discovered and entered on his trail.

Protruding his head for a last glance, before leaving his stand, his eyes were suddenly greeted with a stream of smoke fiercely darting out from a thicket, about half way between him and the supposed locality of his pursuers, and with the instantly succeeding report of a musket, he became sensible that a bullet was grazing the tree and passing between his chin and his breast. Quickly throwing himself at the roots of the tree, so that no further glimpse or shadow of his person could be obtained, he paused a moment for thought. He judged, and rightly too, that the shot came from the Indian he had encountered, who, after sounding the alarm, had run ahead in pursuit, and judged rightly, also, that this Indian, after firing, would not approach any nearer, for fear of a return shot, till his companions should come up. And having settled this in his mind, he rapidly crept away from the screening tree, a few rods into the thickest part of the woods in view, rose to his feet, and turning a sharp angle to the south, and pitching his course towards the place where his company were stationed, made his way through the tangled forest with a speed which was quickened every furlong of his prógress by the fierce yells of his evidently fast accumulating foes in hot pursuit, but a short distance behind him.

CHAPTER XIII.

"The sounds of mingled laugh, and shout, and scream,
  To freeze the blood, in one discordant jar,
  Rung to the peeling thunderbolts of war,
  Whoop after whoop with rack the ear assail'd ;
  As if unearthly fiends had burst their bar;
  While rapidly the marksman's shot prevail'd,
  And aye, as mark'd for death, some stricken warrior wailed."

FOR nearly two hours, after they reached the foot of the
tall dry pine before designated as the appointed rendezvous,
had Noel and his companions in arms anxiously awaited the
return of their adventurous leader.   And as the slow minutes
passed away, and he did not make his appearance within the
time he had specified for so doing, their anxiety began to rise
to feelings of lively apprehension for his personal safety. Noel,
from knowing better than the rest, perhaps, the exactness
with which his superior was accustomed to keep his appoint-
ments, became particularly uneasy ; and having agreed with
his men on a signal for his recall, if any thing suddenly occurred to require it, he left the spot and went down to the
borders of the pond as a more favorable place for distant views
and for detecting distant sounds, which might reach his ear
over the level of the water, indicating the approach of the
enemy, or any commotion there might have been created in
their camp.   Here, after running his eye round the borders
of the pond and seeing nothing suspicious, he lay down on the
edge of the water, and brought his ear near to the motionless
surface, knowing from previous observations, that any weak

or confused noise, at least, is wafted to the ear over a smooth surface of water more than double the distance at which it could be heard on land, and especially a forest covered land, where such masses of objects continuously intervene to disturb and break up the undulations of sound. Here, for some time not the slightest murmur of a sound became perceptible to his strained senses. Soon, however, some distant noise, as if of a sudden outbreak of human voices, came wafting in the disturbed air from the quarter to which his attention was directed. And, in a minute more, a similar, but much louder sound came so distinctly to his ear, that he could no longer doubt, that it was some uproarious shouting of a numerous assemblage of men; while that peculiar shrillness of the mingling tones, which so remarkably distinguish the voices of the American aboriginals, from those of the European people, in all cases of loud outcry, at once convinced the listener that the noise must have proceeded from the camp of the enemy, who perhaps had sent up that fierce shout as one of exultation on detecting and seizing the spy, who had so boldly ventured among them. A boding chill ran over the feelings of Noel; and almost despairing for the fate of his friend, he rose to his feet, again sent a searching gaze round the borders of the pond, and then again fell to listening; when the report of a gun, rising as he thought very near, but a little to the west of the other sounds, came pealing through the forest. There was yet hope, he thought; for a gun would not have been likely to be fired under the circumstances, except at an escaping fugitive. And if Captain Willis was that fugitive, as he suspected, and had not been brought down by the shot, his chance of an escape was by no means a foregone conclusion for one so well known for his fleetness, especially in the forest. With this view of the case, Noel instantly hastened back to his men, and having stated to them his suspicions, and the reasons he had for entertaining them, took two of his most reliable men, leaving the rest to follow on a given signal, and made his way rapidly through the forest, in the direction in which he thought his friend would be most likely to come, that, in case of a pursuit, he might aid in a rescue. After proceeding about a quarter of a mile, in this manner, with his two men keeping pace with him, at short distance on his right and left, he gave the signal for a momentary halt, with the view of listening and reconnoitering for indications betokening the approach and direction of the pursuers; when if any discoveries were made, they would govern themselves accordingly, and if not, move on, but now slower and with more caution.

"Hark! hark, there!" exclaimed Noel, to his nearest companion.

"Ay, ay; but what did you think you heard?" returned the other.

"The yells of approaching Indians, not more than a half a mile in front; and if so, they are probably on the trail of your captain, who must now be near us. Keep a keen lookout for his approach, and see to it that you don't mistake him in his disguise, and fire on him for a foe."

The caution, as the event of the next moment showed, was not unnecessary, and even with it, the same man came near falling into the fatal error, against which he had been just so particularly warned; for the next instant he was seen cocking his piece, and bringing it to an aim, as a quick, stealthy step was heard approaching in the bushes, and glimpses of a human form in an Indian dress were caught by the beholders.

"Hold, there—it is your captain!" sharply cried Noel.

"God forgive me!" said the man, lowering the muzzle of his gun, with a look of horror, at the thought of what he came so near doing.

"A thousand welcomes to you, Captain Willis!" exclaimed the overjoyed lieutenant, now stepping out from his concealment, as the other, with flushed looks, came swiftly gliding

along to the spot. "I have been on the tenterhooks on
your account for the last half hour, and now thank heaven to
see you here in a whole skin."

"Ah!" said Willis, enquiringly, but with his usual calmness. "Then you have guessed out something of the state of
the case, Noel?"

"Yes, in listening closely, distinguished a great shout—
then soon after heard a gun—suspected what was to pay, and
with these two men came forward to this place to help cover
your retreat, and here, a few minutes ago, heard their yells
in pursuit—read it all right, didn't I, captain?"

"We shall find it so, I fear."

"How many do you think are on your trail?"

"Not a large number in the nearest gang—probably, not
more than fifteen or twenty; but others are continually
coming up from the aroused camp and falling into the
chase."

"How near are those in the lead, do you imagine?"

"A hundred rods, perhaps."

"So near! The last time they yelled, I thought they must
be nearly a half mile from us."

"They were. They raised an outcry on discovering the
trail which they had lost, to apprise all other pursuers it was
found, and attract them to the spot. I know where I had
balked the greedy hounds, and before they gave the yell you
heard, indicating that they had again discovered the trail, I
had pulled on nearly a quarter of a mile further, where luckily I came upon a succession of fallen trees, lying in different
directions, and so newly fallen and hard, as to leave no impression of my foot steps, and having run some distance on
these, I jumped off on to a rock, on one side entirely out of
the line of my course. It is at this place, as I judge from
their long silence, that they are now finding themselves so

much at fault. But they will find it soon enough, to give us no time to spare."

" Let us on then to the company instantly."

" Yes ; for we must all get out of the vicinity as far as possible before we make a stand, lest the sound of our guns soon bring down upon us the whole of King Philip's forces, which I found posted where we supposed them to be, not much over a mile from this spot."

" I have thought of all that, too, Captain Willis, and accordingly ordered the company, before I left them, to prepare themselves, and stand ready to march at a moment's warning."

" That is fortunate, for we may not have a moment to lose in keeping clear of them till it will be safe to give them battle. There !" continued the speaker, motioning the others to silence, as a shrill yell of exultation, rising from a point of alarming proximity, rang through the forest,—" there ! did you hear that ? They have found the trail, and are hot on the chase. Now let each put his best foot forward for our company."

With the rapid pace at which the officers and their men now set forward, a few minutes sufficed to bring them to the spot where the main body of their companions stood eagerly awaiting their expected arrival. The eyes of the men sparkled with joy at the appearance of their heroic young leader, and, but for his forbidding gestures, would have given vent to their feelings in the shout of exultation which seemed rising to their lips.

" Thank you, my boys, just as much as if you had," hastily interposed the captain, with an appreciating glance ; " but we have those not far behind us, who would discover our position much quicker by our voices than our trail. And I deem it important to keep good our distance before them, some time longer."

He then, in a few direct words, informed them of their position in relation to that of the enemy, explained the importance of a rapid retreat, and, bidding them scatter into the woods
for separate, but parallel routs, directed them to make their
way with all the speed of which they were master, for the
southern point of a long narrow cove, which made in from the
bay two or three miles of the southwest of them, and which
they would be sure to reach by steering three or four points
to the right of the then noon-day sun. With these orders,
and with the general understanding, that if they were overtaken by the pursuers before reaching their destination, they
should all stop, and rally towards the place where the first gun
should be heard, they instantly started on their race through
the forest. The policy of Captain Willis in scattering his
men widely into the woods, was destined to subserve even
more purposes than the ordinary ones for which it was intended,—those of facilitating flight, and confusing the enemy, in
case of being overtaken. For the Indians, on reaching the
place where the company had been posted, and from which
they had just started, and on finding such a multitude of distinct or separate trails leading off from the spot, supposed the
whites to number as many hundreds as in reality they did
tens, and that the apparent flight was only a ruse to draw them
into an ambuscade. This led to a delay till reinforcements
could be brought up, and then to a caution and tardiness in
pursuit, which afforded ample time to the pursued to reach
their destination and concentrate, before their pursuers arrived in the vicinity. The head of the cove, at which the
company, coming in one by one from their rapid march, had
now collected, curved round to the south within half a mile
of the bay, so as to form with it a narrow neck of land, embracing rough and rocky elevations in the centre, and extending about a mile and a half northward. Here gathering on
the shaded bank of a small brook, they sat down to cool them-
16

selves, after their unwonted exertions in the heat of the day, and take a little refreshment, having first posted, at a little distance in the rear, a few trusty pickets to guard against the surprise, by which they were sadly conscious they were every moment liable to be overtaken.

"I am not without hope," observed Noel, after the demands of appetite had been measurably satisfied by copious draughts of water from the limpid stream at their feet, and portions of food drawn from their knapsacks—"I am not without strong hope, that we have so far outran the red devils that they have given up the chase, and left us exempt from further molestation. What is your opinion, Captain Willis?"

"My opinion is, that you will soon find yourself mistaken. Metacom, now he knows his enemies have penetrated this wilderness, where he doubtless supposed himself secure against their intrusion, will never permit us to get away without an attack, or, at least, without knowing our numbers and how we came here. And I regret to say I have reasons for believing it will be a desperate attack."

"What are those reasons, captain?"

"They grow out of the fact which I think the old fox must have discovered for the first time, in consequence of my visit to his camp to-day; for while *I* made many discoveries there which I deem of great consequence to the public to be known, and which at the first leisure hour I will unfold to you, I think *he* must have made one which I had much rather he should not have known."

"He must have discovered, of course, that there had been a spy in his camp; but what further could he have learned?"

"Who that spy was. Did I not tell you how I came to be detected?"

"No; you told me nothing but to confirm my conjectures that you *were* detected and pursued."

"True; you are right. I had not time when we first met, and this is the first oportunity we have since had to speak together. Well, the only cause of my detection arose from a provoking oversight of my own, in taking my rifle along with me."

He then briefly related the incidents connected with his detection and escape, and resumed—

"Now, Metacom, who well knows who the owner of the only gun like his own is, and who also knows how well acquainted that owner is with the ways of the Indians, their secret forest haunts, and almost every thing that relates to them, will understand at a glance the importance of ridding himself of such a foe. So you now see the force of my reasons for expecting an attack."

"I do; and I think we should lose no time in looking up the place where we can defend ourselves to the best advantage. Have you any such position in view?"

"I have several that would do. But, by way of best providing for all contingencies, I think we had better make for the northern point of this neck of land, where the advantages for making a stand are as good, perhaps, as those of any other place, and where, at least, we cannot be surrounded."

At that instant, two muskets burst in quick succession from the woods in the direction of their outposts, significantly apprising the startled company that the enemy were at hand. Every man, grasping his gun, hied to the nearest tree, and, with cocked piece, awaited in watchful silence for the first appearance of a foeman as a mark for his ready bullet. In two or three minutes, the pickets came rushing in, and reported that the Indians, in large numbers, had reached the near vicinity, and appeared to be stealthily extending their line across the neck about a furlong in the rear. And this intelligence was the next moment confirmed by the appearance of seemingly hundreds of painted warriors rapidly pass-

ing over a partially open hill top a short distance to the east,
and streaming along down the western slope, and throwing
themselves into a line extending from the hill across the entrance of the neck to the bay beyond, with the evident intention of cutting off all retreat for their intended victims along
the shore to the south.

"The red rascals really think they have got us now, to a
dead certainty, I suppose," cheerily sung out Captain Willis to
his men, whom he noticed watching with uneasy looks this
movement of their foes; "but the labor of that cunning
manoeuvre is lost, at least, I can tell them; for I had no
notion, as they seemed to have supposed, of proceeding along
the shore south to give them a chance to surround us on
three sides, instead of one, as they can only do in the place
to which we will now betake ourselves. So, courage, boys,
all will come out as safely for us yet, as it will fatally for our
foes, if they presume to pursue us."

"Ay, I can testify to all that," responded Noel, in the same
animated tones, as he glanced around to the company. "The
captain and myself had just been talking over the matter before we heard the firing, and decided on marching to the
point where there is an open field, which Indians are always
shy about entering, and where there are plenty of large stones
to protect us, if they did. So let them follow us there, if
they like, and we will spot their red pictures for them as sure as
they try it."

"There, my lads," rejoined Willis, "you see that your
lieutenant is of the same opinion with me. Then let us put
ourselves in motion for the point. Take to the right of yonder central ridge in front, for that is the most direct route—
move on lively there, my boys—no trouble in that direction.
All the danger will be in the rear, and that is a post I will
take myself."

Starting off with eager alacrity, under the new impulse

which the encouraging words and intrepid bearing of their cool and self-possessed young leader and his second in command had given their sinking hearts, the men all hurried forward, and, in their haste to reach the favoring location ahead, to which they had been ordered to proceed, soon left their two first officers considerably behind them.

"I thank you," said Willis, as soon as he found himself and friend fairly beyond the hearing of any of the men—"I sincerely thank you, Noel, for backing me with those cheering words. They were timely, and, as you saw, I presume, much needed. The sight of the enemy in such unexpected numbers and frightful appearance, had evidently struck the men with dismay. And I don't much blame them for trembling at our prospect, neither; for, though I would say it to only you, Noel, it is as I feared. We have got to face a desperate onset. But to suffer any misgivings to take possession of the company, would only enhance the danger. Our salvation must depend on our coolness and courage !"

The company, in the meanwhile, hurrying along in a close, irregular column, had entered the long, rocky defile, formed by the sharp central ridge before named, and the steep, ledgy shore of the cove. Having here proceeded about a quarter of a mile in this manner, they were diligently making their difficult way over the fallen trees and rough, briar-clad rocks, when their ears were suddenly assailed by a strange concatenation of sounds, which seemed every where springing up all at once, around and in front of them. It was a peculiar, shrill, quavering noise, or rather combination of similar noises, varied only by the different distances from which they came; here, low and indistinct—there, loud and sharp; but all maintaining the same unearthly, abhorrent tone—a tone resembling something between a hiss and a whistle. With an instinctive shudder, the men all stopped short in their tracks, and exchanged quick glances of inquiry and apprehension.

"What was that?" exclaimed one, with a recoiling motion. "What, in the name of heaven, was that?"

"Yes, what was it? What is it? Oh, what is it?" quickly responded half a dozen others, in the same breath, as the strange music burst forth afresh, and in fast and far spreading chorus, at the sound of their voices.

They all now, with one accord, began to peer in among the rocks and bushes from which the sounds seemed to proceed, when first one, then another, then all who were in front, suddenly started and leaped wildly back among their advancing comrades, at the sight that had greeted their horrified senses. They were in a den of countless rattlesnakes! All along the front, from the insurmountable ledge on the left to the no less precipitous descent of the rocks into the water on the right, scores of the crawling monsters were seen lifting their gray, menacing heads, and brandishing their forked tongues, as if gathered to give battle to the intruders; while the commotion of the leaves, as far back as the eye could reach, told that the whole area of the pass, to an unknown distance in the rear, was alive with the horrid progeny. And it was seen at once that there was no way of getting by or round them, and that the only alternative that remained was to retreat from the defile in the way it was entered, or incur the hazard of the almost certain death of many, if not all the company, by rushing through the frightful array. But the men were not long in deciding on what course they should pursue in the unexpected emergency. One and all declared they had rather face a thousand Indians than run the gauntlet through such a congregated host of death-dealing reptiles, and accordingly the whole company turned and rushed tumultuously back toward the mouth of the pass.

While this singular scene was transpiring among the men, their two officers, whom we left leisurely following on behind, had noticed indications of the movements of their foes in the rear, which had suddenly caused them to change their pace to a speed that soon brought them far into the defile, in which they were vigorously pushing forward, when, to their utter astonishment, they met their company in full retreat from the place.

" Halt !" thundered Captain Willis, to whom the unexpected, and as he now particularly considered it, most unlucky retreat, was wholly incomprehensible. " What in the name of heaven does all this mean ?"

The cause was at once explained to the surprised and irritated officer by his shuddering followers, who described the position and the numbers of the rattlesnakes to be such, that no further progress in that direction could be undertaken except at the imminent peril of all their lives. At first, both Willis and Noel were incredulous, and tried to remonstrate with the men, believing their accounts at least to have been much exaggerated by their fears, and confidently asserting the opinion that two or three persons going forward with long, light poles, could easily clear the way, so that a passage could be effected with entire safety. But with one accord, the men all resolutely demurred ; and when further pressed, absolutely refused to return to renew the hazardous experiment, unitedly declaring that they had far rather face the savage foe, whatever their number, than again attempt to force a passage among the myriads of venomous reptiles that so thickly environed the only accessible way in that direction, and concluded by offering to follow wherever their captain should dare to lead them.

" So be it, then," said the captain, his countenance now changing from the look of mingled disappointment and anxiety it had worn, to one of stern determination. " You shall have your choice ; but I cannot insure you an unmolested march to the point in the only other way now left for us. The red skins, I fear, have before this advanced and taken possession of this long, woody ridge, separating us from the other shore, along which, foes or no foes, we will force our passage to the point which we were to have reached by proceeding on this side of the hill. Throw yourselves into a scattering file, then, boys, and come on. Let not another word or sound of footstep be heard, not a single gun be fired unless to anticipate a shot from an enemy in your path. When we get out to the thick woods, at the southern point of the hill, where we must wind round to the opposite shore, I will plunge on ahead. Follow, and keep up who can."

Noel now falling into the rear, and Willis leading the way, they all, with hurrying steps, silently made their way out of the luckless defile, which had caused them a delay, that at this juncture, they felt, was fraught with especial danger. The moment the captain gained the border of the dense forest, where he had apprised the men they were to double the southerly extremity of the hill, he turned to them, mutely beckoned them on, hastily pointed in the direction he was about to take, glided into the thicket, and closely followed by his whole company, sped his way, with many an uneasy glance around him towards the yet comparatively distant position, which it was now their great object to gain before their change of movements should be detected by their wary foes, who were doubtless looking for them in another direction. Fortunately for these dangerously environed rangers, the trees were so large and thickly planted, and the undergrowth so impervious to the sight in this part of the woods, that they could be seen only at the shortest distance. Favored by this circumstance, and the fact that the attention of their enemies was turned from them, they passed nearly through their whole reach of woods, without the least molestation, or discovering any indications of danger, either before or around them. And, as the long sought opening was now in plain view before them, they began to grow sanguine in the hope that they should entirely escape the open assault or secret ambuscade, for which they had been looking at every step they took in their progress through the woods. But from their pleasing dream of escaping this peril, they were destined to be the next moment most fearfully awakened. Suddenly, and as unexpectedly as a crash of thunder from an unthreatening sky, simultaneously burst the reports of an hundred muskets from a line of low, thick evergreen, within pistol shot on the right, on the astonished band, as, totally unconscious of the vicinity of their silent and secreted foe, they were moving along in close file towards the opening. Captain Willis, who had already reached the edge of the woods, amazed but undisturbed by the perfect shower of bullets, which pierced his clothes, or whistled over his head, gave the first thought for the fate of his men, half of whom, at least, he supposed must have been swept away by the terrible volley. But with a joy equalled only by his surprise, he beheld every man on his feet, and apparently unharmed.

"Not a gun! not a single gun!" he shouted as he saw several of his men raising their pieces to return the fire,—"Give God the thanks for this miracle if you escape under such a volley as that, and follow me through the field to the point of the neck as fast as your legs can carry you!"

"On! on, there!" thundered Noel, from the rear,—"Run! for your lives, run! before the lifting smoke of their guns shall give the balked devils another sight of you!"

Rallying from their dismay at the startling command of their officers, as well as at the conviction, which now flashed over their minds, of the extreme peril to which they would be the next moment exposed, the men bounded forward with a swiftness which the instincts of self-preservation could have only imparted, and were quickly too far distant in the long narrow field, through which their race for life led them, to be harmed by the scattering volleys which their disappointed and enraged foe continued to send after them.

The narrow bushy field, through which the devoted band were now speeding their way before their hotly pursuing foes, opened at length into a rough, stony piece of ground of several acres, from which the forest had been cleared, scattering stumps, a few old logs with an occasional tuft of bushes, only remaining to screen an approaching foe. And it was this open space which constituted the extreme point of the neck, and the position selected by Captain Willis for making his final stand against his savage pursuers; the nearest woods being some hundred yards from the spot he proposed to occupy, and the abundance of loose stones lying near it being capable, with a little labor, of forming a tolerable breast-work for the men. On reaching the point, the captain hastily glanced over the ground, selected the spot he deemed the most favorable for his purpose, and directed his followers, as fast as they came up, to throw down their guns and fall to work with might and main in throwing the stones into an irregular wall, or, as they best could, into a line of heaps, each large and high enough to protect at least two or three of the men. Having put about half the company on this work, he ordered the rest to scatter and throw themselves down behind the best screening objects they could find along the field in front, to watch and fire upon the enemy the moment they should make their appearance. And the event soon showed, that these movements had not been made, nor these precautions taken any too promptly for their safety. For scarcely had that division of the company ordered in front for the protection of those engaged on the breast-work become fairly settled behind the different screening objects, to which they had betaken themselves, before a hideous yell of mingled wrath and exultation fiercely burst from every point along the border of the forest, telling the startled rangers that their far out-numbering foes had arrived, formed a line from one side of the neck to the other, and were now exulting in the certainty of their destruction.

"Courage, my boys," exclaimed Willis, fearing the dampening effect of that terrific shout on the minds of his men—
"Courage! keep up brave hearts. The same Providence that turned away that shower of bullets that were half an hour ago poured upon you, will still protect your lives and bring you off victorious."

At that moment there was a visible movement of hasty preparation among the low-lying and before motionless and silent men all along the irregular line of the outpost; and with the sharp clicking of cocking fire-locks, several voices, from the more advanced positions, were heard in low, eager tones announcing—

"They are coming! They are creeping in whole swarms to the very edge of the woods! See! See! they are fixing for a sudden rush! Aye, some of them have already worked themselves along into plain sight!—Shall we fire, captain!"

"Not yet—keep cool a moment longer, boys," returned the captain, in sharp measured, half suppressed accents, while cocking his own piece and carefully raising it to an aim through the small bush behind which he was lying—"Not quite yet, we want to give them a telling volley at the outset. Lie still as mice, all of ye; and they will soon enough of them be out in sight to give each of you a fair mark. Then make sure of good and certain aims. There! I have got mine! Ready all! fire!"

With the word, the air was rent by the sound of twenty exploding muskets; and the men eagerly peering out from their coverts, exultingly witnessed the effect of their well directed volley, in the wild commotion of the savages who, with yells of rage, were seen hastily dragging back their dead and wounded into the recesses of the forest.

Three loud and quickly succeeding cheers spontaneously

burst from the triumphing band at these palpable indications
of the death and discomfiture which their fire had carried into
the ranks of their hated foes.

"Ho! there, my men!" shouted Noel, who had taken
charge of those engaged on the breastwork—"Spring, now,
every man of you, to the work of tumbling up the stones,
while the smoke of your comrades' fire shall screen you from
the aim of the red skins. For the next five minutes, you are
safe; so on with work with a will!"

And they did so to the letter. If ever men were seen to
put forth desperate physical energies, it was on this emergency; when all felt deeply and tremblingly conscious that if
their ruthless, and now highly exasperated enemy, outnumber-
ing more than five to one, probably their own feeble band
could not be deterred from an open charge and hand to hand
fight, their whole company were doomed to inevitable destruction. And being equally conscious too, that their companions
in front must soon be driven back from the imperfectly screening objects, which they now occupied, and which as those
objects became larger and more frequent towards the woods,
would enable the foe to advance with equal, or greater security, the eager band now assisted by many of those who had
taken post with their arms in front, scrambled, lifted, and
toiled on, as men never toiled before, in perfecting their rocky
defenses. It was not many minutes, however, before their
open movements were detected through the dissolving clouds
of smoke by their vigilant enemies, who had mostly either
retained their old posts, or darted forward to others more in
advance. And quickly a shower of bullets, falling closely
around, and some even striking the very stones they were
grappling in their arms, was sent in among them, and drove
them behind their works to remain till an answering volley
from their outlying companions gave them another chance to
resume their labors, with no other danger than what necessarily

arose from the random bullets which still continued to be
fired in that direction. In this manner, the men alternately
toiling and desisting, as the smoke of the firing screened, or
its absence exposed them, the work and the battle proceeded
together for the next two hours; when the swarming foe,
growing more determined and desperate every moment, and
beginning to work their way among the nearer coverts of the
open field, the beleagered little band, all except Captain Willis
and a few of bis best marksmen, occupying good positions on
the right and left wings, retired behind the works, now sufficiently raised and extended to afford a comparatively good
protection to the whole company.

The battle now became general, and soon the whole field
was enshrouded in smoke, and the surrounding woods and the
distant shores of the bay resounded with the rattling reports
of incessant discharges of musketry, and the hideous yells of
the savage foe. The latter, however, for all their terrible outcries, seemed in no haste to attempt the open encounter which
their opponents alone dreaded. But having already received
enough fatal lessons to teach them the sacrifice of life which
such an encounter would cost them, and now feeling sure of
their victims without incurring the sacrifice, they made only
the most cautious advances, and never exposed their persons
except when rising to fire, or dodging from one covert to another.

The gallant little band of rangers, in the meantime, greatly
encouraged in being thus unexpectedly enabled to keep their
bloodthirsty assailants at bay, and especially in their own
miraculous exemption from either death or wounds, from the
scores of hostile bullets which were almost incessantly whis-
tling immediately over their heads, or rattling like hail against
the stones of their defences, continued, with unflinching
hearts, to ply the work of loading their pieces, and discharging them whenever they could catch a glimpse of a flitting

foe ; and, in despite of their full consciousness of the terrible odds at which they were contending, to hope on, seemingly against all hope, through the slowly succeeding hours of that portentous evening.

With them it had been literally a day of hairbreadth escapes and providential deliverances. And hour after hour after that dread panic of the heart which all more or less feel, it is said, in the first moments of battle, had subsided, they fought on in the faith that in some way or other, though no one could pretend to see how, they should still be delivered from the terrible fate that to all human appearance was now their unescapable doom. But as the sinking sun began to dip on the western horizon, reminding them of the near approach of darkness, for which the now more and more closely pressing, and the more and more fiercely exulting foe, were evidently only waiting to rush on for the bloody work of the tomahawk—as their ammunition was nearly exhausted; and finally as no prospect of succor, nor any earthly avenue of escape from the impending destruction yet appeared to greet their anxious gaze, both their faith and firmness gave way, and soon, in spite of all the arguments of their still unwavering young leader, a look of blank despair settled on every countenance, while

"We are lost ! we are lost !" rose in low, sad accents from many a mouth along the line.

"We are not lost !" exclaimed Captain Willis, in tones that roused every sinking heart to hope and expectation, as, after anxiously running his eye over the bay, he eagerly pointed towards a small vessel bearing down from the narrows above, in full sail directly towards them. "We are not lost ! we are saved ! I know that sloop and her brave master. See ! the crew are armed—they are throwing up planks for a breastwork, and preparing to fire on our foe, by way of covering our embarkation. Three cheers, my boys, for the welcome aid, and then give the enemy your parting volleys to aid in the providential rescue."

Like a flash of light scattering the darkness of midnight, the announcement and the confirming sight of the fast approaching vessel, changed everything in an instant. The cheers were given with a will. The air was rent with the redoubled fire, which, mingling with that of the ship's crew, now coming to anchor near the shore, and sending out their boat, effectually screened the embarkation ; and within twenty minutes, the last man of the rangers was on board, and the sloop was moving triumphantly away, followed by the yells of rage which burst from the balked savages on shore.

CHAPTER XIV.

"The sky is chang'd! And such a change! O night,
And storm and darkness, ye are wondrous strong,
Yet lovely in your strength, as is the light
Of a dark eye in woman! Far along
From peak to peak, the rattling crags among,
Leaps the live thunder! Not from one lone cloud,
But every mountain now hath found a tongue,
And Jura answers, through her misty shroud,
Back to the joyous Alps, who call to her aloud!

And this is in the night;—Most glorious night!
Thou wert not sent for slumber! Let me be
A sharer in thy fierce and far delight,—
A portion of the tempest and of thee!
How the lit lake shines, a phosphoric sea!
And the big rain comes dancing to the earth!
And now again 'tis black,—And now, the glee
Of the glad hills shakes with its mountain mirth,
As if they did rejoice o'er a young earthquake's birth."

OURS is a life of change and contrast. And as we are constituted, it is well that it is so. We owe half our happiness
to its contrast to our misery. So great is the effect of change
and contrast, indeed, that the very absence of pain, after its
severe trials, produces a positive pleasure. And when pleasure palls by continuance, its loss can only be justly appreciated and its possession only regained, through a season of pain
and deprivation. The woes incident to humanity, therefore,
seem necessary to prepare us for the enjoyment of the highest
happiness, and may be regarded as performing the same office in the moral, as storms in the physical world, that of opening the way to bright and happy days to come. By change,

also the pulses of life are quickened, and our greatest energies called into action. Every change brings a new experience, and every new experience adds to the amount of our knowledge and wisdom. It would seem, then, that these violent changes and striking contrasts in the affairs of life, which are so constantly occurring, and of which we are so prone to complain, are alike wanted for the consummation of human happiness and the best and fullest development of human character.

It was sunset; and the perilous strife of the day was over. Imagination could scarcely conceive a greater change than that which had occurred within the last hour in the situation and circumstances of the heroic young officer and his brave little band of rangers, whose fortunes we have been following. One hour ago, parched with thirst, nearly overcome by the intense heat of the broiling summer sun, and half suffocated by the sulphureous smoke, with which the constant discharge of their guns had kept them enveloped, they were engaged in the deadly strife with a merciless foe with no rational hope of escaping the destruction which stared them in the face. Now relieved, alike from their danger, their terrible sufferings of thirst and the scorching rays of the sun, they were quietly reposing around the decks of the sloop, deeply enjoying the physical contrast, rejoicing in the consciousness of safety, and devoutly grateful for their deliverance from the fearful perils from which they had so unexpectedly and so strangely escaped. With them, indeed, it was one of those rare and sudden transitions from darkness to light, which of themselves make the most purely happy moments of our lives.

"Captain Willis," said the hardy looking, free-spoken skipper, who, having been busy with ship duties since the embarkation of the imperiled company, now came forward for a more leisurely greeting to the young officer, as the latter was reclining on the gunwale near the stern of the vessel,

17

and thoughtfully looking back on the receding battle ground—
" Captain Willis, you must have been born to good fortune."

" Do you call it good fortune for a military leader to be
compelled to beat a retreat, and leave his enemies masters of
the battle field ?" said Willis, with a bantering smile, as he
turned to the skipper.

" Yes, in your circumstances. Hemmed in as you were by
four times your own numbers, it was good fortune for you to
escape at all. And now I cannot, for the life of me, see why
they did not close in upon your company with knife and
tomahawk, and annihilate the whole of you. I had supposed
the Wampanoogs had both more cunning and courage."

" Aye, but my assailants were not Wampanoogs."

" Not King Philip's forces ?"

" His forces now, but not his tribe. They were his allies,
the Pocassets, who, with their queen, Wetamoo, entered into
an alliance with him this very morning, as I personally know.
And as these new recruits of Philip were loud in their boasts
of the services they were about to perform, he probably, by
way of testing them, entrusted the pursuit and intended
destruction of my band wholly to them. At all events, I
soon discovered, to my relief, they were all Pocassets, who,
not having the courage to make the open assault, by which
they must have soon overpowered us, were waiting for night,
that they might attack us under cover of darkness, without loss
to themselves and quite as much certainty of success."

" They didn't expect I should come up with my sloop, to
snatch the game out of their hands ?"

" No, nor I either. As I saw the sun beginning to touch
the western hills, and beheld my best men yielding to despair,
I felt myself, I confess, in a strait in which I hope never to
be placed again ; and I was casting about for some expedient
to save ourselves, when my eye caught sight of your vessel.
I need not say, I presume, how that sight gladdened my

heart, nor how deeply grateful I feel to you for the timely and gallant service you rendered us."

"Don't burden yourself much about that, captain. We are involved in a common danger, and you appear to be drawing the brunt on your own head by your brave attempts for the benefit of us all. Your mate—leftenant, I should say—has just been telling me something about your exploits and personal risks to-day, besides what I partly witnessed myself; and if I had not decided to do my best to reach you, I should have deserved the rope's end from the meanest sailor in the ship."

"Then your coming up at the time was not wholly accidental?"

"Oh, no. As I came down the river this forenoon, I learned that your company had crossed over yesterday for an expedition down the eastern shore, and I beat down the bay slowly, with the view of being at hand for just such an emergency as occurred to you."

"That was a kind and patriotic thought in you, surely; but where was you when the battle commenced?"

"A pertinent question, I admit; and I should be ashamed if I could not meet the inference that flows from it. I was lying four or five miles above here; and when I first heard your firing, and for hours after, I was utterly becalmed, and instead of coming downward, I found myself actually drifting up with the inrolling tide. I knew from the direction of the firing, and the cloud of smoke that soon rose and stood over the spot, that you must have taken position near the point of the neck; while from the incessant roar of the scattered volleys, I judged the battle to be a hot one, and I would have given a hundred pounds for a breeze to take us to the spot."

"And yet you could make no headway?"

"Not a mile—for hours, not a mile. Not the slightest

breath of air was stirring. The sloop lay like a log on the dead water. We manned our boat, and by turns tugged at the oars in trying to tow the vessel, till we were nearly overcome by the suffocating heat of the afternoon. But with all our efforts, we could but little more than counterbalance the tide drift; so we threw down our anchor to save what we had gained, and wait for a breeze."

" Which you got at last."

" Yes, after laying there all the afternoon, broiling and panting in the sun, and chafing like tied mastiffs in our impatience to be in motion, a smart breeze, about sun an hour high, came unexpectedly puffing out of the northeast, and as if sent on purpose, lasted, you see, only just long enough to reach and take you away. And that was one of the items I had in mind when I said you must have been born to good fortune. For after having been saved by miracle all day, on land, and found yourself at last, without the least apparent hope of further escape, this breeze seemed to spring up for no other purpose than to snatch you away from death, by water."

" Providence, skipper—the hand of Providence that ordered all that."

" I suppose it is so; but we sailors call it luck, which some appear never to have, others always, even in all small matters which I had somehow got a notion Providence would not be likely to meddle with. But however that may be, you are evidently, under one name or the other, one of the fortunate, and I am glad to have such a man aboard my vessel, especially to-night."

" Why particularly to-night, skipper ?"

" Well, I've my reasons. You have noticed, perhaps, that I've been looking pretty close to get everything in trim about the sloop ?"

" I have; and but for the very fair evening we are having I should have supposed you were preparing for a blow."

" If you *had* supposed so, even as it is, you would not have been very far out of the way."

" Why, skipper, what indications of foul weather can you possibly see in such a clear sky, and such perfect calm as this."

" Several, which I have both felt and seen for some hours."

" Felt ?"

" Yes. When a boy, I used to be perfectly unnerved on the approach and during the continuance of thunder storms. And although I got over that as I grew up, and my nerves became firmer, yet I have always had enough of the same kind of sensations, when the elements were preparing for any unusual battle, to make my feelings the best weather glass I have ever found. The same kind of sensations have been creeping over me now for hours. And besides, there are certain visible things which seemed to point in the same direction. We have had, this afternoon, an unusual degree of heat, and, with the exception of half an hour, just one of those oppressive, dead calms which breed the worst kind of thunder gusts."

" But there are no signs of anything of the kind visible in the heavens now, are there ?"

" Yes, *I* think so. You see those thin, whitish, dingy streaks of cloud that have shot up fan-wise from the western horizon ?"

" Yes."

" Well, they are what we call a mare's tail. And when you see them shooting up in that fashion, after such a day as this, you may count on something that will kick, not far off in that direction. Yes, though I hope to be mistaken, I have made up my mind for something more than a mere capfull of wind to-night ; and I am the more anxious about it, as this narrow East-Bay is not a very pretty place to be caught in when there is much of a gale. Had the breeze continued an hour longer it would have taken us so far down that we could have safely scudded out, when the gust struck us, where there is plenty of sea-room. But as we are not making a rod of progress, and as I have no anchor and cable that would hold the sloop in a gale, I must take it as it comes, and get to Newport as I best can."

"Are you bound any further up the bay than Newport, so that you could land my company near the new fortress they are beginning to throw up at Mount Hope?"

"I can't tell you, Captain Willis. It will depend on directions I expect to receive when I reach Newport, whether I proceed on to Providence or return this way to Taunton river."

"You are going to Newport, I suppose, for freight, which may not be made up without going on to the Providence plantations?"

"No,—nothing of the kind,—I am going to receive a passenger or two who are to be landed to-night, it is expected."

"What! a voyage this distance with a vessel and crew, to take away one or two passengers?"

"I see, you think it strange; but I can't explain. I was not very cunning to say what I did about the object of my voyage; but I am so apt to talk out. The fact is, Captain Willis, I am bound on a sort of secret expedition, with what I consider a perfectly lawful object. And I must drop the matter where it is, and hope you will be content to do the same among the men, both here on board, and when we get to port, where I will land you, if we are permitted to reach there."

"Oh, that you will probably do before morning," replied Willis, after a thoughtful pause, in which he was evidently revolving the mysterious words of the other. "Even by any course you will be likely to take, it cannot be only about twenty miles round to Newport. A breeze, I think, will soon spring up; and I confess I cannot share in your apprehensions that the wind will prove anything more than we shall need for our purpose.

"Ah, I have much less faith in your weather wisdom than in your good fortune, which makes me feel that I shall, at least, have no Jonah aboard to-night," replied the persistent skipper, abruptly turning away and leaving the other alone to his reflections.

It had been, as already intimated, a day throughout of unusual heat and sultriness. And the heat, and especially the closeness of the arid atmosphere, had been growing, as the eventful day wore away, every hour more intense and oppressive. Even the shades of evening, instead of bringing the usual relief to those who have been suffering from a hot day, seemed, in the present instance, but to add to the deadness of the air, and render the undiminished heat the more insupportable. Not the semblance of a breeze fanned the waveless waters of the bay, and the appearance of its dark and dismal expanse, as it lay hushed as if in the sleep of death, was varied only by the visible calorific exhalations which rose in quivering undulations along its heated surface. The sloop, though all her sails were set in readiness to catch the first breath of moving air, lay as moveless on the waters as a dead duck on the face of a mill-pond. The sailors, having done all that was required of them until some change should occur, and feeling too listless for motion or conversation, had dropped down in silence at their respective stations; while the rescued rangers lay reclining on coils of rope or other different objects scattered around the deck, and still more overcome from their greater previous exertions and exposures through the day, seemed drenched with the spontaneous, outstarting perspiration, and literally panting for breath. The skipper, still too much exercised with his apprehensions of perils in store for his charge, to permit him to take any attitude of repose, stood by the midship railing, fanning his bronzed face with his broad-brimmed tarpauling, and anxiously scanning the slowly, but now visibly changing aspects of the heavens. Our heroic young leader, also, too full of his own deep and varied reflections, to suffer him to feel any inclination to give himself up to rest, still retained his place, now running, in thought, over the wild and perilous adventures he had that day so unexpectedly encountered, and so strangely survived, and now reverting to the singular intimations which the skipper had thrown out respecting the purpose of his little voyage, and which he somehow felt might involve the object of his own peculiar solicitude. How this could be, however, he could not tell; and after wearying his mind with fruitless conjectures on that subject, he naturally turned his thoughts to the prognostics of the weather, which seemed to have made so deep an impression on the mind of the skipper, and for the first time he seriously fell to noting the appearance of the clouds, in search of indications going to justify the latter's predictions. Widely spanning the southeastern horizon, and magnificently arching up nearly half way to the zenith, lay quiescently reposing, a single, enormous thunder-pillar, whose thousand vari-form, encircling folds, each beautifully marked and distinguished with their delicately tinted edgings of pink and gold, swelled gorgeously up, one over another, in snowy whiteness, like flower-clad battlements engirding some huge dome, bathed and glittering in the contrasted light of the setting sun. After gazing admiringly awhile on this splendid semblant edifice of the heavens, in which, however, he read naught except its display of mingled beauty and grandeur, he turned to the west, where the alleged indications of a storm were more particularly visible. The pale, thin, upshooting streaks of cloud, before pointed out to him, had thickened up and run together, now forming the ragged border of a long,

muddy looking bank of clouds, slowly heaving up into sight
and stretching far along the darkening horizon.

Faint, but quick and fast coming electric flashes, at first
scarcely more perceptible than the earliest suffusions of the
morning, but growing brighter and broader with each returning flash, soon began to quiver and play over the whole extent
of the vapory parapet.

Being now satisfied that the skipper's predictions, of which
he had been so faithless, were to some extent, at least, likely
to be fulfilled, he turned back to the great bright cloud in the
southeast, which a few minutes before had attracted his attention.   All its bright and gorgeous hues had faded away,
and in their place a broad leaden mass of vapor, rolled heavily
together like a scroll, was darkly brooding over that part of the
horizon.   Once more he turned to the ominous cloud rising
in the west.   As slowly as it had appeared in the distance to
be rising, it had made such rapid advances that it now extended and hung like some vast black pall over nearly a third
part of the visible heavens.   The lightning, every instant
flashing out from some part of the portentous rack, had now
become so vivid and continuous as to leave no room for the
encroaches of night, which had otherwise, by this time, enshrouded the earth with darkness.   And the thunder, till now
inaudible, began to reach the ear in low, broken, but quickly
repeating sounds, like the rapid discharge of artillery on some
far distant field of battle.   Thus far the cloud, except the
long, narrow, rifted belt that seemed to lead the van of the
mustering forces, had exhibited only one smooth, even, uniform appearance over the whole extent of its dark, lurid surface.   But soon its face became ominously varied by several
small masses of wild, angry looking cloud now seen rapidly
pouring up from behind the horizon athwart its lower border
in columns of inky blackness.   The opposite cloud also, seemingly thrown into sympathetic commotion, was undergoing,

in the meanwhile, the most rapid transformations, concentrating all its adjunct, floating vapors, doubling and darkening, as if passing through a series of hurried evolutions preparatory to taking part in the elemental conflict now so evidently at hand.

"Do you see that, and that, sir?" exclaimed the excited skipper, again approaching the young officer, and pointing to first one and then the other of the opposite clouds.

"I do—but you don't anticipate much trouble from·that cloud in the southeast, do you, skipper?"

"Yes, it may be. At any rate I had rather it was away. I have sometimes known two clouds so situated play the very mischief with the winds. You see it is thickening up, and the best we can hope of it is, that it will turn into the same current and prove merely an addition to the great one now rolling down upon us in the opposite direction."

"How far off do you judge the storm to be from us, now?"

"The sound of the thunder, which, when heavy, as that probably is, can be heard about thirty miles, and which has but just reached us, will give the distance of the storm from us now. And if I judge rightly of its speed, it will strike us in just about that number of minutes."

"So soon? Why, you don't seem in much haste to reef your sails."

"No—I have got everything so arranged that I can take in and make all fast in ten minutes; and I want to improve the other twenty in getting down into wider water as far as possible before I yield the sloop to the mercy of the blast."

"I see—we are evidently moving at last."

"Yes, and have been, though slowly, for the last ten minutes. You perceive, the air is freshening fast. There is a low, heavy rush of air from the northeast towards the path of the storm, as often happens under such circumstances. See! it is bearing us along bravely now. We may be able to gain two or three miles before compelled to clew up. I will go forward and see to making the most of it, as the distance gained may be the turning point of our salvation."

Like half-dead men rescued from a coal damp, and reviving in a stream of fresh air, the hitherto listless and dormant crew now began to rouse up from their different lounges, rise to their feet, and send inquiring glances abroad over the heavens, when their looks of apathy and unconcern were instantly changed to those of surprise and alarm at the unmistakable portents of the storm which there stared them in the face. The broad and fearfully black rack of cloud wheeling up from the west had now almost reached the zenith, while its face was becoming rapidly changed and broken by the low, pitchy volumes of the under-cloud that was spreading and sweeping in wild convolutions towards them. Nearer and nearer burst the thunders, and brighter and broader flashed the lightnings; and the deep, dull roar, the herald of an approaching tornado, was already borne to the ear on the undulations of the troubled air. The little craft, in the meanwhile, had been steadily plowing her way down the bay under the strong press of the side-wind, skillfully appropriated for the purpose by the anxious skipper, who stood silent at the helm, now intently bending his gaze forward, during each of the brighter flashes of lightning, at the promontories along the shore ahead, by which he was directing his course, and now throwing hurried glances back over his shoulder to note the progress of the tempest behind. But suddenly the wind died away, and the ominous calm which usually precedes the bursting of the storm again fell on the face of the deep. This did not occur, however, until the gratified skipper saw his vessel shooting past the last headland of the narrows, and safely emerging out into the wide waters of the now rapidly expanding bay, when, quickly calling his mate to take his place at the helm, and throwing another hurried glance at the fast nearing tempest, he rushed forward towards his anxiously expectant men, and exclaimed—

"Now, into the rigging, boys! Every man of you into the rigging aloft! Take in, clew, and make double fast every stitch of canvas to the yards, so that not a rag shall be left loose, from deck to top-gallant! Bare poles may even be too much to stand what is coming. Lively there! I tell ye, there is not a moment to lose."

The sailors sprang to their task like men working for their lives; and, thanks to their captain's previous arrangements, they, even quicker than he had predicted, had put every thing in the closest trim, and came, one after another, quickly dropping to the deck.

"Now, mate, lash me to the helm, and then yourself to some object near," resumed the skipper. "All the rest make yourselves fast to something, or go below. Hear that roar! See that black, boiling mass of cloud rolling down upon us! In three minutes more we are in the whirl of a tornado. Heaven be merciful!"

At that instant, as if dropping down in its attempt to leap the narrowing space of clear sky between the greater and lesser racks of the two upper clouds, now about to join their forces, swiftly descended, within pistol shot of the sloop, a blinding stream of electric fire, and, with a crash that shook the rent heavens and reeling earth for miles around, drove its terrific bolts directly into the boiling waters beneath. Scarcely had the stunned and blinded crew sufficiently recovered from the fearful shock to be conscious of what had happened, before the black, curling van of the swiftly advancing volumes of the nether cloud, now fallen down nearly to the face of the deep, came wildly whirling over their heads, enveloping them in a darkness so intense and impenetrable, that the brightest flashes of lightning from the great upper cloud but barely enabled them to discern the deck beneath their feet. And almost at the same instant, a furious blast, with a roar that completely drowned the loudest thunder peals, struck the devoted sloop with a force which made her shake and tremble in every joint and timber, from keel to mast-head, and sent her madly plunging onward like some suddenly smitten victim fleeing before the blows of the avenger. Another and another followed in quick succession, and at lessening intervals, till they mingled into one continued on-rushing blast, before which the stoutest of human fabrics had been but as feathers on the towering wave, filling the blent heavens and earth with its wild uproar, and forcing the groaning vessel forward through the agitated deep with an impetus that sent jets of foam and spray over the whole length of her drenched decks below, and half way up to the dancing yard-arms above. And thus, with unabated fury, on swept the howling blast, and with it, on flew the brave little craft, now diving like a sea fowl beneath the tops of the crested waves, and now riding high and vibrating on the summits of the rolling billows, with her head tur-baned by the storm cloud, her mast and yards wildly tossing from side to side, and her pathway marked by the long line of white foam which her perilous speed had raised from the cloven waters. On she flew, under the best guidance her drenched and dripping skipper could give her by the feeble glimmerings of the lightning that struggled through the black chaos of vapors that so deeply enshrouded her. On she flew, for a full half hour; when the gale suddenly lulled, stopped, and the next moment its fast receding roar was heard dying away in the distance.

The low, and swiftly flying black, angry scud which accom-panied, and, indeed, seemed to have formed a part of the tor-nado, had now passed away, leaving the upper racks of the two encountering clouds deeply brooding over the earth, and apparently struggling for the mastery in the counter currents which had brought them together from nearly opposite directions. The deafening roar of the wind also had ceased, but in its stead, along with the deluging torrents of rain, the most terrific peals of thunder, like the rapid discharges of some hotly worked battery of artillery, were continually bursting midway in the rent heavens, shaking the solid earth beneath the waves with their fearful concussions, and reverberating in long, bellowing echoes on the distant shores of the bay; while the now unobstructed lightnings flashed fiercely forth in every direction—now shooting perpendicularly down to the face of the startled deep, and now, like the fiery serpents of the fabled Tartarus, crinkling and leaping from wave to wave over the wide arena of their frightful gambols, till the whole bay was kindled into light, and seemingly converted into one vast phlegethon of flames.

"See! see there!" exclaimed the mate, as he came hurrying from the fore deck towards the skipper and the two officers of the rangers, who stood grouped round the helm, witnessing, in mute amazement, the awful electric display going on around them. "What is that? God of mercy, what is it?" he added, wildly pointing down the bay.

The eyes of the group were instantly turned in the direction indicated by the excited speaker; when they beheld, about a mile to the south, and nearly abreast of the outermost headland separating the bay from the broad ocean, a huge black, spiral column standing up out of the waves, and rising perpendicularly till its shafted head became buried in the agitated and seemingly stooping cloud high in the heavens above.

"It is a water spout," responded the skipper, with an air of lively concern, after bending his gaze a moment on the strange and fearfully magnificent spectacle.

"A water spout!" said Captain Willis, in surprise. "I thought they never occurred in these latitudes."

"They do not often. But this is one, and as formidable a looking one, too, as I ever saw in a tropical sea. It is the re- sult of the extraordinary state of the air this evening, and the meeting of the two counter moving clouds we noticed, which have probably by this time got doubled over, and become nearly suspended above. You know I was uneasy about their appearance, from the first, and was looking for something out of the way—even of a more dangerous character than the frightful blow we have already passed through."

"But, are these water spouts dangerous to a ship?"

"Dangerous? Why, that in this case will be as our luck is. If we had a wind, we might tack and avoid it. But here we are again, without a breath of a breeze; and if it moves up and catches us in this helpless situation, it would either whirl us up into its vortex with a crash that wouldn't leave two planks of the ship together, or send us down to the bottom like a nest of small reptiles beat into the earth by the heel of your boot."

While the skipper was yet speaking, the water spout slightly veered, and disclosed to the startled spectators, what, owing to its direct course, they had not before noticed, that the ob- ject of their dread was not only in violent motion, but rapidly approaching that part of the bay where their vessel was slowly floating down towards it, under the spending impetus of the departed gale.

Sometimes veering to the right or left, and sometimes mov- ing in a direct line—sometimes bearing itself perfectly up- right, extending upwards from the water in the likeness of some mighty, straight, smooth, black shaft, till it entered the capping cloud above, and sometimes swaying to and fro, and undulating spirally, like a huge serpent suspended in the air, it steadily bore up towards the seemingly doomed vessel, on whose deck stood the appalled crew mutely watching its awful approach. On, on it still came, presenting, as it neared them a round mass of dark green whirling waters, gleaming in the lightnings, and causing the ocean beneath to boil like a pot along its fearful path through the agitated waters.

With one accord, the affrighted crew now called wildly to the skipper to make some attempt to escape the destruction which appeared so near and so inevitable, to the ship and every soul on board.

" Peace !" responded the skipper, who stood with folded arms calmly and collectedly viewing the terrific spectacle— " Peace ! you should all know that if I could have done anything, it would have been done before this last minute of our crisis. Peace ! and fall to your prayers, as I am doing. If Providence and Captain Willis's good star don't interpose to prevent, our time is come, that is all."

But Providence did interpose to save the despairing mariners. When the frightful column had reached a point in its direct course towards them, within a furlong of the sloop, it again veered a little to one side, and, moving on in a semi-circular path, passed by them with the deafening roar of a cataract, so near as to throw a shower of spray over their rocking ship, and send it whirling into the foaming wake behind.

If ever the hearts of men gushed out vocally in gratitude, it was those of the men who now, after having given themselves up for lost, had thus escaped the awful death that so nearly threatened them. But their dangers were not over. While they were yet indulging in their thanksgivings and mutual congratulations, there rose a cry that the waterspout was returning. The eyes of all were instantly turned in the direction, and but to behold with new horror the meteoric monster slowly sweeping round and coming back in a shortened circle whose curve would bring it directly upon the luckless vessel.

"Now Heaven forefend !" exclaimed the sorely exercised

skipper. "I should not think God *would* tantalize us in that way. Pray again—pray all ye who can, and not depend on me. I feel so worked up, my own prayers won't be worth a rope's end to you, this time."

But the skipper's want of faith was the next moment, signally rebuked by a strange and unforeseen instrumentality. As the waterspout came thundering on, and while getting into fearful proximity with the ship, a large round ball of electric fire, vying with a noon-day sun in apparent size and brilliancy, came majestically sailing through the air and struck the watery shaft midway between the clouds and ocean. A stunning detonation instantly succeeded the contact; when, with a deafening sound of rushing and tumbling waters, a dense cloud of mist suddenly expanded outward from the spot and veiled every thing from view. Within a minute, the misty cloud had dispersed, and the waterspout was nowhere to be seen.

"Surely the devil is abroad to night!" exclaimed the amazed skipper, gazing into the empty space where the waterspout was last seen. "But I think he must have taken himself off with the explosion of that strange fire ball; for I smell sulphur as plain as old cheese, and besides here comes a natural breeze," he added, as a smart blast of wind from the northwest struck the sloop.

"Another gale I fear," responded the mate springing to the helm.

"No matter if it is—I can understand that, and there is plenty of sea-room before us now. But what is that crossing our beam outside the capes there, a half mile or so, ahead?" continued the speaker pointing in a lingering flash of lightning to the dark hulk of a mastless vessel tossing about at the mercy of the waves. "It is some unlucky craft that has been dismantled in the gale. And good heavens! She looks like the very one. Up with the trysail, boys. She is in
18

distress, and drifting towards the inner breakers. Perhaps we can reach her and save the crew."

" *The very one, said you, skipper ?*" eagerly asked our hero, rushing forward. "What one? What vessel do you suspect it to be ?"

"The one I was expecting to meet, I have too much reason to fear. May God help her in her peril !"

"But can't you tell me who are aboard ?"

"No—not to a brother."

"One word more—is there a lady among them ?"

"See ! you can now see the deck—look for yourself."

The young officer now earnestly bent his gaze in the direction, and, during the next bright flash of lightning, could distinctly discern the fluttering garb of a female, who appeared to be clinging to a man, as they stood holding on to one of the shrouds on the canted deck of the wildly rolling wreck.

"God of mercy protect them !" he exclaimed in tones that betrayed his peculiar anxiety—"But faster—faster ! skipper —more sail, or we shall be too late for the rescue."

"Yes, boys, up with more sail. The sloop will bear it," cried the equally anxious skipper—"There, that will do !" he added bending to the helm as the goaded craft went singing through the waves towards the endangered vessel.

CHAPTER XV.

" Look round the spot to faith and firmness dear,—
Finds no rapt spirit fit incitement here,—
Here where the Indian rov'd in nature's pride,
And built his fires and lov'd and warr'd and died ! "

On the banks of one of the tributaries of Taunton river, and within the ancient limits of the town bearing the same name, stands one of the oldest houses in New England. Having been originally constructed in the substantial and massive style of the English cottage architecture of the seventeenth century, when men, unlike those of the present age of lath and plaster, built less for show than durability, this ancient mansion is still, or till recently was, in a remarkable state of preservation. The builder of the establishment, whose name has found a place in our histories, no less on account of its association with that of King Philip, than from the fact that he was the founder in the new world of one of the most numerous and respectable families of colonial planting, was a native of the west of England, and, having immigrated some time during the first twenty or thirty years of the existence of the colonies, had here erected the first iron forge or smithery deserving the name ever put in operation, it is said, in any part of America. This fact alone made it, for many years after its establishment, a place of no little note in the surrounding country; since all classes, both white and red men, were alike compelled to resort here for such kinds of smith-work, as became essential in their various occupations. The white settlers came for their axes, hoes, chains, and the numerous other

tools and utensils required in the prosecution of their different agricultural or mechanical employments. And the red
men came from their forest homes, for hundreds of miles
around, to get their hatchets or tomahawks, knives, steel-traps,
and fish-spears made, and their guns repaired. This constant
intercourse with all kinds of persons, thus kept up for years
by the proprietor in the business of his calling, made him
personally known as widely perhaps as any individual in all
the colonies. And had his character and manner of dealing
been like too many others, his situation in the terrible war
now enkindled, on the very borders of a territory whose dark
forests were swarming with the most active and inveterate of
the savage foe, might have been fraught with peculiar trials
and dangers, either from the jealousy of his own people, who,
in their excitement and alarm, were often so suspicious as to
construe the least indication of a disposition for neutral action
into meditated treason, or from the bullets of the lurking
savages, who all knew him, and would have availed themselves
of the circumstance of the war to avenge any injuries or affronts
they might have previously received. But James Leonard,
in his character and dealings, and especially his dealings with
the red men, was not like those of most others of that day of
narrow philanthrophy and religious arrogance. His enlarged
benevolence of heart and high conscientiousness, together
with his innate honesty, led him to make no discrimination
between the sin of cheating a red man and the sin of cheating a white man. And his dealings were alike, just and fair
with the former as with the latter. His whole conduct and
demeanor, also, were equally kind and respectful towards the
one as towards the other. And yet not even the semblance
of a boast ever was heard to pass his lips. The word, *honesty*,
indeed, so far as regarded himself and his dealings, was never
uttered by him. His moral creed was acted not professed.
And a creed thus possessed, and thus, and thus only, manifes-

ted, was the very thing to enlist the admiration and gain the confidence of the Indians, who are, perhaps, the most search- ing moral critics, and the closest and most accurate readers of men and their motives that were ever known, among all the different races of mankind.

But among all his red customers, there were none who so keenly appreciated the character and conduct of the honest and unbigoted mechanic as King Philip of Mount Hope. And the appreciation of the discriminating and noble hearted chieftain, continually enhanced and made effective as it was by the mental contrast which he was forever drawing between the treatment he had so uniformly received from its object, and that of the arrogant and over-reaching colonists, whom it had been his fortune generally to encounter, gradually ripened into a lively and solicitous regard, amounting to a friendship, indeed, which the hostile relations that the parties were now compelled nominally to assume, had no power to destroy, and which continued, and showed itself alike in words and actions, till the last days of his life.

To the establishment above described, we must now take the reader, to introduce the new characters, and note the new events which arise to mark the progress of our story.

In the long, low, oak-ceiled sitting-room of the mansion just described, on the second evening after the terrible night marked by the fearful incidents whose attempted portrayal occupied the last chapter, sat the worthy proprietor, musing in the twilight, and enjoying that grateful repose, after the active duties of the day, which the laboring man only can ever know. He was a man of a strong, well made frame, plain features, and a frank, kindly, but firm countenance, which, with his quiet, self-possessed manner, seemed equally well calculated to win confidence and command respect. Not sharing in the general jealousy and alarm which had seized upon the people living near the borders of King Philip's dominions, and led hundreds of them to desert their homes for the older settlements, or to immure themselves in block-houses, he had erected no kind of defenses around his build-ings, kept no fire-arms for his own use, employed none to stand on the lookout to announce the approach of suspicious personages, and manifested no apprehensions when any such *did* approach, that they were coming for evil either to himself or family.   And it was therefore with no disturbance of man-ner, and with an air of mere enquiry or curiosity, that he now, as he sat near an open window, in the listless attitude before mentioned, caught sight of an unknown, muffled figure, gliding silently into the door-yard.   The new comer, though accoutred as much like an Indian as a white man, and though the visible parts of his skin were bronzed nearly to the color of the former, yet evidently belonged to the race of the latter; while his erect figure, firm carriage, well formed intellectual features, and the dark, steady eye that beamed over his thick, bushy beard, and from under his once black, but now deeply grizzled locks, plainly showed him to be a man of decision, capacity, and of a more than ordinary strength of character. He paused a few yards from the door, and while affecting an attitude of careless indifference, sent a searching glance around, and into every visible part of the building, in a man-ner which seemed to indicate that he had his private reasons for wishing to know what kind of company he might be lia-ble to encounter if he entered; when, appearing to satisfy himself on that point, he unceremoniously passed into the door, and the next moment stood before the still undisturbed, but wondering owner.

"Upon my word, friend Crocker, I did not till this instant quite know you," exclaimed Leonard, extending his hand to the other, with that brightening up of countenance usually attending the sudden transition from doubt to an agreeable recognition. "You return in a new disguise. How have you prospered in effecting your objects during the month or more elapsed since I saw you ?"

" For the main part, wonderfully well, considering the dubious character of the enterprise; yea, wonderfully, my discreet friend—think I have pretty certainly narrowed down my suspicions to a point, as regards money matters, and as to the other matter of concern you and I discussed, before I started on the expedition, I found affairs worse than I expected; but that, at least, I have effectually remedied."

" How ?"

" The stranger here, with a glance at the doors and windows, as if doubtful about answering the question aloud, drew up and whispered something in the ear of the other, who, with a look of surprise and admiration, exclaimed :—

" Why, you are as adventurous as the old Knight Errants we read about !"

" Ay," resumed the former ; " but I have been through as many perils as St. Paul in effecting my objects."

" From the Indians ?"

" No—*I* am hunted of white men, not red ones. "

" True ; but a bloody war has broke out since you went on your hazardous adventure."

" I know it all, Leonard ; and that circumstance may have added to my peculiar risks, as it certainly has to my perplexities. But I spoke not of that ; I have been shipwrecked, Leonard."

" You have ? Shipwrecked, did you say ?"

" Yea, sir ; but don't be alarmed. I and a certain other person were landed in safety."

" But where is that person, now ?"

" Dispatched to a place of safety, with the safest of attendants."

" I think I understand you in all that ; but not when, where, or how you suffered shipwreck."

"We were wrecked in the frightful storm, night before last, on the south-eastern end of Aquineck."

"Were all the crew saved?"

"Yes, I conjecture so—and the vessel too, probably; and if so, I shall be glad the event occurred."

"Then you must have got separated from the ship, some how?"

"We did, most strangely, and I will now briefly relate to you how we came to be on shipboard, how our perilous passage by water so abruptly ended, and why I think it may be well that it did so."

"Do so. You can talk safely here now, I think; but others may soon be about to prevent."

"I will," replied the mysterious stranger, throwing another glance out of the window, then drawing his chair near that of his host, and speaking in a tone and manner which showed that well understood relations of confidence existed between the two.

"I decided to return mostly by water, because one of the few white men, besides you and Roger Williams, who has my secret, owns and commands a small schooner, which he plies between the head of Buzzard's Bay and the southern ports and settlements. And he, offering to take us round to Newport, and then provide a safe passage for us up to Providence, or to such other place as I should decide to go, we, after many delays, embarked early, day before yesterday morning, and set sail with a good prospect of a run down the bay that would take us to our port before nightfall. But in the afternoon, we were delayed by calms, and with the approach of night, we were overtaken by a terrific tempest, which soon disabled our craft, and at length drove her out into the broad ocean, rolling and tossing about almost wholly at the mercy of the winds and waves, with a rocky lee shore on our right, towards which we found ourselves rapidly drifting. But we

were helpless, and could do nothing but await in gloomy suspense the fate that seemed in store for us all.

" That suspense was for a short time relieved, it is true, by
the appearance of a vessel which seemed to be bearing down
from East Bay, and which our captain hoped would be able to
take us in tow. But in the frequent clear views we obtained of her, in the broad flashes of lightning that were continually leaping out from the receding thunder cloud, and
blazing far and wide over the tumbling ocean, our watchful
captain soon perceived, and announced with a tone of despair
that she had tacked for a more outward course, we by this
time having been driven where she no longer dared to follow.
It was the *captain* of our vessel, as I said, and the *crew* that
were now filled with fear and despair, not I. But for the one
I had with me, I would have preferred to abide the risks of
shipwreck to being taken on board the approaching vessel, for
I had perceived her deck crowded with a crew who were much
too numerous for the purpose of working the ship, and who,
for the most part, did not look like ordinary sailors, and therefore, must have been there for some special object, which I
thought very likely concerned myself.

" But there was not permitted much time, either to the
captain and crew for indulging in their regrets, or to me for
balancing the dubious alternatives I was revolving in my mind.
Before we were aware of our proximity to the land, we were
whirled into a cove and run aground, about a hundred yards
from the shore. The captain believing the vessel must soon
be broken up, decided on trying to get to the land in our
ship's boat ; and, lowering and manning it with two strong
rowers, assigned to me and my companion the chance of first
embarking. This we did, and starting on the back of an inrolling wave, were, in three minutes, safely landed on the
narrow beach ; when we hastily retreated up the bank beyond
the reach of the highest waves, leaving the boat to return for

the rest. But nathless the intent, that, for some wise ordering, was not to be permitted. Just as the boat reached the
schooner, the reflux of a mighty wave, which had lifted her
clear from the bottom, carried her out beyond the points
of the cove, when a sudden flaw of wind from off shore striking her, she was driven out faster than she came in, and was
soon seen nearing the other vessel that appeared to be laying
to in the distance, either to assist us, or—"

"But *you* two?" interposed the other with an air of surprise
at the calmness of the narrator in describing the affair—
"What was *your* situation, thus deserted and left alone in the
night on that woody, uninhabited shore?"

"Alone! Why, for myself I desired to be alone. Night
and woods! Why, sir, for long, long years, they have been
my best safeguards! And my companion, even, might have
had reasons to face them all, in preference to falling in with
the other ship's company. But we were not left to remain
there alone, as we certainly at first supposed we were to be.
A half dozen red warriors soon came gliding to our side."

"And were you not alarmed, then?"

"No, the very thing I should have wished had occurred;
for in the leader of the band arrayed in one of his many perfect disguises, I thankfully recognized the sagacious and true
hearted man who has been my constant friend and protector
from the first year of my ostracism. To you, I need not call
his name."

"No, but how came he and his men there?"

"Why it seems, as I afterwards gathered from him by
piecemeal, that a smart battle had been fought that afternoon
up near the Narrows of East Bay, between a company of
Plymouth troops, who had boldly penetrated into the heart
of Queen Wetamoo's dominions, and a band of her warriors,
that had pursued them to the shore, where, after making a
desperate stand, they were taken off by the same vessel whose

appearance had puzzled me as she came so near us in the offing. And King Philip, who, with his warriors, was waiting the result in the vicinity, having been informed by runners of the unexpected escape of the intruders, and supposing they would be landed somewhere on the opposite shore, had crossed over with part of his force in canoes, at the Narrows above, to intercept them; when on seeing the vessel on the move down the Bay, he kept pace with her, stationing men at intervals along the shore, while he with a select band proceeded on till he witnessed from a neighboring projection their escape into the open sea, as well as the singular event, attending our vessel, by which I and my companion were brought to land."

"We heard of that battle here yesterday, but nothing of the subsequent movements of King Philip, which you have named. It was lucky for his opponents, that they had not been landed as he expected, else they must have fallen into his hands."

"Doubtless they would, but I would like to know who are that company; and especially the man who commanded them with such evident fearlessness and fortune?"

They are a company of hardy young woodsmen, who, on the first alarm, all promptly volunteered to serve under their equally young commander, Captain Willis, who, though acting with his men in a mere voluntary capacity, not being in favor enough at the court of Plymouth to procure a commission, has yet already done more in keeping the enemy in check than all the regularly commissioned companies put together. And since this last bold exploit, the whole country is ringing with his praises."

"Aye, you interest me in the man, friend Leonard. The fact that he could not, or did not, get a commission from the bigot leaders at Plymouth, with me argues in his praise, instead of disparagement, at the very outset. But if the news of this battle was bruited, so as to reach here yesterday, as you say, then the vessel that had them on board, when she crossed our path, must have got into Newport with them that night?"

"She did, as I understood, and brought with her in tow a dismasted vessel, which was doubtless the one from which you were landed in the storm."

"It may be so,—it must be so," said the stranger musingly; yet I would like to know what course this young leader then took with his band,—did you learn?"

"Yes,—they were about to take to the woods to scour the coast opposite to the battle-ground the day before, suspecting, probably, the Indians would come over as you say they did,— but learning ——"

"That may have been their object; and they may have had another. The indications still puzzle me. · But they changed their purpose, you were about to say?"

"Yes,—learning that a body of Indians were threatening Dartmouth, they came up in boats, and, forgetting the fa-tigues and dangers they had gone through the day and night before, pushed on vigorously at once for that place, which, it was thought, they would reach considerably in advance of the regular companies, who had commenced moving for the same destination round by the roads, that morning."

"Doubtless they will, if they took woodmen's direct cour-ses, and their leader is what you describe him,—Willis,—you are sure this young leader's name is?"

"Aye, Vane Willis is his name."

"I have learned something about him this trip, but never saw him, as he has come on to the stage of action since I was abroad in the colonies. And from what I have gathered from you, and what I noticed of Metacom's evident anxiety, at least to keep trace of his movements, I should deem him a person who must soon be conspicuous in the contest. And I should not be surprised if he and Metacom were hereafter to be known as the two great heroes of the war. Yet would to Heaven there had been no occasion for displays of courage, and warlike skill on the part of either. And had justice and honesty prevailed at the court of Plymouth, instead of bigotry and wrong, there would have been none; for you and I know, Leonard, that this war has been most unnecessarily,—most wickedly provoked."

" I may have opinions which it were wiser to entertain in silence than openly express, especially if I would live here in peace, with my own race, while declining to join them in a war upon another race, who have never injured me or mine. This luckless war has placed me in a painful position. This you will the more readily feel, since you, yourself, are brought . by the same means, as you have already intimated, into a situation of equal, if not greater difficulties."

" Greater,—far greater. To take up arms against the men of my own blood, though hunted by them like a wild beast, is what I cannot do; and to take up arms against the red men, who have so long protected and concealed me, is what I *will* not do. To go and reside among the former, is but to court the doom they have hung over me : while to remain among the latter and be found with them, as the chances of war will constantly make me liable to be, can result no better. It is a perplexing strait. And it was the object of consulting you on the matter, and replenishing my purse a little, which now brought me here."

" The last named of your wishes can speedily be complied with ; and while attending to it, as I had better do at once, I will be considering the other. Give us your leathern pouch. How much will you take this time ?"

" Not a great quantity. I don't want to be cumbered with over a pound in weight, and a good share of that in the smaller coins, if you please."

Taking the capacious purse of dressed deer-skin which the stranger now drew forth and handed him, Leonard descended to the cellar, and, proceeding to a dark and distant corner, raised one of the broad flagstones of the flooring on to its side against the wall. Beneath this lay a thinner flat stone, which he also raised, and disclosed a small, rusty, iron chest, sitting in a concealed vault below, but little more than sufficient to contain it. Unlocking the chest, which appeared to be about half filled with various kinds of English and Dutch coins, he selected the required kinds and quantity, carefully made all fast, returned, and handed the purse to the stranger, who, while concealing it beneath his dress, asked—

"The deposit holds out yet, does it, Leonard?"

"Oh, yes—not more than half exhausted, probably."

"So much the better. With my late glimpses of altered prospects, my thoughts begin to go for economizing my fund, which before I cared nothing for. But now for the other part of my business. What would you advise?"

"I hardly know, unless you go beyond the limits of this wretched warfare, to some southern settlement, where you could not be identified by any body."

"That were doubtless advisable, but for the necessity of my being now often in this part of the country to receive and answer the letters passing under cover between me and my secret agent abroad. Still, I would be in a place of safety; for though, six months ago, I would scarcely turn on my heel to save my life, yet now I begin to feel I have something to live for."

"Then you feel confident of success there?"

"I am assured I may do so."

"That is the main thing. But, should that object be accomplished, will you then have the means of effecting the restoration of your rights here?"

"Aye—that was what I meant when hinting about the

discoveries I had made in my journey. I found and took into possession papers which I feared had been lost or purloined, and which, I think, cannot fail to establish the right and bring terrible retribution for the wrong. Ah! the traitor robber little thinks he is now standing on a mine which will soon explode beneath his feet."

At this stage of the conversation, the door was gently pushéd open, and a tall, stately figure, dressed in the usual garb of a sailor, noiselessly glided into the room without word or ceremony. As the rays of the dimly burning candle, which had been lighted for the little business transaction just narrated, fell on his shapely features, which, by some application to the skin, had been brought to the hue of the white man, he would readily have been taken by ordinary observers—unless something peculiar about his deportment had betrayed him—for a stout, good-looking seaman. Carefully closing the door behind him, he stood a moment and met the inquiring glances of Leonard and his guest with a knowing smile, when he advanced, and laying his hand on the shoulder of the latter, quietly and in a low tone remarked—

"All done you wished—all right—all safe, Crocker."

"Thank you, Metacom," replied the latter. "You have done me a service. Let me pay you some money this time?"

"No," promptly responded the chief, with a quick, repellent gesture. "No; keep that to make the white man do good for you, Crocker," he added, withdrawing his hand; and laying it, in turn, on Leonard's shoulder, smilingly asked—

"Leonard is well? The Indians have not killed him yet?"

"No, Metacom," replied the other with the air of one about to qualify his answer. "Killed any of your family?" persisted the chief in the same significant tone and manner. "Killed any of the name of Leonard ?   Touched so much as one hair of their heads, ever ?"

" No," rejoined Leonard, " I have not feared that—it is not that."

" No," pursued Metacom, with emphasis—" no, nor ever will—Leonards always safe, though every other white man of the colony die, and every other house burn, *they* all safe, their houses and property safe always from the red man, who never makes war on those that use him well."

" I know your good will towards me and mine, Metacom," said the other, kindly; " but why, oh why, would you come here at such a time as this ?"

" I came to tell you what I just say, that you are safe," replied the chief, earnestly, " safer than the governor in his house at Plymouth ; because I feared they would make you believe you were in danger, and so lead you to do something to anger my people."

" I hope they will not drive me to that," responded the other, in a deprecating tone ; " but they begin to look coldly on me, because I will not join them in throwing all the blame of the war on you.   And they seem to expect I should assist them in hunting you down, or informing where you may be found.   Did you know they have offered a large money reward to any who shall take or kill you ?"

" Ah !" exclaimed Metacom, starting and recoiling a step, but quickly recovering.   " Ah, that's so.   Well," he continued, with a slightly sardonic laugh, while he bent a keen, searching look upon the face of the other—" well, does Leonard want money ?   If he does, Metacom is here, and his heart would make him weak as a child, if his friend Leonard should put out a hand to take him."

" I shall never try to make you a prisoner, or assist others to do it, Metacom," said Leonard, touched by the visible emotion which the other exhibited in his last remark.

"Leonard can shoot Metacom then, if he desire not to make him prisoner," resumed the hunted chief, in the same mingled tone of melting and reproach. "Metacom will wait till you go to the shop for a gun. Your people make it right if no reward—if any Indian be found without gun, and peaceable, your people make it all right to kill him. The court of Plymouth make fine five shillings for white man to shoot a gun at a rabbit, deer, bear, and everything but wolf and Indian; so all right Leonard, Metacom will wait."*

"O Metacom! Metacom!" exclaimed. Leonard, with increasing emotion and distress, "how you wrong me! But you don't mean it; for you don't understand why I spoke of the reward. I named it because the white men are on the watch for you. And if they discover that you come here, they will call me a traitor for harboring you, and punish me for not betraying you. So, by coming here, you not only endanger your own life, but make me liable to great trouble. O Metacom, cannot this war, which is so painful to me, be brought to an end? Can you not yet listen to proposals for peace?"

"Listen to proposals of peace!" exclaimed the chief, his eyes flashing, and his nostrils distending at the painful thoughts and associations which the unexpected question evoked from the depths of his embittered soul—"listen to new proposals of peace from the court of Plymouth! Has not Metacom been listening for years to their proposals of peace, but to be mocked by treaties made purpose for white man to break, and only for red man to keep? These are the

---

*Soon after the commencement of this war, the court of Plymouth issued the following curious ordinance, which we copy verbatim et literatim from their records—

"It is ordered by the Court that whosouer shall shoot off any gun on any nessarie occation, or att any game whatsouer, except att an Indian or a woolfe, shall forfeite five shillings for any such shot, till further libertie be giuen."

19

only treaties *they* want—the only treaties Metacom ever get. The only peace *they* will have is the peace that gives them to make slaves of the red men. But the Great Spirit never make red men to be slaves and live. Then no peace—no, never, Leonard, till your God make over white man to be honest as Indian—till white man be ready to call Indian brother. Then peace between white men and red men—easy made, easy kept. From the great lakes to the sea, all peace—peace everywhere the sun shines down on the two peoples, then wanting of each other no more than they ready to do or give themselves."

"I could wish I were better able to gainsay the truth of much of what you assert, Metacom," responded Leonard, after a thoughtful pause; "but, as good a cause of war as you may suppose you have, I don't see how you can expect long to maintain your ground against the troops of the colonies, now all united to crush you. *They* are paid and regularly kept supplied with provisions; so that their armies can be kept constantly in the field. Your men have no pay, and no certain supplies. They have already driven you from Montaup, and destroyed all your growing corn. How then can you keep your warriors together after the warm weather is over?"

"Metacom has an answer. When the Plymouth troops destroyed all our much and 'beautiful corn at Montaup, and thought to starve our people, so that our warriors could not be kept together to trouble them, they forgot that just so much of Metacom's corn as they destroyed this summer, must come out of their own villages next winter to feed his people, and they will be very lucky if they see no more trouble than the loss of their corn when his warriors come to get it. They forgot too, that the red warriors have no need to be kept together, like their own, to make them the worst trouble. They forgot how they have some time heard the lone, still going wolf, when he find the great game, raise his long howl to the sky, and every hill top and dark swamp, far away round send back the hungry answer cry of the scattered troop of his swift footed brothers, telling him how quick they will be there to help him. They forgot this; and more, they forgot there is not a beast in the forest from which the red man refuses to take a lesson of wisdom."

"Your words have a dark and terrible meaning, Metacom," said the other shuddering. "God avert the calamities they foreshadow. But suppose," he continued, reverting to the persuasive argument on which he had ventured, to see if he could not turn the proud chief from his fearful purposes—"But suppose you should triumph—even to the extent of desolating the country, do you not know that King James would never consent to lose his colonies here, but would send over large armies, which must soon overpower and destroy your people?"

"Never!" exclaimed the immovable chief, drawing himself up to his full height, and raising his hand as if to invoke the Great Spirit to attest his terrible resolution—"never! While the great wilderness from here to the setting sun has cave or rocky den left to hide the wolf or the bear, or tangled swamp to make a home for the panther, never will the red man tamely yield to the rule of the white man, but retreat from cave to cave and swamp to swamp, fighting for his home and for his freedom as he goes; for he has learned the bitter lesson that to yield is to be a slave. Our language has no word that means 'slave,' Leonard.* We never dreamed there could be one till we saw the white man."

"Then your people, I fear, must eventually perish from the land," rejoined Leonard with a sigh.

"It is well," said the chief. "The Wampanoog at least can die no better."

---

* It is said to be a remarkable fact that none of the dialects of the original Indian language contained a word signifying a slave.

As Leonard was about to respond, a sudden start of the chief, with a hasty gesture of Crocker, as if to impose silence, arrested his attention; when, after a pause, he turned to them and in an undertone said—

"What is it?—What do you think you hear, that disturbs you?"

"He thinks he heard footsteps round the house; and if I err not greatly, I heard the same," replied Crocker, with an uneasy look; while the chief kept silent, with his head dropped in the attitude of intense listening.

"It may be my boys not abed yet," suggested Leonard, though careful to extinguish the candle.

"No—it is no boys make that," quickly returned the chief. "No, nor Indian; but the steps of white men .when they have design. Do they mean me, or you, Crocker?"

"Me, doubtless, I think," answered the latter. "There are those feeling a keener interest in my destruction, than any in yours, and I fear my secret excursion may in some way have given them the means of identifying and so tracing me to this place. Nobody would dream of your being here at this time, or would have detected you in that guise had they seen you on the way."

"Crocker is right," responded the other; "but he shall not be left alone to die, or be taken, while Metacom has a well arm that can be lifted to save him."

"Thank you, Metacom," responded Crocker, warmly. "I may need your help. But how many does your ear tell you there are of them?"

"May be half-dozen near the house, and may be some more keeping back little way," was the reply.

"What course do you think they will be likely to take?" asked the former, anxiously.

"Think they already got station round the house, and waiting now for signal to rush in," answered the latter.

" Then it were my lesser risk to anticipate their intention, by trying to break through their ring and escape to the woods," promptly said Crocker.

The whispered consultation that now ensued between these two brave and high-souled, but unrelentingly persecuted men, whom circumstances, as diverse as were the races from which they came, had thus brought together in the closest bonds of sympathy and friendship, speedily resulted in the arrangement that they both, in the first instance, should only show and use the heavy oaken staffs which they had brought there and set aside as they entered the house. But should they themselves be assaulted with the more murderous weapons, then the knives and pistols which they carried concealed beneath their dresses should be used with all the effect which cool heads and practised hands could give to them. It was agreed, also, that Crocker, as he had before intimated, should be the first to issue from the house, and then do his best to break through the ranks of whatever assailing foes he might encounter in his path, while Metacom should follow close enough in the rear to be ready for any needed rescue. And having thus settled the details of their hasty arrangement, and agreed on a place of meeting at the border of the neighboring forest, in case they became separated in the expected affray, the former noiselessly took his position by the side of the door, which he had carefully opened to favor a quick sally, and stood a few minutes cautiously peering out, and settling for himself the best mode of egress, and the direction then to be taken promising the best facilities for an escape. Presently, however, he shot out like an arrow into the dimly seen space forming the broad, open yard round the buildings, and glided stealthily but rapidly forward towards the highway, about a dozen rods from the door from which he had made his sudden exit. But he had not proceeded half that distance before the alarm was given, and the sharp cries of " *Look out*

there! he is escaping! seize him! seize him!" rang out on the
stillness of the night; and the next instant a half-dozen dark
forms, leaping out from their hiding-places round the house,
were seen swiftly converging into line and bounding forward
in hot pursuit of the fugitive. The latter, however, having
now gained the highway, and putting himself to his utmost
speed, seemed in a fair way of distancing his pursuers, when
another cry of *"Head him! there he comes! head him, Dick!"*
was raised from behind him; and peering forward, he discerned a man advancing, with flurried motions, directly in his
path, and hastily handling some kind of a musket, with the
evident intent of shooting him down on a nearer approach.
With a few rapid feints to confuse the new assailant, and prevent him from getting any certain aim, the now doubly beset
fugitive sprang upon him with the suddenness of a tiger,
knocked down the threatening weapon with one blow of his
cudgel, and with another laid its owner sprawling upon the
earth. But the delay thus occasioned gave his pursuers in
the rear an advantage, which brought them to his back before
he could turn to face or elude them; and the next instant the
whole gang were upon him, and, in spite of all his desperate
efforts to free himself, fast bearing him to the ground, when
suddenly, groan after groan, mingled with cries of surprise
and alarm, burst in rapid succession from their lips. The
avenger, in the shape of the strong-armed chief, was at their
heels, bringing down upon their unguarded heads and limbs a
shower of blows so quick and powerful, that, before they could
recover from their surprise, seize the guns they had dropped
in the *melee*, and put themselves on the defensive, every man
of them was too much disabled or alarmed to offer resistance;
and they all fled, limping and howling with pain and rage,
away from the spot, leaving their arms as a welcome trophy
to the gallant and true-hearted chief, who had so adroitly won
them while effecting the more important object of rescuing

his friend from the grasp of a despicable band of kidnappers.

But who were those kidnappers, who had thus attempted to
seize or slay their intended victim without show of right or
authority, and who could, only by the most untiring efforts
of a secret espionage, have discovered and traced him to
this place through his strangely varied journey by sea and
land, and that, too, as was evident, under a deep disguise ?
Aye, who were they, and by whom and for what dark purpose
instigated ?   The developments of next chapter may furnish
clues, perhaps, to the answers of some of the questions, at
least, which the reader will here very naturally join us in
asking.

CHAPTER XVI.

" Some men are what they name not to themselves,
And trust not to each other."

WHILE the mysterious occurrence narrated at the close of the last chapter was taking place, a scene of a more quiet, but no less significant character was in progress at a small, deserted house, on the road a few miles to the eastward.

In the yard of that lone tenement, on the evening in question, might have been seen through the hour of twilight, a solitary man, in whose peculiar, fat, stumpy figure, nervous, waddling gait, and quick, uneasy motions, no one, who had ever seen him, need have failed to recognize one of the most prominent personages of the fore part of our story, the noted Deacon Mudgridge of Plymouth. He was restlessly pacing forward and backward, with an occasional anxious glance up the road westward, while his moving lips and pantomimic gestures showed the passing of unspoken thoughts that seemed laboring for utterance. And at length those thoughts, with their accompanying anxieties, becoming apparently too intense to be longer repressed, found vent in broken soliloquy :—

" The loitering knaves, why don't they come, or some one of them, to report to me ? It is time they had done something. I doubt me whether they are all, put together, equal to that old praying Wampanoog. Ah, that was rare luck !— luck ? It must be Providence that sent him to me, and I think I can safely take the sending as heavenly sanction of the enterprise I've now put my hand to—yea, rare luck, I do declare, to have thus lit on such a God sent instrument, who, peradventure, was the only one in the whole country, who had seen and known this *man of sin* both among the whites and Indians! Rare luck, likewise, that the sharp-eyed heathen discovered the game embarking, and learned his destination to Newport, and so exactly conjectured what course he would take after landing; and rarer still to have hit on his trail, and dog him to that place so near where he had advised my rendezvous. And what a marvelous swift runner he must be to have come so quick to Plymouth, to notify me of his discovery—then speed to Staunton river, follow up his game to the cage—hie here to notify me, and then back with my men for the capture—and all in time!

"Why, he would surpass the Amalekite runner that brought the news of the death of his great enemy to David. But I will not serve him as David did that runner. No, I will pay him well, if we succeed. Succeed? Why we must succeed. Could anything but Providence have so singularly brought about the discovering and the tracing out of the heaven offending wretch, who was doubtless moved by the same power to come abroad from his lurking places in order that he might be destroyed? And shall I, a chosen leader of the church, with the sword of justice, as it were, put in my hand to execute its God-suggested judgments—shall I hesitate to act on such plain indications of duty? Who am I, that I should, by timid doubtings, and refusing to act, thus in effect thwart the will of heaven?

"But the private motives thereto moving, they will say— 'Who said that?' Sathan! Thou shalt not baffle me by starting such cowardly misgivings! And suppose I had private interest, am I who have been such an arm of sufficiency in building up our Israel, am I to receive no favorings in the things pertaining to private interests —no reward for such continued holy labors, I should like to know? Again, is it not solemn duty to lend ourselves as instruments, on proper indications given, as in this case, to assist in the overthrow of the apostle of the church's enemies? I tell you, John Mudgridge, you are justified—nay, praise-worthy, in moving in this matter thus connected with the temporal and spiritual interests of God's heritage, and not guilty! Guilty? Who said that too? Sathan, once more I tell thee, avaunt! Get thee behind me, foul, meddling fiend!

"Yea, verily I am doing a good thing. Thus I overcome all Sathan-suggested doubts and temptations. So *that* is all settled. And the thing itself whereof I have been thus foolishly doubting, must be settled by this time, I think. Yet it is strange they don't come,—not all, and with him, but one first to report what is done; for Dick Swain knows, if the rest don't, that I would not have him brought here to confront me, but be dispatched on the way by gun-shot, when showing signs of resistance as it were, or escaping. But I hear no gun,—perchance, it has been silent knife-work,—or perchance they have delivered him over bound, to my trusty Wampanoog to be taken into the forest to be dealt with. They will doubtless be here soon, now,—Hark! Wasn't there sounds of footsteps? Yea,—but coming in the wrong direction,—What does that mean? Who can it be? Can that be Dummer, I begin to discern loping along hitherward in the dark? Why, I thought I had put him on a mission that would have detained him all night,—I am most sorry I brought him along with me,—yet it seemed expedient to have him near, so that, in case of any stir or questioning, his presence or accompanying, might be made to throw a sort of sanction over the affair and I think I can manage it, yet, to gain the good of his coming and avoid the evil."

And the desperate hypocrite at once checked the speed of his hurried walk, smoothed his rigid brow, gave a gentle hum,

by way of reducing his harsh tones to pious mildness of voice,
and, as the Shadow came up, cheerily exclaimed,
"Ah! Dummer, is that you? Peace be with thee, my
brother,—What tidings from the army?"

"Nothing adverse, I think, revered Deacon. In fact I
left them all, both officers and men, in just that condition of
feeling, methought, which so savors of godliness and saving
faith as to invite down the needed blessing, and make them
mighty to prevail over the heathen hosts of darkness that are
so threateningly beleagureing our chosen people."

"It truly rejoiceth me to hear your words of faith and encouragement, brother Dummer. I doubt me not,—nor did I
when I proposed your coming here, nor when I especially
urged you this morning to repair to the army,—I doubt me
not, I say, that you have been a favored instrument in greatly
strengthening this temporal arm of our defence."

"I thank you, Deacon, for your confidence in my faith and
acceptableness in intercession. And I trust I may truly say
that my mission has not been a vain one."

"You were well received by the army, then?"

"Aye,—as a humble, service-seeking servant and representative of a prayerful church should be, Deacon."

"And you attended divine service before the troops, and
offered up for their success some of those able outpourings of
prayer which are making you, I may say without flattery,
brother Dummer, a burning light in our church?"

"I did, Deacon, I *did*, I may say safely, I *did* feel, on the
occasion, an uncommon power of prayer on me,—yea, I wres-
tled mightily in calling down the blessing, and truly felt that
I had prevailed, even to the overcoming of the untoward affair that had turned up at the outset to dampen my faith."

"Untoward affair! What was that, my prayerful brother?"

"It was this, and I don't know when I have been so excrcised to keep from crying aloud in holy deprecation,—it was this, Deacon Mudgridge; soon after I came up with the army, which had halted for their mid-day meal, and by kindly permission, was on the point of opening the services, a messenger came post haste to hurry on the troops, affirming that the heathen host had already assailed the threatened village of Dartmouth. But our worthy and considerate General Cudworth wisely decided to delay for the proposed religious exercises, aptly remarking that *prayer and provender hinder no man.* And all the troops but one company reverently tarried."

"All but one company? Why not all? What company was that, who could be so perverse and irreverent as to refuse to tarry to become partakers in such a precious privilege?"

"It was, as you might expect, that froward Captain Mosely, of the Massachusetts volunteers, the same that bearded the authorities at Plymouth a short time ago, and protected that audacious young heretic, called Vane Willis; and his conduct now was equally forward and offensive; for no sooner had the general, nathless the message just received, made known his decision not to move till after service, than he broke out into a terrible passion, and profanely swore he would not tarry one instant for prayer or anything else; when loudly calling on his company to follow, they all rushed disorderly away from the spot, with the beating of drums and the noise of shouting, to the great surprise and offense of every godly-minded man in the army. For myself, I was shocked and scandalized, and still cannot but feel deep concern, Deacon Mudgridge, lest the presence and connection of such men as the two I have just named with our army, will bring down displeasure upon us, and lead to the withholding of the blessing."

"And well may you feel concern in the matter, brother

Dummer—I have agonized and agonized over our remissness of duty, in not purging the land of such heaven-offending misdoers as you have named. But *they* are not the *only* ones, whose suffered existence is keeping back the blessings we should otherwise receive. There is one, abroad in the colony, lurking in disguise, so enormously apostate, heretic, and traitorous, that I cannot but tremble for the land that is tolerating his curse-invoking presence."

" You startle me, Deacon, and the more, as I know you are never prone to speak without good warrant. Who, and where is he ?"

" As a keeper of state secrets, I may not disclose his name, if, indeed, he has any whereby he would be now known in the colony; but we may well call him, as we do, the *Man of Sin*. For years, he has been lurking in obscure and remote haunts among the red heathen, in the wilderness, teaching them his abominations, and instigating them to their present warfare against the chosen. And it was supposed he was out of the reach of earthly justice. But Providence thereunto inciting, doubtless, to the end of punishment, he has recently ventured abroad, been detected, and traced to one of his secret calling places, in this section, by a shrewd praying Indian, who luckily coming along after you left us, and while I was about to proceed to Taunton to strengthen the leaders of the church there, in -fulfilment of my mission, gave us the information. Whereupon my guards, fired with holy zeal, and taking the Indian for a guide, started off in pursuit, and I am now every minute expecting their return."

" You surprise and rejoice me, Deacon Mudgridge. How providential that the news came while you were here !"

" I could not but think so myself, nathless certain doubts, the suggestions of the Vile Deceiver, it may be, crossed my mind, whether it was strictly my province to act, lest it be said I was taking justice and judgment out of the hands of the proper authorities; still I could not but deem there was a duty for me to perform."

"Of a verity there was, and if you were troubled thus with doubts, they must have been, indeed, the promptings of Sathana, ever so ready to turn the faithful from duty."

"Then you would have advised and sanctioned the action I took in the matter?"

"Yea, surely, I would—nay, I would have esteemed myself favored and privileged to have become a helper in the God-bidden service."

"I am truly glad to thus receive your confirming opinions. You have greatly strengthened me, brother Dummer, and I now feel I was but doing an unavoidable and required duty—I feel—stay—what was that? Groans and outcries, with the sounds of coming feet! It must be them, but what can have happened?"

The hireling gang of his unscrupulous tools were indeed approaching, but they were coming to report far different results, and show themselves in a far different plight from what he had anticipated. With great agitation and fierce, incoherent mumblings, he rushed forward a few rods, hurriedly bidding the confounded and frightened Dummer to remain where he was, and then stopped short and began to listen. Presently a fresh and nearer outburst of groans, mingled with imprecations, and expressions indicating lively fears of pursuit, assailed his ears. And the next moment, the balked and crippled band came hurriedly limping and staggering along in wild disorder to the spot, one holding a bruised and nearly broken arm, one dragging a disabled leg, and another tightly pressing with both hands a gashed and bloody head.

"What is all this?" hastily demanded the Deacon, in tones trembling with surpressed agitation. "Where is he? that is, where is the prisoner—What have you done with him? Why, don't ye speak? Dick Swain? Which is Dick Swain?

That! Dick, what is the matter?—what has happened, Dick?"

" Enough !" fiercely groaned the discomfited and smarting minion, wiping away the blood trickling from his smitten forhead—"in the name of all the furies in Tophet, plenty enough has happened! Curse on the hour I undertook this blamed business! I have got my death wound by it. Oh! Oh!"

" That is no answer," persisted the flurried Deacon. "What has befel? Where is the accursed man you went after?"

" Gone back to his place or sunk into the earth," responded Dick recovering a little composure. " That man was no man, but Sathan himself, or one in league with him, or he couldn't have escaped out of our hands in that strange way."

" Escaped out of your hands?" fiercely cried the former. " Did you get him into your hands, and then let him escape without shooting him down?"

" Yea, but could'nt help it, Deacon," deprecatingly replied Dick, cowing beneath the fierce manner of the other. " Old Miles Standish himself had been at fault by coping with such devilish agencies, and when you have heard all, you will say so yourself, Deacon Mudgridge.

He then proceeded with an exaggerated account of " the attempted seizure of the mysterious stranger, at the Leonard Establishment, and the gallant rescue effected by the disguised chief, already related; described the strange, unearthly appearance of the man, when pointed out as the one, by the Indian guide, and seen through the window standing near the light, talking to some unseen person in the room—of the stationing of the men behind different objects round the house, and of himself, with cocked musket, in the road beyond —of the sudden and unnatural swiftness with which the fugitive burst from the house, passed through the line of the surprised liers in wait, and came on towards him in the road, dodging and doubling along like some great serpent running erect on the tail, and with such amazing quickness as to make it impossible to get any aim, and finally, of the unaccountable manner by which he himself had been invisibly approached and struck senseless to the earth. And one of the men, who seemed equally troubled by smarting wounds and exercised by superstitious apprehensions, then took up the narrative and set forth, in vivid colors, the prompt giving chase, and the desperate grappling of the fugitive requiring all their united exertions to hold him, and finally the sudden apparition of something or somebody in the shape of a big sailor, who all at once stood at their heels, as if let down by some invisible winged devil, and who instantly poured upon their unguarded persons such a shower of murderous blows, that they were compelled to relinquish their grasp and scatter to save their lives, as they all did while having the mortification of seeing the fugitive and his questionable rescuer escape to the woods.

"But where is the Indian?" sharply demanded the Deacon who seemed far less disturbed at either the singular apprehensions of his minions, or their alleged dangerous wounds, than at the strange and unexpected failure of the great object in view—"Where is the Indian guide that he don't come with the rest of you?"

"Gone back and still hanging round there, I suppose," answered Dick lugubriously. "After assisting the feeblest of us wounded ones along a piece of the way here, he, though hurt himself in the affray, went back to see, as he said, if he could not trail the unnatural enemy, or, at least ascertain the course they took."

"Ah, who knows but peradventure the thing will turn out right yet," eagerly responded the Deacon, still desperately intent on accomplishing his dark purpose. "That friendly Wampanoog is a fellow of exceeding craft and trust-worthiness; and I can scarce doubt me, but he will again kennel

the game, so that we can come on him unawares and destroy
him, which, inasmuch as he has resisted, and attempted to
take life, will be in the eyes of all, an indubitably lawful act
for any one of us to perform."

"Now prithee, Deacon Mudgridge," rejoined the former in
a tone of deprecation, evidently not at all relishing the thought
of renewing the pursuit as hinted by the other,—"prithee,
consider our disabled and suffering condition, and the mortal
peril we have just escaped, so far as to reach this place, but
which I greatly fear me may not yet be over for us even
here."

"Peril here?" said the other starting, and now, for the
first time, exhibiting signs of relaxing from his blood-hound
intent, at this suggestion of a personal danger,—"peril here?
What peril? What can you mean, Dick? Who is to come
here to beset us? Our brave troops have just scoured the
forests, all round this region, and driven the hostile heathen
to a distance. And touching the matter in hand,—this godless son of Belial and his confederate, why, according to your
own story, there were but two of them."

"True, if you call them mere men," responded Dick, in a
doubtful, hesitating tone; "but such men! I opine they
were *Legion*, though assisting for the most part invisibly.
Then they may have carnal outlying confederates. I expected, every step of the way, in our painful dragging of ourselves hither, to have had them again light down on us."

"So did I," said another of the obviously fear-stricken band.
"The solemn truth is, the whole thing is too uncommon and
devilish appearing, not to give us good reason to have a fearful looking for something out of the way and terrible, if we
tarry here much longer."

Each of the rest of the band, then, in turn, added confirming opinions, and manifested their anxiety to get away from
so near a vicinity to the scene of their discomfiture. And
20

last, the Shadow, who had drawn near and been listening to the dialogue, and its strange development, now crowded forward toward the silent but uneasy Deacon, and, with a perceptible tremor of voice, said,—

"I am not wholly without misgivings myself, I confess, in the matter of further action, nor even of abiding here to-night, so near such a dubious locality, where we have learned such questionable doings and appearances have been permitted to take place.   There is such a thing as the tempting of Providence, Deacon Mudgridge."

The Deacon was still silent : but the trepidation of his manner, and the closeness with which he followed up the rest of the company, as they continued to edge themselves along to the house till they reached and huddled round the door, plainly showed that either conscience or cowardice was fast reducing the stock of firmness, which he first affected to display, to a level with those who had more openly manifested their apprehensions.   Nor did the wild start he the next moment gave, with a sudden leap towards the door, as the sounds of footsteps reached his ear, and the form of some one dimly seen in the starlight to be approaching, caught his eye, less plainly betray the secret apprehensions that were beginning to possess him.   He quickly rallied, however, on discovering that the new comer was the missing Indian guide, and summoning a brave manner, exclaimed,—

"Ah ! our trust-worthy guide returned, it is, I perceive— I am glad he has come in so opportunely to dispel the doubtings, I trust, which, may be, we were over much prone to indulge.   Let us hear what discoveries he has made touching the matter.   Did you get trace of them, and follow them up, my red friend ?"

"Found some trail—found where they go into the woods," was the demure reply.

"But didn't you follow them up then, to discover their

lurking place for the night, which must be near ?" persisted the other.

" No go in the woods to-night—no want to—no want to stay long about there, so come here," answered the former, in a significant tone.

" Why ?" asked the Deacon, with a quick, husky voice. " Why ? Did you discover anything dubious ?"

" Don't know *dubious*," gravely answered the native ; "don't know him you say dubious. But think Wampanoog warriors there in the woods—hear Indian voice, sartain—then Wampanoog signal—know him—think they want scalps—be out soon—may be come here fore morning."

The announcement of the Wampanoog produced, as may well be supposed under the circumstances, no little commotion among his startled listeners. The Indian had, indeed, some reason for his statement. While stealthily creeping across the field, over which the escaping fugitives had passed on their way to the forest, his ear had caught the sound of Metacom's voice, and in it detected the peculiar intonations of the vocal organs of his race ; and subsequently heard the more distinct signal call of the chief, who, for some reason, had varied the place of meeting agreed on, and uttered and repeated his call to apprise his white friend of his new locality.

On this foundation, as he had not the least suspicion of the identity of the great chief with the formidable rescuer of the nearly secured object of the movement, he had not very unnaturally based his ominous conjectures ; nor was it, perhaps, any more unnatural that these conjectures, as groundless as they were, when suddenly disclosed to men already confused and intimidated at what had befel, should have struck them with all the force of an alarming truth, and instantly converted, as it did, their previous undefined fears into an absolute panic.

" The guns ! the guns !" half screamed the now really

frightened Deacon, who, in the strange perturbation that had
seized him on the arrival of his discomfited party, had not
even yet noticed that they were without arms; while the latter also, in *their* strange alarm and superstitious looking for
intangible enemies, had scarcely thought of the fact themselves. "The guns! the guns! I say. Where are the
guns?"

"Our guns! There now! O Lord!" cried Dick, stam-
mering and twisting about in his terror and confusion.
"Why—why, I thought we had told you how we lost them
all."

"Lost them?" fiercely vociferated the other, in a voice
quivering with the strangely mingling emotions of fear and
anger. "Lost them, stupid coward? How lost them?"

"Well, now," said the worse and worse confounded and
trembling minion, "I—I—don't—don't know—know I had
mine safe in hand, when I was struck down and lost my
senses; but it was gone when I came to—and the rest were
then gone too—spirited away some how, weren't they, men?"
he added, appealing to his associates.

Several mouths were at the same instant opened, in mingling jargon while attempting to confirm the strange assertions
of their comrade; but their words were the next moment
drowned in the loud, excited voice of the Shadow vehemently
ejaculating:—

"O Lord, hear and help thy servant in this his extremity.
Lord, the chosen leaders of thy church are in great strait.
The heathen enemy are encompassing us round about, and we
are in mortal peril. Help, Lord, help! Amen! And now,"
he added, in a quaking tone, "now let us flee—flee—flee,
Deacon Mudgridge—let us flee straightway."

But neither the doughty Deacon, nor any of the supple,
though in part, blinded instruments of his dark purposes,
needed any urging to adopt the course so significantly indi-

cated by the terror-smitten Shadow. And with one accord they
made a rush for the road to Plymouth, and went hurrying
and hobbling along in disorderly array on their homeward
destination; the long, lithe-limbed, and fear-impelled Shadow,
with the forward lopes of a giraffe, leading the dimly seen
way, and the obese, duck-legged Deacon, puffing and wheez-
ing like a stranded porpoise, in his desperate efforts to keep
up with the rest, bringing up the rear.

Amidst his tribulations, however, the Deacon was, at first,
sustained by the comforting thought that he should soon have
as much of an advantage over the rest of the company, in lo-
comotion, as they now manifestly had over him; for, being a
bad walker, he had come into the vicinity of the rendezvous,
where we found him, on horseback, keeping along with his
party in that manner, till within a mile or two of the place,
when he left his horse in the barn of another deserted house
on the road, and passed on with the rest, on foot, to their destination. And now, while often throwing timid glances behind
him, and struggling hard to keep from falling in the rear, he
inwardly chuckled at the thought of speedily being enabled
to turn the tables on those, who seemed to him, in his fear
and vexation, to exult in taxing his powers so severely. And
thus the pitiable wretch, agitated alike by his keen apprehensions of pursuit, and his hot wrath at his fellow fugitives for
their desertion, having forgotten that their fears were as
great as his own, and that fear, of all human emotions, is the
least capable of sympathy. Thus he strove desperately onward after the rest, till his longing eyes were at last greeted
by the dim outlines of the building still containing, as he supposed, his trusty steed, which would need only to be bitted
to be ready for mounting. He now began to slacken his
pace and breathe easier, throwing contemptuous glances after
his receding associates, and with fiercely muttered anathemas,
defiantly bidding them push along now as fast as they pleased.

But contrary to his unheeded words, and now even to his wishes, the rushing fugitives in front began to slacken their pace also; and they soon, one after another, halted in their tracks, being evidently thus brought to a stand by the sudden pause and retrograde movement of their file leader, Dummer, who, the next moment, was seen timidly peering along back towards the Deacon, as the latter was about to turn into the barn in quest of his horse.

"Why turn back your footsteps, all at once, brother Dûmmer?" at length asked the Deacon, in a tone of ironical bitterness, which he took little pains to conceal, as he perceived the other to be hesitating, and evidently at a loss how to unburthen himself of the something he appeared to have in mind—"Why not keep straightway onward as best beseemeth one showing himself so prone to lead in the retreat, and to be so unmindful of those who by reason of natural disabilities are compelled to struggle in the rear?"

"Oh, ah, yes," responded the abashed Shadow, now obviously getting an inkling of the state of the case, and feeling it incumbent on him to say something in excuse for his inadvertent neglect. "Why, I knew not but they would be looking to me to take the lead to clear the way, as it were; and then touching my coming back hither now, I did not know, as I bethought me, we were passing the place where you left the horse —I did not know but you would expect— that is, peradventure, you will not take it amiss, that I assist you in equipping the animal."

"Nay, don't trouble yourself," coldly responded the Deacon, suspecting the other's object and hurrying on to the barn. "I can do it myself."

"Yea, but it were no more than fitting," persisted the Shadow, eagerly following after. "And now I bethink me, I noted that this horse of yours is one of exceeding strength and burden-bearing capacity, and would no more mind taking

two on his back than one, and if a somewhat painfully exercised brother might ask for a favor—"

Here the unheeded speaker was cut short by successive exclamations, first, in the tones of surprise, then soon of consternation and despair bursting from the Deacon, who had
found the stable door beaten down, and anon made the
astounding discovery that his horse was missing, leaving evidence in the part of a broken halter left behind, and other
appearances, which, coupled with the known home propensi-
ties of the animal, at once convinced the amazed and troubled
owner, that the hungry and impatient brute had snapped the
tether, beat down the rickety door, clearly escaped, and was
now far on the way to Plymouth!

As terrible as was his disappointment, however, he managed to suppress any further outbreak of feeling, and, withholding, for secret reasons, any distinct announcement of his
misfortune, mutely hurried from the stable, and, gliding
stealthily forward to the road before his approach was hardly
perceived, fastened with desperate clutch on the coat-tail of
the startled Shadow, who stood like an alarmed goose, on the
nightly approach of a fox, apprehensively poking his long neck
out into the deeper darkness intervening between him and the
shadowing barn, in his anxiety to comprehend what had happened, his eager and repeated inquiries for that purpose having met with no response.

"What, Deacon—what—oh what, dear Deacon, has befel?"
blustered out the confused and freshly alarmed Shadow, the
first to speak.

"The horse is gone—broke out and cleared for home,"
replied the other, in a half surly, half desperate tone.

"The horse gone?" exclaimed the other wildly. "What
shall we do? Oh, what *shall* we do?—Lord! Lord! we again
beseech thee—confound the counsels of the pursuing enemy
—hold back the pursuit till thy servants can escape."

"Amen to that," huskily responded the Deacon. "But let us hence quickly. Thou hast marvelous foot speed, brother Dummer, wherein haply we may find the account that the runaway brute be not greatly missed. So, hie thee forward quickly to the front, and lead the way as before, inasmuch as it will throw the men as a guard, as it were, into our rear."

"Then prithee loose thy hold on me, Deacon, that I may do thy bidding more effectively," nervously expostulated the Shadow, vainly attempting to free himself.

"Nay," rejoined the pertinacious Deacon, now the bolder in his persistence as he remembered that luckily he had not betrayed to the other the secret determination he had formed that his horse should be encumbered by no one but himself in the flight. "Nay, I will not. Thou wast about to claim a seat behind me on my horse; and now thou canst not refuse to assist my more imperfect progress. But I shall not impede thee over much. Then straightway, forward, brother Dummer, nor tarry an instant longer in this exposed position, lest, while thus lingering in vain disputations, those blood thirsty sons of Belial, now perchance close on our trail, suddenly come up and destroy us."

Stopping to listen to no more of such ominous intimations, the poor, frightened Shadow began a series of desperate lunges forward, like a frantic horse jerking at a dead weight, and after a while succeeded in pulling the clumsy and shaking Deacon—still desperately grasping the now horizontal coat-tail—into a sort of steady, quickening, elephantine motion; which, by continued exertions, was at length so much increased as to enable this oddly-coupled brace of church-militant heroes to reach the coveted position in front; when, with hurrying step and renewed effort, the straggling column again pressed forward in their continued flight from the ill-omened locality.

But instead of following them further, at this time, in their
harassing panic-march through the night, we will anticipate
their arrival at their first halting place next morning, and, by
change of scene, and, in part, of actors, endeavor to bring
out the now only remaining part of this chapter of singular
adventures.

It was near eight o'clock next morning when Captain
Willis, with his company of victorious rangers, attended by
the staunch Captain Mosely, with his brave volunteers, were
seen, in their march along a road from the southeastern part
of the colony, to be drawing near the point where that road
intersected the great thoroughfare leading from Taunton to
Plymouth. Before them were marching, but without any
pretence of order, a body of one hundred and fifty unarmed
Indians, who, though prisoners, yet evinced not the slightest
disposition to escape, but seemed as unreluctantly and cheerfully pursuing their unguarded way in front as if bound on
some holiday excursion. They were the trophies of the
prompt and rapid expedition of Captain Willis—to which
allusion has already been made—to the menaced village of
Dartmouth, where, arriving at the nick of time, he rescued
the half-burned and plundered town, and, by the boldness and
vigor of his attack, had not only scattered and disheartened
the small, and, when left to themselves, not badly disposed
tribe of Dartmouth Indians, but so hotly pursued the little
band of Wampanoogs who, under the lead of Annawam,
(King Philip's great war captain,) came there to instigate the
assault, that the latter were glad to escape to their own fastnesses in a distant forest. And when this was effected, he had
soon succeeded, by menacing attitudes, feints of surrounding
them, and skillful management in obtaining and conducting
parleys with them, in inducing the warriors of the Dartmouth
tribe to surrender themselves as prisoners of war, as at length
they very cheerfully did, on the condition and sacred promise

of Captain Willis that they should be taken only to Plymouth, and there be fed, well treated, and set free at the close of the war, and as much sooner as might be deemed compatible with public safety.. And in pursuance of these terms, he had started with them the preceding afternoon; and being met on the way by Captain Mosely vigorously pushing forward to the rescue, that officer, rejoicing in his friend's success, at once decided to wheel about, and for a while, at least, unite himself with the escort.

The two captains, as was often customary with this grade of officers on their marches, had mounted some of the horses generally kept in attendance for that and other purposes, and were now riding sociably along together a little in front of the foremost of their respective companies.

" Where do you think General Cudworth and his command are by this time, Captain Mosely?" said Willis, at the point of their dialogue which we have occasion for noting.

" Hang me if I know, or much care," replied Mosely; "but probably halted again for another praying performance. I don't think much of this idea of praying those red-skinned devils into submission, unless by such prayers as are sent along with the cold lead of our muskets."

" Not that you would object to prayers on proper occasions, I suppose, Captain Mosely?"

" Be sure not. Why, even in the pressing emergency I told you about, when naming how I broke away from the rest, as we were ordered to stop to hear divine services, as they said, from a godly emissary of the church; even then, I would say to my soldiers, *Pray boys*—aye, pray boys, as much as you please, *but pray upon the run.* A right sensible fellow that St. James, who said, *Faith without works is dead.*"

" Aye—that is it—that is it. I have as little patience as you, Captain Mosely, with those do-nothing men of faith, who are so certain to be always lagging, when their prompt action is most loudly demanded. You and I will have to do most of the fighting for them, I fancy."

" That, for my part, I expect to do, while affairs are under present guidance and command, friend Willis, though I find it rather tough work to keep the old man in me down on witnessing such outrageous shilly shallying as I saw in them at the army yesterday, when, right in the face of the messenger just come to urge us forward, Granny Cudworth gave order to prolong our already too long halt, to listen to the prayers and preachments of that long, lean, holy-faced marplot from Plymouth."

" From Plymouth, said you, Mosely ? Why you describe Dummer, that mouthing zealot they call the Shadow—Deacon Mudgridge's shadow—because he is found to be a sort of echo to that power grasping personage. But the shadow is always near the substance," added the speaker, after a thoughtful pause—" May it not be, that the Deacon himself is mousing round for some secret purpose, in this section? I have latterly had, Captain Mosely, some strange suspicions about that man, wholly aside from his insufferable bigotry and public officiousness."

" Well, the last is enough for me," rejoined the blunt veteran—" quite enough—nay a little more than I could stand, as you saw, in that miserable attempt of his to get you arrested at Plymouth. I gave him a pretty loud piece of my mind then ; and if I should catch him round here for any of his mischief, he would be mighty apt to get a louder one. But look you ahead there ! How is that, Captain Willis ?" sharply added Mosely pointing forward to the Indians, the rear portion of whom were leaving the road, which here turned to the left, and were now seen to be passing directly forward into the forest on the right—" Your prisoners are scattering into the woods yonder. They are not trying to escape, are they ?"

" No," replied the other, after a quick, sharp glance for-

ward at the objects thus indicated, and then a brief pause—
"no—we are now nearly to the great road, and, between it
and us, lies a narrow point of woods, formed by this road
passing round the left extremity of the swell here in front.
And some of these hindmost Indians, doubtless happening to
remember the locality, are, according to their won't in such
cases, merely cutting across to save distance. All right, I
think, else those jogging along there in front would show signs
of complicity."

The two officers then rode unsuspectingly on some minutes
in silence; when just as they came in sight of the great road,
and the last of prisoners, who had not passed into the woods,
were wheeling into it and disappearing in the required direction,
their ears were suddenly greeted by the sounds of some unusual commotion, accompanied by the sharp, quick exclamations of various voices, as of some surprised and startled company, all proceeding from some point down the great road,
evidently near where the divided band of Indians would again
become united on their march. And the next moment, a loud,
wild outbreak of terror and alarm, in which the mingling cries
of *Help! murder! mercy,* and the tones of vehement ejaculation, were distinguishable, rose in strange chorus from the
spot.

"What in the name of Babel and Beelzebub is all that
about?" exclaimed the astonished Mosely.

"Some party in trouble,—whites evidently, and closely beset,—perhaps by our prisoners. It must be seen to instantly,"
was the calm but rapid reply of the young officer, as lashing
his horse into a gallop, and beckoning the other to follow, he
dashed furiously round the intervening point of the woods,
and, with his friend at his heels, went thundering down the
great road towards the scene of the strange, and to them still
incomprehensible outbreak. Although nothing was at first
visible to explain the mystery, yet, after speeding their course

a few hundred yards along the descending and wood-bordered
way, and reaching the level below, a sudden turn of the road
soon brought them to a small opening; when a scene, less
alarming indeed, but more singular and ludicrous than anything they could have anticipated or imagined, at once burst
upon their view.   On a grass-plat, near a cool spring, where
they had halted, stood, closely huddled together, the fleeing
party of Deacon Mudgridge, with the terror-smitten appearance
of men who suppose their last hour has come.   In the midst
of the group, was seen the gaunt, out-towering form of the
Shadow, with his face turned heavenward, his bony hands
stretched high and nervously above his head, and his whole
body convulsively rising and falling with the violence of his
emotions, as he poured forth to the resounding woods the loud
torrent of his supplications for assistance from above.   The
less excitable Deacon was making little outcry, but his
shrinking motions, the wild glaring of his pig eyes, and the
rapid working of his hard, warty visage, showed the extremity of his tribulation.   And the rest of the party, in their
various manifestations, were unmistakably showing themselves
to be equal sharers in the alarm ; while, peering from the surrounding bushes, on every side, was seen a crowding ring of
grinning Indians,—some in mock menace, poking, with the pretense of taking aim, long sticks towards the affrighted group,
some shaking their fists, some making the motions of scalping,
and all appearing to be vastly amused at the scene before
them.

The whole of this unique affair now stood explained.   After fleeing all night before their imaginary foes, the redoubta-
ble Deacon and his precious gang, a little reassured by the
appearance of daylight, and thence their further exemption from
molestation, had thrown themselves down nearly exhausted at
this inviting spot for rest and refreshment.

But they had scarcely taken a draught from the spring and

become fairly seated on the grass, before their still often repeated wary glances around them fell imperfectly on the main body of the Indian prisoners coming down the road, whom their excited apprehensions instantly converted into a formidable array of their dreaded pursuers, about to burst upon them with tomahawk and scalping knife. And starting up in wild alarm, they began to flee in the opposite direction, but were the next moment intercepted by the other division of the Indians just emerging from the woods into the road below; when supposing themselves entirely surrounded, and giving themselves up as lost, they raised the outcry we have described; while the Indians themselves, though at first surprised and doubtful, yet, with characteristic quickness of apprehension, soon read the true situation of affairs; and being, like all other Indians, thorough despisers of cowardice, they had, through the promptings of curiosity and contempt, gathered up on all sides; when some of them could not resist the waggish desire to enhance the terrors of the thus oddly besieged party by feigned tokens and menaces of violence.

A glance over the ludicrous scene, with what each had known or suspected respecting the prominent personages whom they now recognized in the terrified group before them, was sufficient, as it had been with the Indians, to apprise the two officers of the immediate cause, at least, of the alarm and outcry. And Captain Mosely, after one or two vain attempts to speak soberly, burst out into loud and prolonged peals of obstreperous laughter; while Captain Willis, whose merriment was somewhat neutralized by the suspicions which he had before intimated, and which now burst upon him afresh on seeing the Deacon here, made little or no comment, but spurring his horse forward, cried out to the Indians, who, conscious of their foolish position, were now beginning to look up apologetically towards their captor,—

"What is all this, my red friends? Why are you thus

hedging in these unarmed people? What were you thinking
to do to them?"

"O, ah! notting," replied one of the leading Indians, who,
being the best master of English among them, at once stepped
out and assumed the office of spokesman. "Notting, most
at all, Capun, only see um so scare at Indian with no gun, no
notting, no try—no want hurt um, make much tickle. So
all come up to see—have little laugh—do queer little—have
fun—that all, now, sartain, Misser Capun."

Another explosion of laughter burst from Mosely, so loud
and long as almost to make the forest shake with the reverberating clamor; when as the cachinnation at last subsided to a
sort of inward rib-shaking chuckle, Captain Willis turned
to the wondering, but now evidently much relieved objects of
the rough captain's irrepressible merriment, and said :—

"You see you have been needlessly alarmed now, don't you?
These Indians have no weapons, and not the least disposition
to offer any serious molestation to any man. They are prisoners of war whom I took yesterday near Dartmouth, and we
are now on our way with them to Plymouth, and yonder," he
added, pointing up the road where glimpses could be had of
the sight, and the heavy tread heard of the approaching companies; "and yonder are coming our strong escort."

"Now the good Lord be praised for this, our timely deliverance!" exclaimed the exulting Shadow, the first man of the
now fully reassured and overjoyed party to give utterance to
his feelings.

"A timely happening, verily," muttered the Deacon, in
suppressed tones. "We shall now have a safe escort to Plymouth, where I can be present to advise in these new matters."

"And then the victory," exultingly resumed the former.
"Ah! I felt!—I knew, when such a power of prayer and
faith fell on me yesterday at the army, I knew I had

prevailed even unto the speedy overthrowing of the heathen enemy."

"Now, by Jonah, if that ain't a good one!" roughly responded Captain Mosely, aroused by the Shadow's singular assumption of an important agency in the success of Captain Willis. "Look here, Mr. Dum—Dum—well, Dum Shadow, then—what time was it in the day, yesterday, when you made that wonder-working prayer?"

"About four o'clock in the afternoon, peradventure," replied the Shadow with an offended air. "But what had that to do with the matter?"

"About as much as your prayer had, I opine," bluntly rejoined Mosely. "The victory was obtained in the morning, and Captain Willis had been for hours, before you made that prayer, on his way hither with the prisoners, that is all."

"Why! Ah! Well, now," mumbled the Shadow, taken somewhat aback by the captain's unexpected development; but soon recovering himself continued—"But the carnal minded cannot understand the things appertaining to prayer and supplication. It is the *faith*, not the utterance of mere words, that worketh the effect. And now, I bethink me, I had the power of faith on me early that morning."

"Ah!" said Mosely, with a droll, humorous twist of his rough features. "Well, that is one way to figure it out—one that I didn't know of—that's a fact. But I can't stop to argue that point. I have other business to attend to, before I part with such wise company, as I now must, on my return to the army. And my business is with this Deacon here."

"With me?" asked the latter, with a surprised and uneasy look.

"Yes, exactly so," resumed the captain, with increasing sternness of look and tone. "Yes, and the upshot of what I have to say to your Deaconship is just this, that you are to understand that, firstly, the whole credit of rescuing Dart-

mouth and capturing these Indians belongs to Captain Willis
and his company : and, secondly, that when they surrendered
themselves, they did so on the condition, and his sacred promise of being treated and kept only as prisoners of war, to be
eventually set free—that I have endorsed that promise, and
mean to see the faith of the colony thus pledged, fully carried
out. Now, as you are said to have influence at court, which
I am sorry to believe, and as I have rather slim confidence in
your practices, I plainly tell you, that if you interfere in the
matter of these prisoners, or go to intriguing to give them any
other fate or destination than the one guaranteed them, then
you shall be made to sup sorrow, I swear to you.. Do you hear
that, sir ?"

  " Go to now," exclaimed the Deacon, with the confused
and spiteful air of one whose incipient scheming has been unexpectedly detected—" Go to, now, thou froward and irreverent man ! Who thought anything about interfering in the
matter ?"

  " No one," retorted the other, defiantly—" no one but you,
I presume ; but of you, having seen a small touch of your
managings on a former occasion, I thought such things not
unlikely; hence my warning."

  -" It were an offensive impugning," responded the Deacon,
" yea, and moreover, a needless one. The court of Plymouth,
I wot, will not require to be instructed in their duty touching these heathen prisoners ; albeit they may not be over
ready to be driven, without proper advisement, into the ratify-
ing of terms imposed by those they have never commissioned
for the public service."

  " What do you mean by that, sir ?" sharply demanded Mosely,
with a look of freshly aroused suspicion. " Nobody cares for
your fling at my friend, Captain Willis, here, for he has got
far above your reach ; but the rest of it !—why, hell and furies ! is the man already beginning to scheme how to thwart

21

us? I don't know about such symptoms of wiggling. But I can't stop to dally. Remember my warning, and see that you profit by it, sir," he added, looking hard at the surly Deacon, as he wheeled his horse away to the side of Captain Willis, and after a few private words with the latter, rode away to put his company in motion on the countermarch, for which he had previously ordered them to be in readiness.

On the departure of Captain Mosely and his company, Captain Willis lost no time in starting his own oddly diversified retinue forward on their destination in the opposite direction, the prisoners being allowed, as before, to lead the way, the soldiers of his company marching in order next, and the sullen Deacon and his party, to whom but little heed was now taken either by officers or men, being left to follow as they best could in the rear. And nothing further occurring on the way to delay their progress, they all, near the close of the day, arrived safely in Plymouth; when Captain Willis, without heeding the commotion and rejoicings, which his arrival with such unexpected trophies, on all sides, produced, immediately, with his lieutenant, Noel, for a witness, waited on the governor, announced the arrival of the Indians he had captured and brought hither for safe keeping, and, particularly stating the terms on which they had surrendered, earnestly urged the justice and policy of a strict observance of the conditions by the government. He then formally delivered over the prisoners to the town guards, and, after a delay of an hour or so, to allow his men time for rest and refreshment, and himself opportunity to call on some with whom his still deferred and tantalizing hopes were associated, he again put his company on their march out of town, and on their way back to the seat of war; scarcely permitting himself to doubt, notwithstanding the misgivings of his friend Mosely, that the fate of his prisoners could possibly be otherwise than the one he had promised them, and the one they so evidently, and with such good reason, expected.

But how was this confidence and this just and reasonable expectation of the gallant and honorable young officer destined to be met and requited ? Scarcely had the inveterate Deacon allowed himself time to recover from the fatigues of his fruitless expedition, before he was found besetting the governor with his misrepresentations and miserable religious sophistries, and intriguing with the magistrates, with the object of changing the destination of the prisoners, and within one short week, news reached the astonished and deeply exasperated Captains Willis and Mosely, that the whole body of the Indian captives had been shipped, and were then far on their way to the West Indies to be sold as slaves !

Merciful heaven ! is there no way by which this black page of our early New England history can be veiled from the sight ? Must the damning record of this, and the scores of other transactions of turpitude and wrong, that have characterised our treatment of the children of the forest, forever be read and blushed over by all the succeeding generations that are destined to tread the soil of the Pilgrims ? Sons of New England ! did it ever occur to you, that in view of these things, you, too, may "tremble for your country when you reflect that God is just ?"

> " You call these red-brow'd brethren
>   The insects of an hour,
> Crushed like the noteless worm amid
>   The regions of your power ;
> Ye drive them from their fathers' lands,
>   Ye break of faith the seal,
> But can you from the court of heaven
>   Exclude their last appeal ?"

CHAPTER XVII.

"Here, old men say, the Indian magi made
   Their spells by moonlight, or beneath the shade
   That shrouds sequestered rock, or darkening glade,
     Or tangled dell;
   Here Philip came, and Minatonimo,
   And asked about their fortunes, long ago,
   As Saul to Endor, that her witch might show
     Old Samuel."

FROM the almost sickening task of depicting the frustrated machinations of the desperate Deacon, and the pitiable exhibitions of his discomfited adherents, which mainly occupied the preceding chapter, we turn to the more agreeable one of following the hunted, but a thousand times more noble men, who had so adroitly escaped the toils that had been thrown around them.

On the dispersion and headlong flight of the assailant gang of the Deacon's despicable emissaries, the disguised white stranger, whose capture and destruction was the great object of their secret expedition, at once rapidly struck out wide from the road, a furlong or two, into an adjoining pasture, and threw himself down in the covert of a small clump of bushes, to listen and prepare for any new rallying for the purposes of pursuit which might be attempted by the enemy. But his more practised rescuer and friend, having detected the presence of the traitor Wampanoog among the gang, and deeming therefore the greater caution to be necessary, followed the retreating party some distance along the road, just keeping them in view, and carefully noting their appearance, until he

became convinced that their retreat was no feint, but an
earnest and final one, at least on the part of all the white men
of the gang. He then hurried back to the scene of the affray,
hastily gathered up the abandoned muskets, and, throwing
them across his brawny shoulders with as much ease as if
they had been a light parcel of sticks, bent his steps stealthily
towards a thicket in the woods considerably more distant, and
in a more opposite direction from the course of the retreating
party, than the one which had previously been agreed on as
the place of meeting. And having reached the thicket in
question, and concealed the guns, he next commenced the
series of signal cries to which allusion has been made, rapidly
changing his place, and varying his voice so that it might be
taken for that of different persons, and at the same time cautiously drawing near the appointed rendezvous, till he had
succeeded in attracting the notice of his white friend and
of bringing him to his side.

" How is this, Metacom ?" asked the white man, doubtfully
approaching the expectant chief, who had taken position in
an open place in the woods, that he might be the more readily
recognized. " I do not find you where I expected."

" No," replied the other, " but Metacom thought he had
found reason to change the place he named."

" What was that ? What new discovery did you make to
change your mind ? "

" Why, Metacom discover, as they jump up to run there, a
deserted Wampanoog, who must be the one that dogged
Crocker to Leonard's house. The curse of Manitou light on
the traitor dog ! Metacom's knife was in his hand only one
little minute too late to reach the heart of the quick-fleeing
rascal."

" Ah ! well, that would explain the uncertain glimpse
which I caught of some one in the bushes a mile or two back,
on my way to the house. You may be right; but if so, won't

the skulking knave be returning to dog us here into the forest also, and lead on the rest to another onset?"

"No. You hear Metacom just now make Wampanoog different noises, like scattered warriors in the woods. He may be come back near enough to hear those, but quick turn and run then. Traitor always coward, and the white men all too hurt and frighten to come back ever. No—all safe now, Crocker. We better move on."

" Where?—where do you propose to have me go?"

" Metacom been thinking for his white friend. Crocker has said he must now go where red men and white men will not come together in war. Metacom has thought out such place for him."

" Without going beyond the northern colonies? Where is that place, Metacom?"

" In the great village of the Narragansets, who are not ready to join us on the war-path, but have taken our women and children, and will make safe and welcome any friend Metacom shall send there."

" But will not the colonists, in their jealousy and suspicion, send an army there also?"

"No, they think they have just made treaty with the Narragansets. They have been there with commissioners, and large band of soldiers to force such treaty as they wanted. But the chiefs and warriors all keep out of the way, so the commissioners not find any with power to make treaty; when, at last, they catch two old sachems, too lame and feeble to get away, and make them sign what they write, and then call it good treaty with the whole nation! So they not go there on that reason, nor on the better reason that Metacom will give them enough to do in other places."

" It may be so this fall; but does Metacom, who knows something how those now in rule at court get their treaties with the red men,—does Metacom feel sure, that so long as his women and children are there, the white troops will not, after his warriors have left the field for winter quarters, be sent to fall on the unguarded and defenceless villages of the Narragansets ?"

"Our brothers, the Narraganset warriors, understand all this; and though they will not fight till they are attacked, they will not long remain unguarded and denfenceless. They going to make strong home for winter, on good, dry island, in the big swamp, way down the sunset shore of the bay, ten miles from the sea, where no white troops ever get and live. And Metacom, when the fall fighting all over, will go there with his men, and help make houses and strong fortification about the island. Let Crocker take Metacom's token, go there and show it to Nanuntenoo, the brave young Sagamore, and he then find all safe and welcome. He better start when the next sun rise to light him on his long path through the woods."

"Thank you, Metacom, I think your advice must be good,— I will start, as you suggest, to-morrow morning. But where did you think to take me to-night?"

"Look yonder!" said the chief in a pensive tone, as he pointed over the tree tops of the long slope, which, beginning at the knoll on which they were standing, fell off so rapidly as to leave open a view of the low horizon in the west, where, in the clear, blue sky, the hazy form of the moon, just beginning to be edged with her slender crescent of full light, was seen sinking behind the distant mountain,—"look there ! Do you see that, Crocker?"

"Ay, the setting moon,—what has that to do with our lodging for the night?" said the other wonderingly.

"Metacom will soon tell," resumed the chief. "That the new moon,—this the first night of the new moon,—the time when our people believe the Great Spirit is ready to speak through acceptable powahs about the affairs of his red chil-

dren. And Metacom has appointment to-night to meet the old
Sagamore of Penacook, the great Powah of the North, who
kindly come all the way from his far off retreat in the mountains of Agmenticus, where he go to die in peace, that he
may tell Metacom what fate the great Manitou has marked
out for him in the war."

"But where is the place you have appointed for this meeting ?"

"At the sacred cave near Winnecunnett pond, where white
man's trail has never yet been found, to prevent the coming
of the red man's God."

"In what direction, and how far off, is this pond ?"

"Away through the forest here at the north. An hour's
fast walk, and may be we are there. Crocker is prudent and
wise, and he will not talk of what he sees—Crocker is Metacom's friend, and he shall go and stay there all night. But
Metacom must be away on his path to his warriors before
morning."

The chief said no more, but, after making a few short turns,
and glancing up through the openings in the trees overhead,
to catch glimpses of the prominent northern stars, whose
bearings on his course were to be preserved to ensure its accuracy, now boldly struck a line through the forest, and closely
followed by his white friend, glided rapidly forward in the
direction of the secluded and mysterious locality, for which he
had so hesitatingly announced himself destined. And thus,
without word or pause to vary the monotonous gloom of the
way, he swiftly threaded the silent woods, here turning aside
to avoid a rough steep, and there a tangle of windfallen trees,
but again, with wonderful exactness, ever falling into the true
line of direction—thus he ceaselessly strode onwards, for
more than an hour ; when he visibly slackened his pace, and
at length came to a stand on the brow of a small rocky bluff,
from which the beautiful sylvan lakelet of which they were

in quest, burst dimly on the view. Mutely beckoning the white man to his side, the chief pointed out over the water, and, in low, reverential accents, said to him :—

" Now listen and observe !"

They both did so, in silence, and with the closest attention. For awhile, no sound was heard save the low susurration of the light ripples of the water that were gently kissing the rocks along the shores. Presently, however, a few imperfect notes of the great northern diver, sounding as if broken or interrupted by the feathers into which he had thrust his beak, as he floated half asleep on the water, came trembling over the surface, with its far reaching thrill, from a distant part of the pond.

" Ah, that good—good omen !" hurriedly murmured the chief, who was evidently deeply impressed with the supposed sanctity of the place and the hour. " That the bird that flies so high, and sings so loud and solemn on the wing, to make music for the spirits. It's coming to rest here to-night is a good omen for Metacom and his cause. Now," he added, more directly addressing the other—" Now let Crocker look slow and careful along the shores for sign of those who were to come. *He* has seen nothing yet, but Metacom has."

The white man, while the chief stood curiously watching his motions, then slowly ran his eye round the dark borders of the forest-girt pond, and had nearly completed the circuit, when a feeble glimmering of light, coming through the dense foliage of a dark nook on the opposite shore, shot athwart his yet uncertain vision, causing him, however, involuntarily to raise his finger in the direction, and turn enquiringly to the other.

" Yes, Crocker has hit it," replied the chief, to the implied question. " That the sign, and that the right place. We both see right; but we will both now listen close for sounds there. May be we hear something that tell certain."

They then accordingly both bowed their heads close to the ground, and fell to listening intently. And in a short time, a low, confused murmur of mingling human tones, rising somewhere from the vicinity of the spot in question, came gently wafting to their ears.

"They are there!" said the chief, hastily ‚rising. "Metacom no doubt now. So he will quick prepare, and lead his friend round to the place."

With this, the chief at once proceeded—first to take off the light pack he carried on his back, next, completely to divest himself of every article of his nautical habiliments, next, carefully to wash the light coloring matter from his face and hands, and, finally, to draw forth, and don his best Indian dress and most imposing regalia.

"Now follow close—speak no word, show no sign of fear, and Metacom take care of the rest," said the chief, in a low, earnest, cautionary tone, as he now began to make his way through the dense and tangled woods along the shore, intervening · between him and this Indian Delphos, to which, with trembling expectation, he was now so nearly approaching.

After pursuing their difficult course round the borders of the pond, nearly half its circumference, they at length reached the inmost point of the dark cove, over which, from the darker woods beyond, had shot the feeble pencil of light before mentioned, when the chief paused for further reconnoisance. But before he had made any new discoveries, or decided what part of the seemingly impervious thicket, which here everywhere shot down to the water's edge, he should attempt to penetrate, to reach the place he was seeking, a strangely accoutred Indian stepped noiselessly out from a covert near at hand, and having identified the chief, and silently motioned him to follow, led the way, with many a sharp turn and intricate winding, into the dismal labyrinthian

maze before them. The direct distance to be traversed, however, was comparatively a short one; and they soon and suddenly emerged into the blinding glare of two small but freshly
replenished fires, and the next moment found themselves
standing on the border of a small, level, well smoothed circu-
lar area of ground, of about a dozen yards in diameter, beyond
which, the sacred cave and the red mystics of the forests now
occupying it, stood plainly revealed to the sight. It was a
singular spectacle, and one which could nowhere be witnessed
except in an American forest, and among its native inhabitants—the whole of it, indeed, in view of the solemn hour of
the night, the rugged wildness of the spot, closely surrounded
by projecting rocks, shaggy trees, with their dense, variform
foliage, now assuming a thousand fantastic shapes in the out-
shooting gleam of the fires, and the strange appearance of
the living figures whom the occasion had brought together,
in their outre dresses and wizard equipments—the whole
presenting a scene, of which, even Fancy herself might well
find herself at fault in the portrayal.

In the centre of the entrance of the cave, whose deep recesses were partially disclosed by the light of the fires blazing
on either side a few feet in front, sat the chief actor of the
mystic performances about to transpire, squat on a large bear
skin, in a bowed and stooping attitude, coupled with the
other usual appearances of extreme old age. His body was
enveloped in a sort of variegated mantle, composed of differ-
ently colored choice peltries, and so ample as to wrap nearly
twice around his attenuated frame, and reach from his thin,
tremulous chin, down to his richly beaded moccasins. His
head-dress, alike simple, and significant of his character as
king and conjuror, was coroniform, consisting of a band of
black wampum, closely compressing his lank, silvery locks
below, and rising into a row of sharp tooth-like points above.
This was surmounted by the stuffed and flattened skin of the

Wakon bird, the American bird of paradise, which, being deemed by the Indians, as its name indicates, peculiarly the bird of the Great Spirit, had been procured for him from the great lakes for professional purposes, and which was here made, with its profuse, long, and flowing plumage of green and gold, to over arch the crown of his head, jutting out fancifully over his ears on each side, and waving pendently over his shoulders behind. A single, loosely strung necklace of curious bones, teeth, and bird claws, hanging low over his enwrapped bosom, completed all that was peculiar or noteworthy in his outward equipment. On each side of this old high priest of the ceremonies, sat, in reverential and observant attitudes, first several of his pupilary attendants, who had assisted him on his slow and tedious journey from his distant home; and then a select few of the distinguished powahs, or panisees, as they were sometimes called, of the more immediately surrounding tribes, who had come in to witness the performance, and learn of one with whose great fame they had long been familiar. These were all no less singularly and some even more grotesquely accoutred, some with the stuffed skins of rare wild quadrupeds fitted on their heads—some with pairs of rattlesnake skins tied by the tail behind, and brought round the neck, again knotted, and the heads left dangling over the breast in front—some wearing feathered tunics of deeply contrasted colors—some breastplates or aprons, covered with strange figures, inwrought with shells and fish-bones, and all holding in their hands flattened clubs, magic wands, or consecrated drums and whistles, each marked, as were almost every article of their dresses, with curious mystic devices.

"Son of Massasoit!" exclaimed the old wizard king, at length breaking, with his shrill, cracked voice, the long, dead silence which had ensued after the Wampanoog chieftain had arrived, and fittingly presented himself, by stepping within the

marked border of the sacred circle, and then standing in the
attitude of deep reverence, "Son of Massasoit, thou didst
ask a hard thing of thy father's aged friend, when thou sent
thy runners to invite him here to consult for thee the will of
Manitou, in thy troubles with the pale faces. But Passaconaway much considered—much fasted—much dreamed ; when
he was moved to try making the long journey, and coming,
like a little, weak, tottering child, walking now small time—
resting now much time, has at last, after many days, reached
this appointed place, where he has again fasted — again
dreamed, and is now ready to begin the sacred rite ; for he
feels belief that Passaconaway, who now stands on the edge
of the spirit land, and can look back through a hundred snows
on the doings of men, will be able also to look forward into
the council lodges of the spirits, and learn what Manitou designs for Metacom and his people."

He ceased ; and slowly rising to his feet, began to take off
and cast aside, one by one, every article of his dress and
equipments ; while, at the same time, his attendants took up
the capacious bear skin, on which he had been sitting, and,
carrying it forward from the cave, carefully spread it out to
its fullest extent on the ground, in the centre of the circle ;
when they returned to the old Powah, who by this time had
denuded himself of everything but the scant apron like ap-
pendage hanging from the girdle round his waist.

They then, after joining hands and forming a half circle
around him, assisted him down the rocky offset fronting• the
cave, and, with measured steps, and a low, inarticulate chant,
led him forward between the two fires to the edge of the
spread bear skin, where they left him standing alone, and then
falling back a few steps, awaited the event in demure and expectant silence. He now turned slowly from one to the other
of the four cardinal points of the compass, pausing and gazing
steadfastly a moment at each, when he laid himself down at

full length on the consecrated skin, closed his eyes, and lay a
few minutes as motionless as the dead. He soon, however,
began to exhibit signs of life, and to fumble about him for
the borders of the skin, which he at length succeeded in
gathering over him so as to hide his whole person from view.
When this was effected, his attendants stepped forward, and,
after adjusting the skin so as to leave only his face visible,
and rolling him up as closely as possible, passed under and
around his body and legs a number of ropes, or withes of
twisted grass, the ends of which they carefully tied together.
They then hurried into the cave, brought out all their magic
implements, and resumed their places in the ring.

Another interval of silence and inaction now ensued, during
which the old Powah lay as before without the least sign of
life or motion. At length, the muscles of his face began to
twitch nervously, his lips to move, and his throat to give out
low, gurgling sounds, which very soon grew into loud mutterings of some unintelligible Indian jargon, and to which the
attendant panisees now, in corresponding keys, commenced
adding the accompaniment of their drums and whistles. And
these strange mutterings, now partially dying away, and now
bursting forth afresh, and growing fiercer and louder at each
renewal, were incessantly kept up, till they rose to the wildest
screams and vociferations, and, mingling with the increasing
din of the discordant music, made the startled forest around
ring with the infernal uproar.

The old Powah, whose contortions of face and limb had, in
the meanwhile, kept pace with this clamor, had by this time,
worked himself up to such a pitch of frenzy, that he now
frothed at the mouth, and sprang and tumbled about with
such frantic exertions as, at last, to break the bands of his
ursine shroud, and cause it to fall from his limbs; when starting up wildly, and glaring about a moment, he sunk down

utterly exhausted, and lay stretched like a dead man on the ground.

Feeling now assured that their great oracle had at length attained to what the modern professors would doubtless consider a perfect state of clairvoyance, the attending panisees at once proceeded to lift him from the earth, carry him to the cave, and place him on his bear skin recumbently against the offset at its mouth, with his face confronting the royal subject of the expected vaticination. They then seated themselves on his right hand and left, and, fixing their eyes on his pale face, patiently waited for the appearance of consciousness, or the waking of the spirit, which was to prelude the last act of the performance. And they did not have to wait any unreasonable length of time. In less than a quarter of an hour, he began to open his eyes, so far as to render the still fixed and glassy pupils discernible—then to move his lips, and, in a moment more, he articulately begun :—

"Manitou has kindly granted the vision, and the vision is for Metacom. The son of Massasoit has many enemies,— many as the pale faces in the land. They lie hid, like dangerous serpents, along all his paths, watching his coming that their bullets may drink his blood, and his head be hung up in the places where they pray and hold council. But his totem eagle is a bold and cunning bird; and the white man's bullet is never to kill him. They are mustering thick all round his swamp retreat near the homes of his fathers, but they come near him there only to leave their scalps for his keen-eyed warriors. They think they have shut him up, like a flock of helpless deer in a snow yard, easy to be taken, but he is now, when they think not, seen moving over the country for the great forests towards the setting sun, where they fear to follow him, leaving the hundred trails of his scattering warriors red with the blood of their enemies. Here all the great chiefs of the east, of the north, and of the west, are seen coming to shake hands with him, and offer him their warriors. It has now come the season of the corn harvest and the yellow leaf; and his enemies are gathering strong in the west. But he soon comes down upon them, with the long, still leaps of the panther, and the bands of his divided braves quickly fill the whole valley of the Long river with the war whoop and the shout of victory, rising over the groans and death cries of the beaten and scattered pale faces. It has now come the season of winter, and Metacom's warriors are wandering cold and hungry among the forest hills of the east, where the white men think them too feeble and few to make them more trouble, but soon find them warming themselves at the fires of the burning villages, and eating the corn and cattle they take there. And it has now come the season of the melting snows, the starting bud, and the opening flower. And the forests are swarming with the mustering tribes of red warriors, now all united, like brothers, in the wampum league, with the brave son of Massasoit for their grand Sagamore and war-chief. Their powder-horns and bullet-bags are well filled,—their knives and tomahawks are all bright and well sharpened. The frightened pale faces are every where sending out their fighting men, but only to be every where scattered and leave half their numbers dead on the field of battle. They see the long lines of the avenging red men rushing forward, with shout and war-whoop, towards their great towns and cities for the final blow; and they prepare their ships to leave the land they have stolen to be again possessed by its cheated owners. What shall save them now? See! see, Manitou has at last placed all but within the very grasp of the wronged red men, the birth-right of their fathers! But, ha!" exclaimed the old seer of the woods, whose warning tones had now risen almost into screams of triumph, but who here suddenly paused with an expression of surprise and painful disappointment,— "Ha! What is that? What means it, great Manitou? where are they now?   Where the thick array of victorious warriors a moment ago making their last rush for the prey and the prize? Where,—O where?   But it is so.   A dark cloud has settled over them.   They are nowhere to be seen!   And the vision for Metacom and the red men is shut up for ever!"

He ceased, and with all the rest, sat some minutes musing in gloomy silence; when his eyes again assumed their former dreamy, fixed stare, as if gazing on some thing beyond the material objects around him; and shortly, in subdued and melancholy accents, he resumed—

"Passaconaway can now see away beyond the cloud.   He has more vision; but the vision, this time, is for the pale faces.   From the little narrow past, he sees them spreading out, for three thousand moons, into the great wide future.   He sees them, in long thickening lines, reaching from the north to the south, fast crowding on towards the west, sweeping away the forests of the land they have seized by the right of the strongest, and plowing over the bones of the owners, who have been made to know the fate of the weakest.   They still move on, everywhere leveling the forests—everywhere building houses higher and higher, planting cities and villages thicker and thicker, and everywhere wearing garments richer and richer.   But there is a dark and guilty spot on all their garments, which will not be washed out.   It is the mark of the blood of the red men they have robbed and destroyed. And a voice, long delayed, now goes up from the graves of the wronged race to the Great Spirit, asking how long?   Manitou answers, *Not yet*.   The measure of the great crime is not full. Two thousand moons have now rolled away.   The thickening hosts of the pale faces, now become a great nation, have reached the furtherest shores of the great lakes, and the banks of the great father of rivers in the west.   But still they crowd for a thousand moons more—crowd on further into the last forests, refuges of the dwindling tribes of the red men, who

22

flee only to be again routed, or remain only to die by the
bullet or fire water—on—on they still crowd, till they at length
see the last feeble bands of the hunted victims disappearing
over the last mountains of the setting sun, soon to perish on
the shores of the great sea waters beyond. The pale faces
have now become a mighty people. They laugh at the memory
of the red man, and scornfully trample his ashes under their
feet. They carry their heads high; they boast loud of their
strength and greatness, and kick at the whole world. They
have become rich; they live in great palaces, and now wear
garments of gold. But the guilty spot is still on them all,
grown darker and deeper than before. And again the voice
goes up to the Great Spirit, asking, *How long now?* This
time Manitou returns no answer in word. But presently the
great nation of the pale faces begins every where to shake and
break to pieces; and the fifty little nations now going to make
it up, are soon seen every where marching to make bloody
war on each other. The last thousand moons have run their
courses. The cup is full. But Passaconaway can see no
more. A dark cloud—darker and more terrible than fell on
the leagued tribes of the red men, has at last fallen on them
also, and hid them from his sight. Son of Massasoit!" now
added the speaker, rousing himself from his strange revery,
if revery it could be called, and turning to Metacom, "the
visions of Passaconaway are all ended. He has no more to
say."

"It is well," responded the Wampanoog chieftain, as a
slight shade of pain and disappointment passed over his stern,
gloomy countenance. "Metacom likes it well. He is not to
die by the hand of the white man, nor till he has terribly
avenged the wrongs of himself and his people. Manitou, in
his own time, does the rest. He is content; and his arm is
now made strong for the red work he sees set before him."

To describe the remainder of this strange scene of aboriginal

mysteries, but few more words are wanting. With one accord
the company now broke from the forms and order hitherto preserved, and busily set about cooking the bounteous supply
of fresh fish and venison that had already been provided for
the occasion. Next came the feast; when the short but significant powah dance was made to conclude the wild ceremonies
of the night. After this, Metacom bestowed rich presents on
the venerated old seer of the forest, and lesser ones on each
of all the other powahs present. He then bespoke kind offices
for his white friend, hung about his neck the promised protecting tokens, and departed on his way to the distant camp
of his warriors, leaving the rest of the company to retire
within the cave to finish the night in slumber and repose.

By way of showing the probabilities which we would have
attached to the singular scene which is made to compose the
principal part of the foregoing chapter, it were well, perhaps,
before proceeding with our eventful story, to refer briefly to
the records and legends of the times, in which that scene is
represented to have occurred.

It seems to have been well ascertained, that King Philip,
about the commencement of that terrible war, which came so
near proving the destruction of the Northern Colonies, formally consulted some Indian Seer, respecting the fortunes and
result of the dubious contest; and, with his out-towering position among the red men of the North, it is not to be supposed that he would content himself with having recourse to
any but the most eminent in the land. That Passaconaway,
the aged Sagamore of Penacook, New Concord, N. H., was esteemed such, both by the Indians and white men, scarce a
doubt need be entertained. He had been perhaps a noted
powah or conjurer up, perhaps, to about the middle age;
when succeeding to the Sachemdom of the Merimac Indians,
he became an equally noted hunter and war-chief. But being
like King Philip, with whom of course he deeply sympathized,

although disarmed, and placed under a degrading surveillance by the colony of Massachusetts, he soon relinquished his government to his son, Wonolanset, and retired to the mountains of Agamenticus, in the then wilderness borders of Maine, where he died about the close of King Philip's war, nearly one hundred years old. And it was here, in his mountain seclusion, where he appeared to have resumed his old vocation with a success that threw all his former endeavors into the shade, that he performed those extraordinary feats of sorcery and vaticination, which, next to white witchcraft, made up the greatest marvels of those, and the more immediately succeeding times, and which formed the foundation of more of the wild legends of Indian necromancy than were ever before or since, perhaps, connected with the name of any other individual of that remarkable race. There is one of these legends still in preservation, in verse, which embodies some specimens of the popular traditions and opinions of the general character and supernatural powers of the old chief, and which we will here append as a fitting close of our description.

> That Sachem once to Dover came,
> From Penacook, when eve was setting in,
> With plumes his locks were dressed, his eyes shot flame!
> He struck his massy club with dreadful din,
> That oft had made the ranks of battle thin.
> Around his copper neck terrific hung
> A tied together bear and catamount skin,
> The curious fish-bones o'er his bosom swung,
> And thrice the Sachem danced, and thrice the Sachem sung.
>
> Strange man was he! 'Twas said he oft pursued
> The sable bear, and slew him in his den;
> That oft he howled through many a pathless wood,
> And many a tangled wild and poisonous fen,
> That ne'er was trod by other mortal man.
> The craggy ledge for rattlesnakes he sought,
> And choked them one by one, and then
> O'ertook the tall gray moose, as quick as thought,
> And then the mountain cat he chased, and chasing caught.

A wondrous wight, for o'er Siogee's ice,
With brindle wolves all harnessed three and three,
High seated on a sledge, made in a trice,
On Mount Agiocachook * of hickory,
He lashed and reeled, and sung right jollily;
And once upon a car of flaming fire,
The dreadful Indian shook with fear to see
The King of Penacook, his chief and sire,
Ride flaming up towards heaven, than any mountain higher."

* The old Indian name of Mount Washington.

CHAPTER XVIII.

"They woke to die 'midst flame and smoke,
And shout, and groan, and sabre stroke,
And death-shots falling thick and fast
As lightnings from the mountain cloud."

As has already been foreshadowed in the vision of the old
Indian seer described in the preceding chapter, King Philip,
in despite of the impotent attempts which General Cudworth,
at the expense of the lives of many of his troops, had made
to drive him from his swamp fastnesses on the eastern shore
of the lower Taunton; and despite, also, of the still more
futile attempt which the same sage commander next made to
surround and starve him into submission—in despite of all
these, King Philip and his warriors, laughing to scorn these
contrivances to entrap them, remained their own appointed
time, and then silently and safely transported themselves, one
dark night, on the flotilla of canoes and rafts they had prepared for the emergency, to the west side of the river, and,
before morning, had accomplished nearly half their rapid and
triumphant exodus from their old homes to the wilderness
hills of Central Massachusetts. Remaining here, however, no
longer than to afford him sufficient time to perfect his alliances
with the Connecticut tribes, and with them arrange the plans
of his contemplated fall campaign—allowing, in the meantime,
his restless warriors the pastime of destroying the frontier
village of Brookfield, and of driving back, with the loss of
nearly half their numbers, the Massachusetts Commissioners,
who, with a strong, armed escort, were approaching to attempt

to detach the Nipmucks—the bold and energetic chieftain suddenly burst down from the mountains, like a storm-cloud, into the valley of the Connecticut; and the surprised and comparatively unguarded towns of Northfield, Greenfield, Deerfield, Hatley, Hadley, and Springfield, were soon, and in rapid succession, made to feel the terrible weight of his vengeance. He had now been joined by every considerable tribe of the Indians, from the shores of the Atlantic to the distant banks of the Hudson, with the single exception of the traitorous Mohegans.* And by the wonderful celerity of his movements, his unvarying sagacity in planning his attacks, and the consummate skill of all his military combinations—never surpassed by a Schamyl or Napoleon—he soon, in spite of his rallying opponents, here rapidly concentrating from every part of New England, succeeded in wrapping that beautiful valley in fire and blood, filling it with mourning and lamentation for the perished flower of its youth and manhood, and leaving its history to be saddened by one of the bloodiest pages that ever marked the annals of an American colony.

But as the even'3 of this sanguinary campaign—which, for the next three months, unceasingly occupied nearly the whole force of the united colonies in saving the devoted valley from entire desolation—have no immediate bearing on the thread of our story, now fast approaching its development, we must be permitted, with this cursory notice, to skip over them, together with the time they occupied, in order to be allowed

---

* The Mohegans, whom the great American novelist seems to have delighted to exalt over all other tribes of Indians, were uniformly the servile adherents of the whites in all their wars with the natives, and were therefore every where branded by the red men as traitors to their race. The American people love bravery and independence of character, and perhaps they should be allowed to tickle at the treason once. so useful to them. But is that any reason why they should now any longer be asked to continue their pæans of praise over a nation of traitors?

more space for the description of the great event which was
to close this year of disaster and blood, and whose results,
while exercising as great an influence on the fortunes of the
war as those of any other that occurred in its progress, were
at the same time destined to become the turning point in
the fate and fortunes of nearly all the different personages
whose contrasted characters and varied experiences we have
been endeavoring to delineate.

Slowly and dismally broke the struggling light of the chill
December morning, as the fifteen hundred stern Puritan soldiers, who lay bivouacked round the smouldering ruins of a
block-house, situated on a western arm of Narraganset Bay,
about half way from Providence to the ocean. The united
forces of Massachusetts, Plymouth, and Connecticut colonies,
raised by prodigious exertions, and composed of the most
brave and hardy men that the whole of New England could
furnish, had reached the place the preceding evening, but
only to find the garrison-house of their appointed rendezvous
enveloped in a mass of flames, and its fated score of its inmates and defenders lying slain and scalped around the burning pile, from which they had been driven by the fire to
meet the preferred alternative of dying by the bullets and
tomahawks of the infuriated besiegers. The deed had been
done by an advance party of Narraganset warriors, in retalia-
tion for losses sustained by them the day before, while hovering on the flanks of the army, already within their territory,
and evidently approaching for hostile purposes, in direct
violation of existing treaties. But neither the Puritan officers nor soldiers were the men to think of being turned back
by the loss of a block-house, although it was the only one, on
this long, wild, and dreary coast, which could have afforded
them the shelter of a roof for their headquarters, in a campaign so peculiarly liable, under the circumstances, to disastrous reverses. And besides this, their wayside sallies upon

their flanking opponents, had resulted in an advantage as little expected by them as by their foes. It was understood that the great body of the Narraganset Indians had collected and fortified themselves in some fastness of great strength and difficulty of access, where, like the luckless Pequots of a former period, they might be surprised and exterminated at one blow. The locality of this stronghold, however, was not known to a single man in the army. But among the score or two of prisoners taken in their skirmishes, they found one who was base enough to betray his people, and who not only pointed out the fortified retreat of his tribe, but· offered to guide the army to the spot. And this, in despite of the fact that they would have no place to retreat to but an open snowy field, in case of failure and pursuit, and in despite also of the still more alarming fact that their provisions were utterly expended, and the promised supply of more had failed to arrive —this had led to the bold decision of an immediate march for the retreat of the enemy, now ascertained to be about twenty miles distant.

Although the morning light was still but feebly illuming the thick leaden clouds in the east, yet the whole army were already on the stir. Hundreds of bright lights were blazing from their camp-fires, around which sat the shivering soldiers, partaking their last rations, and gloomily listening to the sullen dashing of the ice-cumbered waves along the shore, or the low, portentous roar of the wind moaning through the surrounding forests. Such dismal sounds now seemed to come in sympathy with their own feelings ; for they were bitterly thinking of the day before them.

Before one of these camp-fires, moodily and alone, sat the veteran, Captain Mosely, his head drooping in thought, and his ear seemingly dead to the noise and commotion around him. Soon, however, his attention was aroused by the sound of an approaching footstep, and looking up, he beheld his friend, Captain Willis, standing at his side.

" Why look so sober ?" said the latter, in his usual calm, cheerful manner—"what are you pondering so gloomily, Captain Mosely?—the pretty day's work upon which we are about to enter ?"

" Yes, Willis, yes."

" Well, it looks dubious enough, certainly; but it is not likely we shall *all* be killed."

" Oh, no; but I am not so sure but every single, damned dog of us all ought to be."

" I don't understand, at all, what you are driving at, Captain Mosely."

" I suppose not. Well it is not the dangers to be encountered which I shrink from—pooh ! no, not that !"

" What is it then ?"

" Why, the fact is, Captain Willis, I have some conscience and religion, and would like to be a Christian in these matters of war. In short, I don't like the questionable character of this expedition. I don't like the idea of this marching an army to massacre a whole tribe of Indian people with whom we are at peace."

" Not at peace now, Captain Mosely. The commissioners of the colonies, who have been invested with full power for such purposes, after a long session at Boston, last month, all united in issuing a formal declaration of war against the Narragansets."

" True ; but how much did that mend the matter ? A declaration of war without cause, is nothing less than a declaration of intention to rob and murder. And what are the causes which these wise commissioners, after a month's drumming about for reasons, were able to set forth to justify their declaration of war ? Why, forsooth, *firstly*, that these hellish

Narragansets had been guilty of exercising the world-acknow-
ledged rights of hospitality towards Philip's women, children,
and wounded warriors, whom we had driven out starving and
mutilated from Montaup. *Nextly*, for being guilty of killing
a two year old bull belonging to somebody. *Thirdly*, for surrounding a man's house till he had paid for something that he
had cheated a drunken Indian out of. *Fourthly*, for a ru-
mored rejoicing at some of our reverses on Connecticut river.
Fifthly, for being deeply guilty of a suspicion of aiding in the
war against us. And *lastly*, and astoundingly, if they had not
already been so, they certainly soon would be !"*

" Nathless, they are as good causes of war as those given
for the destruction of Canaan by the Jews, whose examples our
rulers are so fond of quoting, and so intent on our following."

" Just about—just about. There is where you have it,
friend Willis. Aye, those Jews ! those bloody Jews ! Pretty
fellows they, to be quoted ! Why, of all the remorseless and
coolly calculating devils that ever claimed to be a nation, they

* According to the concurrent testimony of history, the commisioners here
named were incited to set this expedition afoot solely by their fears and suspicions that the Narragansets intended to join Philip in the spring. And
being thus impressed, and being determined at all hazards to prevent it,
they could devise no way of doing so, but by attacking them in their
fastnesses during the winter, where they could be the more certainly surprised and destroyed. But as the colonists were at peace with that tribe,
this could not be done decently without a formal declaration of war, and
it would not do to issue a declaration of war without setting forth some
justifying reasons, or ostensive causes. These were at length luckily discovered, and the difficulty was over. But that no injustice may be done, we
copy them from the document itself :—
" For that the Narragansets are believed to be deeply accessory in the
present bloody outrages of the bloody natives—this appearing in harboring the actors thereof — relieving and succoring their women and children, and wounded men — in their killing the cattle of the colonists, as
is credibly reputed—seizing and keeping under guard Mr. Smith and his
family, and in having, when the news of the disaster at Hadley arrived, in a very reproachful and blasphemous manner rejoiced thereat."

were—well, well, they finally furnished us the blessed Saviour
—though they must needs murder even him—yet they did furnish him for the whole of us lost sinners; so I will be mum
about them. But do you suppose, Willis, that our over pious
rulers, in taking the early examples of the Jews for a pattern,
ever thought of the final fate of the Jews, who, with no other
great national crimes, or, at least, no other half so deserving
divine vengeance, as their wholesale murder of the Canaanites,
were made to become, after a comparatively brief run of pros-
perity, one of the most broken up, scattered, despised, and
God-forsaken people, that the wide earth was ever compelled
to bear upon her loathing bosom ?"

" No. The first band of our pilgrim fathers who landed
on these shores, and who were doubtless one of the purest
flock of Christians ever collected, never spoke of the examples
of the Jews in driving out the heathen. That is the discovery of their degenerate successors in the church after becoming politicians ; and they only wish to avail themselves of it
as a convenient justification of the acts that grow out of their
covetousness and unholy ambition. But we should not, perhaps,
be very forward in judging our rulers, or judging for them. As
to this expedition, however, I must say, I heard of it with surprise, and, as an individual, have scarcely less scruples than
yourself, about the policy and justice which moved it. Still, as
soldiers, we must obey the powers that be, and throwing our private scruples to the wind, do our duty bravely. The responsibility of the right or the wrong, rests not on us, Captain Mosely."

" That is true, thank God ; and I sha'n't be backward in
facing the worst dangers we may be called on to encounter.
Still, if I am killed, the first instant I set foot in the other
world, I will turn State's evidence, and tell them there that I
joined in the affair only from a sense of military duty, and
directly against my will and conscience. But what think you,
Willis, will it turn out a butchery or a fight?"

" Perhaps both, but a severe fight, any way. The Indians always know of the very first movements of any army, and soon gather a wonderful accurate opinion of its purposes. And if they had any doubt about the design of ours at first, our unceremonious assaults on their scouting parties, for the last two days, will teach them what they are to expect from us. They may not know anything about the communications of this traitor guide, and therefore be surprised that we have found them so soon. But even if we reach there to-day, they will be prepared to give us as much fight as we may want."

" A fight it will be then ; for we have not now got the shilly shally Cudworth for a general, but the iron-heeled old governor, Winslow, who, how much soever he might yield to bigot influences at court, would, as a military leader out of it, storm through the gates of hell before he would flinch from his purposes."

" Well, he may have to do it, or something nearly akin to it, before he shall have accomplished his object, if that prisoner's account of the formidable character of the defences of the enemy be true, as, from a close examination of him, I became satisfied it was."

" Do you believe Philip and his warriors to be there to join in the defence of the place ?"

" No, Captain Mosely, there can be no more room there than can accommodate the numerous Narragansets and their guests. Besides, Philip is too active and restless a man, with the extended arrangements he has on his hands abroad, to shut himself up there in idleness. But it must have been Philip's genius that planned and supervised fortifications so strong and so unusual in Indian warfare. Our first struggle will be to get within them ; and then will come the more terrible one of making headway against the then doubly desperate three thousand defenders we shall be sure to find there. It will be bloody work ; but I would not stay away if I could ;

for I am half expecting, half fearing to find somewhere in that enclosure, those whom I would give my life to protect and rescue."

"From what I have gathered and guessed about your secret objects and anxieties, I think I understand you, friend Willis. And if your conjectures should prove true, though I doubt whether they will, I will hold myself in readiness to assist you in carrying out your wishes. But hark! there goes the long roll of the drums, and there rises the stern voice of the old general giving out the order of the march. We must away to our posts of duty."

All was now bustle and commotion in every part of the encampment. And, for awhile, the noise of the hoarsely clamoring drums, and the lively fifes piping out shrilly on the frosty air, of the quick tramp of the soldiery hurrying to their places in the ranks, and the short, stern words of command, grumly repeated from place to place along the incipient lines, by the officers forming their respective companies, the rattling of muskets, and the flapping of standards flaunting on the gusty breeze, together with the appearance of stir and animation which everywhere met the eye, all combined to form a scene in singular contrast with the physical gloom of the hour and a still more striking one with the terrible realities which that indomitable army were destined to encounter on that memorable day. While this was in progress, the aspect of the heavens had been growing every moment more and more gloomy and ominous. The cold, gray, leaden clouds which the first light of the dawn had revealed thickly curtaining the east, had gradually spread upwards and around, continually growing thicker and darker, and ever and anon sending forth those short, hollow soughs of the wind that are known to seamen as the precursors of a coming storm. But neither the portents of the heavens, the discomforts of their situation, nor their entire destitution of provisions, were permitted to deter the hesitating and doubtful troops, from the contemplated march.

" Now on !" rang the loud, authoritative voice of the determined old veteran in command, the moment he saw the last lingering squads of troops taking their places in the line of march.—" On ! on, for that nest of heathen vipers,—on, in the name of God ! for he hath this day delivered them into our hands."

And, accordingly, on they moved with steady, measured tread through the cumbering snows of the sedgy plain, stretching out drearily away before them to the southwest, in the supposed direction of the doomed stronghold of a congregated nation of victims. And thus, hour after hour, they laboriously forced their weary way over the bleak, snow clad hills and plains, which, with their scant forests of pine and oak, intervened in their course, until, after a cold and toilsome march of nearly fifteen miles, without a moment's rest, or a mouthful of food, and cheered only by the sighing of the winds as they swept mournfully through shivering forests, or the croaks of the wild ravens, that, with hurried flight, were occasionally seen winging their way overhead, they, at length, reached the borders of the great swamp, within whose dark recesses was somewhere situated the formidable object, to which they, for many days, had been so fearfully looking forward. But imagination could scarcely picture a place more dismal and forbidding than that which here presented itself to the eyes of the amazed and recoiling soldiers. Far away, as the eye could reach, in every direction in front, lay stretched one dark unbroken mass of thick, tangled and seemingly impenetrable forest. And when the well warranted visions of secret ambuscades, which would probably be sprung upon them on the way, and the death-dealing vollies of a thousand unseen muskets, which would certainly greet them when they approached the dreaded fortress, and before, perhaps, a single shot of their own could be made to count on the enemy, rose in their minds, the stoutest hearts quailed beneath their assumed looks of composure, and the sternest visages blanched at the prospect before them.

"Fetch me hither one Willis, I think they call him," said the general to an attendant, as soon as he had ordered the halt which now became necessary for making some desired alterations in the order of the troops, before entering the swamp—"one Willis, who is said to be here in the army somewhere, with a band of volunteer rangers. Fetch him hither straightway, as I would see him immediately."

The attendant hurried off on the bidding; and in a few minutes the surprised and wondering young officer, who now for the first time had been noticed by any of the military dignitaries of the court of Plymouth, came forward and presented himself before the general.

"Your name is Vane Willis?" inquiringly said the austere old Puritan commander, after sharply eyeing the other a moment in silence.

"It is, your Excellency," respectfully but unobsequiously replied Willis.

"Well, sir," resumed the former, authoritatively, "you and the men who act with you are said to know something of woodcraft, and the fighting of the salvages in their own fashion. If so, I have business for you."

"I am not in commission, sir," responded Willis, with a slight tinge of reproach involuntarily creeping into his tones— "I am not in commission, sir, nor has my company ever been recognized by the court of Plymouth."

"No matter," said the general, gruffly, "you are here to fight, like the rest of us, I suppose; and I wish you to take charge of our Indian guide, and, carefully keeping him within the lines of your men, so that he cannot escape, and following the path he shall point out for you, lead the way with him

forward through the swamp to the stronghold of the Narragansets. Now away to the duty. Some of our best companies will follow you close in the rear, to be on hand in case
of surprise or ambush."

A crowd of bitter thoughts, in view of past neglect, flashed
over the mind of the young officer on being thus deputed, for
his first official recognition, to a service which he knew, and
the general knew, every other company in the army would
shrink from, and if possible avoid. But he prudently repressed his feelings; and knowing that his company could
perform the dangerous duty better, and at a less sacrifice of
life, than any other, he bowed his acquiescence, and hastened
away to prepare his men for entering immediately on the
allotted service. In a few minutes the Indian guide, attended
by a file of soldiers, came forward, and first pointed out, by
the different landmarks discernible from reach to reach along
the low, far-stretching forest in front, the proximate locality
of the distant fortress, and then the circuitous but only practicable way by which it could ever be reached. Having by
these means obtained a pretty correct notion of the course to
be taken, and decided on the most feasible place for entering
the swamp, Captain Willis at once put his company in motion,
and, closely followed by that of his fearless friend, Captain
Mosely, who had claimed the privilege of leading on next in
order, plunged directly into the gloomy depth of the frowning
forest before him. And for the next hour, these bold and
hardy men continued to struggle unceasingly onward through
tho obstructing boscage of the deepening thickets, expecting
every moment to be saluted by the vollies of the ambushing
foe, but happily, thus far, meeting with no other molestation
than what arose from the almost insuperable natural difficulties
they every where encountered on the way. But at length,
after forcing their way through one of the most tangled and
wide-spread jungles they had attempted to penetrate, they
23

suddenly came out upon a beaten track, which at first seemed
to terminate wholly at the border of the jungle, but which a
closer inspection showed to have been made up of numerous
small and scarcely discernible trails, diverging out on either
side towards different and distant points on the borders of the
swamp.   Now readily believing the assertions of the guide—
whose good faith they had begun to distrust—that this path
led directly to the only entrance of the stronghold of the
enemy, they here made a short halt, to await the approach of
the companies more immediately in the rear, and make arrangements for moving on more cautiously, and in a manner
which should better ensure them against surprises from the
secret ambuscades which they would now be more likely to
encounter.   As soon as these objects were effected, they again
slowly advanced along the path about half a mile further,
intently listening for suspicious sounds, and keenly inspecting
every doubtful object in the surrounding woods on either side
of the way, but as yet wholly unable to detect so much as the
sound of a stirring leaf, or discover the least indication of the
presence of an enemy.   All at once, however, the guide, who
had been casting wary glances through the thickets—now
becoming more dense—a little distance from the path both on
the right and the left, stopped short in his tracks, and pointing to an opening here distinctly disclosing itself through the
trees about a furlong in front, hastily, but in low, cautious
tones, exclaimed—

" There ! there the place !—come right straight to it now—
me get kill, me go further."

Finding the guide could not be induced to proceed any further, and having been ordered to keep him under his own eye,
Captain Willis ordered his men to fall back two or three rods
into the woods, and, arranging themselves in a scattered line
on the left, stand ready for service, as a flanking party, until
the forces in the rear should advance by them on the way to

the scene of action. In a few minutes, Captain Mosely, at the head of his company, came up, and, after having been significantly pointed ahead, and briefly apprised of the situation of affairs, pushed resolutely forward towards the opening.

"I don't quite fancy this ominous silence," said Captain Willis to his trusty lieutenant, Noel, as the two officers, who happened to have taken station near each other, were standing, like all their men, with their backs placed against the protecting trunks of large trees. "No, I don't fancy it at all," he added glancing out uneasily into the forest.

"Nor I," returned the other, "nor much less do I like the looks of those freshly fallen thicket topped trees, strung along there on both sides of the way in front, just about far enough back to make the best coverts for mischief."

"Aye," quickly responded the captain, with a look of lively concern—"I see them, and now right abreast of the whole line of Mosely's men. And, by heavens! there is a movement among those dark boughs!"

At that instant the whole forest shook and rebounded, as if from the shock of an earthquake; while countless streams of fire and smoke were fiercely darting out from the suspected coverts upon both flanks of the advancing column, from which strong and lusty men were every where seen pitching heavily to the earth under the leaden storm of death, which had so suddenly burst on their devoted band.

"Charge to the right!" shouted the excited Willis, instantly comprehending the advantages of the secreted foe, and the danger of permitting them to retain their positions a minute longer—"charge those on your right, Captain Mosely. I will find business for all on this side; whether they count by hundreds or thousands. And now, boys," he added, turning to his impatient men, the sharp clicking of whose cocking firelocks everywhere proclaimed their readiness for action—"now, boys, scatter and run like wild horses, till you get round to flanking positions near the hither end of that line of coverts, whence the fire proceeded, and then give the red devils a death doom for every bullet you send after them."

With marvelous celerity the order was executed. And, though the savages, at first, seemed determined not to relinquish their chance for another onslaught on the white forces, whom, with glistening eyes and leveled pieces, they saw approaching the same spot where the first company had been surprised, yet the shots of the closely pressing rangers fell so fast and fatally on their exposed ranks, that they soon broke, and hotly pursued, fled away into the deep recesses of the forest to the south.

"Mosely, I conclude," said Willis, as he fell in with his lieutenant, as they were retracing their steps from the soon relinquished pursuit of the scattered and flying foe—"Mosely, I conclude from the distance and decrease of the firing, has been as successful in scattering and driving off the enemy on that side, as we have on this."

"Doubtless; and as we have now cleared the way for the main body of our forces, nothing remains for them but to close up and finish the work," responded the other carelessly.

"Finish! It is too soon for us to use that word, Noel," rejoined Willis seriously. "What we have done will prove, I fear, but boys' play to what is to come, and the enemies we have seen but a mere handful to those yet to be encountered, and in positions, too, a little different from those formed by a few tree tops."

"But do you fear for the result?" asked Noel, with an anxious look. "With our strong force, I should think we could hardly fail of success."

"That may depend wholly on the manner and places in which we attempt to carry the works," replied the former. "One serious mistake, in this respect, may be fatal to our

success ; and I feel very anxious that any such error should
be prevented.   But I can do nothing—judge of nothing, till
I can get a view of the whole defenses.   That must be my
first business.   And stay !   I *now* see where, and how, I can
effect that object."

" How ?" enquired the lieutenant with an air of mingled
doubt and concern—" how, without exposing yourself to
certain death from the bullets of the intrenched enemy ?"

" You see that dark, thickly limbed spruce fir, here on our
left ?" said the captain in reply, as the two were now creeping
through the screening undergrowth, directly abreast, and
within a hundred yards of the supposed locality of the fortified
enemy.   " That tree, you perceive, greatly overtowers the
shorter growth falling off towards the opening beyond, and its
top must afford a clear view of all I wish to see."

" Yes ; but that is too dangerously near to think of risking
yourself there, Captain Willis," remonstrated the other.

" No," responded the former confidently—" no danger—the
boughs are very thick, and, rising against the black forest
here, will effectually screen me till I can climb high enough
for my purpose.   You keep the red lurkers at a safe distance
here in the rear, and I will risk all dangers from the front,"
he added hurrying away on his hazardous intent.

On reaching the foot of the tree, the adventurous hero rapidly
mounted it to the height of twenty-five or thirty feet; when perceiving himself to be getting above the tops of the trees beyond, he carefully, and, by almost imperceptible degrees,
worked himself up closely on the back side of the trunk some
ten or twelve feet higher.   Here casting about and catching
such imperfect glimpses of appearances without, as to serve
for a general guide, he drew out his pocket knife, and
carefully cut away portions of the boughs, so as to form several
small loop-holes for different views in front.   And then, after
a brief pause, he secured a good foot-hold, grasped a strong

limb with one hand, slowly swung his body forward, and cautiously peered out; when the whole scene burst at once upon his amazed vision.

On a fully cleared, oblong, dry tract of land, embracing an area of six or eight acres, and everywhere surrounded by a deep moat of partially frozen water, stood a city of strongly built log wigwams, ranged compactly in rows, extending laterally from one border of the island to the other, but falling off near the northern and southern extremities, so as to leave broad open space, at each end, for battle grounds. Around the whole island jutting down perpendicularly to the edge of the water, on all sides, was extended a compact, interwoven mass of large, prostrate trees, about eight feet high in front, and nearly as many in thickness; while deeply and strongly inserted between the outward layers of the trees, round their whole extent, stood double rows of heavy, upright timbers, sharpened at the tops, and rising many feet above the heads of the dark lines of the red warriors, who were seen everywhere manning their tremendous ramparts, securely crouching behind their bullet proof palisades. To the whole of this vast and fearful enclosure, there was but a single entrance. At the northeastern extremity, and directly facing the path along which the white troops were approaching, the wooden rampart was left bare of palisades for a distance of about twenty feet; but instead, a rod or two back of the parapet, stood a high block-house, pierced from top to bottom in front, with long, regular rows of dark loop-holes, and fully commanding the single, large tree trunk, which, extending over the water in a line with the path here coming in on the opposite shore to the foot of the rampart beneath the block-house, constituted the only visible place of access, and which was thus made to complete the picture of this formidable stronghold of the doomed nation of the luckless Narragansets.

Scarcely had our amazed and anxious observer found time

to take in, from his lofty perch, all the different objects of his hasty survey, before he noticed a lively, but subdued commotion among the hordes of swarthy warriors, who, before but partially revealed to his view, were now seen rising up from behind every wigwam, log, and stump in the enclosure, and stealthily creeping along, with trailed muskets, towards the open space at its northerly extremity; while hundreds of dark muzzles were being slowly and cautiously protruded through all the loop-holes of the block-house, and every crevice in the palisades, for some distance around it. Following with his eye the direction indicated by these ominous movements, Captain Willis beheld, with emotions of unutterable anguish, the head of the column of his brave companions in arms emerging from the woods, and unsuspectingly advancing with hurrying step, directly towards the end of the log leading over to the entrance, which he had seen to be so fearfully guarded. Overcome by his sense of their danger, and forgetful of his own exposed situation, he shouted aloud to them to desist. But in the intense excitement of the moment, his words seemed to be neither heard nor heeded by friend or by foe; and the next moment his ears were greeted by the loud voice of Captain Johnson, whose company, in the order of the march, came next that of Captain Mosely, and who having reached the water, was now heard sternly crying,

" Charge ! charge over that log upon the works beyond ! and let no man hesitate to take *death or victory* for his watchword !"

Soon, but too soon, was the fatal order obeyed, and but too soon the saddest of those alternatives to be realized. A dozen men, fast followed by more, were seen quickly filing away over the long tree-bridge, and led on by their resolute captain, rapidly making their way to the rampart on the other side. There was then a moment of deathlike silence, during which, many a low crouching head rose to sight, and many a savage eye gleamed triumphantly along the nicely poised barrel of his unerring firelock. And then, sudden as the bursting thunder clap, the rent heavens leaped from the concussion of a hundred exploding muskets. As the whirling cloud of smoke, which had wrapped moat, block-house, and palisade alike in its murky folds, lifted and floated away, that extended trunk was found to bear up not a single man of its late score of occupants. They had all been swept down, dying and dead together, into the dark waters below.

The young officer turned away sickened and appalled. But before he could realize what had so suddenly passed before his eyes, his attention was again drawn to the spot by the rallying shouts of the next company in the rear, who, undismayed by the fate of those that had preceded them, and urged on by their impetuous leader, Captain Davenport, came rushing on to renew the fearful experiment. But scarcely was the fatal trunk covered by the devoted band, before another tremendous volley burst from the defenses of the besieged red men, and another score of their victims were swept into the moat.

"Merciful God!" exclaimed Captain Willis, "is there no other place of assault—no diversion to be effected to prevent this wholesale destruction of our troops?"

And in an agony of anxiety, he quickly withdrew his gaze from the spot, and eagerly ran his eye round the whole circuit of the island; when at length it fell upon a high, leaning tree, luckily standing on the shore on his side of the moat, but a short distance to the south, and tall enough, he was confident, to reach fully across the water to the works on the opposite side. His plans were formed in an instant; and rapidly swinging himself down from limb to limb, from his lofty lookout to the ground, he swiftly made his way back to his company, who by this time, had all come in, and, having heard the firing at the scene of action, were now impatiently awaiting his arrival.

" Our axemen—where are our axemen ?" he hurriedly exclaimed.

" Here, on hand and ready !" promptly replied the two rangers, whose duty it was made, in every campaign, to go always provided with light axes swung to their backs.

" Come on, then ! one and all come on, and you will soon understand what I want," cried the former, striking a line through the woods, with his excited company at his heels, for the helping tree, which was the first object to require attention in his new plan of operations.

" There !" he resumed, with kindling energy, on reaching the spot, and pointing to the tree in question, " fell me that tree square across this ditch of water, as quick as your best blows can be made to do it. Fear not to expose yourselves. The enemy suspecting no attack in this quarter of the island, have all hurried away to help defend their main entrance at the other end, where they are cutting down our vainly assaulting forces by scores. But put in there with your axes, with a will ; and we will have a bridge to their enclosure, and be down on their rear before they know what ails them."

The woods around were soon resounding with the fast falling blows of the strong armed axemen, who, one half hour before, would not have lived to perform a moiety of their task. But, at a little distance, all noises of this kind were effectually drowned by the roar of musketry, which now more and more incessantly rose from the other end of the island ; while every eye near enough for observation, was too absorbingly intent on what was there transpiring, to heed the present movement : for the third, fourth, and fifth attempt had been made to reach the desperately defended entrance : but thus far, only with the same disastrous results. And now the stern and unyielding old Puritan general, who had just reached the sanguinary scene, was heard storming, like a chafed tiger, in rallying the dismayed troops, and in goading them forward for another onset.

"She begins to tremble, captain," now cheerily cried one of the choppers, glancing up the tree, and then over his shoulder to his impatient leader. "There! that last blow has given her the staggers! Now look out for her last kick! he added, as he and his fellow axeman scrambled up the bank to get beyond the reach of the anticipated recoil.

With a sharp crack at the severing stump, and a sudden, toppling bow of the tufted top of the tall stem, the tree, with a booming roar, came crashing down upon the surface of the foaming water, and the smoking parapet beyond, carrying away half a dozen of the strong palisades in its fall, and leaving open a clear path into the supposed impregnable enclosure.

"Now, come on, boys—come on!" shouted Captain Willis, mounting the prostrate trunk, while it was yet vibrating beneath his tread, and bounding along over its half submerged surface, with his whole company hastening on as fast as possible in the rear.

To land, collect, and throw themselves into a straggling line, was but the work of a moment.

"Now, forward!" cried the impatient leader, in a tone that revealed the sternness of his purposes. "On, each for himself, as fast, and in such way as he best can, to the last coverts bordering the scene of action, get positions, and await the order for a cheer and a volley."

Instantly dashing forward, with the rapid, stealthy bounds of panthers for their distant prey—some along the open spaces near the lines of the palisades, and the rest along the narrow lanes winding through the thickly clustered masses of the intervening wigwams, each too intent on reaching his destination, to heed the startled looks of the swarms of women, children, and disabled old men, everywhere encountered on the way, they had all, almost before the minutes could be counted, reached their appointed stations, and, still undiscovered, now stood eagerly awaiting the promised order, within fifty yards of the crowding lines of the multitudinous foemen all too deeply engrossed with the dangers in front, to have a thought to spare for any that might arise behind them.

The expected order quickly came; and the next instant, there rose from the mingling voices of the gallant little band, a shout so loud and wildly defiant, that the sound rose above the roar of battle, and carried its thrilling and welcome peal to the sinking hearts of the army without. And then speedily followed, square into the turning faces of the astonished foe, a volley from the well aimed pieces of the rangers, that brought fifty red warriors to the earth.

Instantly profiting by the confusion into which the enemy had so manifestly been thrown by the unexpected attack in their rear, the daring Captain Mosely, who had just reached the scene of action, and from the absence of the rangers, was looking for some such diversion, ran quickly across the log that had been fatal to so many others, and, closely followed by his whole company, gained with them the rampart in safety; and, the next moment, with the look and roar of the roused lion, he was seen heading a desperate charge upon the recoiling ranks of the amazed and confounded enemy.

Soon rallying, however, from the utter consternation which had seized them, on finding themselves so unexpectedly and suddenly assailed by an unknown force in the rear, and at once perceiving their fatal error in permitting their opponents to profit by their confusion so far as to secure the important advantage of a foothold within the works, the red warriors instantly threw themselves into two dense lines, extending from side to side across that end of the enclosure, and, unflinchingly confronting their assailants on both sides, soon wrapped themselves in the smoke of their own volleys, which now burst like a series of rapid thunder claps along their lines. And then, as fresh companies of the colonial forces, rushing, one after another, through the storm of bullets that greeted their thinning ranks on the way, came pouring into the enclosure,—then commenced a conflict, to which, for ferocity and desperation on the one side, and unwavering determination and disciplined bravery on the other, the whole annals of war scarcely furnish a parallel.

Musket, sword, knife, and tomahawk were wielded in the work of death, as never before, by the infuriated combatants. Here advancing, here receding, and here gathering afresh for more desperate onsets, the living tide of battle swayed forward and backward, like the conflicting waves of a cross sea in an ocean tempest. The dead and the dying, officer and soldier, plumed chieftain and painted warrior, Puritan and savage, lay everywhere promiscuously strewed together beneath the fiercely treading feet of the unheeding survivors, and the beaten earth was everywhere encrimsoned by the out-gushing life blood of the countless victims of the terrific strife, while the incessant and deafening crashes of musketry, the fierce clashing of hostile steel, the agonizing shrieks of the wounded, the hoarse shouts of the indomitable white soldiery, and the appalling yells of the maddened red warriors, all, commingling to swell the dreadful din, rose in awful tumult over the shuddering forests around, and literally

"Flung o'er that spot of earth the air of hell."

The heavens, which, in the meanwhile, had, for hours, been growing more dark and threatening, now began to give earnest token of the near approach of the fearful storm that was destined to close this day of carnage with its superadded sufferings and woes. A tempestuous wind broke howling over the vexed wilderness; and with it, soon came the wreathy undulations of the driven snow beating down fast and fiercely, as if hastening to cover from the sight the gory horrors of the battle field. But the maddened combatants, in the demoniac fury with which they were plying the work of death, heeded neither snow nor tempest, nor aught else coming between them and the objects of their mutual hate and vengeance. And thus, alternately driving and driven across the blood-drenched field, for more than another terrible hour, unceasingly raged the desperate conflict.

At length, however, the force of discipline began perceptibly to prevail; and the red warriors, whose lines had become sensibly weakened by their fearful losses, slowly fell back among the wigwams, and there, for awhile, with the new advantages of partial coverts, made their final stand, fighting with desperate ferocity in their last hope of saving their helpless women and children. But the fierce and rapidly repeated charges of the white forces, exasperated to madness by the sight of their dying and dead companions, over whose writhing or lifeless forms they were constantly treading, soon visibly counted on the now irregular and broken lines of the weakened warriors, who, still desperately disputing the ground foot by foot, gradually retreated from wigwam to wigwam till they reached the last division of the devoted village; where now were soon to be added new and more revolting features to the dreadful scene.

As the dividing bands of the on-rushing troops advanced among the wigwams, the frightened inmates, consisting of women, children, and cripples, poured from every door in the hope of escape, but were everywhere struck down, in their helplessness, by sword, bullet, or clubbed musket, without mercy or compunction. And not content with this, these infuriated Christian soldiers, who had become demons of wrath and destruction, whom their heathen opponents might well have blushed to own as fellow creatures, applied the blazing torch to the inflammable roofs of every cabin in their way, many of which were still filled with deserted infants or bedridden warriors. And the out-bursting flames, which quickly revealed themselves along the whole northern lines of the wigwams, being instantly caught up and swept forward by the blasts of the tempest, went leaping onward, like a swiftly passing army of fiery serpents, from cabin to cabin, and spread with such inconceivable rapidity, that within one half hour, the whole extended village was hopelessly within the grasp of the devouring element. A scene of terrific grandeur, combined with more appalling horrors than all which had yet transpired, now speedily followed. Here, dimly disclosed in the spreading smoke, were seen dark groups of red warriors casting their discharged guns to the ground, and, in the frenzy of their rage and despair, leaping over the charging muzzles, upon their foes, to close in the fatal embrace, and sink with them to the earth. There decrepit old men, unable to fight, but disdaining to flee, were singing their death songs, and then with shouts of maniac laughter, throwing themselves headlong into the flames of their burning wigwams. And there again went up the wild clamor of mingling shout and war-whoop from parties of the exasperated combatants, who had suddenly met and rushed together in deadly conflict; while far and wide, over the whole extent of the fire-wrapped village, rose to the pierced heavens, shrieks after shrieks from the scores of innocent victims, who, unable to escape, were perishing in the flames. But the shouts and war-whoops of scattering conflicts, the outcries of alarm and distress, and screeches of mortal agony, as loud and terrible as they fell on the recoiling ear, were soon overpowered and lost in the explosive out-bursts which now every where, and almost simultaneously, ensued in the progress of the universal conflagration. Then a hundred black columns of smoke shot up, in swiftly whirling eddies, to the clouds, and there uniting, hung, for awhile the broad heavens with the pall of midnight, sending forth, as they ascended, a fierce, crackling roar, which, mingling with the howling of the tempest, might have out-sounded the wildest tumult of a storm-beaten ocean. Then clear and bright, as the jets of blazing furnaces, rose the wreathing spouts of living fire, which, being again struck and leveled, as at first, by a fresh blast of wind, streamed onward in almost unbroken sheets of flame over the whole area of the consuming mass, and converted it into a surging lake of fire, that cast its lurid glow far and wide over the dark forests around, and clothed in crimson the stormy and smoke mingled clouds above.

But we will here cease any further attempts at a general description that must fall so far short of the terrible realities of the scene, and return to the gallant, though still unacknowledged young officer, whose individual fortunes we have undertaken to follow in the expedition, upon the results of which he had exercised such an important agency.

When the regular troops had succeed in driving the savage forces back among the cabins, Captain Willis gradually retreated, so as still to keep the latter between the two fires of their opponents. And thus fighting and falling back, he had reached the southern line of the village ; when he discovered the soldiers setting fire to the wigwams at the other extremity. Seeing, at a glance, that unless a stop was at once put to this suicidal proceeding, the whole village must be speedily destroyed, and with it the provisions and shelter which he believed to be indispensable to the safety of the army, he left his lieutenant in command, and made his dangerous way alone back to General Winslow, and urged him, in view of the hungered condition of the men, and the alarming aspects of the cold and stormy night before them, to order instantly the incendiaries to desist and the fires to be extinguished. But his entreaties and suggestions finding no favor with the bigoted commander and his officers, who sneeringly told him they "came not to save but to destroy the nested heathen," he sadly, and with a boding heart, returned to his company.

By this time perceiving with alarm, from the rapid progress
the fire was making, that the whole village must soon be
wrapped in flames, and urged on by his private anxieties for
the fate of one, who, after seemingly flitting before him for
months, like some illusive vision, must, he thought, at last
be found here, either as guest or captive; he again rushed
forth alone for the hazardous adventure of threading the
crooked, pent lanes of the burning town, for the rescue of the
loved object of his search, who must now be brought or
driven from her concealment by the fast invading flames.
And on he madly plunged through smoke and fire, regardless
of the bullets and tomahawks, that were often hurled after,
and several times wounded him, till he had encompassed
nearly the whole place in the various turns and devious
courses he had taken, in the eager prosecution of his design.
But all in vain. Though he keenly scanned, as he darted
onward, every one of the many flying groups of women and
children he encountered, his eye was greeted with no form
which could be taken for the idolized object of his solicitude.
And he now paused in the partial screen of a freshly bursting smoke cloud, to take breath, and decide what further
measures could be taken in furtherance of his purpose.
While thus occupied, he noticed for the first time that the
firing had nearly ceased on both sides; and at the same time,
he recalled the hitherto unheeded circumstance, that every
group of fugitives, whether of warriors or women, whom he
had seen or encountered, were all rushing in one direction,
and that was evidently some particular point on the west side
of the island, over which a dense cloud of smoke had for some
time been shutting down closely to the ground. Instantly
starting with the new thought which these facts suggested,
he rapidly made his way towards the indicated point of egress
or assembling, and soon reached a stand where the whole
movement stood explained to his view. A rude, but capa-

cious draw-bridge, which had previously been prepared and concealed under the ramparts for such an emergency, had been hastily pushed across the moat, and the entire body of the surviving red warriors had already, under cover of the dense smoke driven by the wind in that direction, made their escape over it into the dark, tangled, and almost impassable cedar forest, closely encircling the moat on that side of the island; while the last straggling groups of their women were then passing over the bridge, and hurrying away into the thickets beyond. But among them, as among all who had been previously scanned, no semblance or trace of the lost maiden was to be discovered. And Willis, sad, disappointed, and weakened by the loss of blood from his wounds, of the effects of which he now for the first time became sensible, was turning dejectedly away from the spot, when he suddenly encountered a doubtfully garbed, unarmed man, who was evidently intent on gaining the bridge to join in the general rush of the fugitives. At first taking him to be one of the enemy with concealed arms, our hero instantly roused himself, and throwing back his sword, stood in the menacing attitude of one about to strike in anticipation of an assault from another.

"Hold!" cried the man, with a calm, fearless look, and in pure English accents—"have you not already here slain enough of the defenceless and innocent, that you would cut down a man who has never been in arms against you?"

"Not against us?" returned Willis, surprised, disarmed, and hesitating, under the undefined sensations created by something he saw or read in the look and manner of the other—"Not in arms against us? How came you here, then?"

"As a guest, sir," replied the stranger fearlessly—"as a guest of this hapless people of the woods whom your army have this day visited with such an unprovoked massacre."

"I have shed no innocent blood," responded the officer,
24

too sensible of the justice of the implied rebuke to permit of angry retort. ' " *I* have shed no blood, except that of opponents in arms against us. But whether you should be ranked among them, I may not perhaps be warranted in affirming contrary to your statement. Nathless, it will be my duty to detain you as a prisoner."

" I will not be made a prisoner," said the other, firmly.

" Then I must force you," rejoined the former, again drawing, but less resolutely.

" Hold! I once more entreat," exclaimed the stranger, quickly stepping up to the very point of his opponent's half-raised weapon, and inspecting it with a keen, earnest look. "It is as I thought at the first glance—it is the one, and a mystery is solved. But can he who is permitted to bear that sword think of imbruing it in the blood of a guiltless, unarmed man, and especially in that of one who—Oh, heaven! what misery in such a forecast!"

" This sword!" exclaimed Willis, in surprise and excitement. " What know you, sir, of this sword? Tell me—tell me instantly!"

" That I may not do," thoughtfully but firmly responded the other. " No, it were better for all concerned that no further disclosure at present be made. But, see! the smoke is lifting from the moat. We can neither of us much longer remain here in safety. Let me go."

" I cannot part with you thus," cried the perplexed and strangely disturbed officer. " I will not. I must know more of you. Trust yourself with me as a prisoner."

" Nay, it were even safer that *you* become *my* prisoner, instead," replied the stranger, throwing an anxious glance at the now blanching and blood-stained face of the other. " *You* could not protect me, even on this field, much less in the settlements, if you and your army are ever destined to reach there. You are evidently a badly wounded man, and cannot keep on your feet much longer. Why, sir, you are already trembling and staggering to the fall."

It was so. The words were scarcely uttered before the wounded officer sunk down senseless to the earth. Instantly starting, the anxious stranger ran back a few rods, to a dead warrior—who had breathed his last in drawing himself towards the bridge—stripped off his blanket, ran back, hastily wrapped it round the swooned officer, lifted him with main strength on to his shoulder, hurried staggering over the bridge with his burden, and quickly disappeared in the forest, where we must leave them for the present, to note the closing scenes of death and suffering which were still to mark this sanguinary and dear-bought triumph of the indomitable Puritans.

All the readily inflammable materials of the wigwams having been consumed, and the fires from the solid timber having so subsided as to permit near approaches, the troops now forced their way over the whole enclosure. But, to their surprise, not an enemy was to be found. They had all vanished, and as the draw-bridge had been removed, no one could tell how or where. They were not, however, left long in their wonder and suspense. In a few minutes, their scattered forces were every where greeted by a sudden, irregular fire, bursting from unseen foes all along the border of the dark forest on the west, and falling on their recoiling ranks with fatal effect. A rally was, indeed, made, and a few volleys returned, but with no other effect than to draw a thicker and more deadly fire from the concealed and evidently unharmed enemy. To attempt to charge into such a thicket, in the gathering darkness of night, were worse than useless; while to remain on the island, where their ranks were so rapidly thinning, and where the lights of the fires made them conspicuous targets for the sharp-shooting foe, were but to court death for their whole army. Then was the blind folly of firing the wigwams brought painfully home to the bigot

commander; and *"Retreat! instantly retreat for the settlement!"* was now sounded from company to company through
the half panic-struck army, who were the next moment seen
hastily gathering up their wounded, and disorderly rushing
from the island.   But what pen can describe the woes and
sufferings of the fearful retreat through the now deep and
trackless snows of forest and field, the intense cold, the blinding darkness, and the pitiless storm, of that terrible night?
And who can tell how, exhausted with toil and hunger, they
ever reached their destination, as history tells us they did
before morning, though with the loss of most of their
wounded, frozen stiff, and cast aside on the way?

Thus ended this memorable swamp fight with the Indians,
which resulted in the destruction of one half of the Narraganset nation, and, including all the resulting deaths, full
one-fourth of the Puritan army.

CHAPTER XIX.

"Not unavenged—the foeman of the wood
Beheld the deed, and when the midnight shade
Was stillest, gorged his battle axe with blood ;
All died—the wailing babe—the shrieking maid—
And in that flood of fire that scath'd the glade,
The roofs went down ;—"

WE will now return to our wounded hero, who, being supposed to be slain and consequently abandoned by his company, had so singularly fallen into the hands of the mysterious stranger, whom the reader has doubtless already identified with the hunted, unknown man, who, passing by the name of Crocker, was rescued by King Philip from assassins at the Leonard establishment, as described in a former chapter.

On recovering his consciousness, Captain Willis found himself lying on bearskins, underlaid with boughs, in a small wigwam, which proved to be one of a scattered group of temporary huts erected and occupied by the Indians, while preparing the more permanent abodes on the island but a few hundred yards distant. The closely interweaving limbs of the thick, dark, evergreen trees above, had almost solely shut out the storm that was howling abroad over the night-shrouded wilderness. The uproar of the battle and the conflagration was all hushed : and the place seemed one of comparative comfort and quietude. A bright fire, over which a small kettle of venison broth was simmering, was blazing near the feet of the wounded captive, if so he might be called ; and his captor was anxiously bending over him, examining and dressing his

wounds, some of which were found to be deep and dangerous.
Perceiving his patient's return to his senses, and noticing his
bewildered, uneasy looks, attended with indications of attempting to rise, the stranger made a quick, forbidding gesture, and
said, ·

"Be calm and content.   You are in safe hands.   By claiming you as my prisoner, whom I would save for a ransom, I
am permitted to do with you as I please, without question or
interference."

"Well, I am in your power," feebly responded the other,
pausing and starting as if in doubt whether the weak, hollow,
sounds he was uttering, could be his own voice—"Yes, I recall
it all, now.   I am wounded, and very weak, and doubtless at
your disposal whatever your intentions.   But first tell me
where I am."

"Within a furlong of the sad scene of this day's butcheries,
which needed not the glow of the conflagration to make the
heavens blush for the deeds of a self-dubbed Christian
colony."

"You speak plainly, sir; and would to God I could gainsay you—at least so far as relates to that revolting onslaught
on the women and children.   But I hear no firing—where are
the conquering army now?"

"Gone—wholly gone.   The warriors, more than half of
whom had survived the fight and escaped unperceived, quickly
arranged themselves along the borders of the thickets on this
side the moat, and as soon as the smoke scattered, poured
such a continued and destructive fire on the now unprotected
and plainly seen troops, that they shortly were compelled to
evacuate the island and beat a final retreat."   ·

"It has resulted, then, as I feared, when I remonstrated
against setting fire to the village.   But what sufferings must
ensue before those exhausted troops can reach the settlement,

over their dark and snow-drifted rout, in such a night of cold and storm as this!"

"Aye, well may you be dubious about their fate. The unwounded may possibly reach their destination; but most of the wounded must inevitably perish. And fortunate it was for you, sir, that I bore you here as I did; for even had you been found and taken by your comrades from the field, you could never, in your condition, have reached the settlement alive."

"It may be so. At all events, I will not repine at the misfortunes which brought me here, nor what Providence may still have in store for me. And who ever you may be, and whatever your motives and intentions—hark!—what is that? —what wild outbreak is that? Is it the herald of a renewed conflict?" added the speaker, as a loud, shrill, prolonged cry of mingling voices, so wild, so unearthly, and at the same time so mournful, as to cause, for the moment, both captive and captor to shrink back appalled, sent its deep vibrating thrill far back into the dark recesses of the forest.

"No," replied Crocker, after a pause; "that is no battle cry. It is the funeral wail of the Indians over their collected dead. They, on learning from the scouts sent out for the purpose, that the white forces were in full and eager retreat, all went over to the island to extinguish the fires of such wigwams as might be partially saved, to rescue what corn they might from the burning store-houses, and to see to their dead and wounded."

The wounded officer was about to push his inquiries, when the other, glancing at his pallid face and trembling lips, motioned to him to desist, and said:—

"These things are exciting you, I perceive. You must keep entirely quiet. I have in readiness here some warm broth for your nourishment. Take it, and sleep as much as the pain of your wounds will let you."

So saying, Crocker, producing from a corner of the hut a small wooden bowl, filled it with the smoking beverage, administered it with all the tenderness of an experienced nurse to the acquiescing invalid, and carefully adjusting his bed and covering, silently took his post as a watcher by his side. In a few minutes, the exhausted invalid had sunk into a quiet and profound slumber, when his anxious nurse and protector carefully rose, put the fire in a condition so that it could not endanger the cabin or its helpless occupant, and then noiselessly stole away to the island, to see what was there transpiring, which it might particularly concern him to know.

On reaching the scene of action, he at once and unhesitatingly mingled among the gloomy and deeply excited throng; when, on looking around, he was surprised to see how much had been effected in the two short hours which, at most, had elapsed since the evacuation of the place. The fires had been effectually extinguished on a large number of the more solidly constructed wigwams, and their log walls, though mostly charred over, were yet left so entire as to be easily made habitable by throwing across them the temporary roofing of poles and boughs, which the neighboring swamp so abundantly supplied. Large quantities of corn, secured in barrel shaped cuts of hollow logs, had been hauled out from the protecting debris, under which they had been buried by the falling of the burning roofs of the store-houses; while nearly twenty of the cabins, which, scattered along next the palisades on the west side of the enclosure, had stood without the range of the wind-driven flames, were left entirely uninjured.

Into these the wounded had been brought, and placed under the care of the women and medicine men. The slain whites, wherever found, had been unceremoniously pitched into the moat—their own dead carefully collected, the funeral wail, already described, uttered over them, and the bodies buried in long trenches hastily excavated in the open space at the southern extremity of the island. And the surviving warriors were now assembled in the light of the still burning piles on the very spot which had been marked by the fiercest of the fight, to hold a grand council for deliberating on the gloomy aspect of their affairs, and deciding what action should be taken, immediately or remotely, to avenge their terrible misfortunes and save the remnant of their bleeding and shattered nation from entire destruction.

Conspicuous among the dark throng of the excited warriors stood, like Saul among the people, with towering form and flashing eye, the brave and chivalrous youthful chieftain, Nanuntenoo, or Canonchet, as he is more often called in history, who, though he had not, till now, broken from the leading strings of the aged king and his advisers, whose timid counsels were, at this period, paralizing the energies of this warlike nation, yet he was the acknowledged heir apparent to the throne, and had that day led on the willing warriors in the terrible conflict which had just so disastrously terminated. Near him was also the ambitious Quinnapin, introduced to the reader in the early part of our story as the suitor of the fiery Queen Wetamoo, who now stood here by his side, as his bride and guiding genius, mingling in the counsels of state and inciting him to action in avenging *her* wrongs, and those which had been this day inflicted on his *own* people.

And around these leading personages, were closely grouped many other noted sachems and war captains of the younger and more ardent class, who sympathized with their bold and independent young chieftain, in his secret feelings of hostility towards the colonists; while a little aloof, with eyes bent dejectedly on the ground, stood the bowed forms of the old sovereign chief and the scarcely less aged counselors by whom he kept himself surrounded. The whole assembly were evidently agitated with emotions which, with all the wondrous self-control of their race, they were not able wholly to suppress. For though these laboring emotions might manifest themselves in the old, only in the silent working of their features, or in their sullen looks of grief and despair; yet, in all the rest, with the withering scowl of hate, that was depicted on their dark, frowning countenances, the loud gnashings of teeth, the hot puffs of fiercely ejected breath, and the sharp, prolonged, serpent-like hisses that ever and anon were bursting forth from the fires of their pent wrath, everywhere gave palpable indication of the terrible intensity of their feelings, now all merged in the one great, overmastering, burning lust for vengeance.

The old chief and several of his counselors had spoken; but their speeches had been all of the same subdued and abject character, all recounting the disastrous extent of their losses, tremblingly deprecating the power and vengeance of the white men, and suggesting no other hope, remedy, or resort for them, but an immediate suing for peace. And the eyes of the warriors were now all anxiously turned upon the last hope of their tribe, the gallant Nanuntenoo, to hear his response to remarks that so illy accorded with the thoughts and desires by which their own fiery spirits were agitated.

After a pause, and a proud glance round upon the eagerly expectant warriors, he spoke, and thus he spoke:—

"Ninigret, our venerable Sagamore, counsels submission and peace! These are not the words of the brave Ninigret, who, thirty years ago, drove back the pale faces, then coming to help our old enemies, the traitor Moheags—drove them back, like trembling deer, to hide themselves from his wrath, in their sea-shore villages.* No, the Ninigret of to-day is old and feeble. His courage is gone with his strength. He is like a little child: and all his counsels are those of a child, and not those of a man and a warrior, who would preserve the

* See Thatcher's Indian Biography for the fact to which allusion is here made.

being, and uphold the ancient glory of his nation. Submission! Where would he and his counselors now be ? where the women and children not already burnt or brained, and where all of us, if we had followed the same puling counsels of peace and submission, which he gave us on the approach of our murderous foes this morning ? Aye, where ? All in yonder red graves, sleeping side by side with our slain warriors, whose blood I already hear crying up to the great Manitou for vengeance ! And if Manitou hears, shall his outraged red people be deaf to the cry? Brothers, hear me—if a thousand warriors should now take the war path, follow, ambush, and fall on the retreating foe, tired, freezing, and staggering blindly along their dark and snowy way, need one be left to carry home the story of their triumphs to-day ? Not one ! Then would our dead brothers be nobly avenged. Warriors, I am ready to lead all who are ready to follow."

Hundreds of young warriors, with heaving bosoms and flashing eyes, eagerly rushed forward to offer themselves for the hazardous enterprise which had been thus artfully presented to their gloating visions of blood and revenge, and which, had it been permitted to be carried out, would, in all human probability, have resulted in the entire destruction of the already twice decimated colonial army. The burning Wetamoo clapped her hands in savage delight, and, while uttering wild exclamations in applause of the braves who were thus evincing their patriotism, impatiently urged, and even absolutely pushed forward her new husband, the less ardent Quinnapin, who, thus instigated, soon took his place as one of the leaders in the bold foray under consideration. And everything, for the moment, promised a prompt and general adoption of the plan suggested by the daring young chieftain.

But here the old chief and his counselors, at length comprehending the character of the movement, came tottering

forward and warmly interposed to prevent its execution. At
first, in authoritative tones, they wholly forbid the movement
as one of folly and madness, and as one which would result
in the certain destruction of all who would engage in it. But
perceiving symptoms of open rebellion among the irritated
warriors, the trembling old chief lowered his tone, and, in
tearful agitation, earnestly pleaded and begged, that the warriors, now the last hope and dependence of their shattered
tribe, might not be further exposed to the terrible power of
the white troops, but all be kept there for the defence of the
helpless. And finding the young chief and the leading warriors still hesitating to comply with his entreaties, and urged
on by his overpowering fears and anxieties, he at last came
out with the humbling proposition, that if this, his last
request, was complied with, he would ask no other favor, but
at once resign the sovereign power into the hands of such
chief as the warriors, in their wisdom, might elect to receive it.

The young chieftain, who, in the meantime, had stood
silently noting this interference, with feelings of impatience
and vexation, which nothing but his habitual respect for the
aged ruler prevented from breaking out in expressions of
open contempt and defiance, again looked anxiously round
upon the faces of the assembled warriors, when perceiving in
their looks indications of the irresolution and doubts, which
the words of those, whom they had so long been accustomed
to honor and obey, had obviously created in their minds, and
which, when indulged in, he well knew to be generally any
thing but an augury of success, he paused awhile with looks
of evident chagrin and disappointment, and then reluctantly
yielded his purpose.

"Ninigret has his wish," he, after a pause, slowly began.
"Yes, Ninigret has his wish, and Nanuntenoo yields, because
he is to yield no more. But warriors," he continued in

kindling tones, as he raised his princely form to its full height, and threw a proud glance on the agitated throng around him— "Warriors, from this sad and humbling day, we are free to act and free to fight. Choose ye now, then, the man ye would have for your sovereign and war-chief."

"Nanuntenoo! none but Nanuntenoo! Nanuntenoo! Nanuntenoo!" burst in one universal shout from the eagerly acclaiming multitude; and the young chieftain stood before them a king confessed.

"Warriors!" at length resumed the chieftain with a stern dignity of manner alike suited to his new position, and the fearful responsibilities he had unalterably resolved to assume in the war—" Warriors, you have this day suffered an outrage which can be atoned for only by the hearts' blood of our foes. The lying pale faces say they have made war upon us because we have received the houseless and starving Wampanoog women, children, and feeble old men, whom they have driven from their homes. Is there a warrior, or a man, or even a squaw in the whole Narraganset nation, so mean and craven but he would do this again?"

A yell of wrath fiercely burst from the exasperated throng in negative response.

"Warriors," continued the gratified chieftain, " your answer is the answer of men who cannot be made slaves or cowards— it is an answer that will fall pleasantly on the ears of our dead braves in their spirit-land homes; and it is the answer the Great Manitou, who is growing more and more angry over our wrongs, would give us. Yield up to be butchered these helpless Wampanoogs? Never! while a warrior among us is left to wield a tomahawk, never! not one! not so much as even the paring of a Wampanoog's toe nail shall ever be given up to the white wolves!* But is that all there for us to do? No! no! a

* The same declaration which this noble but luckless young chief made to Captain Dennison; when, being surprised and made a prisoner a few months

hundred times no! They have made war upon us with a bad cause. We will now show them, in turn, what we can do in a war against them with a good cause. They have destroyed nearly half our warriors; but we will make the other half more terrible for them, than the whole of them before. They have not spared from death our women and children. We will make the land red with the blood of theirs. To-morrow we will begin to fill our bullet bags and sharpen our knives and tomahawks for the bloody work; and before seven suns have passed over us, we will be on our way to the camp of the great Metacom, with the war cry of vengeance on our lips, vengeance to the white man now, and vengeance to the white man forever!"

And " *Vengeance to the white man!*" was eagerly caught up by the maddened throng, and echoed and re-echoed, till the whole forest rang with the clamor of the terrific demonstration, which, at length subsiding, left on the startled ear the shrill voice of the still unsatisfied Wetamoo, wildly repeating, " *Vengeance to the white man! vengeance now! vengeance forever!*"

Thus ended the closing scene of this day's awful drama. And how far the fearful foreshadowing of evil to the colonies which that wild scene had so palpably exhibited were destined to be realized, or in other words, how much this worse than questionable onslaught on a tribe against whom they had no just cause of war was destined to avail the cause of the colonists, let the record of the dozen towns that were desolated, of the five hundred dwelling-houses that were burned, and of the fate of hundreds of men, women, and children, who were slain in battle or massacred at their homes, during the terrible winter that ensued—let the record of these furnish the answer, and at the same time, the lasting commentary on the

later, he was offered his life if he would deliver up the Wampanoogs, and procure the submission of his tribe; and when rejecting the disgraceful proposition with open scorn and contempt, he was shot and quartered by his Christian captors.

whole of that unwashed transaction. We must leave it all to the sad and humiliating history of the times, and return once more to the task of unraveling the web of fate, which, in connection with these public events, had involved the leading personages of our eventful story.

"Oh, what an augury of evil to the infatuated colonists is here!" soliloquized the white man, who having stood at the edge of the crowd mutely witnessing the scene we have described, now turned thoughtfully away, and began to retrace his steps towards his charge in the forest—"Still, who can blame them? Who can blame any, made of flesh and blood, for resolving on such a course under such provocations? This settles it beyond question or recall—a war now upon the colonies by all the united red tribes of the north—ay, and that too, a war of extermination! Yet why anticipate horrors which heaven in its mercy may yet avert? It is enough for me, in my situation, to look to my own safety—guard my own interests. Aye, quite enough; since the forest no longer will be any place for me. Let me bethink myself. Some part of the Providence plantations—Cannonicut or Aquidneck islands—yes, one of them must be my next refuge—at least till it is seen how the approaching crisis in my affairs is to turn; and the sooner I take myself away the better. But this young officer, he must not be left here to perish in the wilderness. No, I could not do that even were he a foe, much less now. No, I must remain here with him, nurse him, and, if possible, save him, and, as soon as he can bear to be removed, take him away with me to some place of safety to him and to me, if I would further commune with him."

Thus anxiously musing, and giving vent to the thoughts that were oppressing his mind, Crocker slowly made his way back to his forest cabin, where his first care was to look to the condition of his wounded protege. But noticing no alteration in the latter, whom he found still sleeping quietly, he hauled

up a supply of already prepared fuel sufficient to last through
the cold and stormy night before them, replenished with solid
logs the low-burning fire, and wrapping closely around him
the warm, ample robe of furs with which he had provided
himself for the winter, laid carefully down by the side of his
sleeping patient, and was soon lost in slumber. After sleeping
soundly many hours, he was awakened by the invasion of the
cold—the woodman's only night signal for rising to prevent a
chill; when, leaving his rustic couch, he first closely noted
the brands of the decayed fire as his only means of judging
the time of the night, which he thus ascertained to be considerably past midnight. Satisfying himself on this point, he
piled on another large quantity of substantial fuel, and then
went forth to examine the aspects of the weather, or whatever
might be passing without. The storm, which had greatly
lulled during the time occupied by the war-council, of which
he had been a spectator, in the fore part of the night, had
again set in with redoubled fury. The snow was sifting down
apace through the interstices of the loaded and bending boughs
of the trees overhead, and the wind was every where wailing
dismally through the muffled forests of the swamp levels
around, and sweeping, with loud, solemn roar, along the more
distant pine-clad hills bordering the swamp on the west. But
all else had given place to these voices of nature and of the
night. The tumult of battle, the roaring of flames, and the
cries of mortal agony, which had made hideous the past day,
were now all over and gone; and no human note was to be
heard, save an occasional stifled groan from some of the
wounded warriors who had been brought to these secluded
cabins, to die here, as they wished, alone and unmolested.
After noting awhile these tokens of the storm—made the more
impressive from the place and the hour, together with the
consciousness of the obstacles which such a fall of snow must
interpose to any immediate execution of his plans for leaving

the forest, he pensively returned to his post in the cabin, and seating himself before the fire, fell into those dreamy reflections which care and solitude are apt to create in the brooding mind. He had not long, however, indulged in his reveries, before he began to be conscious of an alteration in the breathing of the invalid sleeper, which for some time had been growing quicker and more labored. Instantly arousing himself, he proceeded to the side of the latter, where he soon noted symptoms that filled him with uneasiness and anxiety. He ran out, squeezed together a quantity of the fresh snow into a compact ball, returned, and assiduously applied himself to the task of applying it alternately to the fevered brow and parched lips. But as grateful as this cooling process appeared to be to the half sleeping, half-waking, but nearly unconscious sufferer, it did not seem in the least to affect the cause of his sufferings. On the contrary, his symptoms, as the gloomy night wore away, continued to grow more ominous and alarming. More and more restless became every part of his sympathizing system; faster and faster his hurried respirations, and more and more perturbed his uneasy slumbers, which at length were frequently broken by short, stifled groans; while low, incoherent mutterings of the vaguely flitting images of the troubled brain seemed constantly striving forward to lips vainly attempting to give them utterance. Deeply touched by the evident sufferings of his patient, the sympathizing stranger, after doing all he could to alleviate them—but all in vain—despairingly laid aside his appliances, and bending over him with looks of commingled commiseration and anxiety, began to listen to his disjointed murmurings with melancholy interest; when at length, in the jumble of his discordant, half-uttered thoughts and broken accents, the words, "*Madian—loved—lost—persecuted Madian,*" became distinctly articulate. Hastily starting at the sounds, the listener rose and began to pace forward and backward along

25

the narrow space which the cabin floor now only afforded, with rapid steps and visible emotion.

"It is so," he at length said, pausing and looking down sorrowfully on the face of the invalid—"it is so. The heart is taking advantage of the clouded brain, to unburthen itself of its most cherished secret, and the unconscious lips are but doing its bidding. Yes, it is as I conjectured. And now to see him lying here thus!—to see him here in this snow-hedged wilderness, with his life hanging but by a thread, with no possibility of any other than my poor surgery to save him! I would that I could have been spared this painful lot—ay, painful to witness and bear now, but to prove more painful, I fear, in the associations of the future. But how singular this happening! How singular the chance that brought me, in my tardy retreat from witnessing the battle, upon that wounded Pocasset, who could hail and entreat me with his dying breath to slay this young officer, whose scalp, doubtless, at the very moment he received his own death wound from some other quarter, he was aiming to take, to bear it off as a trophy to his queen, for her thanks and reward for destroying one whom he doubtless had discovered to have been her most dangerous enemy! Strange! But may there not be the finger of Providence in all this? And yet, if the man is to die here, to what end was the interposition? Will he live, then, to be restored to his friends and country? God grant it! And as for me, let me trust and believe it, as one more than willing to become the instrument of the merciful purpose."

And from that moment, he *did* trust and believe in the event he had so earnestly prayed for; and thenceforward, and by way of becoming, as he desired, the favored instrument of its fulfillment, he patiently and assiduously devoted himself to the duties of nurse, watcher and physician to his suffering patient, with the best means of cure within his reach, which consisted only of the balsams of the forest around him, for the dressing of the wounds, snow or water for the alleviation of the fever and local inflammation, and the various simples in vogue for sudorifics and stimulants, all applied with the best skill and discrimination, that his observations of Indian methods of cure, and former experience among wounded men, enabled him to exercise. But his faith in success was destined to be severely tested. Day after day, and night after night came and went, with no visible amendment of the sufferer. The fever, in its varying degrees of intensity burned steadily on, constantly disturbing his slumbers by night, and as constantly keeping him by day in a state of stupor or mental wandering. Still undiscouraged, however, by the unpromising aspects of the case, this self-constituted protector and physician continued to persevere in his unremitting attentions to his patient, providing for his comforts, guarding him against the cold, and nursing him with all the tender assiduity of a father or brother, seeming to take no thought of himself, or to regard the storms which were almost continually howling through the wide-spread wilderness around, no further than they might affect the comfort and safety of the object of his unexplained and singularly bestowed solicitude. But faith, hope, and patience, all at length flag under long continued discouragements. And Crocker, finding that all his care and exertions availed nothing, at last began to cast about him for the best means of removing his patient to a white settlement, believing the comforts of a civilized abode, and the attendance of a regular physician, which could there be obtained, would more than counterbalance the risks of removal, in the chances of his recovery. Accordingly he called to his aid several of the ingenious natives, who, as soon as they were made to comprehend the object, went to work, and soon constructed a sort of willow work litter or rather bed-case, which was confined to light runners, so that a soft, springy bed could be laid within, and the vehicle could be carried like a common litter on the shoulders of men, or drawn like a sledge, as the circumstances might require. And scarcely had these preparations been made, before an event fortunately occurred that afforded unexpected facilities for the safe accomplishment of the projected removal. After nearly a fortnight of cold stormy weather, one of those remarkable thaws, which are peculiar only to January, but for the invariable occurrence of which in that winter month, and not in any other, science has yet failed to assign the cause, suddenly made its appearance. And nearly the whole body of snow, then three feet deep on the level, was, within two days, converted, as if by magic, into its original element, leaving all the high grounds as bare as in summer, and all the swamps and lowlands more or less deeply flooded with water. Nothing was now wanting but one cold night to make the way all that could be desired for traveling in the contemplated direction, which led to the nearest point of the neighboring bay, seven or eight miles distant, and for the most part over a low swampy country. Such a night followed the second day of the thaw; and the next morning, the ice was everywhere found sufficiently strong for a safe transit of the invalid and his attendants. As no time was to be lost, Crocker immediately summoned the four native assistants, whom he had previously hired for the purpose; when, having dispatched one of them forward to a designated point on the coast, to procure suitable boats, he with the others gently lifted the unconscious officer into his new traveling couch, carefully covered him with blankets and furs, and at once set forth over the almost continuous glare ice which now, spreading out far and wide in every direction formed the smooth and beautiful flooring of the forest. Under the judicious arrangements adopted, in accordance with which one of the assistants went forward with a hatchet to lop away all obstructing boughs, while the other two drew the vehicle, leaving their leader to walk by its side, to steady, and guard

it from accidents, the party now for many hours diligently
made their way through the most densely wooded part of their
route. They then shortly emerged into a more open, marshy
region, where they encountered so few difficulties, and advanced at such an increased pace, that at the end of six
hours from the time of starting, they had safely reached their
destination at the end of their journey by land.

The place at which they had now arrived was the most inward point of the large, irregular cove, here making some
miles into the interior from the great western entrance of the
bay. Here they found the Indian who had been sent forward
in the morning, in charge of two safe and capacious bark '
canoes, which he had drawn out from a neighboring shanty,
where the Narragansets, it appeared, had deposited their
boats for the winter, and which he had already caulked,
launched, and every way made ready for immediate occupancy. Placing the invalid, litter and all, in the largest canoe, the whole party at once embarked, Crocker and one of
his assistants taking charge of the boat containing the invalid,
and the rest going forward in the other to assist by towing,
and in any other way which circumstances might require.

The keen cold of the morning had now, in the afternoon,
given place to a mild winter atmosphere, and what was still
more important to a favorable issue of the enterprise in hand,
the day throughout had been one of perfect calmness. And
the waters of the bay, the ice of which, including even that
of the cove, had been broken up and dissolved by thaw and
tide, were consequently almost entirely waveless. Encouraged
by these auspices, the hitherto anxious and fearful master of
the expedition, with a few cautions to the rowers to guard
against all sudden and jerking motions, confidently put forth
on this part of the voyage. And so great was the speed with
which these light, feathery crafts were made to skim the surface, under the elastic, steadily applied oars of the strong-

armed rowers, that one half hour sufficed to take them out
into the open waters of the bay, and another to send them
across the channel to the southern point of Canoncut Island.
Here, closely rounding the point, they veered to the northeast, and after skirting this island several miles, struck ob-
liquely across the middle channel, and at length made land in
the vicinity of a solitary but neat-looking farm-house standing on
the western shore of the picturesque Aquidneck, or the well
known Rhode Island, which subsequently gave the name to
the whole of the free born and spirited little State, which
here lies nestling within and around these curiously projecting arms of what may well be termed its fostering ocean.

CHAPTER XX.

*" There was a voice—a small, still voice,
That came, when all the storms were past,
And bade the sufferer's heart rejoice
In hop'd reward for all at last."*

FUGIT TEMPUS! was the commonplace exclamation of
the ancient poets and moralists; and " Time flies—time flies,
O how swiftly!" has been a thousand times repeated and
reiterated, from their day to ours, by every moralizing people;
as, with feelings of mingling interest and concern, they have
noted how swiftly the winged months and years glided irre-
coverably by them in the ceaseless flight of time. With the
healthful and happy, and with the eagerly busy and gain
devoted classes in life, this often quoted sentiment is doubtless
but a melancholy truism. But not so with all. With the
sorrowful and despondent, the days seem to pass slowly and
heavily away—with the weary in waiting, they appear to lag
and linger as if only to tantalize them with hopes deferred;
while with the poor, brain-clouded invalid, time makes no
progress.

Many weary and slowly dragging weeks had elapsed since
the event which last occupied us, transpired. And the modified atmosphere and longer and lighter days, that had succeeded
the cold, short, and dark ones of the previous months, told
that the dreary reign of winter was now fast drawing to a close.
On a comfortable couch in one of the rooms of the solitary
farm house on the island shore, which we left the mysterious
white wanderer of the woods and his dusky associates

approaching, lay the still helpless and unconscious wounded officer. The cottage was occupied by a widowed Quakeress, with a son and daughter, who were old enough to render material assistance to their meek and industrious mother, in all the various in and out-door duties required in her secluded situation, and who, with herself, constituted the good Samaritan little family into whose care the invalid had fortunately fallen. The stranger and his Indian assistants had greatly surprised her by bringing a sick and helpless man to her door; and, at first, she thought she could not receive him. But the former, by the magic of some whispered token, had so touched the secret sympathies of the Quakeress, and so well backed his personal appeal to her humanity by his assurances of pecuniary indemnity, that she soon yielded her scruples, and cheerfully received the sufferer into her quiet domicile; when giving her his instructions in regard to the invalid, and bidding her to act discreetly in regard to himself, he dismissed his Indian assistants to return in the canoes, and hurried off himself, by land, in another direction. From that day the widow had untiringly devoted herself to the care of the patient, who, notwithstanding all her exertions and those of the physician called in accordance with her instructions, had lain there, week after week, without either visible change or amendment. The doctor, however, in his visit on the previous night, had spoken much more hopefully of the case than he had ever done before, believing he had discovered a favorable crisis in the disease, which he called a brain fever, produced as much by the excitement of the battle as the wounds received in it, and predicting with considerable confidence, that when the invalid next awoke, he would do so with partially or fully restored consciousness. And his unusually deep and quiet slumbers, long and easy respirations, and other corresponding symptoms exhibited through the night, having all appeared to go in comfirmation of the doctor's hopeful predictions, the encouraged widow now, on the morning chosen for the opening of the present chapter, had taken her seat with her knitting work in hand near the couch of the invalid, and with an air of solicitous expectation, sat patiently awaiting the promised result of his awaking. She was a middle aged woman, of a rather slight but symmetrical figure, and very comely features, which however, in spite of all the natural vivacity of countenance that enlivened them, bore the impress of many early trials and sorrows. She was not to be kept long in this suspense. For in a short time after she had taken her seat, and while thus employed, with an occasional wistful glance to the face of the sleeping invalid, he fetched a long, deep respiration and awoke.

" Awake at last !" was the first feeble exclamation that escaped his lips. " This must be real," he continued, at musing intervals, to murmur, without looking up, or in any way showing himself aware of the presence of another in the room. " Yes, real, now ; but what a dream !—if it be all a dream ; if not, which the real, and which the dream ? But this "—he added, as with a surprised air he began to glance at objects within the scope of his vision as he lay—" this is not the place ! A finished room ! A white man's dwelling ?"

And now turning his head slightly, his bewildered and enquiring gaze encountered the meek but gratified countenance of his attendant, who, readily anticipating what would naturally be the enquiries which would arise first in his mind, and fearing that he might overtax his new found faculties, now rose, and advancing to his bedside, considerately interposed by saying, with the air of one wishing to obviate all necessity of further questions,

" Yea, friend, thou art indeed in a white man's, or rather in a white woman's house, on the western side of Aquidneck, a few miles north of Newport."

" But how came I here, and who brought me to this place ?"

resumed the invalid, after a seeming effort to collect his confused faculties.

"That," replied the former—"that I would have told thee at once, if I could have done so with any certainty; for I am desirous to save thee, in thy weak state, from worrying thyself by further questionings. But, peradventure, it may be the lesser evil, now the thought is evidently beginning to perplex thee, to say that thou wast brought here by a white stranger and several of the red people, and placed under my care as a wounded prisoner, whom his captors had for some reason decided to convey to the white settlements."

"Yes," responded the invalid, after a thoughtful pause—"yes, it must be the same. I clearly remember now, how singularly I fell into this stranger's hands, and how much surprised I was to encounter such a man under the circumstances, and how puzzled at his words and conduct. There is a mystery about the whole affair, which, if I ever get about again, I shall feel an interest in trying to unravel. But why should he have thrown me on you, a stranger, when I might have as easily been taken to Newport, where I am known to many?"

"I can't pretend to tell thee," said the woman with a manner intended to discourage further conversation.

"How long have I been here?" persisted the querist.

"About six weeks."

"So long! Why, you must have had a hard time in taking care of me, my good woman; but you shall be well paid for all."

"I have been *already* paid."

"By whom?"

"The stranger himself. And he has not only paid *me* well, but left money with me to pay the doctor we have called to attend thee."

"Strange! Strange! All strange—dreams and all—as I

suppose my wandering fancies must have been, though I would like to ask, if you have been my only female attendant ?"

"My daughter Mary, a girl of thirteen, has frequently been with thee," said the Quakeress, with a slightly suppressed and hesitating air; "but why didst thou ask the question ?"

"Because," slowly and musingly resumed the invalid—"because, among the thousand continually coming and going fancies which I have a dim consciousness of having haunted me during my long, troubled sleep, as it appears to me only to have been, there has been one that seems so distinct and abiding, that I find it difficult, and I may say painful, to believe wholly unreal. It was in the form, sometimes of an an angel with white wings, gracefully folded, as she stood wistfully watching by my bedside, and sometimes simply of a youthful female, but always wearing the same sweetly expressive face—always tenderly ministering to my wants, or looking down upon me with the same anxious, and, at times, tearful countenance."

"It is hard making ropes out of sand," rejoined the Quakeress, evading the subject matter of the other's remarks, and affecting to be closely examining her knitting work, as if to hide the sly, roguish expression which was just perceptibly stealing over her features. "Thou will be apt to find it, methinks, rather a fruitless task, friend, to try to make many realities out of such vague fancies as those which we have all been aware were disturbing thy bewildered mind. Thou hadst best refrain now. It only worries thee. Quiet thyself as much as possible, and excuse my absence a little time, that I may go and prepare for thy taking such nourishing beverage as will now benefit thee."

With this, she quietly rose, and, leaving her mystified patient to his reflections, glided out of the apartment. In a short time, however, she reappeared, bearing a small tray containing some kind of smoking beverage, which, turning out and cooling in a saucer, she gently administered, bidding him drink plentifully. He did so ; and then falling back on his carefully smoothed pillow, and, seeming to dismiss all anxieties from his mind, was soon lost again in those quiet and childlike slumbers which as surely, as they do beautifully, mark the rallying of the physical powers in the first hours of convalescence after a long and prostrating fit of sickness.

The doctor, a small, plain, sedate looking man, of few words, and abrupt, well clipt phrases, called, in the course of the morning; and passing, with a simple nod to the family then engaged in an outer room, directly to the bed of his patient, felt his pulse, noted all his symptoms, and, without awaking him, was on the point of leaving the house, when he was hailed by its mistress—

" Thou hast left no directions, doctor."

" None needed—fever gone—brain quiet—small wounds nearly well—great one in the shoulder making no more trouble—sha'n't call again—nature and nursing to do the rest— to be kept quiet, fed moderately, and soon be up again."

" Thou now wilt consent to write to his friends—wilt thou not ?"

" Not yet."

" But they know not, peradventure, where he is, nor whether he be dead or alive."

" Didn't mean they should. Misapplied medicine kills some, misjudging friendship more. Low patients and officious friends should have a double edged sword placed between them. Will write, when he can sit up half a day. Little strength enough then to contend with friends—will need half as much as wanted to meet his enemies in battle. The old fellow who had him brought to your quiet place, with prohibition of notice, knew something. Good morning, madam."

" Stay, doctor—if thou art not to come again, thou shouldst be paid now. What is thy charge ?"

" You pay ? Ah ! Let me see. Ten visits, five shillings each—ten times five, fifty—two twenties, one ten—ay, two pounds ten, that is it, madam."

" Here, count for thyself, doctor," said the Quakeress, who, while the other was reckoning, had stepped to a chest, and now coming forward, held out to him a handful of coin.

" Will—guilders ! Dutch coin—good—know the value— get it right," said the gratified doctor, as he went on counting out the amount of his pay, which he so little expected to re- ceive, at least for the present, till he had finished the agree- able task. " There, all right ; but where did you get this rare coin ?"

" From the stranger. He entrusted it with me for the very purpose of paying thee, or such other doctor as I chose to employ," replied the other, after some hesitation.

" A stranger from the woods with these ! Here's room for peradventures—inferences—guessing," rejoined the doctor, with a puzzled, studying air.

" Ay, but thou wilt oblige me by doing thy guessing mostly to thyself, doctor," responded the Quakeress, with a significant look.

" Ah ! I see—private concernment—unfortunate liabilities or something akin, maybe—but no matter—the old fellow is a gentleman—my respects to him, if you ever see him again— same to you, madam—good morning," said the sententious little man, nodding complacently, and immediately de- parting.

After a day and night passed mostly in peaceful and refreshing slumbers, Captain Willis awoke the next morning so much better and stronger, that, when he had partaken the . light but the most substantial breakfast his careful hostess dared give him, he was smilingly told by her, the bridle she had put on his tongue the day before might now, perhaps, if he desired it, be safely removed for a little season.

"The first use to be made of the privilege," responded the invalid, in the same spirit, "should be, I think, to inquire the name of the kind lady to whose care and attention I am evidently very deeply indebted."

"Nay, nay, friend; I had done but a common duty of humanity, without the compensation I have received—much less, now, could I claim any special thanks from thee. But thou wouldst know my name? It is Rachel Minturn."

"A widow, I think you intimated, with these two hopeful children I have seen here? But I would also know something about your family or personal history, my good lady."

The woman, after a pause, meekly commenced her story, which we will call

THE TRIALS OF THE PERSECUTED QUAKERESS.

"I am," she began—"I am, as thou hast rightly imagined, a widow, with my two children—George Fox and Mary Dyer —and the small farm here which their father left us, for my only hope and dependence. He died about five years ago, after we had occupied here nearly twenty, with a disease traceable to the early troubles which he and I had in common experienced, and which at length drove us to seek an asylum in this peaceful and soul-free island. Yea, it was indeed a dark and angry cloud that gathered over the bright looking path which he and I were beginning to tread together. We were Quakers—that was our crime. We were both reared in the same village in the vicinity of Boston, and at rather an early age were betrothed for a union soon to be consummated; when soon after, some of the earnest disciples of that man of power and of the Spirit—George Fox—who was then moving all England, either as followers or persecutors, came over and began to preach in our neighborhood. Curiosity prompted

me to attend one of the meetings of this new sect, whom the
clergy were all bitterly denouncing, and most of the people
deriding. I went to laugh, but came away to pray.

"I was greatly troubled at what I heard, for I could not
deny its truth, nor reconcile it with the religious formulas I
had been taught to believe essential. I opened the Bible,
and was surprised to find the same doctrine which the preacher
had enforced, breathing through every line and precept uttered
by Him who spake as never man spake; and I now could not
see how it was possible the simple doctrines of love and charity could ever have been twisted into the sanctioning of the
rigid and intolerant requirements of the old churches. The
light seemed all at once to burst upon my mind, like the sun
breaking through a misty cloud. The clogged spirit within
suddenly responded to the striving Spirit from above. I felt
I had been transformed into one of the new sect. I gave in
my adhesion, because God in my conscience commanded it;
and I openly and boldly proclaimed my belief, because I
neither dared nor wished to withhold it from the world. I
was arrested, taken before magistrates, and ordered to recant.
But, instead, I was moved by irresistible impulse to exhort
them to recant. I was then thrown into prison among felons;
but, still unmoved, I went to exhorting the prisoners, the
jailer, my betrothed, and all who came to see me, till all began
to doubt and tremble. 'This pestilent creature must be removed, or she will spread this devilish wild-fire over the whole
country,' said the rulers; and accordingly I was brought out,
banished, on pain of death for return; my tongue—this
scarred tongue—punched through with a hot iron; my ear—
this maimed ear—slit down and cropped. I was then placed
before a constable on horseback, flourishing a long scourge,
and, under the sharply applied lash, driven through the jeering
multitude. Without being allowed to go to my home—which
was with a distant relative—for a change of raiment, I was

forced on to the borders of the next town, in a southern direction. Here I was delivered over to a new constable, already there, and waiting at the town lines to receive me, and, by the blows of a new and untired arm, greatly to increase my sufferings. But my betrothed, the faithful Nathan Minturn, who had resolved to share my fate, and had accordingly provided himself with what money he could command, procured my clothes and hastily packed them up with his own, now, to my great joy, soon overtook us, fell in by my side, and, in despite the curses of my new driver, shielded me, and, as far as he could, took the cruel blows upon his own head and shoulders. The gush of love and gratitude that then welled up from my heart, shook my whole frame as I staggered onward; but I could not express it, save by looks, and that imperfectly, for my parched mouth was filled by my swollen tongue, and the blinding blood from my ear was disfiguring my whole features. But I need not enlarge on the mingled joys, sorrows, and sufferings of that day's terrible journey. Having been thus scourged from town to town by a succession of remorseless officers, we arrived, near nightfall, at the southern border of the colony; when, with a parting lash and a bitter anathema, we were told to go to the land of heretics where we belonged, and never show our faces again, unless we wished to swing on the gallows.

" As soon as this last rude official, who now wheeled his horse and rode off, was out of sight, we involuntarily dropped down, in our fatigue and perplexities, upon a rock by the wayside, and, with our heads on each other's shoulders, truly, as the Scripture hath it, lifted up our voices and wept. We then, after mingling our tears awhile, and comforting each other as we best could, united in a heartfelt supplication to heaven, for support and guidance in our unprotected, homeless, friendless condition. After this, we rose much comforted, calmed, and trusting, and instinctively bent our steps towards Providence, then as now, the city of refuge for the oppressed. Arriving there by daylight, we presented ourselves to friend Roger Williams, then Governor, and rejoicing in the new freedom charter of the whole Narraganset province, which, after so much labor, he had just obtained from England. He received us kindly, ordered refreshments, and then taking a seat beside us, listened to our story.

" ' Poor martyrs of soul liberty !' he exclaimed, with tears starting from his eyes, as we finished our story. ' I welcome you both to our conscience-free plantations. But you must be assisted. Let me see—there is a tract of land large enough for several good farms, on the west shore of Aquidneck, that have not been appropriated. Your unusual sufferings for conscience' sake, entitle you to the best one. You shall have it.'

" He then hurried off, and in a few minutes returning with a freshly written deed—yea, of this very farm, handed it to us for perusal, and keeping. My Nathan read it and hesitated, saying he could not pay for so much land.

" ' Pay ?' said the good man, rebukingly. ' Do you think the Lord placed me here with the means and power, after he had so sorely tried me, for any worse purpose than to give free homes to the persecuted ? Talk no more of pay, but go to your granted home and improve your talent in peace. But children,' he added, after a thoughtful pause, ' you are not married. I am a minister—no formal bans are necessary—it can be done before me, and here on the spot; so rise, my children, and be joined in marriage.'

" At this, we *both* hesitated. The thought of such an event just then, being so unexpected—so strange, and making such a crowning of that sad day's adventures ! But friend Williams thinking it would be best, under the circumstances, we yielded, stood up, and were duly married. After remaining in Providence a few days, we came here to our farm, built a temporary house, and went to cultivating the soil. My hus-

26

Land diligently followed his avocation that year and the next, with none but brief absences.

" But on the approach of the second winter, as he had decided to build a better house the next season, and as he still had property in Massachusetts, which might be sold for enough to aid him greatly in building, he made a journey, with that view, to his old home. Not knowing the fact, which, to his sorrow, he soon ascertained, that a decree of banishment had, at the time of our leaving, been issued against him also, he had not thought of meeting with any molestation. But although, being a prudent man, he had never declared his belief there, or done aught to manifest it, save the part he took while coming off with me, yet he was at once arrested on his arrival as a returned Quaker, and, without being allowed any hearing, thrown into prison. And here he was kept in a cold damp cell, through that whole long and dreary winter, during which he contracted an inflammatory disease, from which he never fully recovered. Early in the spring, however, through the exertions of friends, who made intercession for him on the ground that he had returned in ignorance of the decree, they at last reluctantly released him, and, on account of his infirmities, graciously allowed him to depart without the usual scourging on the way.

" Such is my poor story," added the Quakeress in conclusion. " The people and rulers of my native colony have caused me very many, and very sore afflictions; but I forgive them for all; they knew not what they did."

The invalid, who had listened with deep interest and varying emotions to the simple and touching recital of the Quakeress, failed not to express, what, in view of some of his own experiences, he the more sensibly felt, a warm sympathy for her in her trials and afflictions. Nor did he hesitate to openly and strongly inveigh against the blinded bigots who had caused her trouble. But although the forbearing woman evidently felt the force of his remarks, yet she could not be brought to join him in any words of condemnation, and "it is not for me to judge them," was her only response; for, in common with all her remarkable sect,

> " She walk'd by faith, and not by sight—
> By love, and not by law,—
> The presence of the wrong or right,
> She rather felt than saw."

Still he had evidently by his kind words and frank declarations, which she had hardly expected of one from the colonies from which she had been driven, touched a chord in her feelings which greatly raised him in her regard ; which made him, indeed, henceforth doubly a favorite in the family, and caused the days of his convalescence to pass pleasantly away. And from that time, that convalescence became as rapid as it was thus made pleasant. Within four days from the recovery of his consciousness, he was able to leave his bed, and sat up for hours at a time—within a week, to walk about the house and yard, and, in less than another, to go abroad for short excursions along the shores of the bay, or into the woods with his rifle, which, together with his valued sword, he was gratified to find, had been carefully preserved and brought along with him to that place.

Up to this time he had taken but little thought about leaving his pleasant quarters. He was growing restless, indeed, with his returning vigor of health ; but it was far less any matter of public than private concernment that caused his uneasiness. It was the mysteries attending his late singular capture, connected, as he now more than ever felt them somehow to be, with those still enveloping the fate of his long lost Madian, which now chiefly occupied his mind, and which he was intently but vainly casting about him for the means of solving. Independent of this object of his solicitude, he had formed no definite plans in regard to his own future movements : for, smarting, as he was, under a keen sense of neglect and contumely shown him by the colonial authorities, as his only reward for all his services and sufferings, he felt little inclined to trouble them any further with his presence ; and he was beginning to make up his mind to settle down somewhere among the quiet people with whom his last lot seemed so strangely to have been cast. But events were now at hand which were suddenly to rouse him from his indifference and change the whole current of his thoughts towards a happier and more important consummation. The Quakeress had the week before despatched her son to apprise the doctor of his patient's rapid recovery; and she had been for some days wondering why her communication had not led, as she had understood it would, to visits from the friends of the latter ; when, one evening after dark, as the family were all sitting within, chatting together, they were startled by a loud and heavy rapping at the door.

"That must be a rough customer," said Willis, rising, "let me go, Mrs. Minturn, and ascertain what the man would have."

Accordingly he proceeded to the outer door, carelessly threw it open, and came to a stand on the threshold ; when he discovered the outlines of a stout, burly man sitting on a horse before him, but there was not light enough for any personal recognitions, and for a moment there was a dead pause on both sides. The silence, however, was quickly broken by the new comer, who, in a doubtful, grum, heavy tone, said—

"Can you inform me, friend, of the whereabouts of a certain runaway dead man, once considerable of a creature, passing under the name of Vane Willis?"

"Is not this Captain Mosely?" hesitatingly asked Willis,

without replying to the rough, unceremonious question. "It must be, I think—ay, it can be no other."

"Not very well, I fancy," responded the other; "and now I hear your voice, I know what I half suspected at first—that I am talking to the very chap I am after—have found at last, and now see, thank Heaven! standing like a well man, square on his feet before me."

"Captain Mosely," rejoined the former, "I am as glad as I am surprised to see you. Alight, sir,—alight and walk in."

"Ay, to be sure, I will; for I have no notion of letting you slip through my fingers this time," said Mosely, dismounting and following his gratified friend into the house.

"This is Captain Mosely from Massachusetts, Mrs. Minturn," said Willis as he ushered him into the room.

"He is one of thy friends—is he?" said the Quakeress.

"Ay, and a most valued one.

"He shall be considered one of ours then; friend Mosely, I bid thee a kind welcome to my house and such poor fare as it may afford. George Fox, take care of friend Mosely's horse; and thee Mary Dyer, come, stir thyself, and we will try to make good our words of welcome by preparing something acceptable in the way of supper."

"Now I like that!" exclaimed the off hand captain, taken aback by the words and manner of the Quakeress. "It sounds hearty. I thought the Quakers never paid any attention to politeness; but hang me, if there an't more of the quintessence of politeness in these few words she has just spoken here, than in all the fine phrases I ever heard at a Boston dinner table! Captain Willis, I don't wonder at your safe recovery in such keeping."

When these word-tokens of mutual, amicable, and happy feeling, had been thus pleasantly exchanged, Willis and Mosely retired to the private apartment of the former, for the

double purpose of more freedom of conversation, and of relieving the females of their restraining presence during the hospitable preparations of the kitchen.

"Now, Captain Mosely," said Willis, as the two became
seated, "now for the news from the colonies—the progress of
the war, and all. Your coming has re-awakened something like
the old interest which I used to feel, but which I thought I
should never feel again, in their public affairs there."

"News?—Progress of the war?" exclaimed Mosely, with
a look of surprise. "Why, don't you know, Willis? Hav'n't
they told you what has been happening the past winter?"

"No, how should I? From the night of that desperate
swamp fight, which closed over me in a swoon from loss of
blood from wounds, which I was hardly aware I had received,
I have known nothing distinctly till within the last fortnight.
And since then, I have scarcely felt interest enough in events
abroad to enquire. And if I had enquired, it would not have
availed me in this secluded family of Quakers, who never
enquire or talk about the events of war. No others have I
seen to enquire of, except the doctor; and him I only indistinctly remember, as he discontinued his visits about the time
I fairly came to myself, and so managed, as I began to suspect, that I should not immediately have any other visitors."

"Ay, very likely—a queer old stick, that doctor. It was
he who wrote to a friend of mine, giving us the first news
we had of you, whom, as you were not to be found when we
retreated, we supposed to have been killed and dragged off,
or taken prisoner and then killed, and in coming into this
section, as I immediately did, I had to go to this doctor
for directions to the place where you might be found."

"Ah! Then it would seem he has been keeping up a sort
of supervision over me, during my convalescence, and chose
his own time when I should come into the world again. Well,
he may have judged correctly. At all events, it has been a .

matter of indifference with me. But to the news you were about to tell me."

"The news, I am sorry to tell you, Willis, goes to make up a sad and gloomy tale. The events of the war since I saw you, present an almost unvarying picture of blood, plunder, and conflagration. Our wicked assault on the Narraganset village, and our indiscriminate massacre there, as dear as it cost the Indians, cost us still dearer. Every tribe in the country seemed to make common cause with the survivors, in the work of revenge. They were before that time, simply ordinary enemies, since then they have been infuriated fiends. As we slew unoffending women and children at that battle; so they, in turn, have spared neither age nor sex in their subsequent warfare upon us. The villages of Lancaster, Medfield, Groton, Warwick, Marlboro, Bridgewater, Sudbury, and Scituate, have been successively sacked and laid in ashes, and large portions of their inhabitants made victims of the bullet and tomahawk ; while the scattered settlements of nearly the whole frontier of Massachusetts have shared the same melancholy fate. It has seemed as if all hell had been let loose upon our devoted colonies."

"But our troops—where have been our troops in the meanwhile?" exclaimed the astonished and horrified young officer.

"They have been everywhere—ay, and everywhere on the chase after the enemy. But it has all amounted to little or nothing. We would hear of them concentrating in large numbers to assault some particular town, and we would make a forced march for the place. But when we arrived, the mischief was done, and the red devils were off to emerge from their fastnesses, two days after, perhaps to bring the same doom on some other equally unprepared town fifty miles off in an opposite direction. And even when we were lucky enough to come across, and engage any of their roving bands, they have, I am ashamed to say, generally succeeded, by their ambushes, traps, and other devices of their devilish cunning, in killing two of our numbers where we killed one of theirs. They are, however, giving us a little respite just now, having gone, it is thought, over to Connecticut river. But they will probably soon be back upon us again, and in larger force than ever. In short, matters look rather squally for us, I can assure you, friend Willis. We must have *you* in the field again."

" I am in no condition to take the field at present, Captain Mosely ; and besides that I have resolved never to enter the service again without a commission. I have already fought and suffered enough for one who is to receive scorn and neglect as the only reward for his perilous services. You know the part I took in the swamp-fight, and how I was then treated."

" Ay, and I know also, that but for your masterly movement in gaining the island and assailing the foe in the rear, that victory, if victory it could be called, had never been won. And I further know your gallant achievments, on that terrible day, have in no way been noticed by our bigot-blind superiors. The people, however, I find, understand it. And your reward, brought about by their clamors in your behalf, cannot be, I think, far distant. But enough of this. I will now hear, as far as you could know them, the circumstances of your mishap in the battle, capture, manner of getting out of the woods to this place, and recovery   The old doctor gave me some vague and mystified hints about it ; but I want to hear it from you."

Accordingly Captain Willis proceeded to relate all, with which our readers have been made acquainted, respecting the singular occurrences embraced within the scope of the other's enquiry ; when, as the two, both almost equally in the dark respecting the mysteries in which the whole subject was still involved, were discussing the probable character of the stranger, and the motives which could have actuated him in his friendly, liberal, but extraordinary and unaccountable course and conduct towards an entire stranger, and before they could hit upon anything that looked like even a probable solution, their conversation was interrupted by a new and unexpected arrival.

" Friend Willis," said the Quakeress, gently throwing open the door, " there is a youngerly red man here, who desires to see thee ; but both of thee had better come out now, as our supper is nearly ready."

Casting at each other looks of inquiry, slightly mingled with surprise, the officers at once rose, and, without remark followed their hostess into the kitchen.

" That is friend Willis," said the Quakeress, pointing to the younger officer, while directing her words to a young Indian, who stood near the outerly entrance, demurely looking down upon the floor ; but who, thereupon, with a keen glance at the person indicated, advanced a step, and held out a letter.

Captain Willis, with a look of lively interest came forward, took the letter, at once opened it, and, after glancing over the contents, and hesitating a moment, read aloud,

" As soon as Captain Willis is able to travel, which I trust is now, his late captor, or prisoner, or nurse in the woods, would be gratified to see him at Providence. Enquire of Governor Williams for

CROCKER."

" There ! by the George, Willis," exclaimed Mosely, slapping the other on the shoulder, " in that short and sweet epistle, I see the spot where the light is to come from out of that cloud of mist and mystery, we were just bothering about."

" Then you would advise me to go there, would you ?"

" To be sure I would—there is a meaning in this queer affair."

" When, and how would you go, Mosely ?"

"To-morrow, and with me. I came by way of Providence—left my horse there—came down in a little schooner, which returns to-morrow from Newport, where I landed and took horse hither. You are well enough for the trip, and will be in a fever till you know what is to come out of the business. Yes, go with me to-morrow; I will stop in that town till you can tell me something of the discoveries you may make; for I'll be whipped if I ain't getting to feel as curious about it as a little girl over a riddle."

"I will do it, Captain Mosely," responded the other cheerily; "so we will call it settled."

"But art thou to leave us, then, to-morrow morning, friend Willis?" asked the Quakeress, with visible emotion.

"It would seem so, my good lady," replied the young officer, tenderly.

"Then to-morrow will be the saddest day we have had this long time," responded the Quakeress with starting tears.

"Oh, it is not for a final separation, I trust, my kindest of friends," rejoined the other, feelingly. "Oh, no! I can never forget this family—no, never; and however the journey contemplated now, may turn out, I shall often visit the peaceful abode where I have been placed under so many obligations. But I must have a word with the messenger," he added, turning to the Indian. "When do you return to Providence, my red friend?"

"Part way—up, long four, three mile, where left canoe, to-night, may be—rest part way, next sun—morrow morning."

"Well, as you will doubtless get to Providence first, you may tell the man who sent you here, that I shall probably reach there some time to-morrow afternoon."

"Yas. Me go, now," said the native, turning to depart.

"Nay, nay, red friend," interposed the kind Quakeress,

"thou must not go till thou hast had some food. Come, we are about to take supper, and, if these gentlemen here don't object, we will give thee a seat with us at the table. The Lord, according to our creed," she added, addressing the readily consenting officers, as they all now seated themselves round the well loaded board—" The Lord created all men equal, whatever their race or color; and it is not for us, his poor creatures, to be the first to set up distinctions."

CHAPTER XXI.

" They talk of short-lived pleasure—be it so—
Pain dies as quickly : stern, hard-featured pain
Expires, and lets her weary prisoner go.
The fiercest agonies have shortest reign ;
And after dreams of horror, comes again
The welcome morning with its rays of peace."

                                                 BRYANT.

IT was spring—auspicious spring—that season which alike
gladdens and delights the doubting heart of the Christian
philosopher and the raptured eye of nature's poet. For, as
the thronging idealities which she brings in her rejuvenating
train, burst on his mental vision, the one sees in every bursting bud and germ, springing into new life from the perishing
seed, the cheering type of the new life in store for him, when
he too, like the seed, shall be mingled in the dust. The other
as he beholds nature gradually spreading her flowery carpet
beneath his feet, and unfolding her leafy banners to the whispering breeze above his head, is regaled with the purest em-
blems of moral loveliness, and the most delicate forms of
beauty, which poetic thought can appropriate, either to hoard
for its own silent pleasures, or elaborate for the gratification
of others.

Near the top of the southern declivity of the fine elevation, around and over which, now cluster the conspicuous
edifices of Providence, the city of the beautiful early record,
and, with the progress of a just and comprehensive liberty,
of constantly brightening early memories, there stood, at the
period of our story, a cosey little cottage, so far removed from

all others, and so poorly provided with approaches as to give it the air of solitude and intentional seclusion. But any drawback which might be found in its loneliness, was amply compensated by the unrivaled prospect which its peculiar situation afforded. A variegated landscape of field, forest, and waters, lay stretched to an almost limitless extent before and around it. And these views, as striking as they were at all times, were now, on the pleasant spring afternoon, when we would bring up the spot to the notice of the reader, especially beautiful and magnificent. Reanimating nature was making her great yearly toilet, and everywhere rejoicing in the beauty and fragrance of her vernal attire. Far away on the right, dotting the country in lessening perspective, lay the green hills kissing the skies. On the left, the eye wandered, with fewer prominent land-marks indeed, but with other objects of scarcely less attraction, over river, plain, and woodland, till the vision melted away and was lost in the blue distance; while in front, the long, wavy line of the bright waters of harbor and bay, now glittering in the rays of the descending sun, lay sleeping in their resplendence, like young Beauty reposing in an illuminated cradle.

In the front room of the secluded cottage we have just de-scribed, and close by the side of an open window, sat a beau-tiful, dark-browed girl, wistfully gazing out on the bright scene before her. But her eye was not now feasting itself on the natural beauties of the landscape. It was fixed on a small vessel that was seen heaving round a distant headland, and slowly creeping over the undulating waters towards the quiet little haven which lay embosomed among the surrounding hills and forests, almost at her feet. She now rose, thrust her head through the window, as for a nearer and clearer view, and scanned the approaching craft long and intently, when she hastily withdrew from the window, and taking a long, relieving breath, stood awhile musing and murmuring, "It is

the one! Coming at last! coming at last! Oh, if *he* knew
of this agitation—this half-dreading, yet intense longing to
meet him, how he must despise me! But thanks to woman's
instinctive arts of reserve for concealing what cheapens her
in the eyes of those she would enchain, and revealing enough
to ensure the permanence of the thrall—thanks for these, he
will never know. So, now for the schooling."

Accordingly, while slowly pacing the room, she commenced
the proposed process of trying to reduce her rebellious feelings
into subjection and calmness, or rather to school the tell-tale
countenance into such expressions of quiet indifference, or
mere polite interest, as should, at least, decently conceal the
tender tumult within. All her resolutions to this end, however, did not prevent her, at every turn in her walk which
brought her near the window, from sending a quick, eager
glance out upon the water, to note the inward progress of the
vessel which was thus riveting her attention. This she
continued to do until she had seen the lagging craft, that
seemed to her, in her impatience and suspense, to be forever
in reaching its destination, at length driving up to its wharf,
the grating hawser thrown around the confining-post, and the
crew leaping ashore. With cheek made eloquent with the
coming and going shades of hope and disappointment that
successively flitted over it, she stood noting, for some time,
with unsatisfied eye, each individual form of the ship's company, as, one after another, they now made their appearance
on the wharf. At last, however, one form came in view,
which the keen eye of love instinctively told her could be no
other than the original of the picture she carried in her own
bosom; when, suddenly letting down the curtain of the window, and removing the chair from before it, she took a book
from a shelf, and seated herself in a different part of the
room. After sitting in this position for the next, and, to her,
the almost interminable half hour—now abstractedly turning

over the leaves of her book, now trying to read, and now shutting the volume, to open it again and go through again the same empty performance—the sound of an approaching footstep without at length reached her quickened senses, causing her to start; and the next moment, a gentle rapping on the door brought her instantly to her feet. With flushing cheek and fast-heaving bosom, she flew towards the door, and, forgetful of all her self-training in the emotions of the moment, quickly threw it open, gave one earnest look, and, with both arms extended, rushed forward to her greatly surprised, but still more greatly overjoyed lover.

There was an attempt to speak, on both sides; but on both sides it was equally a failure. The starting tear and quivering lip were the only interpreters of their overcharged feelings, and, hand in hand, they mutely passed into the house, and seated themselves facing each other in the recess of the window.

"Excuse me," said the girl, as soon as the silent language of the emotions could be made to yield to the less eloquent utterance of the tongue. "Excuse me, Mr. Willis," she repeated, in low, broken, and tremulous accents, as she wiped away the tear-spray that had bedewed her fair cheek; "I did not think to be so childish. But to see you alive, after I had, in thought, buried you; and now, after such a sickness, to see you looking so unexpectedly well! Oh, Vane, Vane! how much I have suffered in mind on your account!"

"And *I*, too, dearest Madian, have suffered both in mind and in body, it may be said, on your account. But I am richly compensated for it all in the happiness of this moment. And so much the more joyful the meeting, because, at this time, so unexpected."

"Unexpected, Vane? Ah! I bethink me, now; the finding *me* here *might* be unexpected."

"Yes, finding *you* here *now*, though I confess I expected

to meet one here who might, I thought, assist me to find you. But where is he? This is the house, surely; but where is Mr. Crocker, and who is he, Madian?"

After hesitating an instant, the maiden, who had by this time regained her usual composure, looked up a little archly, and said—

"Yes, this is the house; but you are throwing upon me a whole heap of questions all at once about other folks, when we have had scarcely five minutes together to talk about our own affairs."

"Oh, no, not much of a heap—only a simple question or two; and it was for the very reason I fancied they might have some bearing on our affairs, that I was prompted to ask them."

"But you will be asking me for my adventures, since we parted, next, won't you?"

"Certainly shall I, next, or now, if you choose it, Madian; for never have I been so utterly at fault about any thing in my life, as about your movements, since your mysterious disappearance from Plymouth up to the present time."

"Very well, sir, you shall be immediately gratified with my whole story, provided you will allow me first to furnish a sort of practical preface, which I trust will not be the least agreeable part of the performance. So, here my brave friend, who is said to be proof against ambuscade and surprise—here take this volume, and amuse yourself during the brief absence I must also be allowed in furtherance of the matter."

Thus playfully remarking, the now joyous and animated girl, with a sort of roguish, knowing smile, lightly tripped out of the apartment, leaving her lover utterly at a loss to comprehend the meaning of her enigmatical words, or to form a guess of the object of her singular movement. He was not long left, however, to the indulgence of useless conjectures. In a few minutes, she reappeared in the entry, with a countenance

lit up with joy and pride, and walking arm in arm with a well
dressed, dark complexioned, elderly, but vigorous looking
gentleman. Captain Willis instinctively rose at their appearance, glanced keenly at the face of the man, hesitated in evident uncertainty an instant, and then doubtfully uttered—
" Mr. Crocker—I believe."
" Ay, sir, till I get a new christening," said the other
smiling and throwing a significant glance at Madian.
" Captain Willis," said the maiden, with an impressive air,
and in tones made tremulous with emotion—" Captain Willis,
this is *my father, Colonel Richard Southworth.*"
After the young officer, who, it will be needless to say, was
as much delighted as astonished at this unexpected denouement, had received the congratulations on his recovery now
warmly proffered by Colonel Southworth, as we should now
call the mysterious stranger heretofore passing under the name
of Crocker, and, in his own turn, expressed his deep gratitude
for that care and attention of the other to which he had doubtless been indebted for his life, and of which the bestowal had
been to him such a matter of mystery—after these gratified
words and thoughts had been exchanged among this happy
and interestingly situated trio, Madian turned to her father
and said—
" Father, I had promised to give Captain Willis the particulars of my secret flight from Plymouth last summer, and of
my subsequent adventures, whereof, unwisely I have since
feared, I kept him in the dark ; but as *my* adventures would
be mainly embraced in a relation of *yours,* which he will also
wish to hear, I will, if you please, appoint you spokesman for
us both."
After a pleasant preliminary remark or two about his good
fortune in being no longer under any necessity for further
concealment, either of his identity or his thoughts, he signified
27

his ready acceptance of the appointment, the results of which we will place under the heading of

THE ADVENTURES OF THE OUTLAW AND HIS DAUGHTER.

" The crimes, as my daughter here knows, and as you, sir, have doubtless heard—the unpardonable crimes which were laid to my charge, and which occasioned my flight from civilized society, to escape an ignominious death on the block or the gallows, consisted in my hearty service, under the lion-hearted Cromwell, in aiding the overthrow of the corrupt monarchy of England; and also, in fearlessly asserting, after my settlement here in the colonies, the claims of religious liberty for all, and especially in behalf of the persecuted Quakers.

" The decree of my banishment as a Quaker, as I was assumed to be on account of my open defence of their rights, which had been rather timidly agreed upon, and then kept in abeyance, I cared little about; for I had determined to appeal to the people and fight it out. But when the news came that my name had been at last added to the list of those who, from time to time, had been doomed to the scaffold to appease the royal vengeance of the new Stuart; and with the news, came also, as I was secretly apprised, a warrant for my arrest and transportation, with a large reward set on my head for so doing, I lost no time in escaping into the wilderness, being resolved that my head should never be made to sanction or to grace the triumphs of one who, not *by the grace of God*, but by the weakness of the degenerate people, had reached the throne of England.

" Having been inured to fatigue, and the privations and discomforts of the worst kinds of out door life, by years of experience in the hardships of the camp, I hesitated not to elect the forest as my refuge. And I accordingly at once made my way into the wooded highlands of the west, and took up my residence among the Nipmuck Indians. Here I was treated, as every white man going among the natives with honest purposes ever will be, with uniform kindness and courtesy. In accordance with their just notions of politeness, they forbore to pry into my affairs, or even to ask my name. And I, on my part, while falling quietly into their modes of life, minded my own business, made no explanations, and left them to judge for themselves of my character, and to designate me by their own terms, as they soon did by an appellation which meant *stranger*, but which sounded so much like Crocker, that I concluded to assume that name.

" I built me a substantial cabin in a secluded location, and lived very comfortably, my money bringing all the game I wanted, which I could not take myself, as well as my breadstuffs. And in this manner, I continued to live here many months, without much fear of molestation from any quarter, apprehending nothing from the Indians, and believing that the officers of the law must have, by this time, given over their search for me. But I was mistaken. I at length learned from some members of the tribe, who had returned to their old haunts from sojourns round Boston and Plymouth, where, in becoming praying Indians, and constantly mingling with the whites, they had picked up all the news, that the authorities were not only hanging Quakers, but were still scouring the country for the man who had run away from Plymouth, and was now said to be somewhere in the Nipmuck country.

" I knew well enough what all that portended, and at once laid my plans to remove to some less exposed situation. In pursuance of these, I wrote a short letter to my agent in Plymouth, (you both have reason to know who that agent was,) renouncing civilized society, and intimating that I should probably never return. This missive I entrusted to a praying Indian, whom I paid for carrying it to Plymouth. In a day or two after this, I feigned to be taken by a fatal and infectious disease, warning my Indian neighbors to keep at a safe distance, and telling them that I was about to crawl off to die in some cave in the mountains. I then made up my pack, and, having thus provided against all chances of discovery or pursuit, stole away that night from my cabin, and stealthily made my way out of the territory of this tribe, in a southerly direction.

" After wandering and temporarily sojourning in the woods a few weeks, I at length reached the western shore of Narra-ganset Bay, purchased of an Indian á good bark canoe, rowed over to the long, crescent-shaped island, lying westerly of Montaup, skirted its northerly point round nearly midway the island, landed on the eastern shore, and penetrated about half a mile into the woods to a beautiful little pond, cosily situated at the base of a sheltering pine hill. Soon deciding on this sequestered and beautiful spot as an abode promising security against molestation, and, if I was threatened with it, the best of facilities for escaping by water, I went leisurely to work with my hatchet, and, in a week or two, succeeded in erecting a good, weather proof cabin.

" For the first three months I lived a complete hermit, subsisting on the bag of corn, and a package of dried venison I had bought of the Indians before I left the main land, together with the fresh fish and water fowl taken around the island by the fishing gear and fowling piece with which I had provided myself before leaving home. I was, as I wished to be, wholly cut off from the world. Not a single person, white or red, had to my knowledge approached the island; and the only human forms that greeted my senses, indeed, during that whole period, were those whom, from my lofty lookout from a pine tree on the hill behind my cabin, I could discern on the decks of the distant coasters, lazily pursuing their way to or from some of the ports above.

" About this time, however, needing some necessaries, I

concluded to go over to the main land and visit the Wampanoogs at Montaup, feeling the less hesitation in so doing,
because I knew there was but very little intercourse between
this tribe and the colonists, on account of the mutual growing
jealousies which even then had made considerable progress
towards the disastrous and unnecessary war now pending. I
made the excursion, and the result was a reception which soon
led to established relations of mutual confidence, and the most
friendly intercourse with them all. And Metacom, who had
then just succeeded to the throne, especially became my friend,
my protector, and finally my confidant, having given me not
only the red man's faith, but the faith of one of the most
high-minded men I ever knew; and it was a faith which was
never withdrawn or broken.

"Thus securely located in my pleasant island retreat, and
thus befriended by this powerful chief and his willing subjects,
I continued to live on, year after year, with a good degree of
contentment and safety, but with little to vary the monotony
of my half-savage life. After my fears of betrayal and pursuit, however, had measurably subsided, I ventured to make
excursions, in disguise, to several of the nearer white settlements, where I had several former acquaintances, whose
trustworthiness I had tested, and whose sympathy I felt sure
would be, for different reasons, readily accorded me. These
were our friend Roger Williams, of this town; James Leonard, of Taunton; Nathan Minturn, the husband of your
late hostess; and Captain Alden, the owner and master of a
ship usually plying between the head of Buzzard's Bay and
the southern colonies. All these received me as I expected,
and all in turn became masters of my secret. Mr. Williams,
who had then lived down his former miserable persecutions,
and become favorably known even to the Government of
England, was *more* than kind to me. He warmly but discreetly enlisted himself in my behalf, and volunteered to try

to obtain a reversal of my sentence of outlawry at the British court, where he had made some influential friends while there, when he was procuring his great charter. My trusty friend, Leonard, also rendered me good service in procuring for me money from my banker in Amsterdam, and faithfully keeping it to supply me as my necessities required; while both of the others I have named were ever equally faithful in guarding my interest and contributing to my peace and comfort.

"In this manner I continued to reside there during a period of nearly seven years, during which I pretty much lost all interest in the affairs of civilized life, and all desire of ever again returning to it, associated as it was in my mind with the bitter experiences of the past. But events were now at hand which were destined to modify these feelings in some degree, or at least to lead to a change of residence and mode of life. On one of my secret visits to my friend Captain Alden, I found him fitting out his ship for South Carolina, when he invited me to accompany him on the voyage, which he said could be made without risk on my part, as he had the right kind of crew, and we should fall among the right kind of people when we reached our destination. Soon concluding to fall in with the proposal, I went back to my residence, made my arrangements, paid flying visits to all my confidential friends, and returned just in time to embark on the proposed voyage. In due time we arrived at Charlestown, where I found myself among so many defiant refugees for conscience' sake—Quakers, Huguenots, and king-haters—that I soon felt myself quite at ease; and before my vessel was ready to return, I made up my mind to remain in that country, and accordingly I proceeded, with some congenial acquaintances I had formed at the port, to their residence at an interior settlement, where I settled down, and continued contentedly to reside for a period of over two years.

"But, by this time, the short supply of funds I had brought

with me began to run low; and besides, I was beginning to
entertain projects of purchasing landed estate. In view of
these circumstances, I at length decided on taking a voyage to
the north; and having ascertained when my old friend Captain
Alden was again expected with his vessel, I repaired to the
port, luckily found him there on the eve of departure, embarked, and, after another pleasant voyage, once more found
myself on the shores of New England.

  " This was less than a year ago ; and I, of course, found the
country in a state of feverish excitement and alarm from the
fast thickening portents of a war between the Colonists and
the Indians, and especially that spirited and intelligent tribe,
with whom I had mainly consorted. I fearlessly went among
them, however, and was kindly received, though I could
plainly perceive that they were laboring under feelings of
suppressed indignation from an increasing sense of their
wrongs, and that the presence of a white man among them,
was now attended with irritating associations. Metacom had
lost none of his friendship for me. He was very kind, but,
at the same time, very thoughtful, and evidently much oppressed in prospect of the fearful responsibilities which he
clearly saw were about to devolve on him, as the already
selected leader of the red men of the North in the impending
contest. He spoke with much feeling of the new wrongs
and indignities that had been heaped upon him and his people,
and said it required but one drop more to make the red man's
cup of bitterness overflow, when he could not, if he would,
restrain his warriors from hostilities any longer. That drop
I saw madly added, a short time afterwards, at Plymouth ; but
I will not anticipate. From Montaup I proceeded by night
to this town, and remained secreted, a few days, in the house
of my never to be forgotten friend, Governor Williams, who,
by this time, had become, quite unexpectedly to me, fully
warranted in opening to me the cheering prospect of a favora-

ble issue, at no distant period, of his efforts at the British court for a reversal of my outlawry. He also apprised me, for the first time, of the death of my wife; and gave me some vague intimations, which he said had been made to him as vaguely, that my daughter, then grown to womanhood, was less pleasantly situated, and less certain of obtaining her just rights there at Plymouth, than she should be. The opening of this new prospect for me personally, filled me with sensations which I before thought were dead within me. I began to wish to see my family, and know how my affairs at Plymouth had been managed in my absence; and the desire for this was not a little enhanced by the intimations I had received respecting them. It was perfectly useless for me to try to sit down contented under the new train, that had so unexpectedly been lighted in my bosom. On a succeeding night, therefore, I made an excursion to the residence of my friend Leonard, who, instead of relieving my anxieties about my home affairs, gave me information that still more startled and amazed me. Although a portion of the few hundred pounds that Leonard had drawn for me from my banker in Amsterdam, still remained in his hands, yet, on my departure for the South, I gave him authority to make another draft, which he was to hold in readiness for me in case I lived, and needed it at the South—if not, to keep it for my family. He had made the application, but the bank had refused to honor the draft, intimating that the fund was nearly, or quite exhausted! What could this mean? Mudgridge had no authority to make but one draft, and that of but a tithe of the fund; who then could have drawn all the rest, and how? My wife, or Deacon Mudgridge? But could either have drawn it without my authority? and if they had, what had become of it? Here was a mystery which was as dark as it was startling. At all, and every hazard, I must immediately fathom it, and, at once, I formed the bold design to visit Plymouth in disguise, and investigate the matter for myself.

Accordingly, in the well studied disguise of the dress, complexion, character, humble appearance, and broken English of a praying Indian, with a piece of an old Bible in my hand, I made the journey by night to that place, which I reached on the morning of the trial of the Indians. Having made for my retreat a temporary camp, deep in among the pine thickets adjoining the town, I sauntered out at an early hour, and mingled, unnoticed and unquestioned, in all the different crowds and gathering of that memorable day—saw everything—heard everything, ascertained much about the situation of my own family—much about the extent of the possessions of Deacon Mudgridge, and, on my way back to my retreat, at ten o'clock at night, looked into my own house; but will leave it to my auditors," added the speaker with a roguish smile, " to guess whom I probably saw there.

"After my return to my camp, I sat down and sadly reflected on the events of the day. The discoveries I had already made, in connection with the revolting public scenes I had witnessed, had given me a great deal of new light on what I now plainly perceived to be the dangerous character and influence of the man, who had, as I now had become satisfied, built himself up on my ruin. And coupling this with the intimations I had previously received, I began to feel for the first time really uneasy for the situation of my daughter. But as I had thus far learned nothing to warrant much alarm on that score, the feeling soon gave way to gloomy forebodings of the consequences which I saw must follow that bloody day's work of the infatuated court of Plymouth. Full of these fancies, and prompted by the displays of superstitious fears I had that evening witnessed in the streets, I was moved to help on the excitement. And remembering, that when I was at the head of Cromwell's thunderbolt regiment, as he was pleased to call it, I had the unusual power of voice to make my words of command, when ordering an onset, clearly distinguishable to the distance of a full mile, I ascended a pine tree, and from its top held forth to the distant multitude in such utterance of denunciation and warning as came uppermost. This I repeated for many subsequent nights; for I had a design, from the execution of which I wished to keep public attention diverted. That design was secretly to make myself known to my daughter, and thus obtain, before leaving the place, much or all of the information I wanted. In accordance with this project, I loitered round in sight of my door, the next day, till I saw her in the yard, when I respectfully approached her, asked for a cup of water, received it, contrived to have her look me full in the face, and departed; trusting something to the operation of that mysterious sympathy often felt by stranger kindred, when unknown they meet, to create in her feelings an interest for me, which should save her from any alarm, and me from a repulse at another interview. I had not miscalculated. The next time I called, which was at twilight, several days afterwards, when I found her again in the yard among her flowers, I at once read in her countenance the very interest and spirit of curious enquiry that I had desired to create in her mind. But perceiving that she was looking for some reason for my calling, I asked her to read to me a little from my fragment of a Bible. She did so, scanning my countenance at every pause closer than ever. I then told her if she would be found sitting in her open window at dark the next evening I would call again and tell her news. Upon this I turned, and in my natural voice and manner, said, as she was moving towards the house, ' Good night, Madian ;' when glancing back, I saw her suddenly stop short in her tracks, and stand like a post, gazing after me in blank bewilderment. The next night I called—found her at the proposed window, and, as will be anticipated, at length made myself known, explained all, and received from her in turn, a frank expose of all that concerned her personally, and all she knew which concerned me and my affairs. The result was another and more secret interview. And the result of that was an arrangement to decamp together, the next night, at midnight, on our way to Providence, where she was to remain in private, while I retired to some safe retreat, at no great distance, to await the issue of the negotiations going on in my behalf in England.

" In execution of the safest plan I could devise for effecting our object, I set off that very night for the residence of my friend, Captain Alden, near the head of Buzzards Bay, reached there the next morning, let him into my plans, engaged a couple of his trusty sailors as oarsmen and assistants, and with them traveled over the neck to a fishing station on the outer coast, chartered a good boat, and rowed up to Plymouth in the evening. Landing about eleven o'clock at a small, familiar cove making into my own farm, and agreeing on a signal call in case I wanted help, I left the sailors to keep the boat till my return, and proceeded to my house to notify my daughter. But the servants, from whom we had agreed to keep the secret of our flight, lest through them we should in some way be traced, had but just gone to bed; and she would not be ready before the appointed hour of midnight. There was yet a long hour to wait; and feeling restless, I took in my hand a light package of choice linen, which Madian had already made up to take with us, and left the house with the first intention of going with it to the boat. But when I got out I was moved by a sudden inclination to patrol the streets. All was silent; and there were no lights to be seen, save a solitary one that was feebly glimmering through a distant window. I followed it up, and found it proceeded from a ground-floor bed-room in the costly dwelling-house of Deacon Mudgridge. Perceiving the window which opened into the garden to be raised a few inches, I took it into my head to go round and peer into it. A dimly burning night-lamp sat on a table near the foot of the bed, while in the broad, scamy, upturned face which lay exposed to view on the bed, I readily recognized the well-remembered features of the veritable Deacon. The muscles of his face were twitching nervously, and his lips were moving with incoherent mutterings. But so far from blaming him for having a conscience-laden dream, it suddenly occurred to me, that if I could get into the room, I might add a counterpart or finale to the probable burden of the dream with wholesome effect.

"Accordingly, after noting the best way of ingress from without, I proceeded to the outer door, and finding it unfastened, hastily wrapt about me a white sheet taken from my package, stalked into the bed room, carefully setting all the doors open as I went, and gave a loud rap on the table. The troubled sleeper started, and with a rapid glance over the room, bolted upright in bed, riveted his gaze on me, and sat glaring me in the face, his eyes opening wider and wider, his looks growing wilder and wilder, and his hair gradually rising up like bristles on his head, as, without the power of moving he continued to gaze on in his speechless fright. After gravely encountering his looks a moment, I silently and solemnly pointed upward, then at him, then downward, and then, with my eyes still frowningly fixed on him, slowly backed out of the apartment.

"Having no more time to lose, I left the Deacon to his own thoughts and conclusions, and hastened back to my house; when finding my daughter in readiness, we at once proceeded to the boat, embarked, and were soon rapidly cutting our way through the waveless waters, and in the light of the rising moon, which now fortunately combined to favor our nightly voyage. On reaching our landing, after two or three hours' snug rowing, we found, as had been arranged, a carriage in waiting for us; and immediately starting overland, we made

such good speed that, before it was fairly light, we were
safely ensconced in the house of Captain Alden.

"As the captain was to sail south again in a few days, and
was to touch at Newport, from which he thought he could
promise us a safe passage up Narraganset Bay, we remained
there in private till the vessel was loaded; when we embarked
wholly undiscovered, as I then supposed, and, after a variety
of adventures, which it will probably now be unnecessary to
particularize, at length arrived at our respective destinations,
Madian having been escorted to Providence, and I passing
round by land to the great village of the Narragansets."

"You have thrown," said the young officer, who had been
listening to the developments of the other with the most intense interest—"Ay, sir, you have thrown a flood of light on
a mind which, now for almost a year, has been groping in be-
wildering and painful darkness. Most of the mysteries that
have been thus defying my powers of fathoming, stand explained; but not quite all. Let me ask you, therefore, what
day or night was it you passed from the waters of Buzzards
Bay into those of the Narraganset?"

"That is a part of our story which I thought you probably
had pretty nearly ascertained at the time. At all events, I
was fearful you or your crew had, or would, I recollect," replied the colonel, smiling. "But as it seems that you did
not suspect the truth, I will inform you that our voyage was
made on the day of your battle and lucky escape at Pocasset,
and on the night of the terrible thunderstorm that followed."

"And it was then indeed Madian and you, who were put
ashore, when your dismasted vessel grounded, and was supposed to be in danger of going to pieces? I *did* suspect
something like the truth, at least, so far as she was concerned;
for when your vessel crossed our path, a flash of lightning

distinctly revealed to my sight a female figure, standing on her deck, which, from some inadvertent words dropped by the skipper, who must have been partly let into your secret I think, I hoped, or rather feared, at that terrible moment, might be hers, whose fate I was so anxious to ascertain.

Yet, when both our vessels got into Newport, the next morning, your trusty friend Alden, whom I questioned, so adroitly concealed your secret, by leaving me to infer, that it was a praying Indian and his squaw that I had seen put ashore, that I gave up my impressions, and forebore the pursuit I was intending. But how and when did you get away from that wild and desolate looking shore ?"

" In the canoes of those, who were more friendly to us, than they might have been to you, had they caught you. I asked no questions, but gathered that they followed you down the bay, keeping themselves invisible in the shadow of the western shore till after dark, and then part of them getting ahead of you till the storm struck ; when they made their way by land, till they saw you out of reach in the open sea. And having seen us landed, they came forward, identified me, and sending back for their canoes, offered to take us up the bay with them. Accepting the offer, we embarked with them as soon as the water became smooth enough, and long before morning, reached the vicinity of Montaup, where I relinquished Madian to be rowed by one of them up to Providence ; while I kept on with the rest, to be landed at the mouth of Taunton river."

" A bold step for you, Madian—was it not ?" asked Willis, with a look of doubt and surprise. " Did you not hesitate to go thus ?"

" Why should I ?" replied the maiden, with quiet assurance —" Why should I hesitate to trust myself with one who had proved himself my father's friend, and who, at the same time, was the safest of boatmen ?"

" Who was he, Madian ?" rejoined the other, still wondering and doubting.

" It was KING PHILIP, in the disguise of a sailor !" answered the girl in a low, impressive, and slightly rebuking
tone.

" Ay, and that was not the last good office he did me,"
warmly interposed the colonel. " A night or two afterwards,
I met him at Leonard's, where he rescued me from the very
grasp of the kidnappers or assassins, who there unexpectedly
assailed me."

" Kidnappers !" exclaimed Willis starting—" kidnappers,
Colonel Southworth ? Who were they, and by whom instigated ?"

" I do not know—that is with any certainty—but have
strong suspicions," returned the other thoughtfully.

" And so have I, now," rejoined the young officer leaping
to his feet, with the air of one recalling something that goes
to confirm some damning conclusion—" so have I *my* suspicions too ; and I will give you my reasons for them."

And he then related the singular and questionable circumstances, under which he overtook Deacon Mudgridge and his
band, while on his way to Plymouth with the Dartmouth
prisoners, which event, by comparing notes with the colonel,
he found must have occurred the next morning after the assault at Leonard's, and concluded by asking—

" And yet, how could that old fox have discovered you were
alive, and in the land ?"

" I was, at first, at a loss to know, myself," answered the
other. " But subsequent reflection led me to believe that,
after his fright was over, his devil's cunning converted the
supposed ghost into a living reality, threatening his ruin
unless traced out and destroyed. And that, thereupon, he
had sent out a band of spies, some of whom must have identified me by his description, when I embarked with Captain

Alden, and perhaps got an intimation that I was coming into
this region, which led the whole of them, with their master,
to come where they accidentally discovered and dogged me to
Leonard's house.   And it is now clear that I was right.   The
black hearted hypocrite intended not only to seize me, but
designed, I am satisfied, to crown his iniquities by causing me
to be assassinated.   But the day of reckoning is now close at
hand."

" What do you propose to do ?" asked the former.

" Go to Plymouth," resumed the latter—" go there to-morrow or next day, and openly arraign the miscreant before the
whole court."

" But have you any tangible evidence, to warrant so bold
a step ?" enquired Willis, anxiously.

" Am I not rather too old a soldier to go to battle, except
in full armor ?" responded the other, significantly.

" But can you make the journey, and then your appearance
in public, with safety to your own person ?" persisted the
former.

" At all events, I shall try it," replied the determined colonel, with eyes flashing with their old fires.   " But you may
not find me so unprepared for the contest as you fear.   There
has been an arrival lately from the old world.   No ; I go, as
you will see, not wholly unprepared ; but I wish you to accompany us."

" I will do so," responded the other, musing.   " Ay, I will
go, and I think I can aid you, at least, in exposing that last,
and most flagitious of all that man's wicked attempts.   I
know who was the chief tool, as he has long been in other
matters, in that dark transaction ; and as he is one of those
rats most ready to desert a sinking ship, I think I can use him
for a better purpose than punishing him with his master ; but
I may require time.   I think I had better go on one day in advance of you, to prepare matters ; and I have a trusty friend

in town, Captain Mosely, who will accompany me. And—
why, there !" he added, glancing through the window—" there
is the very man, now, approaching the house in company of
our friend, Roger Williams."

The personages thus announced now entered, and the required introductions took place ; when in the conversation that
at once sprung up between the mutually attracted Colonel
Southworth and Captain Mosely, the unexpected but delight-
ful discovery was made that they were not wholly strangers,
but had known each other in an interesting connection in the
old world :—Mosely had been a young subaltern in the colonel's own regiment; was, in fact, distantly related to his
family, and, like his leader, having, in his hatred to kings,
left the country at the Restoration, had, after a wild life with
the buccaneers a few years, settled down in the colonies. The
old battles had of course to be fought over again, and it was
an animating and joyful scene all round; but it was not yet
quite ended.

The good and venerable Williams now rose and waved his
hand for attention.

"*All* reunions," he said, in his usual pleasant and self-possessed manner—" *All* reunions of friends and kindred are
things of joy ; and *these*, which have been witnessed here to-
day, are so especially such, that I think they may be well sig-
nalized by special tokens. I, on my part," he added, drawing
forth a document, and with it approaching, and lightly rapping on the shoulder of the wondering Madian, " have here
a small one, of which I beg this fair and noble maiden's acceptance, merited as it is *every* way, and particularly so by
her many weeks' devoted attentions in nursing and aiding to
restore our gallant friend Willis here to life and usefulness."

" Mr. Williams," here exclaimed the surprised and blushing girl, with a look of charming confusion, and with a playfully menacing shake of her beautiful head; " you, sir, it ap-
28

pears to me, are exceeding your license of speech; he did not know, and I did propose he never should know that."

"Ah! Why?" rejoined the good old man, with a kind but slightly quizzical air. "Why, my fair friend, you are delicate over much. But that is ever the way with the riddle, woman—go through fire and water at the call of duty and affection, but shrink from the veriest trifle squinting adversely to her sense of female pride and propriety. Well, it is too late to retrieve my error. But Captain Willis won't think much worse of either of us, I fancy, for the disclosure?" he added, glancing inquiringly to the surprised and gratified young officer.

"Oh, no," eagerly responded the latter: "no, indeed, no; and I thank you, sir, for the revelation of a fact which I should know, that, if possible, I may repay the precious favor. And I am gratified also in the disclosure, in that it clears up a mystery in which that sly Quakeress but the more befogged me. But it seems the eye of love will be true, though the brain wanders. Rogue, Madian, I half mistrusted you!"

"This," resumed Williams, presenting his paper anew, after this by-play had passed—"the paper I have here in hand is a deed of the handsome tract of land adjoining that of our most worthy and Christian friend, the widow Minturn, whom most of those present have so much reason to remember. It runs to Madian Southworth. Will she accept it?"

"Why, sir," replied the hesitating maiden—"why, I hardly know what I should say or do. What should I, father?"

"Oh, don't appeal to him," said Williams, "but ask Captain Willis. What does he say?"

"I have no answer to make," responded Willis, with emotion. "The father and daughter have both conquered—doubly conquered me. Their decision in this, as well as in matters still more nearly concerning me, I should try to make my own, even if disagreeable."

"It will not be disagreeable, I trust," interposed Colonel
Southworth, now stepping forward, with moistening eye.
"Daughter, arise; and you also, Captain Willis, if you will.
Here, sir," he continued, placing Madian's hand in that of
her lover. "I was aware of the relation in which you two
have stood towards each other; but here is her lawfully
bestowed hand. As you have been privately, without parental
sanction, so be you now, with a parent's full sanction, publicly
betrothed. Choose your own time and place for the consum-
mating forms of the law, only let every thing be open and
above board. God bless you, my children!"

"I was not," remarked Williams, after the emotions attending the tender ceremony had subsided—"I was not, I confess,
wholly without selfish motive in my gift. I had hoped to
induce—and may I be allowed still to hope that my friend,
Captain Willis, whose views, I have reason to believe, in some
respects coincide with my own, will in reality be induced to
settle down on my beautiful Rhode Island, and help make it
what I intend and confidently prophesy it shall become—a
moral beacon-fire, which, with the passing years, shall grow
brighter and broader, till, in its expanding light, the whole
American people shall see that no *true* civil freedom and no
true piety can long flourish but in the unrestrained exercise
of the principles of religious liberty."

After their venerated friend, Williams, had departed, Colonel Southworth and his congenial guests went into an earnest
secret consultation in relation to the important expose yet
remaining to be made at Plymouth, the results of all which
are reserved for the next and concluding chapter of our
eventful story

CHAPTER XXII.

"In his lair,
Fix'd Passion holds his breath, until the hour
Which shall atone for years; none need despair;
It came, it cometh, and will come,—the power
To punish or forgive—in *one* wo shall be slower."

WE have at last, in the progress of our story, found our way round to the place whence we started. We are again in Plymouth, the town of Pilgrim memories—memories of many a stern virtue, in the times in which we write, it is true, but memories also of

"That faith—fanatic faith, which, wedded fast
To some dear falsehood, hugged it to the last."

It was twilight; and the shades of night were falling deeper and deeper over the green lawn and unfolding shrubberies surrounding the quiet and secluded mansion of the singularly fortuned Southworths. The two faithful old domestics, Taffy and his wife Maggy, who, since the mysterious disappearance of their young mistress, had been the unmolested and unguided occupants and managers of the establishment, were now both, after the labors and duties of the day, listlessly sauntering about in the yard, occasionally pausing, the one to draw forth his pocket knife and prune a scraggy shrub, and the other to stoop and scratch round the roots of some flower-plant, just peeping through the old grass, dry leaves, or other rubbish of winter. They had been kept in utter ignorance, not only of the fate of the daughter, but also of her astounding discovery before she left them, that the father was still in the land of the living; for the latter, knowing their ardent temperament, and consequent liability to reveal by some unguarded word, or leave to be inferred by their actions a secret which he believed of great consequence to him to remain unknown and unsuspected, for the present at least, decided that the only safe policy to be pursued would be to keep them equally in the dark with the public at large.

" What ye dumping and duling aboot there, Taffy?" asked the woman, after a second enquiring glance at her husband, who stood at a little distance with his fingers thrust into his long, sandy hair, and in the attitude of one in a deep study.

" I wull tell ye, Maggy, an ye first tell me what is that long ward the minister uses sometimes, whan he's spinning out his sarment, near the eend on't, and says, from this, or that, I draw the following—what is the ward he draws, Maggy?"

" *Inference?* inference, it is, ye forgetful loun, Taffy."

" Ay, that's the ward, it is, aweel, its an inference I'm trying to draw, Maggy."

" Aboot what thing,—what cunning maggot's got into yer head, now, Taffy?"

" It's aboot the why is it that church carl, the Deacon up town, don't come speering round the wark an things here, as he used to. He's not been here once since our young leddy went off so strange. Seeing she's gone, I expectit he'd come the more; so it an't nothing about that, I opine, Maggy."

" Sure enuf—ye sets me thinking; but what yer think *is* the why, Taffy?"

" It was jest that vera why I was trying to draw the inference aboot, Maggy. It may be because he thinks his game is up; an he can't mak any more out of her, or so much as he was mintin."

" More like it he's found out somethin, Taffy—found out,

maybe, she knows more aboot her rights than he thought she knew, the carl! an *she* don't know none *too* much, I opine. The kurnel once had heaps of money, an *all* of it never came into *this* family *I know*. Taffy, I never said much aboot it, but I rather suspicion that man, if he *is* high Dacon."

"Aweel, whether ye suspicion right or wrong, Maggy, we are glad of one thing, an't we? We are glad the wark has gone on jest as weel without the Deacon's speering an contrivin, an that we've been done prudent and saving of our young leddy's property, as we shuld, an she were here hersel· Ay, we're glad of that, an't we, Maggy? for she sure be somewhere, an will be back, soon, I've faith, to receive her own."

"Amin to all that, Taffy; for 'twud mak my auld heart jump to see her agin; an' if that goodly young man culd only come too! But he is dead in the Injun battle, they say. How our young leddy will gret an' grieve aboot it, to be sure!"

As this confabulation now sunk into silence, Maggy slowly retired into the house, leaving her husband to continue at will his musings in the yard. She had been seated in her room but a few minutes, however, before she heard him raise a strange, sharp outcry, which seemed to be forced from his lips by some sudden surprise and alarm. Starting instantly to her feet, she sprang for the outer door, when she encountered him rushing through the hall towards her, gibbering in quick, suppressed tones and with startled looks.

"A wraith! a wraith! I've seen the old kurnel's wraith standing in the yard, as sure as a gun, Maggy!"

"What?—fiddle-stick!—Why, yer clean gone daft, Taffy!" exclaimed the woman, with look and tone, in which the emotions of surprise, contempt, doubt, and fear, were strangely mingled.

"I'm na dafter nor you, Maggy; it's true as the Book!" responded Taffy, sufficiently reassured by the braver bearing of his wife to speak connectedly—"it *is* true, Maggy! But, O Lordy! what has we done to bring him up on us so? *I'se* done nothing, sure—I wull swear that. It must be *you.*— What has *ye* done, Maggy?"

"Na a single thing!" promptly retorted the woman, who, besides being naturally of a firmer nerve than her husband, was now nettled into daring by his last intimation—"na the *least* thing, for cheatery or offence; an' I daur go an' face him on it, this vera minute!" she added, making resolutely towards the door.

Taffy made a confused attempt to catch and detain her, as she brushed by him; but it was in vain. The next moment, she threw open the door; when her eye falling on the questionable figure she was looking for, standing in the path with face averted towards Willis and Madian, then just coming into view, she stopped short on the threshold, and gazed out in the utmost perplexity and astonishment.

"Gude guide us! if the old mon ben't right!" she at length muttered—"dead or alive, that's the kurnel, sure, now! But what's that?" she continued, now catching a view of Willis. "Why, there is another of them! and—and—no—yes—yes, thank God, it is! and flesh and blude, too, every inch of her, I *know*. And here goes for *her*, any way."

So saying, she bounded forward through the yard, and giving a wide berth to each of the ghosts as she passed them, pounced upon the surprised Madian, like a hawk upon a dove, and threw her arms around her neck with a scream of joy.

It was many minutes before the newly arrived company could discover and comprehend the cause of the singular appearance and behavior of the two old domestics, especially of Taffy, who stood timorously peering out from behind the door as mute as a fish; and it was equally long, before the latter could be made to realize that his old master was still alive, and really there in flesh and blood. But when he at length did, he became almost crazy with delight, dancing about, leaping up, throwing his hat into the air, and exclaiming—

"Huz—huz—huzza! huzza for the kurnel! in the body and bones, worth a dozen empty wraiths! Huzza for our young leddy, who outwitted the Deil and the Dacon! Huzza for the young Captain, who wasn't killed by the bludy salvages! Huzza for everybody, and auld Oliver Cromwell besides!"

"Look out there," laughingly said the Colonel—"have a care, Taffy, or King James will serve you as he did me."

"Dang King Jeems!" returned Taffy snapping his fingers—"dang *all* kings—I'se a rip publican! Dang the Dacon, an' every body that ever speeched, thought, or did any thing against the kurnel or our young leddy; for the dead be comed to life, the lost be found, an' I wull kill that fatted calf the morrow mornin'—I wull!"

"Ter—ter—Taffy!" interposed Maggy, choking with emotions of the same joy, but of the opposite manifestation—"Taffy, yer acting like a fule; yer daft, ye auld child."

"Fule an' daft, is it?" retorted Taffy. "Which be the biggest auld child fule: to be sniveling and skirling like a great booby, as yer doin' there, or to be caperin' an' laffing like I do? Ha! ha! ha! Huzza!"

"That's right; let it off, now you are at it, my man," here broke in the grum, half-laughing, half-choking voice of Captain Mosely, who, unnoticed, had approached, and stood witnessing the scene, a little aloof. "All right, sir, and no blame; for, really, I don't see much to choose in the plight of any of you," he added, chuckling, and dashing away a tear that had started in his own eye as he glanced round on the company, who all seemed to have caught the infection of the

old domestics. " But, colonel, you are not so prudent a
commander as I had counted. After leaving your carriage
and sending it back, when two miles off, so that you could walk
into town in the dusk undiscovered, this display in the open
yard, where the neighbors will be so likely to hear and
suspect, hardly comports, does it?"

" True," responded Colonel Southworth, seeming to recollect himself—" true, Captain Mosely, true. So, now, all hands
into the house; for it is agreed, for certain reasons, to keep
close mouths and a close garrison to night, and till the hour
arrives for showing ourselves to-morrow."

On this intimation, they all soon disappeared within the
newly honored walls of the old homestead, where we will leave
the happy circle to the social enjoyment which the circumstances were so well calculated to impart—to the enjoyment
of emotions as pure and felicitous, probably, as ever gladdened
the home and hearth of any family on earth.

It was about nine the next forenoon when Deacon Mudgridge, who had not been out in the street that morning,
suddenly started from a reverie in which he seemed to have
been for some time deeply buried as he sat alone in his room,
rose, went to his desk, took out a thick parcel of deeds, and
counted them over, muttering to himself something about
their respective values as he glanced at each and laid it aside,
his mind being evidently engaged on a sort of running
computation of the amount of his possessions.

" Twenty farms and ten houses. Ay, a full score of
valuable farms, and half as many good tenements, besides my
money bonds; and I should like to know how any body is to
get them away from me?" he said, putting up the papers, and
beginning to pace the room with a certain look of unrest and
secret apprehension, which sadly belied the boastful and
defiant words he was uttering. " Then, what need this

uneasiness—this boding fear that the Lord, who has so long blessed and favored his servant above other men, is now about to desert him and give him over to the buffetings of Sathan? There is none! Then, begone with ye, phantoms! I will not—but, hush! hark! Was that not a rap on the door? Ay, it is Dummer's rap. COME IN! Come in, brother Dummer. I know you by your rap almost as well as I do by your voice. Sit down, and tell me the news. I am glad you dropt in, brother; I was feeling quite lonely this morning."

"A little lonely, peradventure, our honored Deacon may sometimes feel; yet he is never alone—the Lord is always with him," observed the Shadow, obsequiously.

"Your words are of kindly intent, albeit they do over much exalt me in the matter of spiritual desert, brother Dummer," rejoined the Deacon, with affected meekness. "Yea, verily, I fear so; but I was inquiring about the news —is there any thing in particular stirring abroad in the streets this morning?"

"Why, not much," replied the Shadow, slightly hesitating. "Nothing, in truth, I may say, save the assembling of the court, which seems to be going on, and the which—"

"Assembling of the court!" interrupted the Deacon, starting—"Assembling of the court, Dummer, and I know nothing about it?—I not consulted—not even notified! What does that mean? What is it for? What is to be done there, Dummer?"

"Well, touching that, now, Deacon," replied the Shadow, "I can't say as I know myself, exactly. As I was going by, I noticed people going into the court room, and was moved to drop in it also. But though most of the usual sitting magistrates were assembled, I heard no announcement whereby I could hear the occasion thereof."

"But didn't you hear anybody say what matters were to

come before the court to-day, Dummer?" eagerly persisted the other, with a disturbed and suspicious air.

"Yea," said the Shadow—"yea, Deacon, now I bethink me, I *did* hear one man tell another, that he guessed the court were going to try some criminals. But there was no show of any such questionable characters there to confirm it; albeit, there *was* one there who *should* be held as a criminal by the whole household of faith—I mean that scoffing Captain Mosely, who so audaciously obstructed the course of the law here last summer, in the matter of the contumacious Vane Willis, and who then again afterwards, broke away so offensively from service, at the time I made my great prayer for the strengthening of the army."

"That Mosely—that bold scoffer, do you mean? Are you sure it was he you saw there, Dummer?" sharply demanded the Deacon.

"Verily, it was the same man, Deacon," answered the Shadow, looking up inquiringly at the former, as if at loss to account for his disturbed manner. "It surely was the man; though I could but marvel how his presence could be tolerated there as it was. But you do know, Deacon, how strangely his forwardness has been winked at by some of our temporal rulers; and more so than ever to-day, methought; for I saw him actually whispering with the governor."

On this the Deacon hastily rose, and, with visible perturbation, rapidly paced the room several minutes in silence; when turning short on the Shadow, he abruptly asked—

"Dummer, where is Dick Swain?"

"Well, now, really, Deacon, I do not recall having seen him this morning," replied the other; "nay, I have not, nor even yesterday, as for that matter. He don't seem to have been about as usual."

"Worse and worse," muttered the Deacon to himself, as he resumed his hurried walk, with increasing agitation.

" Things all point one way—my bodings had a meaning. It has come ; but it must be met boldly. Dummer," he continued, again stopping before the wondering Shadow, with an effort at calmness—" Brother Dummer, you always professed to be my friend—stand by me to-day—I greatly suspect some evil is designed against me ; but it is a device of Sathan to destroy my influence, and must be put down ; and may I not safely count on the aid of your powerful spiritual arm, in case anything untoward shall befall ?"

" Of a verity you may, my honored Deacon," warmly replied the Shadow, his enthusiasm instantly kindling at this flattering appeal, as little as he could comprehend any necessity for making it. " But what is there untoward that *can* happen ? And what has my Deacon to fear, if there should? Doth not the Scripture say *the arms of the wicked shall be broken ; but the Lord upholdeth the righteous ?*"

" As steel sharpeneth steel, so do your words of faith re-assure and strengthen me, brother Dummer," responded the Deacon. " I shall feel strong with you battling by my side. But do not be baffled by Sathan into any doubts and misgivings in the matters of accusation he may instigate against me."

" Nay, I will not," rejoined the Shadow, boldly ; " I will put on my whole armor and dare the adversary to his face."

" Then let us hence to the court room," said the Deacon, hurriedly taking his hat and leading the way out of the house.

On reaching the court room, the presentient Deacon and his church-militant champion, found the governor, his assistants, the minister, and the licensed religious teacher, all occupying the bench in silence, and with no apparent business before them. At almost any other time the Deacon would have entered the room under the confident expectation of being immediately conducted to a seat on the bench, by the attending officer, or, of being beckoned thither by the governor, the ex-officio Chief Judge, since he had often been called to sit among the magistrates as one of the representatives of the over-shadowing ecclesiastical part of the government. But now his conscience-suggested fears and forebodings had so deeply shaken his self-confidence, that he made no expectant pause as he passed the officer near the door, and scarcely ventured a glance at the governor for the notice by which he had been so frequently distinguished on entering the court room, on the eve of a session. And therefore, after a sort of hesitating lingering in front of the bench, for a moment, he passed on to a seat among the scattered audience, and with an assumed air of unconcern, began to look around him a little, closely scanning the expressions of the countenances of the leading laymen present, and finally ending his inspection by a sharp, but covert glance at the different members of the court. But his anxious eye was greeted with little to comfort or assure him from any quarter. The governor appeared unusually moody, and an air of stern resolution was visibly brooding upon his countenance. Two of the assistant magistrates sat with their heads together, and with solemn, regretful looks, appeared to be discussing, in low, subdued tones, some subject mutually painful and repugnant to their feelings. And all the rest of the officials, as well as many leading men among the spectators, appeared singularly thoughtful or disturbed; their looks, which were often turned furtively towards the door, plainly indicating a more or less defined expectation in their minds that something very unusual or unpleasant was about to transpire.

At this juncture, a slight bustle at the door instantly drew all eyes in that direction; when the brawny figure of Captain Mosely was seen boldly pushing forward into the room, followed by Captain Willis, and another and unknown personage, with a slouched hat on, drawn down low over his eyes, an Indian blanket wrapped around his shoulders, and brought up so high and close on each side of his face, as, with the hat, wholly to conceal his features from the view of all gazers. One after the other, the strongly contrasted trio stalked mutely along the aisle, passed on in front of the court, and turned into a conspicuous seat in the rear of the bar at which criminals were usually brought for their arraignment. The two officers had removed their hats on entering, but the other kept his on, and still retained it, together with his blanket muffler, in place, after he became seated; exhibiting, as he sat with low, drooping head, both in outward rig and deport- ment, the general appearance of some sullen Indian prisoner, as he was taken to be by most of the spectators. Presently, Captain Mosely slowly raised himself to his feet, and looking round over the gathering crowd, with a sort of mock gravity, till his eye had singled out the squat, cowering form of Dea- con Mudgridge, and then turning to the court, and balancing himself on his toes a moment, he bluntly asked the governor if he was ready to proceed to business? · And, taking the affirmative nod of his excellency as a satisfactory answer to the question, he quietly drew his broad palm across his mouth to smooth down the mischief-boding pucker which had gathered there, and soon began—

" Well, then, I suppose your honor and others will remem- ber a little bit of a word fracas we had in this town, last summer, over an attempt to detain Captain Willis on charge of Quaker- ism, or some such trumpery matter, at a time, when he and I, with our companies, were pushing on to the frontier to help put down the Indian outbreak ; and when every minute's delay might cost the scalp of a white man, and the lives of his wife and babies. And your honor will pretty likely remember, likewise how I interfered—a little roughly, may be, to get the object of that muss off so that he could go about his business, which God knows was urgent enough, at the time. Well, sir, as now the captain, after good service, finds himself, while getting well of wounds received in battle, with the leisure and disposition to meet all claims the authorities may have on him, I have brought him here to deliver him up, so that a certain Deacon I wot of, who seemed to be the stirrer up of that notable affair, shall not say that *I* have robbed him of the chance of displaying his righteous indignation in the matter he appeared so intent on prosecuting. And here is the man, sitting on my right, so that his saintship yonder, the devil helping, may now work his will on him," added the rough soldier, motioning carelessly with one hand to Willis, and pointing significantly with the other to Deacon Mudgridge.

The court—especially the governor, seemed to be taken with surprise by this singular announcement. It had been as we presume the reader has already inferred, privately intimated to his excellency what developments might be expected, respecting the character and crimes of Deacon Mudgridge—developments that, for reasons, which his observations the past year had supplied, but which he had prudently kept to himself, he was not wholly unprepared to witness; and he had that morning, with feelings of the deepest chagrin, made partial revelations of the painful occurrence to his assistants. But neither he, nor they, had any expectation that the forthcoming disclosures were to be prefaced by any such presentation as Mosely, through some policy or whim of his own, had made in relation to an old, gone-by case, which, even at the time, was considered, to say the least, very unadvisedly got up by the Deacon. And his excellency, scarcely knowing, therefore, what response to make to the strange communication, which seemed to be left so as to invite some action or remarks on his part, turned, after a doubtful pause, to his assistants, and went into a brief whispered consultation with them on the subject. But the affair evidently had a very different effect on the troubled Deacon. He had from time to

time been casting uneasy and suspicious glances at the strange
muffled figure, sitting mute and motionless near the two
officers whom he had followed into the court-room.   As soon,
however, as Captain Mosely had brought his communication
to a close, in a manner to lead to the supposition that
nothing more was intended than what it purported to be, the
countenance of the Deacon began visibly to brighten, and
perk up into something like his old airs of assurance and holy
antagonism.   Mosely's movement had misled him, and believing the danger of the dreaded developement to be over,
he drew a long breath, as if relieved of an overpowering
burden, and began to rally his controversial forces for an
emergency, in which, if that were all, he felt himself strong
to give battle.

"I *did*," he said, at length floundering on to his feet, with
hands, looks, and voice all in a flush—"I *did*—and it shameth
me not to confess it, though scoffers may revile and speak
tauntingly—I did, at the important crisis mentioned, verily
believe we had a duty to perform, in rebuking the crying
heresies, which were bringing the displeasure of Heaven on
the land, as seen in the threatened war with the heathen salvages.   And, wherefore, I *did* move in the matter of the
reported pestilent Quakerism of the man, Vane Willis, even
unto the pointing him out for the action of the authorities.
And I am bold to say, it was a daring offence, and one argu-
ing a guiltiness of the charge, for him to put them at defiance
in the contumacious way and manner he and his confederate
did, on that disgraceful occasion."

"Amen!" here loudly chimed in the Shadow, suddenly
bobbing up from another part of the crowd, like a startled
kangaroo.   "I, for one, can truly say amen to every word
just uttered by our God-loving brother, Deacon Mudgridge,
who has done but his conscience-directed duty, in striving to
purge the land from the abominations of its heresies, unto

the turning away of Divine wrath, from a greatly sinning people."

" Ay," rejoined the Deacon, warming up, " brother Dummer hath spoken truly touching the dangers of our remissness, in tolerating the pestilent heresies of the day. They are the great curse-breeders of our American Israel. And yet," he continued with the air of an injured man—"and yet, for my honest strivings against the alarming evil—for the attempting my God-bounden duty, in that behalf, I am held up here, in words of profane levity and scoffing, for the invited reproach of a Christian court! Ay, held up here as one called to account, as if, forsooth, faithfulness to duty were some crying offence !"

" Peace !" said the governor, who, having finished his hasty consultation, had been listening, for the last few minutes, with evident impatience, to the Deacon's back fire, as all in the secrets of the hour, at once perceived it to be—" peace ! this discussion is needless. Nobody is to be called to account in anything relating to the untoward affair of last summer, whereof mention has been made. There is no charge against Captain Willis before this court. On the contrary, I deem it a duty to say here openly, that since witnessing his gallant conduct in the taking of the Narraganset fort, and then investigating for myself his previous course and character, I have felt an increasing conviction of the injustice that has been done him. But the error, I trust, will now soon be atoned, by conferring on him the rank and commission, which shall not only make amends for past neglect, but induce him to continue his valuable services for the future."

" There it is, at last !" said Mosely with a low, exulting chuckle, turning to the young officer at his side, who appeared like one doubting his own senses in what he had just heard— " there it is, right from head quarters ; and done like a man, too ! You now see what I was after, don't you, Willis ?"
29

"Ay," responded the other in the same undertone. "Ay, and many thanks to you, sir, for bringing it out as publicly as were the slights I have received. But I confess it has taken me wholly unawares."

"Well, my boy," gleefully returned the other, "you are evidently not the only one taken by surprise by such words from such a source. Just cast your eyes round over that squad of the Deacon's worshipers, that have gathered near him, and see what wondering and wriggling there is among them! and the Deacon himself! Only look at him, casting doubtfully about him like a man in a blue maze! But hush! The court speaks."

"Captain Mosely," said the Governor turning from another brief interchange of opinions with one of his assistants, "if you have further presentments or communications to make, you can now proceed with them."

"I will," promptly replied Captain Mosely, rising, "I will proceed, at once with *my* part in the forthcoming matter, which I am happy to say consists merely in introducing another, who is abundantly able to do his own speaking, and make his own presentments of the extraordinary transactions that have driven him here to-day for justice. And I accordingly announce the man sitting here on my right, and bespeak for him the favor—the only favor he asks—of the unprejudiced audience of this honorable court."

The muffled *unknown* who had been indicated by the last speaker, and to whom all eyes had thus been drawn, now quietly disrobed himself of his disguising outer rig, and calmly rose to his feet, revealing to the wondering spectators the ensemble of an oldish, dark-visaged, but richly appareled English gentleman, of an unusually commanding person and countenance. A low buzz of eager, broken whispers ran through the crowd, and some half-uttered name seemed struggling on the lips of many a doubting inquirer; but no word or exclamation was heard, even from the Deacon, who, however, turned very pale, and, involuntarily starting partly to his feet, and recoiling back against those crowding up from behind him, stood, with one hand thrown forward, palm outward, as if for defence, mutely glaring at the apparition that had so suddenly emerged into view.

"There may be those here," said the object of this curiosity and commotion, in clear, self-possessed accents, after a momentary survey of the mingled assembly—"there may be, and doubtless are, those here present, both on the bench and among the spectators, who will recognize in me Colonel Richard Southworth, formerly a citizen of this good town of Plymouth, but latterly a hunted outcast, and a homeless wanderer in the woods, or among strange peoples abroad. But I come not into this presence to complain of the acts which drove me from home, or to speak of the adventures or misadventures that befel me during the long, dark period of my compulsory exile. I come for a different and more important purpose. I come to claim the indubitable rights which have been wrested from me in my absence. And in this behalf," he continued, glancing defiantly around him, and raising his deep-toned voice to a pitch of startling loudness—"in this behalf, I arraign before this honorable court, Deacon John Mudgridge, on charge of the willful embezzlement of my property, of gross fraud, and of other still more heinous crimes and misdemeanors!"

"I deny! I remonstrate! I protest!" shouted the Deacon, in quick, husky tones, rising almost to a scream. "Yea, I do solemnly protest. I do deny the man's right to appear before this court at all. He is an outlaw; and instead of allowing him to come here to malign and arraign innocent men, the authorities should see to it that he is arrested himself—and, verily, I do suppose it is their bounden duty to do it—and send him back to expiate his offenses in England. Can't you seize him, Mr. constable? Why don't you seize him there? Any of you—all of you! I order it! I command it!"

"Yea, and I, too," here rang out the loud voice of the Shadow, whose tall form, at the first pause made by the Deacon for breath, was seen suddenly shooting up over the crowd, with the jerk of an opening jack-knife—"and I, too, must add my protest, my most signal rebuke, to such unheard of doings; for I can hold my peace no longer, when words so audacious, even unto the assailing of the very pillars of our Israel, are permitted to be—"

"Will the gentleman," interrupted the colonel, glancing from the court to his opponents—"will *both* the gentlemen spare their breaths till I can show, as I was about to do before, my right to appear in court as I have, which the gentleman has so pointedly denied. And here is my showing—here, in this document," he continued, drawing forth a parchment and triumphantly waving it aloft—"*here is a free and full pardon* and reversal of my cruel sentence, and a restoration to my former rights and privileges, and all under the royal seal of KING JAMES OF ENGLAND! Will that satisfy the gentleman with whom I am about to deal? Here, Captain Willis, please pass this up to the court," he added, pausing till the document could be examined.

"Yes, the paper is evidently authentic; so you can proceed, colonel," at length said the governor, with gloomy sternness. "This thing, strike where it will, must be met. It is due to the character of this court and colony, that there should be no shrinking, even from the most painful of duties. Proceed, sir."

"I said I arraigned John Mudgridge for embezzling my property," resumed the fearless accuser; "and I do so charge him, your honors. When I left Plymouth, I had ten thousand pounds deposited in the bank of Amsterdam, only one-twentieth of which has ever been drawn out for my personal use, in my absence. He, as I am prepared to prove, has drawn the rest."

" It is false ! I deny it ! that is, he can't prove a word of it—no, not a word. And suppose I *did* draw, had I not authority for it ? Yea, even under his own hands, and I defy him to gainsay it !" exclaimed the Deacon, blending his denials and admissions all in one breath, in his confusion, as he returned desperately to the fight.

" It is true," coolly rejoined the colonel, pausing and casting a contemptuous glance at the accused—" it is very true, your honors, that I *did* give him discretionary power to draw one thousand pounds for the use of my family in case of need. But not one half of even *that* sum was ever expended by or for them. Now, where was his authority for drawing the rest ?"

" I was his agent. I was—I was his agent, I say," stammered the more and more confounded Deacon, halting in his strait between the dangers of persisting in his denials, and those of compromising himself by further admissions, while attempting to find justification by avoiding both. " Yea, his general agent, and he can't deny it—ay, the manager of his whole property, and thereby could rightfully, supposing I had drawn it, could rightfully draw the whole of it. I say, supposing I had ; but it all rests on his assertions—yea, the assertions of—"

" Not on my assertions alone, as you will soon find, equivocating miscreant," impatiently interrupted the colonel, bending his withering gaze upon the cowering Deacon. " I have not come here to bandy words, empty handed of proof to back my assertions. Here," he continued, producing a package of papers and holding them up to view—" here are the original drafts, orders, and certificates, procured by my agents abroad from the bank itself, all duly authenticated, and all clearly showing where the money went to. Here they are ! I pass them up for the examination of the court; and we will see who will be the best content to abide the consequences of the damning evidence they contain."

There was now another considerable pause in the war of words ; and while the court were engaged in examining and comparing the papers which had been thus submitted to their inspection, the whole assembly sat in breathless silence, with their excited countenances turned expectingly on the court.

" In looking at those papers," resumed the cool, but deter-mined accuser, rising, as appearances indicated that the examination of the papers was essentially concluded, " the court will perceive that the first draft, in the order of time, is signed by myself, and for the thousand pounds I have already named, as drawn by the accused with my sanction. Next, within the same year, another draft for five hundred pounds, with my genuine signature also attached, but drawn by ano-ther agent for my personal use, while in exile. Then follows, under consecutive dates, two others drawn by the accused, and signed by him as my agent, together with an accompany-ing letter full of singularly false representations. And then, as seen in this certified statement, the banker declining to honor any more drafts so signed on account of some fears that all was not right—then, at intervals, follow two others for the remainder of the fund, which purport to have been signed by myself, but which the court, I think, by comparing them with my admitted, genuine signatures, and the general hand-writing of the accused, cannot fail to believe to be, what *I here fearlessly pronounce them,* — bold and shameless FOR-GERIES !"

The whole assembly, as may well be supposed, were thrown into commotion by these last more definite disclosures and ac-cusations, which had been wound up by this astounding an-nouncement. The Deacon, whose intense anxieties had before brought him to his feet, stood a moment like one suddenly transfixed by a bolt from the heavens. Then his features began to work and twitch, showing signs of reviving oppugnancy. And then he fell to gesticulating violently with both hands, while his lips moved rapidly, in the evident attempt to speak. But his flustered voice had become so hollow and husky, that the half uttered word *fa—fal—false !* could only be distinguished, as, with the sounds dying away into incoherent mutterings, he dropped into his seat and covered his face with both hands to hide his overwhelming confusion.

The Shadow—the poor, trusting, honest, but sadly duped Shadow, even looked blank and bewildered, and glanced this way and that, uneasily about him, a doubt of his great oracle's infallibility now evidently for the first time crossing his simple mind. And the whole audience, astonished at these unexpected disclosures and accusations against one who stood, as they supposed, immeasurably above the possibility even of the imputation of crime, and still utterly unable to bring their minds to the reluctant belief, everywhere gave token of intense excitement, and with one accord, after exchanging a few hurried looks and words among themselves, now turned again eagerly to the court, and sat waiting in feverish anxiety, to catch their response to the extraordinary charges they were known to be considering.

That response at length came. Governor Winslow, after an attempt, and then a successful effort, to conquer his emotions, drew a tremulous sigh, and said—

" We have somewhat carefully examined the evidence you have submitted to our inspection, Colonel Southworth, and sad and humbling, indeed, is that duty which constrains us to say that we cannot resist the painful conviction of its conclusiveness, rebutted, as it only is, by confused denials and unsupported assertions. This, especially in regard to the wrongful appropriation of your property by the wretched man before us. The *property*, however, can, and in truth shall be, promptly restored ; for, if he will not voluntarily make legal transfers of enough of his ill-gotten possessions, if he has them, to make good the loss, process and decree shall at once issue from this court to effect that object—yea, the *property* can be restored ; but what shall wipe away the foul stain of reproach which has been brought on the good name and fame of this Christian colony, by acts of such amazing turpitude ? The accused, howbeit, in the matter of the felonies which are alleged, and we fear with too much reason, to have been coupled with the embezzlement, must be allowed the ordeal of grand jury and trial by God and the country, and I wish I could better hope for his safe deliverance. Thus much for what has thus far been brought before us. Are you through with your presentments, Colonel Southworth ?"

" Not yet, your honor," said the latter, promptly returning to the charge—" I have not done with the accused yet. In addition to those I have specified, I now presentment make of another, and not the least in the dark catalogue of his offenses. I charge him with having, within this very year, secretly conspired and attempted to take my life ! I here fearlessly aver that he, last summer, having through a singular incident connected with the rescue of my daughter from his infamous attempt to coerce her into marriage with a creature of his own—he having discovered that I was alive and habiting obscure places near the southern borders of this colony, and carefully keeping the secret of my identity to himself, did deliberately, and with murderous intent, put upon my track, a band of his hireling spies and assassins, who dogged me to the house of a friend ; where, with their base instigator and employer hovering near and giving orders for the deed, they seized, and but for my timely rescue, would have despatched me on the spot."

With that lightning-like flash of thought which is sometimes, in terrible emergencies, known to encompass heaven

and earth in an instant, the wretched Deacon, in the mental
reaction that in some measure succeeded his paroxysm of
shame and guilt at his exposure and condemnation on the
previous charges, had glanced over every part of the dark and
dubious prospect before him. He had at first given himself
up as irretrievably lost. But as his mind rallied, he saw, in
the law's delays, in the chances of invalidating testimony, or
of corrupting judge or jury, together with what his own tor-
tuous scheming could effect,—he saw in these enough of hope
for escaping punishment and saving a good portion of his property to raise him once more partly out of the black gulf of
his despair. This new and totally unexpected charge, therefore,
fell upon him with much the same effect as would naturally
be produced by the fresh and ruthless assault of a conquering
aggressor on one who, with gathering hope of life, was just
rising from a murderous blow, the repetition of which was
wholly unanticipated. His countenance at first became the
picture of pitiable distress. But after pausing a moment in
his new and aggravated perplexities, his mind seemed to rally
with the belief that the accuser could not possibly, in this
case at least, be in possession of any tangible proof to support
the accusation, and with a last desperate effort at mustering
his forces of resistance, he made shift to hiss out his old as-
severations—

"It is false !—false as Sathan himself; and I do—yea, I do
defy him to prove it !"

"I again accept his challenge !" promptly exclaimed the
bold and confident accuser. "As little as I expected the man
would find assurance to give it, I cheerfully accept this challenge also; and I trust the required proof will not be long in
forthcoming. Mr. Richard Swain," he added, calling aloud
to the recently enlisted Dick, who had been sitting unnoticed
in an obscure corner of the room—"Mr Swain, will you step

forward to the witnesses' stand, be sworn, and testify to what
you know about the case on hand?"

Dick, with a sort of self-abased, deprecatory air, now hurriedly shuffled forward, took the stand, went through the
forms of the oath, and with the eyes of the excited, but
breathlessly silent crowd bent intently upon him, proceeded
with sundry apologetic remarks about having been deceived
and acting from a mistaken sense of duty, to relate what, in
the progress of the story, may have already been learned or
inferred by the reader, respecting the secret and dastardly
attempt of Deacon Mudgridge and his hireling band of spies
and assassins, to pursue, entrap, and destroy the identified
Southworth; and having hurried through the general history
of the affair, he particularly described the last damning
details of his secret instructions, accompanied by the promised
reward of a farm in case of success, and wound up by lifting
his eyes to the court, and firmly emphasizing,

"I aver, then, that he *did* commission me to do the deed,
which I thank Heaven, I was spared the guilt of actually
committing at his instigation—*he did employ, and especially
enjoin me to* MURDER COLONEL SOUTHWORTH!"

The whole assembly sat almost aghast in the astonished
witnessing of such amazing depravity. And how felt he,
who was the loathed *object* of this significant demonstration
of universal abhorrence?—

> "And how felt he, the wretched man,
>   Thus all unmask'd, as memory ran
>   O'er many a year of guilt and strife;
>   Nor found one sunny resting place;
>   Nor brought him back one branch of grace?"

With soul-chilling awe, have we several times caught the
last conscious look of men about to perish by sudden and unforeseen accident; with painful sadness, have we stood and
looked on at many a sick-bed, when the hope-cheated sufferer

was at last called to look death in the face as an instant, unescapable reality ; and with melancholy interest have we often
even noted the look of the death-doomed brute, glancing
wildly up at the descending axe—we have noted all these, and
found in them all, whether human or brute, the same strange,
frenzied look—the same indescribable expression of mortal
terror stamping the countenance, in those awful moments.
And so looked the wretched Mudgridge. With a first instinctive impulse for life and safety, it is true, he cast a rapid,
furtive glance at the door, and began to sidle along in that
direction. But the quick eye of the secretly instructed Sheriff
in attendance instantly detecting the movement, and promptly
confronting him, he turned round with a look so despairing,
so frenzied, and so fearful, as to cause an involuntary start
through the whole crowd of shuddering beholders. Then his
face suddenly blanched to a corpse-like pallor, and then, as
suddenly, came the fatal revulsion of the blood towards the
gorged vessels of the brain, suffusing, one after another, neck,
lips, cheeks, and temples, till they glowed with crimson red-
ness. The next moment, with a quick, frightful glare, he
wildly threw up his arms, staggered, drooped, sunk crippling
to the floor, gasped, and was dead.

CONCLUSION.

THE action of our tale is not yet, in all its parts, fully concluded. We wish it were so. It were, indeed, but a pleasing office, if that was all, to glance over the bright picture of the domestic felicity enjoyed by those in whom we have seen virtue and faith so signally rewarded, while casting the veil of forgetfulness over the acts of those in whom we have also seen vice and crime as signally punished. But gladly would we be spared the melancholy task of depicting the closing scene of that frightful drama of war and desolation which came so near resulting in the annihilation of the infant colonies of New England. Even for the credit of the conquering race would we avoid, as we shall, many of the sickening details that stained the laurels of their final victories. It is not so much for them, however, as for the saddening duty of following, to the last, two of the active personages of our story—for whom, we trust, we have, in despite of their wickedly blackened memories, succeeded in enlisting a share of the reader's sympathy—that we add the concluding picture. For in that closing scene, the heroic and unfortunate Metacom, and the faithful and fiery Wetamoo, were both destined to perish—but to perish, as they wished, otherwise than by the hands of their foes: in the case of the one, a fratricidal hand extinguishing the great light of the American forest forever; and in that of the other, the embittered soul, by her own act, voluntarily ascending, as an accusing spirit, to her long worshipped Nemesis, to demand retribution for the terrible wrongs she had suffered at the hands of the pale-faced aggressor.

It was nearly four months subsequent to the occurrence of the extraordinary developments at Plymouth, which brought the main part of our story to a close in all that the reader's fancy could not readily supply. Since that time, the contest had assumed its most fearful aspect, and resulted in the most disastrous consequences to the distressed and straitened colonists. Three different corps of their bravest troops, with their gallant leaders, had been successively cut up, routed, or utterly destroyed, by the thickly mustering and frightfully vengeful foemen. Four flourishing villages, within twenty miles of Boston and Plymouth, had been successively assailed in open day, and the bones and ashes of their helpless inhabitants left mingling with the red ruins of their plundered and desolated homes. The storm of war, indeed, rolling on nearer and nearer, and growing darker and more portentous with every hour of its appalling progress, had already approached to the very confines of the populous towns and cities of the coast, threatening the immediate destruction even of this last line of the strongholds, and the refuges of the alarmed residents and the frightened and fast ingathering people of the surrounding country. And both rulers and people, perplexed and amazed at the overshadowing portents of the hour, seemed almost equally at loss which way to turn to escape the terrible doom that, to all human appearance, must soon overtake them. But, happily, their fears were not to be realized. All at once, the storm ceased to advance. The expected bolt fell not. Why this strange delay of the beleaguering foe, at a moment when they seemingly had the keenly coveted prize of victory all but within their very grasp? What unseen hand had stayed that woe-freighted avalanche? Yes, why was all this? The question has been answered in almost as many number of ways as the number of different original writers who have attempted to grapple with it, but never answered to any general acceptance. To this day, it is one of the mysteries of history; and no satisfactory explanation has ever been furnished, unless it be not found in the remark made by one of the prisoner chiefs to his taunting captors, after the red man's calamity had fallen: "You could have never subdued us," he said, "*had not the Englishman's God suddenly made us afraid.*" Indeed, it *did* seem as if, at this fearful crisis, the finger of Providence had been suddenly extended, and that the whole of that formidable wampum-league, like a blight-smitten tendril, or rope of sand, had withered and crumbled at the touch.

And so it was; at the very hour when the prospects of the victorious avengers of the forests were the brightest, and those of the trembling colonists were the darkest, the tide of fate and fortune not only ceased to flow forward, but was mysteriously thrown upon its reflux. The time of the former had come; that of the latter was yet in the untold distance. The prophetic doom cloud, seen by the aged seer, as described in a former chapter, had at last fallen on the devoted red men; and their souls sunk within them under the dark and chilling prefiguration. They felt that their day of war deeds and daring was over and gone. And with the conscious departure of their power and prestige, the confederate tribes slunk away fearful and dismayed to their old separate recesses in the distant forests.

Like the frost-smitten leaves of their own woods, they all shrunk at the strange moral blight, scattered, and passed noiselessly away—all but the lion-hearted Metacom. He, though at first amazed at the unexpected and shameless desertion—he yet quailed not under this terrible blow to his cause; but his proud spirit seemed to grow more defiant and indomitable, in proportion as fell the crushing weight of his misfortunes. He and his faithful and still undaunted Wampanoog warriors, one and all, lifted up their hands and swore by the red man's God, that *they* at least would fight on to the bitter end; and that now returning to their old dear haunts and homes, they would take their last, desperate stand over the graves of their fathers.

And consequent on this, the excited colonists, who had not yet become apprised of the great, but silent turn of affairs in their favor, were soon thrown into fresh consternation and alarm by the sudden appearance of King Philip and his supposed numerous army of warriors, in the forests surrounding the great ponds of Middleborough, once the seat of populous native villages, but now almost in the heart of the Plymouth colony. Sufficient military forces were already in the field, under Major Bradford, fit successor in the command of the Plymouth troops to the imbecile Cudworth of the previous year.

But Bradford and his troops did nothing, except to march from town to town along the public roads, and keep at a safe distance from the places where their presence was most needed, and the universal voice of the alarmed people had gone up to their rulers for the appointment of more efficient military leaders. Captain Willis who had speedily wed, after the great denouement we have described, and retired with his blooming bride to her gift farm in Rhode Island, had been offered, before leaving town, a commission for raising and leading one company into the field. This honor he had declined, ostensively on the ground of his unwillingness to move with a force so inadequate to the emergency.

But he was not to be let off so. The current of favor at the court of Plymouth, since the death of Deacon Mudgridge and the consequent change in its counsels, had now set as strongly for, as previously against the gallant, but shamefully slighted young officer. A second commission, empowering him to raise double the force first specified, and conferring the rank of Major, soon followed him into his retirement. This also he respectfully declined. But the same messenger that carried back the declination, returned post haste, within two days, with a third commission, with plenary powers to raise all the forces he could, assume an independent command, and lead them against the enemy with the least possible delay.

Yielding this time, but rather from the convictions of duty than any desire for exchanging his domestic elysium on the quiet shores of the beautiful Aquidneck, for the honors of a command conferring a rank little less than that of General, he tore himself away from his weeping wife, and at once entered on the duties of the contemplated campaign, with a promptitude and activity commensurate with the urgency of the occasion. And so rapid and successful were all his movements and measures, that within ten days he had raised, with his old company, who promptly rallied at his call, a force amply sufficient, as he believed, to effect his purposes; since they were all men who would never hesitate to follow where he would dare to lead them.

And with these, after a series of daring adventures and achievements, which were never perhaps equaled in Indian warfare, he had slain hundreds, taken hundreds of captives, everywhere routed the foe, and driven them from forest to forest, until they had reached the fated goal, at which they had been steadily aiming—the spot of hallowed memories, where their last stand was to be taken.

Sadly to them broke the morning sun into the last encampment of the doomed Metacom and the still unyielding remnant of his faithful Wampanoogs. It was a deeply secluded spot, near the southern slope of the ever memorable Mount Hope, opening to the sunny bay in front, and everywhere hedged in and surrounded by a wide and densely wooded morass in the rear. The forest lay hushed in the breathing silence of nature, and no sounds were heard save the occa-

sional trill of the thicket-loving wood bird, and the low, sullen dashing of the waves as their long inward swells broke
soughing along the cliffy base of the neighboring elevation.
All nature seemed dressed in smiles, but her smiles brought no
animating gladness to the gloomy souls of the hunted warriors
and their sternly forlorn chieftain.   He had effected by war
and diplomacy more the past year than the world's greatest
warriors, in the same space of time, and with such uncertain
elements for instruments, had ever accomplished.   He had
also endured more of disappointment and affliction than any
of them ever suffered, and more than any but the sternest of
heroes could suffer and live.   He had seen himself suddenly
forsaken, apparently on the very eve of a final triumph, by
fickle or foolishly panic-struck allies.   And then, as with
proud resolve, he turned his face homeward, he had found
himself betrayed by basely deserting friends and kindred, at
almost every step of his progress.   And to crown all, and
pierce his soul with redoubled anguish, he had seen his beloved wife and darling son, surprised, captured, and sold into
slavery by his remorseless pursuers.   And yet, under all this
mountain of accumulated woes, his proud and unsubdued
spirit faltered not, nor entertained one thought of submission.
That terrible red legion of two thousand warriors, whom, one
short year ago, he led forth, in all their confidence and pride,
to scatter over the land in their incursive warfare, had now,
by the losses in battle, sickness, and capture, wasted and
dwindled to nearly half as many hundreds.   And these, the
sad remnant of his devoted followers, having, a day or two
before, and unknown as they supposed to their foes, reached
their final destination, had now gathered round the central
council-fire of their idolized chieftain to soothe his bursting
heart, and still take from his imperial lips their law of guidance
in the gloomy emergency.   Moody and silent he sat, like some
colossal iron statue in their midst; while on his sternly com-
30

pressed countenance rested that fearful expression of mingled anguish and desperation, which seems to court death, and at the same time to defy his approach. By his side sat the faithful and keenly sympathizing Wetamoo, the beauteous, but vengeful warrior queen, who had resolved never to desert him so long as he had an arm to raise against the pale faces. In front of these, flanked on either side by rows of his grim and sullen warriors, sat the stalwart old Annawan, long the great war captain of the tribe, looking, with his rough, scarred visage, giant contour of frame, and fixed ferocity of countenance, like some gnarled, ancient mountain oak, that laughs at the winds, and defies the bolts of heaven.

"Last sleep I had a dream," at length slowly and gloomily said Metacom, while all eyes were turning with eager expectance to his opening lips—"I stood on the shadowy side of the silent river that gently murmured along its half lighted way between this and the spirit land. Soon, a small, feeble, flickering blaze of fire began to be in the air, just over the water about midway the stream ; and growing stronger and broader as it went, moved slowly on from me across the brightening expanse, till, in the shape of a beautiful cloud of gold, it floated over the far-reaching throng of departed warriors, who, with shining faces, thickly lined that happy shore. I looked on as one looks who sees a great wonder. There, beneath bright, blue, smiling skies, and among green, pleasant forests, watered by sparkling streams, stood the red host of rewarded braves. The faces of all were bright ; but the faces of those slain in battle with pale faces were the brightest. Their bullet scars glittered like spirit lights on their bodies, and wreathed scalp-plumes floated, like clustering stars, from their heads. There stood the Narraganset braves, who died fighting to save our wives and children, and with them the bold Nanuntenoo, towering high over the rest. And there also, in the fairest, brightest spot of that shining shore,

stood gathered the proud array of our dead Wampanoog warriors. My father, the good old Massasoit, was there. On
his face seemed to rest a shade of regret for having spared
and warmed into life the nest of white vipers, to sting his
family and tribe, instead of crushing them at first into the
earth with his heel. By his side stood my murdered brother,
the noble Wamsutta, with his face, like an unsatisfied spirit,
turned wistfully towards the land of life, as if to ask of us
one more deed of vengeance to appease his troubled soul. I
sprang wildly forth for an object on which to do the welcome
bidding, and, in the effort, awoke."

"Oh, my husband! my poor, poisoned husband!" wildly exclaimed the excited Wetamoo, goaded to frenzy by the chief's
dream-wrought picture of the appearance of her lamented lord,
as seen in the spirit land. "Oh for another blow at the accursed pale faces!—Oh for another scalp—one more scalp,
good Manitou, that I may take it, when I go, to lay it at his
feet, as an acceptable offering to his unsatisfied vengeance!
Metacom, I thank you. It was a good—oh, it was a good
dream!"

"Ugh! Ugh!" approvingly roared the old war captain, in
a voice resembling the low bellowing of a bullock—a voice so
remarkable for tone and compass as to have found a place in
the histories of the times. "The words of Wetamoo are the
words of a brave, and she has read the dream with a clear
eye. The dream shows things in the spirit land that are
right to be true. My old chief, Massasoit, does well to be
sorry he did not crush out the hatching nest of the pale faces.
My young chief, Wamsutta, whom they made to die the death
of a poisoned dog, does well to want more vengeance. Annawan is an old warrior, and his war-paths are strewed with the
bones of his white enemies. But his arm is still strong, and
his tomahawk is sharp. The starry scalp-plume he will carry
to the spirit land, is already big; but he would make it big-

ger.   Yes, the woman warrior is right.   The dream of Metacom is a good dream !"

"No, the dream is a bad dream," said one of the warriors,
in a confident tone.

"How ?" exclaimed Metacom, starting, and bending on the
other a look of mingled surprise, doubt, and suspicion.

"Much 'fraid the dream a bad one," responded the former,
moderating his tone, but evidently inclined to persist in his
opinion.   "No good to see faces of the dead in a dream.
And the fire kindled in the air without hands, and moving
away from him who sees it, is the fire, the old medicine men
say, that comes to light his way to the spirit land.   And it
will soon be the fire to light *all* our paths there, if we stand
out much longer against the pale faces, who are gathering
round us, a hundred to our one, to kill us in battle.   When
we were many, we were strong-hearted to fight, because we
had hope.   But now we are few—we are nothing—we have
no hope.   There is no fight in our hearts.   It is no use to
try to fight any more.   We had better lay down the bloody
hatchet.   I advise Metacom to get terms and surrender."

"Surrender !" shouted the astonished chieftain, springing
to his feet, with a countenance all fearfully alive with the
rapidly succeeding shades of pain, chagrin, and fiery indignation, that quivered and flashed over it—"surrender, to be sold
and become whipt, cringing, groaning slaves, as my wife and
son have been !   Surrender, on promised terms, and then be
secretly poisoned to death by the base, double-tongued white
cowards, as my noble brother was treated by the miscreant
crew !   Was it," he continued, his every feature glowing and
gleaming more and more fiercely in the gathering intensity of
his terrible emotions—"was it a Wampanoog warrior who
made that damning proposal ?   And shall one of our hitherto
undisgraced tribe, who still claims to be a warrior and a man,

be suffered to utter such baseness, and live? No! by the eternal Manitou, no!"

Quick as the lightning's flash, the arm that had been lifted high in the utterance of the irrevocable oath, descended to the belted pistol, and whirled the gleaming barrel to the line level of the quailing object of the frenzied denunciation. Then there was a momentary, an awful pause, in which a cold shudder ran visibly through the surprised and recoiling assemblage; and then, suddenly, the steel gave fire, the bullet sped—the warrior died!

"It is well," growled the fierce old Annawan, the first to rally from the general amazement that had seized the awe-struck warriors at the quick and terrible punishment that had awaited this first sign of weakness and misgiving in their devoted band. "Yes, it is well; it is well that he should die before his heart grew any softer."

"Ay, it *is*—it *is* well!" eagerly responded the warrior queen also. "It is more than well; it is *right*, it is *just*, my brave brother, who has been driven to make the painful sacrifice to preserve unspotted the proud totem-eagle of his tribe. Let every such weakness, in whomever betrayed, meet the same punishment, and with the same swiftness. Load up your pistol again, noble Metacom; and if you see even the poor, weak woman, Wetamoo, growing faint before the foe, send the mercy-meant bullet through her heart, and her undishonored soul shall thank you with every wing-flap of its flight from here to the spirit-land."

Not another word was uttered aloud by any; yet the quickly exchanged glances, and the varying shades of sensation which flitted over the faces of the dusky warriors, evidently showed that a busy thought-council was in progress in their sympa-thizing bosoms. And, almost the next moment, the rapid subsiding of the flashings of excitement, and the keenly questioning expressions that had at first marked their startled

countenances, made it equally evident—followed as they at
last were by low murmurs of satisfaction—that their silent
deliberations had resulted in a general verdict of approval of
the summary proceeding of their sovereign chief, and that he
was to be sustained by all—all, with one solitary exception.
That excepted one was the brother of the slain warrior. *His*
brow, as he gloomily looked on, grew darker and darker with
displeasure and meditated revenge ; and soon rising, he took
his gun, edged away from the throng, and disappeared in the
forest.   An uneasy and suspicious look passed over the face
of Metacom, as his eye fell on the retreating figure.   But,
either from that strange apathy that grows of despair, or from
his ignorance of the fact that his white foes, though as yet
unapprised of the location of his camp, were already within a
mile of him in the rear, the chief made no corresponding
movement, sent out no scouts, and stationed no guarding outpost; but, with the rest of his devoted band, soon relapsed
into the stern, moody silence which had been broken by the
occurrence of the sad scene we have been describing.   And
another gloomy hour passéd away without incident or alarm.
But the dread moment of doom had now, at length, arrived.
Suddenly as the breaking thunder-clap, burst from a concealing
thicket near by a deafening volley of musketry, and a shower
of bullets was poured in upon the devoted camp.

Leaping for their arms, the surprised and dismayed warriors instantly scattered, fled, and quickly disappeared among
the protecting and supposed unoccupied thickets of the swamp
in their rear.   Not yet venturing to make their appearance,
the small party of white assailants still kept close and quiet
in their coverts ; and all, for a brief interval, relapsed into
silence.   Presently, however, the report of a single musket
sent its ominous peal through the forests, and the next moment, a fierce shout of exultation, portending no common trophy, burst from one of the secreted bands of the stealthy

invaders, and being quickly caught up, went ringing, with
fresh outbursts of hurras, from station to station along the
whole extended line of the ambushing troops. The shout
was soon repeated at the starting point : and this time distinctly came the words, " KING PHILIP IS SLAIN ! *slain by
the bullet of the deserting Indian ; and the great enemy is at
last overthrown !*"

These jubilant demonstrations had scarcely died away, before they were succeeded by other sounds, that fell on the ear
in sad and painful contrast. From every part of the distant
thickets rose the wild wail of the red warriors, who, but too
well comprehending what had befell, had paused in their
flight thus to give voice to their grief and despair at the fall
of their idolized chieftain. Then was heard the stentorian
roar of old Annawan, in rallying the fugitives to come to a
stand, and avenge the death of their great leader. And for
a few minutes the woods resounded with the battle cries of
the combatants, and the scattering fire of the pursuers and
pursued. But the shots growing fewer and fainter in the
distance, and soon followed by another shout of victory, told
that the brief contest was over, and that all was lost, forever
lost, to the red men.

But where, in the meanwhile, was the luckless, woe-wed
Wetamoo ? Had she escaped here, as had many of the
wretched remnant of her people, only soon to be captured
elsewhere, and sold into slavery, or shot as was the lionlike
old Annawan ? No; she had resolved to have her destiny
within her own keeping ; and hers was to be a more befitting
fate, and one far more consonant with her high-wrought feelings and desperate purposes. With a strange prescience of the
calamity at hand, she had, at the moment of the alarm, instead
of fleeing into the thickets of the swamp with the rest, instinctively made her way to the water side. And here within
the covert of the scantily screening coppice, she stood, still

unmoved and unquailing as the flinty rocks at her feet, and awaited the result in silence, until the dread announcement of the death of her royal brother fell on her anguished ear; when she joined in the general death cry then raised by the scattering warriors, in a wail so shrill and loud as instantly to bring upon her the pursuit of a party of her foes, who had by this time reached the camp she had just left.

She then, with her pursuers pressing on hotly behind her, rapidly forced her obstructed and difficult way along the shelvy and precipitous shore of the bay, winding up the adjoining elevation, till she had nearly gained the summit; when she caught sight of another party of her foes coming up the opposite side of the hill to intercept her course, and with those in her rear, make sure of the prize of so noted a prisoner.

In the quick glance she threw around her, in her now hopeless emergency, she caught a glimpse of a tall perpendicular cliff, rising from a partially screening clump of bushes, a short distance to her right, and beetling directly over the dark chasm of the ocean waves dashing against its base far, far away down beneath, and her eye sparkled with fierce joy at the sight. In one moment her resolution was taken, and in another she was standing on the dizzy brink of the cliff, towering up in the wild beauty of her matchless form, like the chiseled marble on its pedestal, and frowning her defiance on her despised pursuers, who, having closed up within a few yards of the rock on which she stood, were pausing in their doubts of her questionable purposes.

"So," she at length exclaimed, with a look of ineffable scorn and hate, "so you think to take the warrior queen to lead round, with boasts of the brave deed of capturing a lone, unarmed squaw, and show her to your scared and wondering women and children, who have so often turned pale at her name—you think thus to make her a thing of show and triumph, till you get ready to give her over, like a sold dog,

SUICIDE OF WETAMOO. 473

to the lash of the slave-driver as you did the wife and child of the slain Metacom—you think to take her *alive* for such ignoble purposes, do you, ye white wolves? Wetamoo's long strained heart is ready to burst. She is ready to die, but not by the hands of the hated pale faces. She goes to join her poor, poisoned husband in the spirit-land, who is there constantly besieging the Great Manitou to send death and desolation on the race of his cowardly murderers. She goes, but she leaves her bitter, her crying curse on *you*, ye pitiful, double tongued thieves, and on the whole land you have stolen from the red man and fattened with his blood, and let that curse be her fare-well, to remain on you and your guilty land, till the Heaven-heard cries of the wrongs and blood of a plundered people shall all be appeased in the terrible atonement."

She ceased ; and while the thrilling sounds of the last of her high-heaped anathemas were yet echoing among the rocks around, her exasperated assailants made a sudden rush to seize and drag her down by the feet. But her wary eye was too quick for the baffled woman hunters. With a quickness of the outstarting antelope, she leaped, with a wild cry of exulta-tion, out wide from the fearful brink, and then descended, like a bow-driven arrow, to her watery grave below.

THE END.

INDIA

AND THE

INDIAN MUTINY

COMPRISING A COMPLETE

HISTORY OF HINDOOSTAN,

From the Earliest Times to the Present Day,

WITH FULL PARTICULARS OF THE

RECENT MUTINY IN INDIA.

ILLUSTRATED WITH NUMEROUS ENGRAVINGS.

BY

HENRY FREDERICK MALCOM.

This work has been gotten up with great care, and may be relied on as

COMPLETE AND ACCURATE;

making one of the most THRILLINGLY INTEREST-ING books published. It contains illustrations of

All the great Battles and Sieges,

making a large 12mo. volume of about 450 pages, and is sold at the low price of $1.25.

NOTICES OF THE PRESS.

The tragical events of the war will not only be read with thrilling interest, but the history of India will be studied by all classes. The work before us is well calculated to impart the knowledge of India and the Rebellion, which is sought by those whose curiosity has been excited, as it gives, in one volume, a popular history of the country at different epochs.—*Rural New Yorker.*

This work appears to be one to meet the demand for information respecting India.—*U. S. Journal.*

T. S. ARTHUR'S WORKS—*Continued.*

A BOOK OF STARTLING INTEREST.

THE ANGEL AND THE DEMON.

A handsome 12mo. volume.   Price $1.00

In this exciting story Mr. ARTHUR has taken hold of the reader's attention with a more than usually vigorous grasp, and keeps him absorbed to the end of the volume.   The book is one of STARTLING INTEREST.   Its lessons should be

IN THE HEART OF EVERY MOTHER.

Onward, with a power of demonstration that makes conviction a necessity, the Author sweeps through his subject, fascinating at every step.   In the union of

THRILLING DRAMATIC INCIDENT,

with moral lessons of the highest importance, this volume stands forth pre-eminent among the author's many fine productions.

NOTICES OF THE PRESS.

A story of much power, imbued with that excellent moral and religious spirit which pervades all his writings.—*N. Y. Chronicle.*

This volume is among his best productions, and worthy of a place on every centre-table.—*Clarion, Pa., Banner.*

This is a most fascinating book, one which the reader will find it quite hard to lay aside without reading to the last page.—*Albany, N. Y., Journal and Courier.*

THE GOOD TIME COMING.

Large 12mo., with fine Mezzotint Frontispiece,.............Price $1.00

It is like every thing emanating from that source—worth reading.—*Toledo Blade.*

It is characterized by all the excellencies of his style."—*Phila. Bulletin.*

It is a book the most scrupulous parent may place in the hand of his child.—*Providence Transcript*

T. S. ARTHUR'S WORKS—*Continued.*

Lights and Shadows of Real Life.

With an Autobiography and Portrait of the Author.   Over five
hundred pages, octavo, with fine tinted Engravings.   Price $2.00.

NOTICES OF THE PRESS.

In this volume may be found a "moral suasion," which cannot but affect for good
all who read.   The mechanical execution of the work is very beautiful throughout.—
New Haven Palladium.

It is by far the most valuable book ever published of his works, inasmuch as it is en-
riched with a very interesting, though brief autobiography.—*American Courier.*

No family library is complete without a copy of this book.—*Scott's Weekly Paper.*

No better or worthier present could be made to the young; no offering more pure,
charitable, and practicable could be tendered to those who are interested in the truly
benevolent reforms of the day.—*Godey's Lady's Book.*

The paper, the engravings, the binding, and the literary contents, are all calculated
to make it a favorite.—*Penn. Inquirer.*

This volume cannot be too highly recommended.—*N. Y. Tribune.*

More good has been effected, than by any other single medium that we know of.—
N. Y. Sun.

The work should be upon the centre-table of every parent in the land.—*National
Temperance Magazine.*

LEAVES FROM THE BOOK OF HUMAN LIFE.

Large 12mo.   With Thirty Illustrations and Steel Plate.   Price $1.00.

A single story is worth the price charged for the book.—*Union, Newburyport, Mass.*
"It includes some of the best humorous sketches of the author."

The following Books are bound in uniform style as "ARTHUR'S
COTTAGE LIBRARY," and are sold in sets, or separately, each
volume being complete in itself.   Each volume is embellished
with a fine Mezzotint Engraving.]

THE WAY TO PROSPER.
AND OTHER TALES.

Cloth, 12mo., with Mezzotint Engraving, ...Price $1.00.

TRUE RICHES; OR, WEALTH WITHOUT WINGS.
AND OTHER TALES.

Cloth, 12mo., with Mezzotint Engraving, ...Price $1.00.

ANGEL OF THE HOUSEHOLD
AND OTHER TALES.

Cloth, 12mo., with Mezzotint Engraving, ...Price $1.00

PERILS AND PLEASURES

OF

A HUNTER'S LIFE.

With fine colored Plates. Large 12mo. Price $1.00

From the Table of Contents we select the following as samples of the Style and Interest of the Work.

Baiting for an Alligator—Morning among the Rocky Mountains—Encounter with Shoshonees—A Grizzly Bear—Fight and terrible Result—Fire on the Mountains—Narrow Escape—The Beaver Region—Trapping Beaver—A Journey and Hunt through New Mexico—Start for South America—Hunting in the Forests of Brazil—Hunting on the Pampas—A Hunting Expedition into the interior of Africa—Chase of the Rhinoceros—Chase of an Elephant—The Roar of the Lion—Herds of Wild Elephants—Lions attacked by Bechuanas—Arrival in the Region of the Tiger and the Elephant—Our First Elephant Hunt in India—A Boa Constrictor—A Tiger—A Lion—Terrible Conflict—Elephant Catching—Hunting the Tiger with Elephants—Crossing the Pyrenees—Encounter with A Bear—A Pigeon Hunt on the Ohio—A Wild-Hog Hunt in Texas—Hunting the Black-tailed Deer.

HUNTING SCENES IN THE WILDS OF AFRICA.

COMPRISING

The Thrilling Adventures of Cumming, Harris, and other daring Hunters of Lions, Elephants, Giraffes, Buffaloes, and other Animals.

T. S. ARTHUR'S WORKS.

[The following List of Books are all written by T. S. ARTHUR, the well-known author, of whom it has been said, "*that dying he has not written a word he would wish to erase.*" They are all gotten up in the best style of binding, and are worthy of a place in every household.]

TEN NIGHTS IN A BAR-ROOM,

AND

WHAT I SAW THERE.

This powerfully-written work, one of the *best* by its *popular Author*, has met with an immense sale—ten thousand copies having been ordered within a month of publication. It is a large 12mo., illustrated with a beautiful Mezzotint Engraving, by Sartain; printed on fine white paper, and bound in the best English muslin, gilt back. Price $1.00.

The following are a few of the many Notices of the Press.

Powerful and seasonable.—*N. Y. Independent.*

Its scenes are painfully graphic, and furnish thrilling arguments for the temperance cause.—*Norton's Literary Gazette.*

Written in the author's most forcible and vigorous style.—*Lehigh Valley Times.*

In the "Ten Nights in a Bar-Room," some of the consequences of tavern-keeping, the "sowing of the wind" and "reaping the whirlwind," are followed by a "fearful consummation," and the "closing scene," presenting pictures of fearful, thrilling interest.—*Am. Courier.*

There is no exaggeration in these pages—they seem to have been filled up from actual observation.—*Philadelphia Sun.*

We have read it with the most intense interest, and commend it as a work calculated to do an immense amount of good.—*Lancaster Express.*

We wish that all lovers of bar-rooms and rum would read the book. It will pay them richly to do so.—*N. Y. Northern Blade.*

It is sufficient commendation of this little volume to say that it is from the graphic pen of T. S. Arthur, whose works will be read and reread long after he has passed away. He is as true to nature, as far as he attempts to explore it, as Shakspeare himself; and his works, consequently, have an immense popularity.—*New Haven Palladium.*

There are many scenes unequaled for pathos and beauty. The death of little Mary can scarcely be surpassed.—*N. Y. Home Journal.*

WHAT CAN WOMAN DO?

12mo., with Mezzotint Engraving, ... Price $1.00

Our purpose is to show, in a series of life pictures, what woman can do, as well for good as for evil. We desire to bring her before you as a living entity, that you may see her as she is, and comprehend in some small degree the influence she wields in the world's progress upward, as well as her power to mar the human soul and drag it down to perdition, when her own spirit is darkened by evil passions."—*Extract from the Preface.*

T. S. ARTHUR'S WORKS—*Continued.*

GOLDEN GRAINS FROM LIFE'S HARVEST-FIELD.

Bound in gilt back and sides, sheep, with a beautiful Mezzotint En graving. 12mo. Price $1.00.

NOTICES OF THE PRESS.

It is not too much to say, that the Golden Grains here presented to the reader, are such as will be productive of a far greater amount of human happiness than those in search of which so many are willing to risk domestic peace, health, and even life itself in a distant and inhospitable region.

These narratives, like all of those which proceed from the same able pen, are re markable not only for their entertaining and lively pictures of actual life, but for their admirable moral tendency.

It is printed in excellent style, and embellished with a mezzotint engraving. We cordially recommend it to the favor of our readers.—*Godey's Lady's Magazine.*

"Arthur's Home Library."

[The following four volumes contain nearly 500 pages, Illustrated with fine Mezzotint Engravings. Bound in the best manner, and sold separately or in sets. They have been introduced into the District, Sabbath-school, and other Libraries, and are considered one of the best series of the author.]

THREE ERAS IN A WOMAN'S LIFE.

Containing MAIDEN, WIFE, and MOTHER.

Cloth, 12mo., with Mezzotint Engraving,.....................Price $1.00.

"This, by many, is considered Mr. Arthur's best work."

TALES OF MARRIED LIFE.

Containing LOVERS and HUSBANDS, SWEETHEARTS and WIVES, and MARRIED and SINGLE.

Cloth, 12mo., with Mezzotint Engraving,.....................Price $1.00.

"In this volume may be found some valuable hints for wives and husbands, as well as the young."

TALES OF DOMESTIC LIFE.

Containing MADELINE, THE HEIRESS, THE MARTYR WIFE, and RUINED GAMESTER.

Cloth, 12mo., with Mezzotint Engraving,.....................Price $1.00

'Contains several sketches of thrilling interest."

TALES OF REAL LIFE.

ontaining BELL MARTIN, PRIDE and PRINCIPLE, MARY ELLIS, FAMILY PRIDE and ALICE MELVILLE.

Cloth, 12mo., with Mezzotint Engraving,.....................Price $1.00.

"This volume gives the experiences of real life by many who found not their ideal".